Schythium

W.S Wilcox

By: W.S. Wilcox

ISBN: 9798410304320

Dedication

This book is dedicated to my parents, Bill and Joanne Wilcox, who instilled in me the love of the written word from an early age. They opened my eyes and imagination to the infinite possibilities that can be contained between the covers of a book. If it wasn't for my mother reading to me every night as a child and for my father constantly introducing me to new books, genres, and ideas, I doubt that I ever would have begun writing my own works. I owe them both endless gratitude.

CONTENTS

CHAPTER ONE

The standby light fills the hold of the dropship as we make our descent. I stare through my visor at the familiar glow as my mind drifts into the past. I think back to when I bathed in its muted light for the first time. When we were recruits, young, dumb, and fresh out of Boot. Excited to finally be deployed on our first drop.

Back then, the red light made us sick with nerve-racking excitement as we sat on our Wargon mounts, waiting to land. We had been through an exhaustive amount of training to get to that point and were itching for some action. After countless drills and exercises, we were finally being put to the test. Our confidence was high. Hell, I doubt anybody is more confident than a cavalry soldier fresh out of training. I also doubt anyone is as foolish. Although, it wasn't really our fault. Our egos were inflated from a year and a half of being told that cavalry soldiers were the meanest combat units in existence. A lack of life experience didn't help much either.

To make matters worse, the process of becoming a cavalry soldier is difficult to the degree that anyone who makes it through naturally has feelings of superiority over others. After all, if you weren't good enough to become cavalry, then what good were you? To make it into the program, we had to pass a grueling selection process designed to eliminate all applicants who weren't deemed mentally or physically capable of surviving the training. At least, it felt gruelling at the time. Once we made it to boot and the actual training began, we saw that the selection process was only the beginning. Even if you were selected and made it through the training, you still weren't guaranteed a spot. In order to be a cavalry soldier, you needed a Wargon partner, and Wargons can be picky about who they partner with.

After we endured the toughest, hard-core training the Federation could imagine and were lucky enough to find a Wargon willing to let us ride them, we assumed we were ready for anything. Prepared to take on the galaxy. It didn't take long for reality to set in, and we quickly realized how wrong we were. Us recruits were all too eager to jump headfirst into any combat that came our way. Didn't matter where we were or what we were fighting for. We were just excited to prove how tough and brave we were. Too excited to enter a war, that for most of us, would never end.

All of us on that dropship were combat virgins except for Sgt. McKenzie and her Wargon. A hardened veteran in the truest sense, she was one of the last of the original cavalry soldiers. One of the glorious few who had ridden with General Jaxxon in the battle for the Wargon homeworld of Grimble. It was on Grimble that the Federation came to the Wargons aid, and the alliance between our species was forged. The battle marked a turning point in the Bug war as it was the first-time humans rode Wargons into combat, giving birth to the modern Federation cavalry. Even though Sgt. McKenzie was only a private back then. She quickly earned a reputation as a revered cavalry soldier.

I doubt that I will ever forget the sight of those two warriors stoically sitting at the front of the ship. Armoured Wargons are always an impressive sight, even to those of us that spend most of our time with them. Unarmoured, they look like an unnatural union between a Siberian tiger and a wolf. If that union pumped itself full of steroids and growth hormone, started bodybuilding, and then grew up in a warrior society. Titan strength paired with a predator's teeth and dagger like claws made these furry monsters the rulers of their world. Standing eight feet tall at the shoulders, these barrel chested, four-legged beasts weigh around two thousand pounds.

Now, take that one-ton beast and clad it in a thousand pounds of powered battle armour. Fit it with a rhinoceros-like plastanium horn. Add an armoured cavalry soldier mounted on top of it, armed to the teeth with Federation hardware, and you start to get the image of a typical cavalry pairing. However, Sgt. McKenzie and her Wargon were anything but typical.

The rest of us wore second-generation cavalry suits built from lightweight plastanium. Each plate was seamlessly formed and interlocked perfectly with the next. Completely self-contained, the armoured suits provide their wearers with the ability to fight in almost any environment. Like the Wargon's armour, the cavalry suits augmented the soldier's strength, giving them even greater combat ability. They were the most cutting-edge battle suits that the Federation had designed. Impressive works of engineering, the pinnacle of over five thousand years of human armour development.

Sgt. McKenzie and her Wargon did not wear this armour. Like most veterans of the early days, they preferred the older first-generation battle suits. They may not have been as advanced as the newer version, but what they lacked in technology, they made up for with their commanding presence. The sheer intimidating sight and sounds of the older metal suits gave their wearers a heroic quality, reminiscent of the epic stories we were told as children. Their cold industrial nature made them look like they belonged in the sketchbooks of mad scientists from Old Earth's pre-computer age period, not on starships.

McKenzie's armour was painted the same dull grey colour that the Federation used to paint everything. It was scratched, burned and scarred. Some parts had been clearly welded and repaired. You could see the tiny worm-like welds that hadn't been polished out. It's not that the older suits couldn't be flawlessly repaired; the veterans intentionally left them in rough shape. To them, each imperfection told a story of past battles fought. They were a testament to their combat experience.

Little colour could be found on her suit, except for her right shoulder. Here, she wore the three gold sergeant's chevrons beneath the same Mongols insignia that we all wore. Mongols is our legion's official designation, getting our name from the Old Earth horse soldiers that dominated ancient battlefields.

Even if McKenzie had worn the newer armour, she would still have stood in complete contrast to the rest of us. As we shifted anxiously on our mounts, eagerly awaiting our landing, she stood stoic and calm. Neither she nor her Wargon moved as our dropship hurtled towards its position. They both sat utterly still. Waiting.

I remember how my stomach turned as the adrenaline built in my body. Even though my battle suit kept me at a constant temperature, I felt a cold sweat coming over me. My skin grew slightly tighter as the hairs on my arms and neck began to stand up. My stomach was in knots, and I had the overwhelming need to shit, even though the meds we took before launch made that physically impossible. It wasn't fear of what was waiting for us that got to me. Instead, it was an intense need to get off that fucking dropship so that we could get on with the business of war.

I increased the oxygen level in my suit in an attempt to calm myself before my nervousness spread to my Wargon mount. The fact that I even attempted such a move was a sign of my inexperience. Wargon and rider are mentally linked through a jack the Federation installed in our heads. Any emotion is transferred instantly to our Wargon in a sort of simulated psychic connection that lets us communicate. They felt what we felt.

It wouldn't have mattered anyway. You could see everyone was on edge through the burning red glow of the standby light. Hell, even with no light, or jack in your head, you'd know how tense and nervous everyone was. You could feel it in the air like a living, breathing presence.

Our anxiety was abruptly interrupted as Sgt. McKenzie broke her stillness. When she began to move, the room fell completely still. All twitching and nervous action ceased instantly. It was the smallest of motions, but it had the most immense impact because it was the first move she had made since getting on the ship. She lifted her head and straightened her spine ever so slightly. Then she spoke.

"The Federation believes that the cavalry is the weapon that's going to turn the tide of this war. They're calling us the perfect Bug killing machine, and I couldn't agree more."

She paused to look us over.

"Do you know what I see when I look around this room?"

The room grew even stiller as our nervousness shifted to anticipation.

"Killers! Hard ass, no bullshit, ready to die for the Federation, killers."

At these words, we all sat a little taller on our mounts.

"Now, I don't know what kind of shit show we're going to be riding into down there, but I do know one thing. Those Bugs are in for one hell of a fight, because there isn't anything in the galaxy better at smashing Bugs than the Federation cavalry!"

Whatever nervousness was left in us receded as every soldier in the dropship responded with a loud guttural "huha!"

"Ready yourselves. By the time this engagement is over, those of you lucky enough to still be alive will no longer be recruits. You'll be veterans and you'll have earned the right to wear that armour. Earned the right to call yourselves cavalry!"

Another loud "huha" erupted from our ranks.

As it did, I felt primal aggression rising in me, purer and more animalistic than anything I had ever felt before. As if a beast that lived deep inside was waking up from its slumber. Ready to release a lifetime of frustration and anger on anything that would be unfortunate enough to cross its path. I felt like my blood was getting warmer. No, not just warmer. It was getting hot like it was about to boil. The jack in my head felt like it would burn right through my skull, then I realized what was happening. I had never experienced that feeling before because it wasn't my feeling at all. It was my Wargon's.

Our being roused by the Sergeant's words had fired up and excited the Wargons. We were getting worked up, and those savage beasts loved every minute of it. Their blood lust grew with every word the Sergeant spoke.

Sgt. McKenzie continued, "Get ready you filthy apes. Glory waits for no one."

The red light flashed three times as the shrill electronic buzzer sounded. Thirty seconds till landing. Thirty seconds until we learned the hard way what this fucking war was all about. Thirty seconds till we found out that glory might not wait for anyone, but death waits for us all.

A third of the soldiers on that ship never left the planet. The Sergeant was part of that third. Less than a quarter of those soldiers are here with me today. Our losses were massive in those early days. The Federation carelessly threw us into battles that we had no business in, just to see how cavalry would perform. Throughout human history, militaries have suffered from the same problem. No matter how great an army and its soldiers are, if they aren't used properly, they're going to be little more than cannon fodder. Luckily for us, they figured out how to properly deploy cavalry units while there were still enough of us left to be useful.

The loss of human life wasn't a big deal. Thanks to Federation-sponsored breeding efforts, we've managed to acquire enough soldiers to occupy the better part of the known galaxy. If half a million soldiers die in some backwater shit hole, nobody will take notice. But when it's Wargons who are getting killed, it's a problem.

Unlike us, the Wargon species, until recently, was restricted to one planet. They didn't have a galaxy of space and resources to support an ever-expanding population. Because they were a race of hunters, their population was limited even by planetary standards. Add this to the fact that they lost half of their population when the Bugs invaded, and you can begin to understand why Wargons are more valuable than humans. There just aren't as many of them to waste.

This doesn't mean they stopped sending us on suicide missions. They simply put more thought into picking which suicide missions would be worth sending us on. It's okay to be slaughtered, as long as some faceless officer that's never been remotely close to a battlefield has punched the numbers and decided it's worth it.

As we sit here, once again basking in that familiar red

glow of the standby light, I wonder how long they thought about this suicide mission. I wonder what the number crunchers over at Fleet considered when they decided how many of our lives could be spent to take this hellish rock of a planet.

Now that I wear the sergeants three gold chevrons on my shoulder, it's no surprise that I'm thinking of Sgt. McKenzie. When she sat stoically at the front of our first dropship, was she wondering the same things I am? Did the same questions plague her mind as they do mine? It occurs to me that maybe the reason she sat so still was that her mind was wrapped up in the same turmoil that mine now is. If a recruit was on this ship, would they look at me the same way I looked at Sgt. McKenzie? Would I appear as stoic and calm?

Was she wondering about the who and the why of the hell that awaited us? Or maybe she didn't care about the details. Perhaps she followed the Old Earth poet's words that said, "theirs not to reason why, theirs but to do and die." After all, those words were written about a cavalry unit and their doomed charge. A group of men who put aside all fear and followed orders because that's what soldiers do. Maybe a millennia later, those words still hold true. Or maybe, in the fast-paced reality of mounted warfare, there's no time for the irrelevant issue of the why. Only the how matters. How to fight. How to die. How to win.

My thoughts are interrupted by the growing roar as our dropship punches into the planet's thick, hostile atmosphere. The entire ship groans under the strain. This is the point in the drop where Sgt. McKenzie would have tried to fire everyone up with some rousing words. Those words that inspire young recruits to put aside their fear and try their hand at becoming heroes. Turning their anxiety into blood lust. But I'm not Sgt. McKenzie and my squad aren't new recruits anxious about their first real fight. My squad are all experienced veterans. Disenchanted with heroic dreams. All with more cavalry drops under their belts than Sgt. McKenzie ever had. We also have far superior battle suits that carefully regulate our adrenaline levels and ensure that we don't get too worked up.

The number crunchers realized a statistically higher rate of mistakes when cavalry had elevated adrenaline levels. I wonder how much time they wasted on that study. Any non-commissioned officer in the Federation, or any army in the history of humankind, could have told them that when the blood lust is high, soldiers fuck up.

No, the soldiers and Wargons on this ship don't require grand speeches about the glory of war. They all know the truth of it. They have all been around long enough to have experienced the cold hard reality of war. This war in particular. All the morale-boosting and chest-thumping doesn't change the fact that we have a job to do. It may help the recruit whose most significant challenge is overcoming the anxiety of their first engagement. Still, for experienced veterans, it's of little use. What we need is the ability to focus on the job at hand and keep our heads long enough to complete it. All too often, we have seen Wargon and rider fly into uncontrollable blood lust and rush off to certain death.

By the sounds of it, death may be sure enough on this drop without the added liability of enraged blood lust. This is the biggest single planet assault that the Federation has ever launched, and the death toll will be incredible. They say that this rock must be taken no matter what it costs. I can't help but think how easy it is to say that before the cost has been paid. They might have a different opinion once the death toll and bills for destroyed Federation assets are calculated. It's one thing to say that you'll pay any cost. It's another thing entirely to live with the knowledge that something has cost you everything.

The shrill electric buzzer sounds in its predictable tone as the standby light flashes the thirty-second warning. The sound that used to fill my body with anxiety, preparing me for imminent combat, now holds no more significance than its designers intended. It's just light and sound, nothing more. The truth is, after enough drops into unforgivably brutal combat, you remain in a constant state of readiness. You never turn it off. The warrior is always there, waiting, ready for battle. You couldn't get rid of it if you wanted to.

I think about saying something to the squad. Some last bit of inspiration that will somehow make what we're about to experience seem less horrid, but there's nothing to say that could do that. Everyone on this ship, human and Wargon alike, knows damn well what fighting Bugs is like. No matter what you do, you'll never be prepared for what you encounter when the blast doors open. Not really. Especially on an operation of this scale.

So, we wait, still and silent. Listening to the roar of the thrusters as we position to land. We brace for the coming impact of the ship landing a little harder than it should. They always land a little harder than they should.

Boom. Impact. Each Wargon and rider grows tense and alert as they ready themselves. I feel my legs flex, squeezing my Wargon beneath me. I tighten my right hand on the grip of my battle rifle as my left grabs the front handle of the saddle. I feel a surreal sense of calm coming through my jack from my Wargon, the calm before the storm. With a slight hydraulic groan, the locks on the blast doors disengage. Then there's a split second of silence. A split second that feels like an eternity before almost instantly, the hulking plastanium blast doors spring open.

CHAPTER TWO

Forty-eight hours before the drop, we are summoned to the final officer's briefing.

I'm not an officer, but due to the inconvenient tendency for large amounts of cavalry to be wiped out in short periods of time, field promotions were a regular occurrence. To help mitigate the effect this has on active units, the Federation decided that it would be best for NCOs to be included in officer briefings. That way, if an officer got taken out, there would be a lineup of people ready to step into their role and the meat grinder could keep moving.

The officers also appreciated us being there because it meant that we could take a more active role in briefing the troops. They claim that NCOs doing briefings helped build the chain of responsibility, but I figured they made that up because they didn't feel like doing it themselves.

All large-scale briefings are held in virtual reality to save space and time. In the past, command ships housed large auditoriums specifically for briefings. Apart from being a poor use of space on an already crowded starship, it required people to physically shuttle to the command ship. This cost valuable time and was often a logistical nightmare. Of course, these were sensible reasons to hold briefings in VR, but they were not the only reasons. The main reason that meetings were held in VR was that the Federation was afraid of having too many high-ranking officers in one place at the same time. If an enemy found out about a meeting, we would be highly vulnerable. An entire invasion could be stopped before the first dropships or bombers were launched. This was a reasonable concern, but the Federation denied that it played a role in their decision to hold virtual meetings. They felt that admitting that they could ever be vulnerable would be an unnecessary sign of weakness.

I get word that the briefing is about to start, so I put on my headset and jack in. I find myself sitting in a large auditorium. As I look around the simulated room, I'm floored by how many different legions are here. I know this was being touted as the biggest invasion in history, but I guess the reality of what that meant hadn't yet settled in. If I didn't know better, I would have guessed that every officer in the Federation was currently sitting in this room.

Lieutenant Jeanceon, who is sitting beside me, leans over and says, "Get a good look Sergeant, nearly every legion in the Federation is represented here. Make no mistake, this invasion will be one for the history books. I can promise you that."

I think about telling him that almost every invasion

would be part of our history books because the Federation records nearly everything, but I keep it to myself. Best not to sass the Lieutenant right before a drop.

"Look," the Lieutenant says, pointing across the crowd. "They even called in the reserves and the expeditionary forces."

"No shit," I reply as I look to where both groups are sitting.

This is surprising because reserve forces are only ever called in when enough regular troops aren't readily available, but we have practically every regular force in the Federation here.

The presence of expeditionary forces is also extraordinary to see as part of an invasion. They are highly trained soldiers, but they're specialists who mostly stick to exploration and small scrimmages. Typically, they're deployed on unexplored planets in the far reaches of the galaxy. Although they could hold their own in the specific style of guerilla warfare that they're trained in, they had little to no experience in open war. Including them in a full-scale invasion just didn't make sense. Which raises the question as to what the fuck they are doing here?

"Why would the Federation include the expeditionary forces in an invasion?" I ask the Lieutenant.

"It's all about numbers Sergeant. The Federation has called in every available person capable of holding a weapon and following a battle plan. This is an all hands on deck situation."

Did the Federation really think that this operation was going to require this many bodies? We have never needed this many boots on the ground to fight Bugs. Usually, air support and heavy armour do most of the work in a Bug fight.

Seeing these forces reminds me of something that sends a chill down my spine. I remember reading about how legendary Old Earth conqueror, Genghis Kahn, used to send in waves of captured soldiers at the beginning of a large assault to soak up enemy arrows. His generals knew that assaulting certain locations would cost a particular number of lives. It didn't matter how well trained those soldiers were. The same number would die. So he would use the prisoner armies to do the majority of the dying before sending in his own skilled troops. By the look of this crowd, I'm starting to think the Federation is using a similar approach. The only difference is they're going to use reservists and expeditionary forces instead of prisoners.

I look at the Lieutenant.

"Sir, this is going to be a blood bath, isn't it?"

The Lieutenant says nothing. He just looks at me and

gives a considerate nod.

Three beeps sound in my ear, signalling the start of the briefing, and at once, the immense crowd falls silent. All eyes turn to Chief Fleet Admiral Holoiday as he walks out on the stage in the center of the digital auditorium. Dressed head to toe in the finest military uniform that the Federation has to offer. He is the spitting image of a desk jockey officer. On his chest, he wears more medals than I've ever seen on a single person. I didn't even know a uniform could hold that many medals. I guess sitting behind a desk, sending real soldiers to their deaths, requires a lot of recognition. Someone has to receive praise for their sacrifice. No point giving awards to soldiers that won't be around long enough to wear them anyway.

The Admiral addresses the crowd.

"Good evening. We stand here on the edge of the largest invasion in the history of our species. What will happen over the course of the next few months will undoubtedly decide the future of the Federation."

I find it funny how the Federation advertises every drop as the biggest event in history. I suppose soldiers are more eager to fight to the bitter end if they think they're part of some larger purpose.

My VR switches from the auditorium to an image of

a planet as the Admiral continues.

“This is Excalibur. With a radius of 6500km, it’s just a little bigger than Old Earth. However, apart from its approximate size, it shares little else with our beloved homeworld.

“Excalibur is a cold, barren rock not capable of sustaining human life. Its atmosphere is comprised mostly of argon, which means it will choke the life out of you. There is no water or natural fauna of any kind. If you’re thinking of catching a tan while on planet you’re shit out of luck because there isn’t any direct starlight either. The planet is covered by a thick layer of low-altitude orange cloud that blocks most of the light. These clouds also create a magnetic field that disrupts our guidance systems, making air travel extremely difficult.”

The Admiral continues listing reasons why Excalibur is a giant shit hole for a few more minutes. When I think the planet couldn’t sound any worse, he mentions the Bugs.

“Even though this planet should be completely uninhabitable, the Bugs have adapted extremely well to it,” the Admiral says before subjecting us to a long lecture about the adaptability of the enemy.

I really couldn’t give two fucks about most of what he had to say. The fact that “due to atmospheric pressure, the exoskeletons of Bugs on this planet are projected to be thirty percent stronger than previously encountered, making them more resistant to small arms fire," matters little to an armoured soldier riding a fully suited Wargon, capable of putting its colossal foreleg through a plastanium door.

The only thing that matters to me is that since there is no local food on this planet, the enemy must be storing their own food somewhere. This means that finding and destroying food supplies will be a high priority. Other than that, the only other thing of importance was the number of Bugs that we'd be up against. Excalibur is an enemy stronghold, with more Bugs than any other planet we've come across. Intelligence couldn't produce any solid numbers but said that it was safe to say there would be no shortage of hostiles to kill.

As the Admiral yammers on, my mind begins wandering as I try to figure out the point of all this. So far, we have an uninhabitable planet packed full of hostiles, and for some reason, we have massed the largest invasion Fleet in human history. But why? If the goal were simply to knock out a Bug stronghold, why not just unload a few planet buster bombs from orbit and be done with the matter. There must be a reason why the Federation wants this shit hole intact, but for the life of me, I can't imagine what that reason is.

Finally, my attention returns to the Admiral as he begins to explain.

"Taking all that into consideration I'm sure you're all wondering why the Federation would bother sending an invasion force in the first place. Why not just bomb the planet into oblivion?" the Admiral asks.

The rhetorical question must have been an intentional attempt to ensure that he had everyone's full attention. It is clearly the question on everyone's mind because all eyes are fixed on him once again.

He continues, "The reason that we don't simply bomb the Bugs off the planet is because we can't."

This grabs my attention even further since I've never heard of the Federation not being able to bomb something. Sure, there were many situations when decimating a planet with bombs is impractical or immoral, but it's always possible.

"The reason we can't bomb the Bugs off this rock is that the planet is made almost entirely out of schythium."

Gasps fill the auditorium, followed by unintelligible chatter.

"Well, no shit," I say aloud to nobody in particular.

If this planet is made up of schythium, it makes it the most valuable planet in existence. This is because schythium is a nearly indestructible metal that, until now, has only been found in minimal quantities. Most of the schythium that's been discovered has been found on asteroids. To our knowledge, humans are the only species that have been successfully able to mine and work it.

The Admiral waits for the chatter to die down before speaking.

"Now, I'm sure you can understand why we are pouring so many resources into this invasion. Our mission is to take the planet and strip it down to its core, claiming every ounce of schythium that we can get our hands on. That much schythium will allow us to not only manufacturer all future battle armour but entire starships. We could assemble a near indestructible battle Fleet that will give us an extreme edge in this war and any future wars that we might find ourselves in. When we take this planet, its resources will protect the Federation from all enemies, present and future."

I wonder what future enemies they might be concerned about that would require a schythium clad Fleet to defeat. But my ponderings are cut short once more by the Admiral.

"Don't get too excited. The schythium is the prize and prizes are for winners. We haven't won anything yet."

The Admiral shows us endless amounts of incomplete maps and blurry photos of the planet as he explains the battle plan. Due to the thick cloud cover and extreme magnetic interference, Intelligence was limited in their ability to adequately scout the planet. From what we are able to see, it looks like Excalibur is the worst possible place to fight Bugs that one could imagine.

With deep canyons and towering razor-sharp peaks, Excalibur looks like the place where nightmares are born. There were practically no open spaces on the entire planet, just cliffs, tunnels, and jagged rock. This will make the fighting an up close and personal experience. The limited open space means that our heavy cannons will have a minimal field of fire. It also means that air support would be basically useless. With the rock being made of schythium, we could drop our biggest, meanest bombs, and they wouldn't make a fucking dent. Due to the thick argon atmosphere, the Fleet's favourite tactic of firebombing will be off the table too. The Bugs are going to have every advantage here.

The Admiral points out that there are five flat areas large enough to land enough ships to establish proverbial beachheads. The invasion force will be divided up between each landing zone, labelled Alpha through Echo. The Mongols were assigned landing zone Bravo, along with the Hussars, who are a cavalry legion much like our own. The two legions will give us close to twenty thousand mounted soldiers to back up the other ten million personnel assigned to landing zone Bravo. This was the smaller of the five landing sites, which is why our numbers were so few compared to the other zones.

Over ten million soldiers might sound like a lot, but considering the enemy will likely be over a billion strong, and we will have almost no air support, this is going to be a cluster fuck.

The problem is there simply isn't enough physical space to land, and house, the required soldiers. Unlike Bugs, humans need space to live. We need supplies and facilities to prepare food, recharge suits, store power and extra weapons. Humans also need an area off the front line to let soldiers rest. Soldiers left on the line for too long start to degrade in quality. They get strung out, lose focus, and their ability to make good decisions on the fly disappears.

A Bug can be left in the field indefinitely because their warriors don't have the burden of needing to think for themselves. Their mental processes are a little more than simple animal cunning. They detect threats and adapt as required, but any real thinking is done by the Queen. A horde of Bugs given the instruction to ambush a target will do so with finely honed instincts and effectiveness. It might even appear to be thinking, but it's really just reacting to stimuli and adapting its tactics as needed. If they're told to hold a line, they will do it effectively until ordered to stop, or they die of starvation.

Our landing site is a few square kilometres of flat ground in the shape of the number eight, only with the top circle being a third the size of the bottom. On the North, the site is bordered by razor-sharp mountains that appear utterly impassable above ground. They are, however, filled with unmapped tunnels. The battle plan states that the Hussars are to lead the way into these tunnels, backed up by light infantry and an expeditionary unit. After the tunnels are taken, they will be closed in with plastanium airlocks and will serve as part of the base that will be erected.

East of the LZ was much like the North, with high jagged cliffs but with a few surface passes through the rock. The passes weave up through the cliffs and into the thick cloud cover. Not seeing what is at the top of the cliffs will be a disadvantage, but it can be overcome by how easy these tight passes will be to defend. With the right amount of reinforcement, the enemy could hide four armies up in the cliffs and not pose a severe threat to the base that will be constructed below.

The west side of the LZ was nicknamed the Surf because it looks like the meanest waves from the roughest ocean imaginable, only instead of water, they are formed from razor-sharp schythium. The tight geography will give the Bugs almost limitless cover, making the Surf a living hell for the soldiers tasked to take it. The only saving grace is that there is enough room between the waves for Goliath suits to maneuver.

Our area of deployment is going to be on the south side of the LZ. Where a series of canyons create a maze in the towering southern cliffs. Most canyons are wide enough for three Wargons to ride side-by-side and have sufficient room to fight. This will be advantageous for us cavalry soldiers because superior numbers won't count for much when the enemy can't line up more than four or five wide.

The plan, as it pertains to us, goes as follows. An hour before the first dropships land, Fleet will begin bombing the planet. The hope is that if they hit the planet with the biggest bombs available, they will clear the Surface of Bugs. They also hope that the resulting shock waves will stun anything close to the Surface, buying us time to land and exit our ships. Rather than just bombing the LZs, the Federation will hammer the entire planet in an attempt to hide our intended LZs. Although those bastards have the nasty habit of always knowing when and where we'll be dropping.

The Mongols will be the first to drop on the Southside, landing at the edge of the flat and quickly getting into formation. Once in formation, we will deploy a quarter of our forces on the eastern side of the canyons. Pushing as far forward as possible before turning west to hit the bulk of the approaching enemy in the flank. The remaining forces will charge straight into the canyons hitting the Bugs head-on. The Samurai heavy infantry will follow behind and help support the center.

The goal is to clear the area of Bugs so the engineers can construct a base and reinforce the location. With pre-built buildings and sections of wall, they should be able to put a base up relatively quickly. Reinforcing the outer perimeter will take more time, but with the Bug population in the area smashed, they should have a week or two to get everything up and functioning.

I hate the idea of building a base. Anytime we've tried a take and hold strategy in this war, it has turned into a fucking mess. By picking a piece of land and trying to hold it, we're basically putting up a flag and telling the Bugs to come and get us. They have the numbers and ability to hatch reinforcements to launch assault after punishing assault. Their resolve never breaks. But after watching your friends being ripped apart, day after day, our soldiers will eventually find their breaking point. After all the battles we've fought, it's become clear that the only winning strategy is to find the hives and destroy them. If it's a barren planet like this, you can target food supplies as well, but hiding behind the walls of a fort-like ancient Babylonians is a sure-fire way to die.

The Admiral claims, "I know this might not sound like the most ideal option, but it is the only option. We would much rather assault their hives directly, only we can't find them. So, we're going to do this the old-fashioned way."

Old fashion is always code for stupid. It's no surprise

that the egg heads at Military Intelligence couldn't find the hives. Those stupid fucks couldn't find their dicks to take a piss without someone telling them where to look first.

The Admiral finishes his briefing with some "never give up, fight till the last," bullshit that I can't be bothered to listen to.

I was too busy thinking over the details of the dip shit plan that we've just been handed. I swear the Admiral took notes for his battle plan from the romantic Middle Ages of Old Earth. Building forts to hold territory like some kind of iron age king. We have starships and dropships, so why not sit safely in orbit and launch assaults from there. Instead, we are going to paint targets on our asses and sit still. It occurs to me that the Admiral thinks this is the best option because he is far too stupid to think of anything else. Here's a better option, fire him and promote someone smarter, like a fucking monkey.

After the pointless applause that follows any address from a high-ranking officer, Lieutenant Jeanceon looks over at me.

"Well, we have our orders. You have forty-four hours to get your squad briefed and geared up. Next time I see you will be on Excalibur, good luck Sergeant."

At that, I turned off my VR and was greeted by a view of my luxurious five by ten-foot room. I figure the one silver lining of the Admirals plan is that I probably wouldn't be seeing this room again.

CHAPTER THREE

"All due respect Sergeant but are you fucking serious," Corporal Wilson pipes up after I laid out Chief Fleet Admiral Holoiday's battle plan.

"There's no way they're that stupid, are they?" Wilson asks.

By the looks on everyone's faces, I can tell they all have the same question as Corporal Wilson.

"It's not that they're stupid, it's a matter of the fact that the material Excalibur is made from is worth far more than our lives are. So, if every one of us needs to die in order to take it, that's exactly what we're expected to do. We're cavalry soldiers, taking shit orders and making them work is what we do best," I reply.

Looking at the faces in the room, I ask the group, "Do you know how much of an advantage an entire Fleet of Schythium battle ships would be?"

"But Sergeant," Private Crang responds. "The shields on our battle ships are already practically impenetrable to any weapon we've come across, except maybe a few of our own. How much more impenetrable do we need our ships to be?"

I explain how if we have weapons that can puncture our current shields, there is a good chance that someone else out there has them too. There is a hard reality in war that today's best technological advancement is yesterday's outdated relic. I remind them that just because we haven't run into anyone with a better aptitude for war than us yet, it doesn't mean they're not out there. There was a time that we didn't know about Wargons, or even Bugs, for that matter. Hell, there was even a time when people were openly mocked for even uttering the idea that there might be life on planets other than Old Earth. It's a common human weakness to think that our current perception of the galaxy reflects reality.

"Need I remind you that we still don't know how Bugs move from one planet to another. They're highly intelligent but the lack of anything remotely resembling hands makes building things like star ships out of the question. So, how then do these filthy Bugs end up on planets all over the galaxy? What's more, how do they invade planets? The only guess I've heard that makes any sense is someone is doing the moving for them. Someone capable of getting a hive into a planet without being noticed. If this is the case, whoever is doing it would have to be fairly advanced technologically," I say.

This has been a very controversial opinion that the Federation is very quick to shoot down. There isn't any good reason for them shooting it down other than they feel that it somehow challenges their authority. Suppose it turned out that there was a species superior to or even equal to our own. It could affect the power structure of the Federation. Most planets, colonies, and even space stations, remain loyal to the Federation simply because there is no other option. The Federation is, as of the present, the dominant power in the galaxy.

The fact is, we don't know how the Bugs get from planet to planet. If someone is moving them, we definitely don't know why or how. All the Federation knows is that one way or another, our position in the galaxy would be a lot more comfortable with an indestructible Schythium Fleet.

I change the subject.

"All that aside, think about the difference that much Schythium would have for the boots on the ground. I for one would feel a lot better riding into battle with a full Schythium battle suit. With just one Schythium clad cavalry legion, we'd be able to smash any hive we come across."

Most of the squad starts nodding in agreement until Corporal Wilson points out that all the Schythium cavalry suits in the galaxy wouldn't make one lick of difference if there weren't any cavalry left to wear them.

"If there aren't any cavalry left to wear the suits, that means we're all dead, and it won't be our concern anymore, will it, Wilson?" Corporal Wenjack says, putting that concern to rest.

Corporal Wilson shrugs his shoulders, conceding the issue.

Making an attempt to get our focus back on the mission, I continue.

"To be honest, this plan isn't as bad for us as it could be. The tight canyon walls will provide us with a few advantages. Our flanks will be protected so we'll only really have to focus on fighting what is in front of us, rather than being constantly worried about getting hit from the sides. The Bugs biggest advantage is their numbers, but the tight walls will considerably limit that advantage. The Bugs will only be able to stand about four side by side, so it will be three Wargons against four Bugs at a time. Not bad odds for us."

"This plan assumes that the Bugs will be mostly attacking up the center," Corporal Wenjack adds. "If we're unlucky and they come down the flank, we'll be jammed up pretty quick."

"It would actually be for the best if they did. If they directed their main assault up our side, all we would have to do is hold the line and wait for our main force to swing around and crush them," I say.

"As long as we can stay alive long enough for our main force to get there," Corporal Wenjack says.

"Shit Wenjack. If we make sure to die in the right spot our corpses will jam the passes shut long enough for them to arrive. It's a win-win," Wilson says.

Corporal Wilson's comment would seem like a sarcastic attempt at humour to a civilian observer, but he was dead serious. Civilians tend to think that their lives are so valuable that they would only be worth sacrificing for something significant. Modern soldiers realize that our lives are anything but valuable, with trillions of humans populating the galaxy. Giving our lives to achieve any goal, no matter how important, is not only commonplace but expected. If a soldier's job is to hold the line, nobody cares if he does this task while dead or alive. Success is the only important factor.

I go over the plans a few more times with my section until each soldier has memorized them completely. We meticulously analyze every detail of the briefing packet, making damn sure that everyone knows exactly what to do when we land. The Bugs have the advantage of being controlled by a single hive brain that allows them to move flawlessly as a cohesive unit. Every Bug operates as part of a larger whole. We do our best to reduce this advantage by being extremely diligent when going over plans and ensuring everyone is on the same page. By the end of the briefing, every member of the team should be able to explain the jobs of every other member without fail. It wasn't as smooth as being controlled by a single brain, but it did help us move with a united goal, which was close. We could position and move as one entity through our detailed planning, intensive training, and drill, which might appear like we were controlled by one brain to the casual observer.

We also had the distinct luxury of being able to mentally communicate with our Wargons. Wargons are naturally able to communicate through a genetic link that they all share. We haven't been able to figure out how it works precisely, but it allows them to instantly share a certain level of thought, which is very useful in the heat of battle.

This link is what forms the groundwork for how we communicate with our Wargons. The egg heads at Fleet discovered a way to communicate with Wargons by sharing emotion and intention through a simulated psychic link. Although, I've never been capable of understanding the science behind how it actually works. The idiots' explanation that I was given was the jack installed in our heads captures electrical signals in our brains and transfers them to our suit's computer. This signal is then sent to the Wargon's suit, translated, and delivered through their jack. My understanding of such things begins and ends with that simple explanation because a cavalry soldier understands science as much as a scientist understands being a cavalry soldier. All I need to know is that it works.

One area where not having a single hive brain is an advantage over our adversaries is experience. Each member of my team is a battle-hardened veteran with extensive combat experience. That means when we're preparing for a deployment, we have twenty-four unique perspectives making predictions. The value of this can't be understated. In combat, battles are often lost because someone failed to predict a possible point of failure in the plan. By having each soldier go over the plans with their unique perspective, we can anticipate far more possible scenarios and ensure that we're prepared for them. This is something that the Bugs simply can't do. They are limited by the intellect and experience of the particular Bug doing the thinking for the rest of the hive. No matter how smart that Bug is, and make no mistake, those fuckers are really damn smart, they are limited in their perspective.

Our briefing is interrupted by a loud knocking on the briefing room's door frame. A gargantuan man who looks like he is the product of a breeding experiment between a gorilla and a brick shit house walks in. He must be around six-foot, ten and weighing at least three hundred pounds, none of it slack bellied. The standard light infantry soldier in full battle suit was just barely the same size that this son of a bitch is in coveralls.

He speaks with a voice so deep that its vibrations

travel through us so that we can feel it almost as well as we can hear it.

"Sergeant Braddock?" he asks.

"Yeah. That's me."

"I am Sergeant Kato, from the Samurai heavy Infantry legion," the large man says in an accent typical of a Samurai.

I hold myself back from asking him about his name. It had become fashionable for members of the Samurai legion to adopt Japanese last names. Every soldier who wasn't Samurai found this practice laughable. It made an otherwise impressive military legion look like role-playing children. Asking Samurai what their real name actually was, became a sure-fire way to get under their skin.

Every legion was named after famous armies from Old Earth's pre-Federation history. The practice was adopted in an attempt to remind Federation forces where they originally came from. It was supposed to give us a sense of unity by reminding us that even though we might have grown up on different planets, we all originally came from Old Earth. The soldiers also loved it. Everyone likes the idea of having their own symbol and feeling like they belong to a special club. Humans are ridiculous like that. But most of us wouldn't go so far as to pretend that we actually are those units from history.

I'm a Mongol, and I take pride in the fact that my legion is named in honour of Genghis Kahn's legendary horse soldiers. I'd even be willing to admit that having the name Mongol printed on my armour inspires me to fight a little harder than I otherwise might. But it doesn't mean that I'm going to change my name to Baatar and start drinking fermented horse milk.

The Samurai were different. They gobbled this shit right up. Changing their names, adopting new accents, and even going so far as to carry a pair of swords into battle with them. Granted, those swords did come in handy when the Bugs got close, and things started getting messy. Most soldiers are completely fucked when a Bug fight gets up close and personal, but the Samurai live for those moments. They love nothing more than the idea of dying with one of those stupid swords in their hands. This is because they chose to adopt the ancient Japanese code of Bushido. At least what their interpretation of Bushido was. Imperial Japan folded over a thousand years ago when the first atomic bombs fell. So, any information on Bushido had to be the best guess based on digital copies of old books. I'm sure whatever they currently believe is a far cry from what the code initially was.

All the role-playing bull shit aside, they were one hell of a legion, and I was more than happy to have them backing us up on this drop. That's why I decide to avoid asking him about his name. Better not to piss off the guy who's going to be watching your back. Especially when he's holding a mini cannon or Gatling laser. In general, it's also a bad idea to say something that could start a fight with someone who could fold me in half and use me as a fuck toy. So, I let him continue.

"Sergeant Braddock. As you know, we will be providing your back up for tomorrow's assault. It's my understanding that you will be leading the charge up the outer most section of the flank. Is this correct?" he asks, speaking in a steady, measured tone that's typical of Samurai.

"Yeah, that's right."

"Very good. My section will be responsible for handling your rear."

As he speaks, I can hear a couple of my soldiers start to chuckle. The immature humour is lost on the big man, and he continues.

"I just wanted to meet you face to face before the drop and assure you that your rear will be secure in our hands," he says, completely deadpan.

I continue trying to keep an air of professionalism, but his continued comments about our rears were becoming a source of amusement for many in my section.

"Thank you, Sergeant. It's ah, good to hear that our rear will be handled by someone with experience, in that area," I say, trying not to laugh.

"Yes, we are very experienced and have handled the rear many times. You won't have to worry about your rear as long as it is in our capable hands," he says.

At this, a few of my soldiers can no longer hold back their amusement and crack out laughing. I can see the rest going red in the face trying to keep it together. I think that this guy must be fucking with me right now because there is no way he doesn't realize what he is saying. Maybe someone put him up to it in an attempt to lighten the mood before the drop, but the deadpan look on the giant's face gave nothing away. Samurai weren't exactly known for their sense of humour either, so it was a rare pleasure if it was a joke.

Luckily, I manage to keep my own laughter stifled, and he continues with no acknowledgment of the laughter in the room.

"My soldiers are some of the best and we have been through many battles together. I would gladly trust my life to any one of them and often do. You can take comfort in the fact that if you get held up, we will be close behind," he says.

Despite his comments about our rears, I appreciate his words and thank him for his sentiment.

"Good luck to you and your soldiers, Sergeant Braddock."

With that, Sergeant Kato turns and leaves the room, ducking to clear the door frame.

I hear one of my privates blurt out, "Fuck, I'd like to handle his rear for a while," and everyone in the section breaks out laughing.

The laughter continues for a minute before falling quiet. The unexpected bit of humour is a welcome, albeit temporary, distraction from the seriousness of the situation. Although this close to a major drop, it's typical for the humour and positivity to, all of a sudden, be sucked out of a room as the sense of what's to come settles in. It feels like Death himself just walked in and put his boney hands on your shoulders. No matter how many drops you make or battles you fight, you can't prevent it from happening. You just learn to accept it and even respect it.

After a pause, I break the cold silence.

"I think we've beat this thing to death long enough and have covered all that we can. Tomorrow, we'll meet up at the muster location in hanger five. There we will have our final equipment briefing before suiting up for the drop. You've got nine hours, so grab whatever sack time you can because it might be the last time you sleep in a bed for a while. Section dismissed," I say.

"Nighty night, keep your buttholes tight," Corporal Wilson says to the group.

"Won't do you any good with ass man Kato lurking around. That guy could crack your cheeks open like an egg," Private Crang adds.

"Don't threaten me with a good time," Private Powel says, and the section all laugh as they stand to leave.

All the soldiers file out of the room except for Corporal Wenjack. Wenjack was the only soldier that I'd known for my entire career. We were part of six who had attended Boot together and ended up getting assigned to the same dropship. It's now rare for a dropship to have that many recruits from the same Boot, but in those early days, it was more common. The other four had all bought the farm somewhere along the way. Only Wenjack and I now remained. Corporal Wilson was the only other soldier in our section that was a veteran of our first drop. The drop when Sgt. McKenzie led us into combat for our first time, and her last. Everyone else had either been transferred to other sections or bought it. Of those few remaining soldiers, only Wenjack and I shared the bond of surviving Boot together, and that is a bond that is never forgotten.

For us, Boot is like your childhood and those recruits that went through it with you are your brothers and sisters. No matter what happens in your life or career, you are always happy to run into someone you booted with. It's like seeing family. Years could have gone by, and you could have served with thousands of different soldiers, but you still feel a special connection with your first family of recruits.

We leave the room together and head down the passageway toward our quarters.

As we walk, Wenjack asks me, "So, what's your honest opinion about this drop?"

"Honestly? I'm not sure what my opinion is. On one hand I'm eager to get after it. This is the biggest drop in history and I'm excited to be a part of it. I think the plan is kind of fucked and the odds of us making it through this one are pretty low, but that's firing me up even more. The fact that we might be charging to our deaths isn't scaring me, it's just making me impatient."

Wenjack gives me a questioning look.

"Not that I'm looking forward to dying or anything. It's just that if death is waiting for me down there, I want to know. I'd rather ride out and face it head on than sit here waiting," I say.

"I know what you mean. They train us for fighting not sitting around waiting. Which is funny because we spend far more time waiting than fighting. But, I think when this thing kicks off we're both going to wish we were back here and not down there." Wenjack says.

We walk a while longer in silence before he speaks again.

"What do you think are chances are on this one? Think we're fucked?" Wenjack asks.

I take a hard look at him before I respond, "Maybe, but then again maybe not. I think we're going to be in for the hardest fight of our lives, but I'm not sure if it will be the last. It's not the initial assault that worries me, I think we'll perform pretty well there. What I'm worried is going to break us down is how long we're going to be down in the shit. We've got some long fighting a head of us, this planet isn't going to fall into our hands after a few battles. Its going to be a long and drawn-out engagement and I'm not entirely sure that the Federation remembers how to deal with that. Only time will tell."

"What's troubling you then?" Wenjack asks. "I can see that something is weighing on you. There's been a sense of dread coming off you all day."

"It's that obvious?" I ask.

"It is to me at least," Wenjack answers.

"I am troubled," I admit. "My problem is that unless I die early, I'll be leading soldiers to their deaths, day after day, battle after battle. Slowly we'll lose more and more people. That's what's got me troubled."

Wenjack looks at me, carefully considering my words before he speaks.

"Well Sergeant, it sounds like whether or not we're fucked is out of our control. So, what's the point in worrying about it."

"I'm not sure if there is a point to worrying. It's just something that's hard not to do."

Wenjack nods his head and gives me a look of genuine understanding.

"I'm reminded of an old earth fable about a monk."

Of course he is, I think to myself. Everything reminds him of a story of something, but I choose to say nothing and let him continue.

"There was this monk you see, and one day he was out for a walk when all of a sudden he runs into a tiger. Big fucking tiger too, a real man eater, that could tear a man's flesh off without even breaking a sweat."

"Do tigers sweat?"

"Not the point of the story Braddock. So anyway, the monk is like, 'fuck, a tiger' and starts running. The son of a bitch is so scared that he runs right off a cliff. Luckily, he lands on a tree branch, and he's pretty happy. That is until he looks down and realizes that there are two even bigger tigers waiting on the ground beneath him. So, he's fucked. There are tigers everywhere. If he climbs up, he'll get eaten by a tiger. If he jumps down, he'll get eaten by two tigers. Just then, he looks forward and sees a single berry on a plant growing out of the rock, right in front of him. So, he eats the berry, and it was the best berry that this stupid shit ever ate."

I've never heard that story told quite that way before, but I understand what Wenjack is saying.

"I see your point," I tell him.

"Anyway, we should probably go grab some sack time."

He looks at me with a big grin and says, "Not me Sergeant, I've got a date with a cute weapons tech. I'm going to eat some berries."

He turns and walks away. Usually, I would have discouraged it the night before a drop, but I knew Wenjack could eat berries all night and still show up at a hundred percent the next morning.

On the way back to my quarters, I stop and look out a porthole, or at least that's what they call it. It was actually a digital screen linked to an outside camera. Putting a physical window of any kind in a starship would be beyond stupid.

As I look out the window, I am taken aback by how many ships are out there. Thousands of ships of every class are spread out as far as the eye could see. It looks as if the entire human race has come to fight. I imagine that this is what the Greeks must have felt like as their Fleet approached the beaches of Troy. I am overcome by the inescapable reality of how big the operation really was. No matter what horrors I would soon bear witness to, I would remember the beauty of this site. Humans from all over the galaxy united in one common goal.

CHAPTER FOUR

We file into the armoury briefing area with two hours remaining before the drop. Each soldier takes a seat as the armoury briefing officer enters the room. You can instantly tell that he's a tech and not a fighting man. His soft physical appearance gives it away as much as his weak presence. He holds the air of someone who hasn't been forced to come to terms with the hard facts of life, and yet, still considers himself an experienced military man. There is no mistaking the superior ego that is common among techs. They always think they're better than soldiers because we generally don't understand the engineering complexities that go into our battle suits and weapons. Of course, despite all their knowledge, they hadn't the foggiest clue what goes into actually using a suit. They tend to assume that you could put any monkey into one, and it would become a soldier.

Their attitudes were always more of a source of amusement for us rather than an annoyance. They can claim superiority all they want. It won't bother us one bit because last time I checked, human history wasn't filled with stories of great weapons techs. I can't recall one story of the weapons techs that supplied the battle of Troy or the ones that equipped King Arthur and his knights. Mongols never sang songs of the men that armed Genghis Kahn and his warriors. No legends are told about the man that handed Julius Caesar his sword before the battle of Alesia. I am comfortable assuming that this man's name will be forgotten too.

As we sit in our ranks waiting for the briefing to start, I hear Corporal Wilson whisper to anyone listening.

"This guy better not start talking about handling our rears."

This results in a burst of stifled laughter rolling across our ranks.

"Listen up," the briefing officer barks.

"You lot wouldn't be laughing if you knew what you were in for."

This makes us all laugh a little harder. Someone who's never seen combat telling a section of veterans that they didn't know what they were in for is utterly laughable.

He continues, "If you guys want to get killed, that's fine by me. But you're going to be wearing expensive Federation property and I'd appreciate if it was returned in one piece."

I quickly respond, "Is that an order, Sir?"

I wasn't trying to be insubordinate, but this guy is

pissing me off.

"Yes Sergeant, that is an order. An order from a superior officer," he snaps back.

I decide to let it go because if there was ever a time to be reprimanded for insubordination, it wasn't hours before a drop.

"Unless there are any more stupid questions from the peanut gallery, let us continue," he says as snarky as possible.

"Quick question Sir," Corporal Wilson says with his hand raised.

"Yes, what is it?" the tech says in annoyance.

"What's a penis gallery?" Wilson asks and nearly the entire section begins to laugh.

"What the fuck is wrong with you?" the tech snaps. "You are moments away from the biggest moment in Federation history and you think it's time for jokes?"

"No jokes Sir," Wilson says sincerely. "I was just confused. I've never heard of a penis gallery before. Which is weird because that sounds like a really cool place."

The rest of the section now fights to hold back their laughter as the tech's face goes beat red.

"You know damn well that I said peanut gallery. Not penis," the tech screams at Wilson. "Now, if one more of you fucking morons makes one more stupid joke, or talks back even slightly, I'm going to fucking court marshal every last one of you."

This tech clearly hasn't spent enough time around soldiers to know that a lot of us use humor as a way of coping. It keeps things light before they get dark.

"I'm sorry Sir," I say apologizing for Wilson. "We're just nervous is all. We also clearly lack the maturity required in the presence of an esteemed officer like yourself. Please continue."

The tech takes a deep breath.

"Alright. Well, let's continue. I'm not going to waste my breath explaining details of the upgrades that have been made to the suits because you probably wouldn't understand them anyway. All you need to know is they're going to work a little better than the last time you used them. Fast twitch programing has been increased, which means better reaction times. We've also done some other things that you couldn't possibly understand to increase overall strength and speed," he says.

Despite their repulsive personalities, I was happy to have these dorks on our side. Federation techs were geniuses when it came to setting up suits.

"The biggest changes that you need to be aware of, were made to the life support system," he says with a strange grin that I find off-putting. "Since you will be out in the field for extended periods of time, each suit has been equipped to supply your body with five days of nutrition and hydration, with an added supply of two days emergency level rations. This means that you will be able to function for up to one week before your body begins to die."

I wonder if they are really expecting us to be in the field that long without supplies.

"We have also set your suits up with enough tranquilizers and stimulants to put you to sleep and wake you back up six times," he adds.

Sleeping in a battle suit can be hard enough at the best of times, and doing it while in hostile territory is damn near impossible. For this reason, the Federation had battle suits equipped with a stimulant and tranquillizer system to help soldiers sleep in the field.

The officer turns on a screen behind him, including a list of weaponry that we will be equipped with.

"You'll be carrying the standard cavalry kit on this drop, but only more of it," he says.

"This is a kill everything that moves kind of drop, so the Federation has cleared us to equip you with the maximum amount of ordinance possible. The power capacity of your kit has been increased and extra power packs have been included. You should have enough power and explosives to fight all day and not worry about running out."

I have to admit that I liked the sound of that. Nothing is more frustrating than running out of firepower while in the middle of a Bug-infested shit hole.

The screen changes to a picture of a thermal Lance, and the armoury officer smiles.

"This, ladies and gentlemen, is the new and improved thermal lance."

A thermal lance is simply a long-shafted melee weapon that resembles a spear. The only difference is that once ignited, the tip burns hot enough to slice through Bugs like they weren't even there. They were a standard cavalry weapon and convenient in a pinch, but they had one major flaw. Once lit, they couldn't be put out. You had thirty minutes of continuous burn time, and then they were useless.

"This new model burns almost twice as hot and for over five times as long," he says with a grin. "It also has the added advantage of having the ability to be turned on and off."

The soldiers erupt in indistinguishable chatter. This will be a game-changer in the closed-quarters combat that we are undoubtedly riding into. With these new lances, we are going to cut the enemy to bits.

After the chatter quiets down, the officer goes over a few more changes to our kit, but nothing is as exciting as the thermal lance. The briefing ends with one and a half hours till drop.

We leave the briefing room and file into the armoury itself. Here we are attended to by an army of techs that help us into our suits. It takes three techs to get a soldier suited up and run through all the diagnostics required before a drop. All we soldiers have to do is stand still and be patient as we are bent and pulled at. I always wondered if this was what the ancient Knights of Old Earth felt like as their squires dressed them for battle. There was no way of knowing, but I think the thought of it helps me feel less like a piece of meat being caged for the slaughter.

After being suited up and our systems checked, we're given our armaments and sent into the hanger.

The hanger of our transport ship is probably the largest room that I've ever been in. It is big enough to hold twenty thousand soldiers, Wargons, and the dropships to carry them all. There is something to be said for the sight of that many soldiers and beasts standing in perfect ranks, all dressed in armoured battle suits.

Throughout human history, drill has always been an integral part of military training. It was expected that the better an army was at marching and standing in ranks, the better it would perform. A commonly held opinion was a well-drilled army was a disciplined and effective army. The end goal was always to appear as machine-like as possible.

Luckily for us, we required minimal instruction on the matter. With modern battle suits, you are simply required to follow the prompts on your heads-up display, and the computer does the rest. It tells you exactly where to stand, how to move and what to do. The result is an army that can execute a perfectly drilled parade with little to no effort. The Federation could suit up a million new recruits and, after half a day's training, have them execute a parade with each soldier moving to the exact inch that they're supposed to. The generals of the past would be green with envy if they could see us now.

As we march toward our marks, we pass the Samurai. The brilliant red, blue and gold of their suits stand in complete contrast to the dull grey of our own. They always keep their suits in pristine condition. Colours were never burnt or scratched, and the mirror-polished gold-coloured plastanium accents always shined bright. With all of the colours and flair, they weren't much for camouflage. Although I guess blending in doesn't matter when your armour is made from thick plastanium plates, and you're carrying the biggest handheld weaponry that the Federation has to offer. Samurai are essentially walking tanks.

As we pass them, the size difference becomes unmistakable. On average, they have about two feet of height on us and at least another foot in width. The actual size difference is in the thickness of our armour. Everything about their suits is thicker and heavier. They outweighed ours by at least five hundred pounds, which says a lot considering the relatively lightweight of plastanium.

If I tried to describe what a Samurai suit looks like in person, I'd say that you need to look up a picture of ancient Samurai armour. Then imagine if it was double the size and made from smooth plastanium plates. Now swell that imagined image up, like the suit had an allergic reaction. Add some bright metallic colour, and that will give you a pretty good idea of what these guys look like.

We march further through the hanger until we finally see our Wargons, waiting for us already in ranks. When I see my Wargon, I'm no longer aware of anything else. All I want to do is get over to him and jack in. There is an indescribable connection that is formed between a Wargon and its rider. It is like the bond shared between anyone who has been through combat together, but only more so. The bond of the shared experience of war is amplified by the emotional link that comes through our jack. We share every aspect of the trials we face, physical, mental and emotional. Maybe shared isn't even the right word because that still implies some level of separation. What we are experiencing is complete oneness.

After serving long enough with the same Wargon, you grow close. So close that you become part of one another, one mind occupying two bodies. It's a strange feeling, and it takes some time to get used to. At first, it can be very disorienting and confusing. If you're not careful, you can lose your sense of self and become lost in the experience.

One of the essential parts of cavalry training is dealing with the experience of being mentally linked to another species. To jack successfully, a person needs to have a strong enough sense of self to not be overtaken by joining the two minds. The ability to distinguish one's human emotions from the primal whims of the Wargon mind is critical for a successful connection. For the two to work effectively together, the human must supply emotional control. The Wargon brings the instincts and intuition of nature's perfect apex predator. Too much of one or the other, and the pairing doesn't work. It needs to be balanced.

If the human influence is too great, the Wargon loses too much of its natural desire to fight. It becomes overly docile and begins to lack the aggression needed to take the initiative required in combat. Part of why Wargon mounted cavalry are so effective is that soldiers are tapped into the Wargons instincts. They can draw from the Wargon's natural cunning that has been developed through millennia of hunting and war. When a Wargon loses that natural instinct, they're of little use.

On the other hand, if the pair is subject to more Wargon influence than human, they lose their ability to think clearly and follow orders. Often they become overwhelmed with directionless aggression and either start fighting with other cavalry or charging forward, they attempt to attack targets on their own. After a while, they become more animal than human and have to both be decommissioned.

By the time training ends, you've proven whether or not you're able to handle the link. At least you've proven that you can handle being linked, but the stress that you don't expect is when the link is separated. When we're suited up and jacked into our Wargon, we feel whole. However, when we're out of our suits and separated from our Wargons, we feel like a part of ourselves is missing. That feeling can be the hardest to deal with, a constant feeling of emptiness. Some soldiers can't deal with it and eventually end up snapping. Suicide is rare because we're so closely monitored, but it does happen. Most of the time, the ship's head shrinkers can tell when the separation is getting to someone, and they medicate the shit out of them. The medication turns people into social zombies but keeps them in good enough shape to fight.

We spend all of our ship time separated. Wargons don't travel well, so they spend most of their time hibernating in stasis chambers. After a long transport like this one, we can't wait to see our Wargons again.

When we finally get to our Wargons, we climb onto their high backs and lock our legs into their mounts. Then finally, we get to jack in. I can feel that he is as happy to be reconnected to me as I am to him. The separation is as hard on them as it is on us, perhaps even harder because they don't have the added benefit of the psychological assistance training that we do. We are one, and that bond is felt equally between us both.

Most of us had named our mounts, even though the so-called experts told us not to. They said that Wargons had no use for names, and calling them by one would only confuse it. Like most things experts told us, this too was wrong. So, I named my Wargon Sleipnir after Odin's horse from Old Earth's Norse mythology. Even though my Sleipnir would have used Odin's horse as a chew toy, I thought it was still a good name.

Once I get reacquainted with Sleipnir, I look around the hanger. As I do, I notice a dropship off to the side that is different than the rest. It's much smaller than the ones that we use, probably closer in size to the personal transports used by high-ranking officers. Only it's not like those vessels either. This ship is far more streamlined than the standard dropships, which are relatively bulky in appearance. The standard dropship is built to be able to move troops quickly but sacrifices maneuverability for cargo capacity. Whatever it was, it appears to have been designed with maneuverability in mind, almost like a cross between a dropship and a light fighter.

If its size and shape aren't enough to set it apart from other ships, its strange colour definitely is. In fact, I can't decide exactly what colour it even is. At first, I think it is a dull blue colour, but then it appears to be grey, then black, then purple. It is almost as if the colour is constantly changing, shifting between shades and hues. As soon as I think I know what colour it is, it shifts and becomes a different one. I eventually decide that this must be some kind of new camouflage that hadn't made it into mainstream production yet. I wonder who this strange ship is for and what its purpose is.

My ponderings are abruptly halted as I see the vessel's intended passengers. Riding across the hanger is a Wargon and its master, the likes of which I haven't seen before. To the best of my knowledge, Wargons are strictly used for cavalry legions. I hadn't heard of them being used for any other purpose. However, the Wargon and rider that I see before me are certainly not standard cavalry. Their suits appear thinner and of much lighter construction than our own. The Wargon's suit has an entirely different leg and hip construction than ours, with far larger actuators and joints. Increases in the size of the running gear coupled with the streamlined design make me guess that this armour was designed primarily for speed. Both of their suits bore the same colour-shifting ability as the ship.

My attention is drawn to the Tikka long barrel precision laser rifle slung across the rider's back. The weapon looks to be of comical proportions as it is almost as long as she is. I recognize the Tikka from the few campaigns I had fought against enemies of the non-Bug variety. The weapon was the rifle of choice for Federation snipers due to its incredible range and adjustable power settings. Having the ability to adjust from a low power shot that could kill an enemy without leaving an exit wound, to a high-power blast that could put a hole straight through an armoured vehicle, make it an optimal sniper weapon. You just didn't see them too often in the Bug wars because precision sniper fire wasn't of much use against a horde of a million Bugs. This was a war for rapid-fire and explosives. I wonder what reason this rider could have for carrying such a weapon.

In addition to the Tikka, she carried a cut-down Remington battle rifle, a Colt high-energy pistol and one of the new thermal lances. The Remington was built from the same base platform as our own rifles, but it had an adjustable stock and a much shorter barrel. It also appeared to have a larger power cell than was standard issue. The weapon was assembled for up-close fighting and stood in complete contrast to the long-range sniper weapon.

The combination of long and short-range weapons reminds me of the way hunters would arm themselves. Carrying a long-range firearm to shoot what they're hunting and a short-range high-power sidearm in case something decides to try hunting them. The high-speed lightweight armour they wore would be helpful for a hunter, but what purpose would a hunter have here. Bugs aren't exactly hard to find, and they definitely didn't require a hunter to track them. Much like a sniper, a hunter would have no place in a war against billions of Bugs. So then, what purpose did these two serve?

Given the light armour and quick speed that I imagine they have, maybe she's a scout? Even though I have never heard of a Wargon riding scout in all my years as a soldier. Most of the time, scouts wear a specially designed suit that looks more like a communications center on legs. They had little to no combat ability, intended strictly to travel fast and relay information back to command. This suit didn't appear to have any added communications equipment. Even though she looks too lightly armoured for heavy combat, she is too heavily armed for scouting.

I want to ask the Lieutenant if he knows who this mysterious woman is, but I know better and keep my mouth shut. If I am supposed to know who this strange rider is, then someone will tell me. The cavalry operates on a need-to-know basis, and I didn't need to know. Still, I am curious.

The lights in the hanger flash amber, signalling that it is time for us to board the dropships. I hear Lieutenant Jeanceon's voice in my ear.

"You know the plan Sergeant. Once we land, get your section into position as fast as possible".

"Copy that, Sir," I reply.

The entire hanger comes to life as sections start loading into their corresponding dropships. Everything moves with precision, like parts of a well-oiled machine. You would think that many people and Wargons moving in the same space would become chaotic, but we all move as if flawlessly choreographed. We appear more like robots than an assembly of individuals, just a bunch of plastanium soldiers marching where they are told. A perfect machine of blind obedience.

When it is our turn to load, we march into position and enter through our ship's large plastanium blast doors. As section leader, I take the head position in front of the doors. Section leaders are always the last ones on and the first ones off. This sometimes leads us to be the first ones killed, but that creates plenty of opportunities for newer recruits to move up the ladder through battlefield commissions. Once we're all in position, we're locked into place.

The hulking plastanium blast doors spring closed in front of me. They won't open again till we touch down on Excalibur. The red standby light turns on as the dropship launches from the transport. We sit there, letting the red light wash over us, ready, waiting.

CHAPTER FIVE

The blast doors open, and Excalibur greets us with an image of Hell itself. Even if the Bugs hadn't claimed this planet, infesting it with their murderous hordes, it would still be hellish by its nature alone. Upon laying eyes on its barren landscape, I feel a new comfort in the fact that we're going to mine it into oblivion, stripping it down to its useless core. A planet like this only exists to punish people for being foolish enough to test their bravery on its evil Surface. It doesn't need to exist.

The wicked traits of this hateful place are intensified by the dull orange light that radiates through the nearly impenetrable cloud cover. Before us, we can see about a kilometre of flat before the canyon walls rise out of the ground like towers of grim despair. They rise up to the limits of merciless orange clouds that fill the malicious skies.

We quickly exit the ships, and as we hit the ground, I notice how clean it is. I thought that we'd be dropping into a slick film of Bug guts sprinkled with fragments of bomb debris, but the ground is spotlessly clean. Fleet had bombed this place relentlessly, but since the ground was so hard, it repelled the force of the explosions. The result was all force being pushed outward, taking with it any trace of Bug or debris. Whatever Bugs were unlucky enough to be here when the bombs fell are long gone.

General Jaxxon addresses us over the command circuit, "Form up and get moving. Any Bugs who were stunned by the bombs won't take long to shake it off. We need to seize the advantage while we can".

Our heads-up displays flash with instructions, and we spur our Wargons into action. The explosive power of our Wargons, enhanced by their battle suits, launch us into a flat-out run. Within seconds, we are charging across the flat ground at a hundred and twenty kilometres an hour. Unlike cavalry armies of the past, we're able to form up into ranks while moving at full speed. Our heads-up displays guide us perfectly into position, so after only a short distance, we are already riding in flawless formation.

It feels good to be riding again, flat out across the plains. Even though we're probably only short moments away from embracing the complete chaos of war, I take time to appreciate the temporary peace as we ride. For a few seconds, I'm free of all the burden and stress of command as I ride out ahead of the others. With nobody in sight, it's just me and Sleipnir riding hard against the wind, and it feels incredible.

My serenity is short-lived as my heads-up display flashes instructions to move. I signal Sleipnir, and we cut hard to the left as we approach the entrances to the canyons. The cracks in the schythium walls gape at us like openings into the depths of Hell itself. The last opening on the left is outlined by a green light on my HUD, signalling our entry point. We ride hard for the gap, the armoured feet of Sleipnir and the other Wargons pounding hard against the unforgiving schythium ground. As we approach the gap, Corporal Wenjack rides up and takes the position on my right while Corporal Wilson takes the one on my left. The rest of my section files in behind us. Behind them are the other two hundred cavalry that make up our portion of the left flank.

Spaced three wide, we hit the entrance to the canyon flat out. I wish we could form a more expansive line, but the narrow halls of the canyon wouldn't permit it. So, three-wide would have to be enough. Our Wargons push hard, navigating the winding paths with impressive speed. Every time we turn a corner, I can feel my hand squeeze the grip of my rifle in excited anticipation. Focused, my eyes are constantly scanning for Bug activity.

"Come on you filthy bastards, where are ya?" I say in a whisper.

We are about a kilometre into the canyons and still no Bug contact. I guess the pre-landing airstrike had a more significant effect than I thought. Just then, I'm hit by the realization that I haven't heard anything over the coms links for the past minute or so. I check the connections, and sure enough, they're all dead except for the one linking the soldiers in this branch of the canyon. I run another scan and can't pick up anything. I cycle through my HUD, trying to get locations on the rest of the flank. Again, nothing. The high schythium walls are somehow blocking our communications.

The effectiveness of any army is directly related to its ability to communicate and coordinate. We are now able to do neither. We're essentially riding blind into one of the biggest fights of our lives. With the speed that we're moving forward, we could easily find ourselves deep behind enemy lines with no hope of reinforcement.

Through my desperate need to figure out what's going on, an idea comes to me. I decide to attempt something that I have never tried before. Something that, to my knowledge, nobody has ever tried before. I figure that since Sleipnir is mentally linked to the other Wargons, and I'm linked to Sleipnir, there must be a way that I can tap into the other Wargons through him. By focusing on my link with Sleipnir, I should be able to sort through his mind and find any emotion or thoughts that don't belong to him. Anything in his head that isn't coming from him, or I, must belong to another Wargon.

I relax and focus on Sleipnir's mind, looking for the link. Sleipnir is singularly focused on the charge, utterly uninterested in anything else. His mental clarity makes it easier to find the link. I find it and focus on exploring what can be found. Pushing past our own thoughts and feelings, I begin to feel others in his mind. I feel aggression, pain, excitement and a whole other cocktail of emotions that are uniquely felt by someone in the heat of combat. The others have no doubt engaged the enemy, and the fighting feels intense. Soldiers and Wargons are dying everywhere, and we still can't make contact. I can't find any thoughts, save our own, that don't suggest combat. It looks like we're the only ones that have yet to engage the enemy.

"Ride harder you apes!" I command, determined to join in the fighting.

Soon I hear it. The unmistakable sound of thousands of giant pointy legs striking the ground. Like the sound of millions of corn kernels popping all at once. At last, I see our enemy up ahead. A steady flow of Bugs begins pouring around the corner.

"Bugs!" I yell over the coms link as I open fire.

Immediately, Wenjack and Wilson join me in laying down a blanket of laser fire as we charge forward. The powerful blasts from our rifles make short work of the Bug's exoskeletons as they come apart under our heavy fire. I feel Sleipnir speeding up beneath me, trying to reach the Bugs before our laser fire does. He wants to get a piece of the Bugs for himself. But for now, he must be satisfied with feeling the

Bugs corpses crush beneath his feet as we ride over their dead.

We continue charging and shooting until we can no longer shoot the fuckers quick enough, and the Wargons finally get a piece of the action. Our Wargons lower their plastanium horns before we smash into the enemy with titanic force. Horns gore the Bugs as the Wargons incredible suited strength overwhelms them. The Bug's tough exoskeletons are no match. They crack and pop as Sleipnir, and the other Wargons crush them against the schythium walls and underfoot. When the Bugs' resistance becomes almost too much for us to push through, the second and third lines push up from behind, driving us forward. The combined power of our Wargons appears to be unstoppable in the tight confines of the canyon.

The Bugs break upon our ranks as we drive forward like a freight train of destruction. We continue shooting as our Wargons crash, crush, and smash through the Bugs. Our relentless laser assault leaves the air thick with bloody mist and vaporized bits of foul Bug bodies. Blood, limbs and laser fire pollute the air, all the while we drive forward, always forward, never giving an inch. Yard after yard, kilometre after kilometre, we take this horrid landscape away from the mindless bastards, spreading their blood and corpses as we go. Painting the canyon walls with our abstract art.

We hammer through them until there are no more left

in our way. I can feel through Sleipnir's mind that not all of our brethren are sharing in our success. Somewhere out there, cavalry are dying. I can feel them being ripped, torn and crushed as they fall. All the pain, loss, and death flood into my mind as I wish that I never opened this fucking link. But all the wishes in the galaxy won't help me escape from the mental onslaught that I have brought upon myself. There's no running from the torment of the dying and those that must witness it. I can't hide from their grim despair any more than they can. All I can do is keep going and kill as many of these fuckers as I can. Ending this thing as soon as possible.

Continuing forward, we venture deeper into these dammed canyons. It's not long until we hit another wave of Bugs. Digging deep, we smash through them with the same violent force as we did the first. Our Wargons crushing them with armoured foot, head and horn. Within the tight walls of the canyon, we create an unescapable meat grinder as we massacre every six-legged bag of shit that comes our way. Hundreds, thousands, tens of thousands. It doesn't matter how many come. We ride over them all. Fueled by the pain of our dying brothers and sisters. Fueled by our Wargons primal hatred of the filthy plague of Bugs. Fueled by our legion's pride. It doesn't matter how many Bugs we are thrown up against. The Mongols would not fail because our pride simply won't allow it.

Again and again, we repeat this dance, slaughtering

wave after wave until eventually, the Bugs stop coming. I wonder if we have finally passed their lines, but I can't be sure without an established coms link to the rest of the flank. We ride on until eventually, my HUD flashes the indication to turn at the next fork.

"Hard right!" I instruct, and we all bank to the right.

The fork turns us ninety degrees west from our southern direction. With little resistance, we're able to quickly cover ground as we head west. If the prompts on my heads-up display can be trusted, this change in direction means we are finally lined up to make our assault on the enemy's flank. At least, we hoped that was what we were doing. Given the technical issues we have already been dealing with, faulty HUD prompts would be consistent with our luck. If we are heading in the right direction, we should be linking up with Lieutenant Jeanceon and the rest any time now. If they're still alive.

So far, we've had no problem getting through the canyons. Hell, we haven't even had a single casualty yet. But I knew from tapping into Sleipnir's link, not everyone was as lucky as us. Mongols are dying. I can only hope there are enough of them left to join us when we finally hit the enemy in the flank. Assaulting millions of Bugs with two hundred cavalry wouldn't be sufficient enough to take the pressure off the main assault. If no other Mongols survived the run-up the flank, our only support would be the Samurai, and they're way behind us by now.

With no time to loiter, we continue west, slowing slightly as the canyon walls change for the first time. The walls widen, allowing us to temporarily ride five wide, almost doubling the width of our line. Smooth canyon walls give way to razor-sharp, jagged ones. This area looks like liquid metal had been splashed into the canyon and cooled instantly, creating waves of hardened schythium. All around us, tunnels and alcoves open everywhere.

"Keep your eyes open!" I say as a Bug leaps forward from an alcove, knocking Corporal Wilson straight off his Wargon.

"Ambush" I yell as all Hell breaks loose around us.

Bugs spring forth from every tunnel, crack, and alcove. Instinctually, we all turn to face outward in a defensive formation and start unloading laser fire in every direction. We respond to the ambush almost instantly, but the Bugs were still right on top of us.

The Wargons buck and thrash as we fire, but there are just too many damn Bugs. They are fucking everywhere.

"Lances!" I cry out as I drop my rifle, letting it hang suspended from its harness, and I reach for my thermal lance.

In one motion, I pull the lance from its holster and swing it at the enemy. Lighting the lance, it blazes to life as I swing it in a hard arc, severing any dirty Bug limbs that get in its way. The rest of the soldiers follow my lead, and soon we're a mass of stomping Wargons and swinging lances. Bug limbs and blood rain through the air as we kill without hesitation.

I'm forced to watch as a big fucking Bug grabs Wilson around the middle with its thick mandibles. Raising Wilson into the air, it snaps its mandibles closed, cutting him in half. Blood and plastanium shards rain down as the two halves of his body fall to the ground.

Wilson's Wargon rears up in a show of God-like power before bringing its full weight and rage down upon the Bug that was painted red with Wilson's blood. The enraged Wargon breaks ranks and begins wildly killing Bugs with careless abandon. There is no fear or control in the beast as it cascades blow after crushing blow onto its enemies. We do our best to hold ranks as it rampages around, enraged by the loss of its rider. Eventually, the mass of Bugs proves to be too much and bring it down. Shredding plastanium and flesh.

It couldn't have fallen more than fifteen feet away from us, but it may as well have been a mile because we couldn't break ranks to help. We can only watch as they tear open the plastanium suit and ravage the soft flesh that lays inside. Like a pack of scavengers ripping the insides from a shellfish, only with more blood. So much more blood.

By the time the Bugs stop coming, the canyon is a mess. Smashed carcasses are mixed with shredded plastanium and unrecognizable body parts that used to be Federation property. We do a quick assessment of casualties and find that we have only lost twenty-seven Mongols, no injured. It could have been a hell of a lot worse. If we didn't have so many experienced veterans, it probably would have gone differently.

I wonder if the rest of the flanking force had run into similar ambushes. That could explain the pain and loss that I felt through the link. Maybe the others didn't fare as well as us. Perhaps we're all that's left.

Typically, we would call in a retrieval ship to pick up our fallen brethren, but with no communications, that was going to be impossible. We despised the idea of leaving our fallen soldiers here, mixed in with the smashed corpses of the Bugs, but what other option did we have. If we didn't keep moving, more Mongols would die. We'd have to come back for them later, assuming we're going to be fortunate enough to have a later.

We ride on, trying to force the fresh memories of what just happened from our minds. Corporal Wilson was a friend, and I had just seen him torn to pieces before my eyes. The same way I've seen so many friends go over the years.

I've seen friends ripped up, shot up, and blown up. Even though you never get used to it, you learn how to push it into the dark corners of your mind. Push them down so deep that they can only Surface when your mind's defences are dimmed by the stillness of sleep. Only then can you remember, as the faces of those left behind come forward and call to you. They ask why they are dammed to suffer in darkness while you still have the privilege of walking in the light. Not a night's sleep passes without them calling to you, beckoning you to take your place among them. These things would be of little concern, though, if we don't manage to live long enough to dream again.

We continue west toward the main force, always looking for signs of the rest of our flank. Riding past fork after fork, we expect they should be pouring out to join us, but so far, no one came. We take some comfort in knowing that Sgt. Kato and his Samurai were working their way up behind us. I hope that means that we don't have to worry about too many Bugs coming out of those openings after we pass. Then again, we've been moving along at an incredible pace, and I doubt that Sgt. Kato and his men are close behind.

I wonder if we've been moving too fast. Was the rest of the flanking force behind us somewhere, wondering if we were all dead? I focus on Sleipnir's link. I can tell that we're not the only ones left. There are more, just not as many as there should be. I can feel them getting closer as we push through the canyons until finally, I hear new voices coming over our coms link.

"Sgt. Braddock," Lieutenant Jeanceons voice breaks over the coms link.

Words can't describe how happy I am to hear his voice.

"Sergeant, how many soldiers have you lost," he asks.

"Twenty-seven Sir," I respond.

There is a short silence before the Lieutenant speaks again.

"I don't think you heard me Sergeant, I asked how many you've lost not how many you still have."

I reply, "I heard you loud and clear sir. I still have one hundred and seventy-three Mongols with Wargons to match."

There is another short pause before the Lieutenant says, "Good work Sergeant, those are impressive numbers given the situation. Best we can tell we still have just over five hundred Mongols on the flanking force".

Five hundred was a far cry from the two thousand that we started with, but five hundred Mongols were better than none. We would have to hit the flank even harder to make up the difference.

"We're just up a head of you on the right Sergeant. Keep riding and we'll merge in with you as you pass," the Lieutenant says.

I order my soldiers to spread out, leaving extra room in our ranks. We ride about half a click before seeing the fork where the Lieutenant and the rest of the Mongol flank are waiting. As we reach the fork, they ride forth and merge seamlessly with our ranks. The Lieutenant takes the center position, becoming the lead rider, and I settle in on his left. The position that Corporal Wilson previously filled for me.

I want to ask the Lieutenant how we had lost so many Mongols this early into a drop, but the battle suits of the surviving soldiers told as much of the story as I need to know. The layers of both human and Wargon blood mixed with Bug guts spelled it out pretty clear. They had ridden into Hell and paid dearly for it. Many Mongols gave their lives to get us to this point, and we needed to make it count. We held the flank. Now we needed to use it to our advantage and kill as many of these fucking Bugs as possible.

CHAPTER SIX

The camouflaged dropship circled the outer perimeter of the LZ before finding the perfect place to make its drop. A small section of rock on the Northwestern ridge line was just flat enough for a single Wargon to traverse. Not exactly a trail, but a skilled rider could make do, and she was definitely a skilled rider. Perhaps skilled is an understatement as she is, and has always been, one of the best riders that the Federation has ever produced. She could do things on a Wargon that most cavalry soldiers would claim were impossible. Then again, how could they know what was truly possible when they didn't know that riders like her existed. As far as they knew, they were the only ones privileged enough to ride the ferocious beasts.

The dropship hovered over its chosen drop zone, popping its blast door in mid-air. The camouflaged pair effortlessly jumped from the ship, landing smoothly on the small section of rock. Shooting up through the thick cloud cover, the dropship left its passengers standing on top of the towering cliffs. They stood there as motionless statues as if they were carved from the cold schythium itself. Stoic silhouettes, a thousand feet above the LZ.

From her high vantage point, she watched as the first

dropships penetrated the blanket of orange cloud as they hurtled toward the Surface. It was as if the entire sky had opened up all at once and begun raining thousands of little plastanium ships. They came down as fast as the laws of physics allowed, not applying the breaking thrusters until the last possible moment. Each ship slammed into the ground the way that two magnets might snap together with great force and then immediately cease all movement.

She watched the cavalry unload on the southern and northern landing zones, pouring out of the dropships. Even to an elite rider like her, it was impressive how they could exit the ships at a full sprint and perfectly form up on the move. Their coordinated movements were so smooth that it almost looked like they were being controlled by a single mind. Ironically, they moved like Bugs. From her high perch, they even looked like Bugs, just a horde of tiny warriors blindly following instructions.

There was a cold mechanical nature to the entire invasion, and everything moved in perfectly synchronized order. As one dropship emptied, it immediately shot back up, and another slammed down, taking its place. This provided an endless flow of troops, and the cavalry was able to seamlessly offload without a break in their ranks.

After the cavalry had all deployed, the bright and colourful Samurai took the southern field. Their ridiculously vibrant armour stood in complete contrast to her own. Everything about them stood in contrast to herself. She preferred to go unseen and have her existence be unknown, as where the Samurai needed everyone to know everything about them at all times. They acted like their very existence relied on people believing in them. Despite all of this, they were a spectacular sight.

Through the telescopic lenses of her helmet, she could see them clearly as they exited their ships. They formed up quickly, although it was noticeably slower than the cavalry. With precision, they marched into their ranks, carrying their massive weapons. Most infantry carried a version of the standard-issue Remington battle rifle. It was an excellent weapon with plenty of firepower, but it wasn't enough for the Samurai. Instead, they carried Gatling lasers, heavy automatic weapons with twelve rotating barrels. These weapons were more commonly found mounted atop walls or inside pill-boxes rather than in the hands of soldiers.

Despite the incredibly high rate of fire produced by a Gatling laser, the Samurai felt like they needed more. So, one in ten gave up the Gatling laser for a heavy blaster cannon capable of taking down a small ship or fighter. When these cannons were aimed at a horde of approaching Bugs, their blasts made a colossal mess of their ranks. The combination of the two weapons was absolutely devastating. Although for the Samurai, nothing spelled success quite like excess, so they also brought with them enough rockets and grenades to reduce a small city to rouble.

She watched as these walking armouries formed up and charged off into the distance. Running towards the towering southern canyons. The tall cliffs presented formidable geography, but the Federation had chosen the soldiers well. The combination of Mongol cavalry and heavy Samurai infantry should be able to turn those tight canyons into a slaughterhouse.

To the north, the Hussar cavalry offloaded much the same as the Mongols had. Despite all of the inter legion rivalry bullshit, Federation cavalry legions were basically all the same. Their names and legion insignias were about the only things that separated them.

Instead of Samurai, the Hussars were backed up by legion after legion of light infantry. These soldiers might not have been as heavily armed and armoured as their Samurai counterparts, but they made up for it with sheer numbers. They couldn't engage Bugs in hand-to-hand combat, but they were highly effective at using their vast numbers and advanced battlefield tactics. They were well-trained and dedicated soldiers, as ready to lay down their lives as anyone. Which was good because light infantry tended to have the highest casualties.

The northern tunnel network they were assaulting

was slated to be an integral part of the base to be built. That meant that the tunnels had to be cleared one yard at a time. They had to be entirely sure that no Bugs, or eggs, lay hidden in some out-of-the-way passage. Nothing could be missed. The fact that those deep tunnels were almost certainly crawling with Bugs was why the Federation was throwing so many soldiers at it.

She watched as the countless rows of soldiers formed up and charged into the tunnels. Their bravery still fresh in the dull orange light of the day. Whether or not their courage would hold in the dark tunnels when the silence was broken by scuttling Bugs and endless screams of the dying was yet to be seen. It's easy to be brave before bravery is truly required.

To the west, she watched as dropships unloaded a mixture of light infantry and armoured support. The armoured support units wore the massive Goliath suits. Standing over twenty-five feet high and carrying a multitude of heavy laser weapons and projectile explosives, the Goliath units carried the most firepower on the battlefield. They were arguably the most effective ones too. These heavily armoured suits were capable of continuing to fight while Bugs hung from their hulking mechanical limbs. The only way they were ever brought down was by being completely overwhelmed and torn apart, piece by piece.

The large suits took point and led the infantry into the

gauntlet of razor-sharp rocks nicknamed the Surf. Wave after wave of infantry poured into those horrid rocks, endlessly charging forward into the abyss.

She looked to the eastern LZ beneath her, watching the ships unload the same configuration of troops there as they did in the west. The eastern edge of the plains consisted of steep hills and winding paths. Beside the far-reaching paths lay a striking geological feature that was being referred to as the falls. The falls were a long steep slope of schythium that roughly resembled a massive waterfall. Its nearly vertical drop was believed to be too steep for Bugs to traverse and was therefore avoided.

Standing watch as ship after ship delivered countless legions onto the battlefield, she observed it all. Making sure that her suit's computer recorded everything she saw. After a while, the landing legions stopped rushing to combat and instead focused on constructing defences. The battle had barely started, and already the Federation was making itself at home. Pre-constructed buildings were landed in place as large machinery was unloaded from transports. The engineering legions used their massive suits to begin erecting gigantic plastanium walls.

Despite the name, an engineering suit wasn't actually a suit at all, but instead a forty-foot tall piece of heavy equipment. It might have taken the rough shape of a headless human, with two arms and legs coming out of a long mid-body, but it wasn't a suit. Suits were worn over a person's actual limbs and merely augmented the wearer's natural movements. Their limbs had no ability to move on their own. An engineering suit was controlled by the engineer who sat in the middle of the suit's main body. All movements were controlled by a pair of joysticks that operated in conjunction with the onboard computer. They were piloted rather than worn.

The engineers picked up and moved the giant pieces of wall, like children playing with blocks. She marvelled at the speed at which this base was being put together. The organization and coordination of the engineers rivalled, if not surpassed, that of any combat unit she had seen.

After standing watch for what must have been the better part of two hours, she turned and made her way into the cliffs. Her Wargon hopped lightly from rock to rock as it effortlessly traversed the dangerous path, never breaking momentum, bouncing from one place to the next. The giant beast moved with unpredictable grace as it made its way. Eventually reaching one of the eastern passes, well behind enemy lines.

Quickly, she moved down the pass until hearing the unmistakably familiar popping noise of thousands of pointy Bug legs running towards her. Silently, she ducked into an alcove just as Bugs came around the corner and into her line of sight. There she sat, perfectly still, letting the camouflage do its job, as the horde of Bugs approached her location. She went utterly unnoticed as she sat, watching them pass mere feet from her face. She signalled her suit's computer to save a copy of what she was seeing. Noting as many things as possible about the Bugs as they cross the opening to the alcove. Their colour, shape and size are inspected and carefully recorded.

Once the horde passed, she carefully slipped from the alcove, her Wargon moving in almost complete silence. The pair of them jumped on top of the pass's rocky walls and headed after the horde. They ride fast and easy, bounding from rock to rock as they chase after the Bugs. It takes no time at all for her to catch up to them. She moved into a position that gave her a clear line of sight to the back of their ranks. Lifting her long-barreled Tikka laser rifle, she took aim at the last Bug in the horde. With expert precision, she adjusted the power down to the point that ensured the laser wouldn't produce an exit wound. Effortlessly steadying the large rifle, she focused her aim on the small spot where the creature's massive head met its thorax and gently squeezed the trigger.

A silent shot left the barrel of the rifle and found its target with no interference. A small spurt of blood exited the Bug as it went limp and collapsed to the ground. The horde continued on, completely unaware that their ranks were just a little bit smaller.

She waited until the horde was far enough away before moving in to claim her prize. Silently she rode up and dismounted beside her fallen prey. Grabbing some instruments from a plastanium saddlebag, she began taking various measurements of the Bug. Everything was recorded on her helmet's computer as she went over the Bug inch by inch. From the Bugs tapered legs to its huge mandibles, each part was diligently examined. She pressed a button on one of the instruments, and a large needle sprang forth from its side. Gently she inserted the needle into the Bug and drew out a sample of its blood. The dull green screen of the instrument flashed to life as it transmitted its data.

She secured the instruments back into the saddlebag before firmly locking it closed. With subtle grace, she mounted her armoured beast and rode hard into the East.

CHAPTER SEVEN

With the Lieutenant leading us, we charge forward through the canyons. The plan was to hit the Bugs in the flank and take the pressure off the main force long enough for them to build up momentum. By now, they have most likely gotten bogged down, and their advance has slowed. Us thinning out the Bugs ranks should hopefully give our main forces a chance to restart their charge. Although with only five hundred Mongols, it will prove to be challenging to kill enough Bugs to make a difference, but we'll sure as hell try.

Lieutenant Jeanceon is riding hard despite looking like he had just ridden through the deepest depths of hell. I can't help thinking that he really embodies everything that a cavalry officer should be. He is solely focused on completing the objective and wastes no energy thinking about the past. Hell, I bet if this hard son of a bitch lost all of his soldiers, he would charge forward on his own. The fact that we were only five hundred didn't seem to bother him one bit.

Maybe that was one of the keys to being an officer, though. No matter what you feel, you have to keep it inside and carry on. As a leader, you aren't permitted to show any weakness because if you do, you'll be giving your soldiers permission to do the same. There is no room for weakness in the cavalry, no room for it in war. At least not in the Bug war. Perhaps when you're fighting like-minded species, you could permit a slight weakness. It could lead to acts of compassion that help bring a practical peace after the war, but not with Bugs. With Bugs, it's kill or be killed, and there's nothing else to it.

"Sergeant," the Lieutenant barks.

"Change of plans. We don't have the numbers that we originally predicted, and our communications aren't worth a damn right now. I was supposed to locate the main assault force in order to know where to hit the Bugs, but that's no longer possible."

The Lieutenant pauses slightly and clears his throat as if he is preparing to say something difficult.

"At the next fork we come across I want you to split off with half our force," he says.

I reply with an abrupt, "Yes Sir."

"That's not all Sergeant," he continues.

"From there, I want the forces to continue splitting in half at every fork until they are reduced down to squads of twenty-four. We can't afford to split into smaller groups than that. I'm sending out number designations now so everyone knows who to stick with," he says.

This order would clearly result in the deaths of many Mongols, but I understand his reasoning. With our communications down, we have no way of knowing where the main force is. We are charging around blind, hoping that we might get lucky enough to end up in the right spot. Together, we have the strength to stand and fight, but without the foggiest fucking clue where we are, there would be no point in making a stand. So, we are fucked either way. Either we maintain our strength by sticking together, which would likely result in us not finding the main force and failing to complete our objective. Or we split up, severely weakening our forces but increasing our chances of finding the main enemy force. At least the second option would give us the opportunity to deliver some kind of damage to the Bugs.

The smaller groups of twenty-four will still be strong enough to charge through the tighter canyons relatively unhindered. As long as they keep moving, they will stand a chance. The biggest problem is, if a force that small gets ambushed, it would meet almost certain death. It also means that if the main enemy force is found, whoever finds it will have to make a suicide charge. Either way, it looks like many more Mongols will be meeting the reaper before the day is out.

"I know it's not the order that anyone wants to hear and believe me, I don't want to give it. But it's our best option right now," the Lieutenant says.

"Yes Sir. I understand," I reply.

No more needs to be said on the matter. We had come to understand each other through our few words, and that was good enough for us both.

"Sergeant, I'm getting low on sergeants and need to make a battlefield promotion. Any suggestions?" He asks, changing the subject.

"Corporal Wenjack, Sir," I say.

I recommend Wenjack for the promotion with a heavy heart. He's a great right-hand man, and I hate to lose him, but the Lieutenant needs a Sergeant and Wenjack is the best for the job.

"Right, Wenjack is a good man," he says.

"Corporal Wenjack," the Lieutenant snaps.

"Yes Sir," Wenjack answers as he is added to the link.

"You've just been promoted, you're a temporary Sergeant. Congratulations," says the Lieutenant.

Wenjack always fancied himself a career Corporal, but with our numbers dropping, he knew there was no refusing this promotion.

So he excepts with a, “Thank you Sir.”

“Sergeant Braddock, the first fork is coming up on the left,” the Lieutenant says.

Up ahead, I can see the fork, with one path sharply cutting to the left. I quickly check my HUD to ensure that my half of the force is keyed in. As I do, I get a warning from part of my subconscious that has been developed through years of combat. I sense what it is, first from Sleipnir, and then I hear it for myself.

“Bugs,” I yell out as a horde of the dirty monsters come spilling around the corner.

The last thing I want to do is abandon fellow Mongols seconds before a fight, but these Bugs belong to the Lieutenant and the newly minted Sgt. Wenjack. So, we ride forward with everything we have. Riding hard in an attempt to make it to the fork before the Bugs hit our lines and cut us off. The Lieutenants troops are riding just as hard to engage the Bugs before they reach the fork. Together we ride, each Mongol pushing their Wargon to greater and greater speeds as the Bugs close in. Racing each other and the Bugs.

Despite my every effort to be the fastest, the Lieutenant pulls ahead of me and meets the Bugs just meters before the fork. With the force of a tidal wave, he smashes into the enemy line. His Wargon crushing the bastards beneath its feet and against the canyon walls. The rest of his forces flood in behind him, joining in the slaughter. Briefly, I witness the Lieutenant and Wenjack steamroll over the fuckers, before I'm forced to turn and head down our side of the fork.

We don't get far before I hear more Bugs coming our way. As we turn the next bend, we are met with about a kilometre of straight canyon with another massive horde at the end of it. With this much straight canyon between us, we are about to turn the place into a shooting gallery. I can tell Sleipnir knows it too, because the Wargon speeds up. His massive stride covering vast amounts of ground. Again, he wants to get a piece of the Bugs before our laser fire cuts them all down.

As we ride, I level my rifle and open fire. The Mongols on my flanks do the same. At the far end of the canyon, we can see the Bugs as they're cut to bits. As soon as a Bug makes it to the front of the ranks, it's immediately blasted. Our meat grinder is working in full force, and the mindless fucks are just running into it, one after another.

We continue to close the gap, and when we are only three hundred meters away, I command "Grenades."

Without hesitation, the Mongols behind me begin launching a volley of grenades overhead. The round balls hurtle through the air before landing with explosive concussions among the Bugs. The rigid schythium walls of the canyon reflect the force inwards, magnifying the grenade's destructive power. Every Bug in the immediate vicinity of the explosion is turned into a cloud of brown mist. The ones slightly further away are simply reduced to random bits of flying debris.

Through the brown mist, we ride, firing our weapons as we're bombarded by the mangled limbs that now rain down from the sky. So much blood and Bug guts had coated the canyon floor that I can feel Sleipnir fighting not to slip as he runs. The grisly mud only gets thicker as we continue using volleys of grenades and laser fire to push our way forward. But still, we press on through the mist and the growing slop.

Another fork waits for us just beyond the next bend, so I warn the soldiers, "Prepare to split!"

As we round the corner, two things happen. The canyon immediately split in two, and we outrun our volley of laser fire. Violently, we slam into a wall of Bugs. Seizing the opportunity, Sleipnir begins unloading his pent-up hatred upon them with tyrannical force. His violent fury is unleashed so rapidly that all I can do is hold on and try not to fall victim to his brutality.

The Bugs come from both sides of the fork, and their numbers are felt in their strength. Their spindly bodies lock together and push back against us. Sleipnir slows against their tremendous force, but he refuses to stop.

It takes a lot to stop a Wargon, especially an armoured one, but the force of this many Bugs in such a tight space makes it a hard slog. I can feel the Wargon behind me ram its shoulder into Sleipnir's ass to help push. Another jolt is felt as all the Wargons behind us begin doing the same, and the added strength is enough to keep us moving forward. As we drive, the Bugs snap at us with their greedy mandibles and strike out with their cursed fucking legs. Trying to get a piece of us.

The schythium walls prove to be our biggest advantage in this fight. Not only did they amplify the destructive power of our grenades, but they provide an unforgiving Surface against which we crush the Bugs. Being caught between an armoured Wargon and a schythium wall has the effect of fruit being put through a machine that makes jelly. Exoskeletons are broken as the gooey middle is squeezed out.

After what feels like an eternity, we finally ride through the last of the horde, only to find another fork. As per our orders, we split our forces in half again, and again at the next fork and so on, until I was only followed by one section of twenty-three Mongols. In this hostile place, riding with these few soldiers makes me feel naked and exposed. We still have the strength to ride over a small horde, but any resistance like the horde we just faced would likely be our end.

We ride the next four kilometres without seeing a single trace of Bug activity. This is strange because if we are heading towards their center, we should be seeing more Bugs, not fewer. I wonder if we had become lost? We hadn't doubled back because we would see corpses if we had. Through Sleipnir's link, I can feel fighting, anger, and death, all around me. The chaos of battle was felt by so many, but they didn't feel close. I know that we must be deep in what was still enemy territory but where the fuck was the enemy.

I instantly regret asking myself the question as we find them. All of them. In front of us, the canyon intersected with the most extensive run we've seen yet. Bigger than we even knew existed in these canyons. The run is at least a couple hundred meters wide, and the Bugs are using it as a superhighway. I'm baffled as to how Intelligence managed to miss this place but realize it must have been a combination of the high walls and thick cloud cover. Those fucking clouds. If it wasn't for them, we would be able to cover this area with air support and shut this Bug highway down. Instead, we'll have to do it the old-fashioned way.

This route is obviously the main route for the Bugs. If we could shut it down for even a minute or two, it should give our main assault force the time it must need. Give them a chance to form up into a full charge and clear out the rest of these horrid canyons. The only question was whether or not we were capable of that. Could twenty-four Mongols hold back millions of Bugs in a space this large for that long? It was more likely that we'd ride in and die instantly, but as the old pome declared, "Theirs is not to reason why, theirs is just to do and die."

Stopping a short run away from the intersection, I turn and face my section.

"Mongols! This is it. This is what we've come for. We need to break their line, no matter the cost. The numbers aren't on our side so we're going to need to hit them as hard as we fucking can," I say.

"Huha!" they reply.

"Once we are ten meters out, throw every fucking grenade you have. Don't try and save any because you won't be getting another chance to use them," I order.

"Huha," they bellow again.

That simple, guttural sound said more than any words ever could. It told me that not only did they understand the order, but they understood that it was likely the last one I would ever give. They understood that death waited for us, and they were ready to meet him with open arms. No words could ever express as much.

With nothing else to say, we wheeled around and charged for the intersection. Sleipnir and I lead the way as the rest follow close behind. Our Wargons feet thunder against the ground as we ride towards certain death. Just as I ordered, when we are ten meters from contact, we begin hurling every grenade we have. The corresponding explosions are massive and blow a path straight through the enemy's ranks. We continue lobbing grenades as we ride through the newly opened break in their line. Some of the grenades were of the high-energy pulse variety that were designed to knock down small buildings. When they went off, they vaporized large circles of Bugs, sending a superheated brown mist of blood into the air that rains back down.

As the grenades run out, we finally make physical contact with the enemy, hitting them with all the force we can summon. Crushing the Bugs underfoot, we rip through their ranks like wind through tall grass. Wargon against Bug, their strength is tested. My left hand holds onto my mount for dear life as I wield my rifle with my right. With this many enemies, there is no need to aim, so I blindly fire into their ranks.

Fearlessly pushing forward with all the might one could ever hope to possess, we hammer through the enemy's line. Our initial assault is devastating, but ultimately the force against us is too great. Without verbally making the command, our Wargons instinctually spread further apart, relieving the pressure on our line by letting some of the Bugs past us. With the enemy all around us, we forgo our rifles for lances.

Igniting the hot spears, we begin cutting down Bugs. Frantically swinging our lances, we try and limit the number of Bugs that slip past us. Slashing through them as fast as we can, but it's not fast enough.

On the edge of our right flank, Private Powel's Wargon is brought down. A Bug grabs its leg in its mandibles and, in one smooth motion, flips the beast onto its back. Private Powel is thrown to the ground as the Wargon is toppled. Without hesitation, the valiant Private jumps to his feet, holding his lance in a ready stance. He quickly splits an approaching Bug nearly in half before he is grabbed from behind and hurled through the air like a dog's chew toy. Another Bug impales him, mid-air, with its forelegs before ripping him in half with its mandibles.

Quickly we lose another Mongol as a Bug comes up behind him and snips off his head before getting to work ripping into his Wargon.

"There's too many of them," Private Talve yells.

"Suck my dick you six legged freaks," Private Crang roars as he thrusts his lance through the head of a lunging Bug.

"Fuck! Fuck! Fuck!" shouts someone else.

"Hold the Fucking line you apes," I command, barely able to get the words out between swings of my lance.

Soon we're down to only fifteen Mongols, then fourteen, then nine.

"Fuck," I mutter under my breath.

I wonder how much longer we can hold out and what death awaits me. People say that if you're torn in half, you still live for a few seconds, completely aware of what's happening. Maybe I'll be lucky and have my head cleanly nipped off and never see it coming. All I know for sure is that no matter how they kill me, I will make them earn it.

Sleipnir rears back on his hind legs in a last show of defiance and power. As he does, I swing my lance through the air and for a split second, we stand there like gods towering over the surrounding horde. We stand as a challenge to every Bug that lays before us. Challenging them to do their worst.

Then out of nowhere, all the Bugs around us start exploding. No, not exploding. They're being ripped apart by heavy laser fire. I look to my left and see the massive figure of Sergeant Kato leading his Samurai across the canyon. The bright colours of their hulking battle suits stand out against the dull landscape as they charge towards us, firing lasers and cannons all the way.

"Sgt. Braddock, so nice to see you," Kato says over the coms link as if we were casually bumping into each other at the mess hall.

"It's a lot nicer to see you, I can promise you that," I respond.

"Let's kill some Bugs," he says as he lets a series of rockets fly.

The Samurai quickly make their way up to our position, forming a new line. I move in behind them with the rest of the Mongols, using our elevated position to fire over their heads.

The amount of firepower that the Samurai could lay down is genuinely incredible. Holding nothing back, we stand there, unloading on the horde with laser fire, canons, rockets and grenades. We mow the Bugs down by the thousands as they approach. Our laser fire chewing them up, blasting their front line into oblivion as the Samurai's canons rip gaping holes through their ranks. But the bastards keep coming. No matter how fast we cut them down, they come faster than we can shoot them. Like the tide encroaching onto the shore, they move forward. Slowly but relentlessly, they come.

We needed to hold this ground for as long as possible. Every second we stand gives our main forces just a little more time. Let's them build a little more speed and ensures that they have to face just a few less Bugs. Every Bug we kill here is one less Bug that can destroy our brothers and sisters. Here on this line, the outcome of this battle will be decided.

The Bugs soak up our fire and their casualties without hesitation. Endlessly they push forward, and soon they will be on top of us. What I wouldn't give for some fucking air support right about now. A few bomber loads of high explosive anti-personnel bombs would be enough to send this horde straight to hell, but we wouldn't be that lucky. Not here. Not on Excalibur.

The enemy's line creeps closer, so close now that I drop my laser rifle and light up my lance. As I do, every Samurai in line drops their firearms, drawing the two plastanium swords from their waists, and all hell breaks loose. The Bugs hammer into our lines. Mandibles and legs clash with lance and sword. It doesn't take long for the cold mechanical fighting style of the Samurai to degrade into something resembling a barroom brawl.

Not being ones to pass on a good brawl, Sleipnir and I get to work. I ruthlessly guide the burning tip of my lance through Bug after Bug as Sleipnir stomps, kicks and swings his massive, armoured head like a battle mace. Chaos rules this battlefield, and we embrace it as every soldier fights, ready to give their last. There is no quit in us as we cut, blaze and smash our enemies.

I witness one Samurai who had lost his swords pick up a laser cannon by the barrel and start swinging it like a club. He cracks open Bug exoskeletons like grim piñatas, spilling their gory surprise over the ground. Another who was unarmed takes on the Bugs with nothing but his armoured suit itself. Punching, grappling and kicking at the Bugs. In a show of immense power, he grabs a Bug by its upper and lower mandible and rips it in half before being knocked down from behind. Bugs swarm his body as he falls. His armoured suit proves to be too hard for one Bug to crack, but they worked together to separate him from his limbs.

I see Sgt. Kato's mountainous form fighting with a level of skill that could only be developed through a lifetime of experience. He smoothly swings his swords with practiced intention as Bug strikes glance off his thick armour. Amongst the scattered brawl, Kato stands out as he moves with the steady rhythm of a symphony conductor. There was almost something beautiful about his movements as he massacres his foes with measured focus and power. As the rest of us desperately slash and struggle, he has the deliberate concentration of an artist working on his masterpiece. For a moment, I wonder if he is capable of fighting through the entire horde by himself.

He may yet get the chance. Even though each one of us fought harder than anyone could ever expect, our numbers fall fast. We have held the Bugs for longer than we ever thought possible, but our time was almost up. I feel no fear in this moment, knowing that we have done what we set out to do. Against all odds, we have done it. We have bought the needed time and thinned the enemy ranks enough for our forces to ride over what remains. At least, I think we have, but without communications, there is no way of knowing.

Then again, maybe we haven't held out long enough. What if there are even more Bugs than we predicted, and it just wasn't enough? What if the main assault force was already dead? If soldiers as good as us were falling this fast, would any of the others really stand a chance? My fearlessness turns to panic, and I fight on. Killing as fast as possible now, with no concern for myself or others. I can feel Sleipnir's rage building as his blood lust rises. We ride the verge of going into a blood frenzy, careful not to lose all control, though I know that soon, either all control will be lost, or we will be killed. There were no other options.

Amid my blind fury, I feel something hit me through Sleipnir's link. I sense Wargons approaching, and before I know it, my HUD springs to life with locators. At first, I think that it might be another section riding in from the flank, but I quickly realize that there are far too many locators for that.

"Oh fuck yeah," I say to myself.

My HUD flashes again as the legions main coms link finally regains its connection.

"Fucking move!" a voice commands over the link.

I look back and see thousands of charging Wargons coming our way at full speed. It was General Jaxxon leading our main assault force, we had given them the gap, and now they are coming our way. Coming our way really fast and will run over anything standing between them and their target.

At this, Sgt. Kato and his remaining soldiers break contact with the Bugs and start running for the canyon wall. They would need to reach those walls fast and hug them tight to avoid getting trampled to death. As they ran for cover, I quickly weigh our options. I decide to take my remaining five Mongols and charge headlong at our assaulting forces.

"What the hell are you doing Sergeant? Do you have a fucking death wish?" General Jaxxon barks across the coms.

"Sir, just joining the party, Sir," I respond.

We ride with all the speed our Wargons can muster until we are halfway towards the approaching line. Frantically, we swing around in a sweeping U-turn and start riding as fast as possible, hoping to build enough speed to join the line instead of being crushed by it.

"Bold move Sergeant. Stupid, but bold. Better hurry up though or I'm going to run you down," the General says, in surprisingly good nature despite our current situation.

They must have been having better luck than we

were.

By the time they catch up to us, we can match their speed. We file in with their ranks, and it feels good to be riding with full numbers again. I can feel Sleipnir begin to calm down to a normal battlefield level of stress as we charge forward. Gripping my rifle, I take aim and unload on the horde that had almost claimed my life. The feeling of satisfaction that I experience as we mow them down is entirely indescribable. We slaughter them without mercy and keep on going.

We continue charging through the canyons, running down anything and everything that gets in our way. The Bugs attempt ambushes at a few different points but to no avail. They get a few of our riders here and there but mostly just get trampled by our superior force.

It takes us a few more hours to completely clear the canyons, but in the end, we wipe out everything with more than four legs. After their main force had been trampled, there was little else that could resist our assault. The invasion was a success, at least our LZ has been, as it's too soon to tell how the others have done. For us, victory was here. Temporary as it may be. As any army in history could tell you, there is a big difference between taking land and holding it.

We faced an enemy capable of reproducing an army the size of the one we had just fought in a matter of months.

They don't get tired. They don't get distracted, and they never give up. We have won the day, but until the Federation has successfully mined every ounce of schythium from this hell hole of a planet, we haven't really won anything.

CHAPTER EIGHT

With the canyons finally cleared out, we're able to catch our breath and count our losses. The main assault went better than expected, with a casualty rate of only twenty percent. Out of the ten thousand Mongols that took the field, we still had eight thousand left. Those were surprisingly good numbers despite everything. However, it should be noted that casualty rates on an unhospitable planet like Excalibur aren't directly comparable to a life-sustaining planet like Earth.

Casualties on a planet like Earth are a mixture of dead and seriously wounded. Out of two thousand casualties, only six hundred might actually be dead. On a planet like Excalibur, however, two thousand casualties mean two thousand coffins will be filled. Two thousand letters will be sent to two thousand families. Two thousand lives that once held infinite promise are reduced to statistics.

Our battle suits do a great job of protecting us, but when they are breached, we are left exposed to the ruthless elements. If you lose an arm on a planet similar to Earth, there is a good chance that you won't die. You might be in so much pain that you'll wish you were dead, but you will live long enough to regret your loss. On a planet like Excalibur, if you get your arm torn off, the air will leak from your suit and the planet's cold atmosphere will seep in and choke the life out of you. Our two thousand casualties didn't include any injured.

Even though the main assault force faired pretty well, our flanking force did not. Out of the two thousand of us that took to the flank, less than a hundred made it out alive, giving us a ninety-five percent casualty rate. Like always, the Bugs somehow knew we were coming and laid ambushes everywhere. The numbers of the main forces were large enough that the ambushes had little effect, but for the smaller flanking forces, they were devastating. Especially when we started breaking into smaller sections. When these sections ran into ambushes, they were almost always overwhelmed.

The lack of communication was also a major fuck up. If we had had functioning coms, we would have been able to relay the information about the ambushes. Instead, each unit had to discover them for themselves, with dire consequences. Having functioning communications would have also allowed us to avoid breaking up once we had taken the flank. Since we didn't know where the main force was or where the majority of the Bugs were moving, we had to split up, and that decision cost us a lot of Mongols.

I ride through our ranks, assessing our losses and waiting for orders as I hear a voice call to me.

"Well, if it isn't the hero of the Bug highway," Sergeant Wenjack says as he comes riding up beside me.

"Wenjack! You son of a bitch. Didn't think your ugly ass made it through this one."

He raises his hands in a gesture of surprise, "What, no faith? It's going to take a lot more than a few billion Bugs to take me out," he says through a laugh.

"I knew that you'd made it through, the entire force is talking about Braddock and Kato, the heroes of the Bug highway," he says.

I was surprised to hear that we were being called heroes, seeing as how we would be Bug food if it wasn't for General Jaxxon showing up when he did.

"Hero?" I question him. "As nice as that sounds I feel like I was more of a damsel in distress than a hero. If Kato didn't show up with the sushi brigade when he did we would have been dead long before we were able to do any good. Even then, if it wasn't for General Jaxxon we would have all been fucked. A lot of good soldiers died in there. We were just the ones who were lucky enough to make it out in one piece," I say.

"Lot of good soldiers died in a lot of places today," he says in a sullen tone. "And you and I both know that a lot of the real heroes didn't make it through. But, the Federation needs living heroes to inspire more foolish soldiers to give up their lives, and for the time being it looks like you're one of them."

I don't like the sound of that at all, but Wenjack makes the good point that nobody really gives a shit about what I like. The only thing that matters is what the Federation likes, and right now, that's pumping up false heroes.

"The way people are telling it, you and Kato took on a few million Bugs by yourselves, fighting back-to-back, standing on top of a mountain of corpses. They say you did it all with nothing but swords and lances. Real King Arthur kind of shit," Wenjack says excitedly while gesturing with his hands as if he was wielding imaginary swords.

"That's fucking ridiculous," I say with a laugh.

"Oh, I agree. I know that you fight like garbage, but nobody else seems to know that," he says.

"What about you?" I ask. "What were the real soldiers doing while we were getting our asses kicked on the highway?"

Wenjack paused for a moment before answering.

"Getting ambushed mostly," he says. "Honestly I'm surprised to have made it through in one piece and wouldn't have if it wasn't for Lieutenant Jeanceon."

"I was going to ask if you knew what happened to

him."

He responds in a low, sullen voice, uncharacteristic to his usual upbeat demeanour, "The Lieutenant was one of the real heroes of this battle, if it wasn't for him I wouldn't be standing here talking to you right now."

Wenjack goes on telling me how the Lieutenant had led them through the horde without issue. They even made it through an ambush without losing too many. The real problems began when the forces started splitting up, and the ambushes came more frequently.

"You should have seen the way that the Lieutenant fought," he tells me. "Like a man possessed. I've honestly never seen anyone kill Bugs as quickly as he did."

Wenjack tells me how the Lieutenant led them through ambush after ambush. They plowed ahead despite their numbers rapidly shrinking from splitting up and the mounting casualties.

Eventually, they made it to an area where the canyon walls widened out to four times their average width, and the mother of all traps was sprung. Bugs poured out from every crack and alcove in the rock. Behind them, the path they had just taken, filled with a horde that had been following them, waiting for them to reach the trap. Their only hope was to shoot for the tighter gap ahead, but with so many Bugs closing in around them, they thought they would never make it.

Without hesitation, the Lieutenant ordered the Mongols closest to him to hand over their pulse grenades. When they did, he commanded them to make a break for the gap. They did just that, riding for the gap, throwing grenades as they went to keep the attacking Bugs at bay. The Lieutenant and his Wargon charged in the other direction, headlong into the horde.

Wenjack says that he looked back as he rode and watched the Lieutenant fall and become quickly swarmed. Wenjack tells me, at this point, he knew what was about to happen and ordered his troops to ride harder. The next thing they knew, the sound of twelve pulse bombs exploding at once echoed through the canyon.

The shock wave almost knocked them off their mounts, but they had managed to ride far enough for it not to be lethal. Lieutenant Jeanceon had given his life, without hesitation, to save the rest of his soldiers. He was indeed one of the real heroes.

"He was a true cavalry officer, through and through," Wenjack says remorsefully.

"Oh well, let the dead worry about the dead," he says. "We are alive, and I'm still happy to be here. Well, maybe not here in particular, but on the right side of dead, I mean".

"Yeah, me too. For now at least," I agree.

Wenjack tells me that before he found me, he was checking the deceased and noticed that out of the twenty-four soldiers from our original section, thirteen were still alive.

"That's a little over a fifty percent survival rate. Compared to the dismal five percent for the rest of the flank, that's pretty good," he says.

"Must have been a lucky dropship," I say.

He tells me that it probably had something to do with their Sergeant.

"He's a hero after all," he adds, and we both laugh.

"Speaking of heroes, have you seen Sgt. Kato around?" I ask.

"As a matter of fact, I have, he's with the rest of the Samurai back east of here," Wenjack answers.

I was about to make a joke about thanking him for handling my rear so well when I receive a summons to meet with the other section leaders.

"Looks like we're back on the clock," Wenjack says.

We meet the other section leaders in an open area that was serving as an impromptu command post. Captain

McArthur rides up, and we form a semi-circle around him.

"Good evening, Sergeants," he says.

On planets like this that didn't have clear days or nights, it became a permissible bit of humour to always say good evening, no matter what the Federation standard time actually was.

"Since Lieutenant Jeanceon's command has come to a heroic end, I will be taking over his responsibilities until a replacement is found," he says coldly.

"First off, I was told to extend congratulations from Chief Fleet Admiral Holoiday, on a well fought battle."

Nobody gave a flying fuck what Holoiday had to say because we all knew that he was an out-of-touch desk jockey.

"General Jaxxon also wanted to extend his congratulations."

This meant far more to us because he was a well-respected cavalry soldier who had actually taken part in the battle, unlike desk jockey Holoiday.

"The General said that you all made him proud today, and you were perfect examples of what cavalry soldiers should be," he says.

That was high praise coming from a man like him. I

only wish that we could hear it from the General himself.

"We've taken the canyons and had a chance to catch our breath, but now we've got work to do. The Mongols are being divided into three groups. Group one will oversee the retrieval of our fallen, group two will be responsible for roving patrols of the outer canyons, and group three will be providing security for an engineering legion that will be coming in," McArthur says.

I hope beyond hope that we don't get group one. Watching your brothers and sisters die in combat was one thing but scraping their mangled corpses off the battlefield was another. Nobody wanted that job, especially after the shit we've just been through.

"You lot are in group three," he says.

Everyone simultaneously lets out a sigh of relief. Even though I was confident that we have just begun to see all the death that this planet has in store for us, I'm relieved that we don't need to witness anymore today.

A man in an engineering command suit walks up and stands beside Captain McArthur. His suit is a smaller version of the far larger engineering construction suits, which are the size of small buildings. These command suits are built to specifications required for the oversight of construction projects. I don't really know what those requirements are because I'm not an engineer, and I couldn't care less how they do their job.

"This is Lieutenant Drummond of the Sapper engineering legion," McArthur says.

Lieutenant Drummond steps forward and says, "Look soldiers, I understand that you must be tired, but the Federation needs a little more out of you."

I think about how arrogant this guy must be to believe that he can speak for the entire Federation.

"The Federation needs a little more? How about you go fuck off and die, you piece of shit," I feel like saying, but I hold my tongue.

He continues, "It cost a lot of lives to take these canyons and the Federation doesn't want to hand them back over to the Bugs. However, as you know better than anyone, these canyons are too big to feasibly hold in their current state. So, the Federation has a plan."

That's no surprise to any of us. The Federation always has a plan. The question is whether or not the plan they come up with is worth a Wargon's ass.

"The plan is to lock this place up tight with a series of walls. Each wall will be protected by guard towers and sentry guns, so that any Bugs that attempt to retake the canyons will find themselves in a heavy crossfire. Each wall on its own, won't be able to withstand a full assault, but with enough of them, we should be able to hold the canyons indefinitely," he says.

As Federation plans go, this isn't the worst one I've heard. Most of the runs are narrow enough that these walls should stand a good chance of severely slowing down any Bug assault. I doubt they will be able to hold out indefinitely, but they should be a suitable deterrent against the Bugs coming this way.

"The only pass that will remain open will be the highway because it will serve as a valuable way for us to move troops and equipment through the canyons. However, it will be heavily reinforced with enough armour and defences that any Bugs foolish enough to go that way will be vaporized.

"The Federation also acknowledges that the communications systems have been a massive restriction, so we will be installing coms gear in the canyon walls. That way, in the future, we will have the ability to communicate.

"Lastly, we will be rigging these canyons with a shit ton of explosives. In the event that the Bugs somehow manage to retake the canyons, this time we will be the ones with the traps," he explains.

I like the sounds of that. See how they like being

ambushed for a change.

"Our engineers will be handling the work. We just need you to make sure we aren't surprised by any Bugs while our heads are down. Your assignments will be sent directly to your HUDs, with all necessary instructions. Dismissed," the Lieutenant says.

Technically he wasn't authorized to dismiss us, but the Captain lets it go, and we go our separate ways to report to our assigned engineers.

I take a minute to go over my assignment and notice that I would have the distinct privilege of providing personal security for Lieutenant Drummond. Maybe he wasn't as pompous as he first appeared, or perhaps he's worse. Either way, orders are orders. I was lucky enough to be assigned four of the surviving Mongols from my section so I wouldn't have to suffer alone.

We meet Lieutenant Drummond at the rendezvous location.

"Sergeant Braddock reporting for duty Sir."

"At ease Sergeant," he says, even though I wasn't standing at attention because my ass was firmly secured to Sleipnir.

"Let's get moving, we have a lot of ground to cover,"

he says.

We head down the first canyon run with two Mongols riding out front and two in the back. I ride in the middle with the Lieutenant walking beside me. It feels good to be riding while an officer has to walk beside you, even though his command suit was about as tall as I was on Sleipnir.

Our job was simple and boring, protect the Lieutenant as he goes around overseeing the work being done. After the past day's events, a boring job sounds just fine to me, so I take the assignment for what it is.

As we walk, the Lieutenant asks me, "Do you know why I chose you to be my escort?"

"I could have chosen anyone from your legion, officers included, but I chose you. Do you know why that is, Sergeant?"

Not only did I not know, but I also didn't exactly give a shit.

"No Sir," I answer.

I purposely don't ask him why because I know that he's going to tell me anyway.

"Because Sergeant, I'm no fighting man."

That much was straightforward and went without

saying.

"Sure, I have extensive training in advanced battlefield theory, and I understand the theory behind building defenses as well as anyone. I'm also no coward, if the need ever arose, I'm not afraid to pick up a laser gun and zap some Bugs," he says.

Calling a battle rifle a laser gun and saying that he would zap some Bugs made it clear that he has never been close to combat or combat soldiers. He sounded like a complete moron.

"But I'm no fighting man," he says again.

"I wanted someone with me that had extensive combat experience. Someone that has firsthand knowledge of what the Bugs can do in combat. I might know all the theory, but I wanted a practical opinion on what we're doing out here."

That was probably the most sensible thing he's said yet.

"Sir, that doesn't explain why you requested me. Every Mongol has been combat tested, and most of our officers have more combat experience than I do," I tell him.

"True, but those other Mongols aren't the hero of the Bug highway," he says.

"The other Mongols riding with us were there too, and to be honest, if it wasn't for the Samurai, none of us would even be here right now. Believe me Sir, I'm no hero," I say.

"Bullshit Sergeant. You led your soldiers bravely and helped win us the battle. I would agree that Sgt. Kato and his Samurai are heroes as well, but between you and me, Sgt. Kato is a bit of an oddball," he says.

I now wonder, more than ever, if Kato's rear handling comments were normal behaviour for the giant man. Possibly it was just part of his own strange sense of humour. I suppose it doesn't matter one way or the other.

As I ponder the oddity that was Sgt. Kato, I realize that I hadn't responded to the Lieutenant for a while, and the air between us has now grown awkward. In an attempt to break the awkward silence, the Lieutenant changes the subject.

"So, what do you think about the plan to fortify the canyons? Give me your honest answer," the Lieutenant asks.

"Honestly Sir, I think as far as plans go, it's okay. I know you think that these canyons will be impenetrable when your done with them, but when it comes to Bugs, nothing is impenetrable. No matter how hard you plan they will find a way to fuck you. The plan has some good points, communications and the laying of explosives for example, but if you think a wall and some guns will be enough to stop the enemy indefinitely, you're going to be disappointed. Given your options I would say the plan is good enough, but it isn't perfect," I say.

He takes a second to consider my answer before speaking.

"Just good enough, hmm. I thought it was a bit better than that," he responds defensively.

I try and explain with as much tact as possible.

"Look, these canyons are just too damn big and the Bugs come in too great of numbers. This plan will definitely make it easier to control the canyons, but they will be far from impassable. Realistically, this plan will probably succeed in slowing down a counterattack, maybe even discourage one. If there is an easier route to the base, they will likely focus on that instead. But if they really want to retake the canyons, no amount of walls will stop them. Even the explosives won't completely stop them. You have to realize that we're dealing with an enemy that can hatch a few million warriors in a afternoon. If they really want to take the canyons back, they won't stop until they succeed," I say.

He ponders that for a time and then asks, "In your opinion, what will stop the Bugs?"

"In my opinion Sir, the only thing that can stop Bugs is finding their hives and destroying them. As long as they have hives, they can keep hatching more warriors and keep attacking," I tell him.

That was the honest truth. No amount of walls or sentry guns could ever stop the Bugs. They needed to be hunted down. A lesson that we had learned time and time again, that the Federation has seemed to forget.

"Fair enough Sergeant," he says and doesn't press the subject farther.

It's not long until we come upon the first construction site at a fork. The engineers were working away in their gargantuan suits, stacking plastanium blocks and welding them firmly into place. They work with incredible speed as they assemble the massive wall. I had doubts about whether or not they would be able to wall up every run in the canyon, but with the speed that I'm now seeing them work, I would say it is possible.

The wall itself is about seventy-five feet high and ten feet thick. The top of the wall is lined with covered ramparts that hold several heavy Gatling lasers. From there, soldiers would be able to defend the wall from a location of relative cover. To add to the firepower provided by the defending soldiers, the engineers would be installing a series of sentry guns along the length of the wall.

I'm still not convinced that this would stop a full-on Bug assault, but it could repel a moderate-size horde. Hopefully, for the sake of whichever soldiers are unlucky enough to defend the wall, moderate hordes are all they will encounter.

"So, what do you think now?" The Lieutenant asks, with an irritating amount of smugness.

"I'm impressed, Sir," I say with complete honesty.

"Anything you would do differently?" he asks.

"Yes Sir," I say, pointing down the canyon toward the direction we had just come from.

"The sentry guns back there need to be moved," I say.

"Why, what is wrong with the sentries?" he asks with genuine interest.

"You've got them too spread out. I noticed that you have them for the entire approach, when they should all be mounted closer to the wall," I tell him.

"Those guns are placed like that to thin the attacking ranks, in order to take pressure off the wall. Why would we move them?" he asks.

"Because the Bugs will take them out in no time out

there, they are basically useless," I respond.

He pauses for a good while, and I can only guess that he's giving me a look of complete bewilderment beneath his helmet.

"Sergeant, those sentries are about a hundred feet up the canyon wall. How exactly do you think that the Bugs will be able to take them out" he asks.

"Sir, they will simply climb on top of each other to get up there. A horde of Bugs could form a mound big enough to get up a hundred feet in a matter of seconds. However, if the guns were all focused around the wall they would be able to cover each other and the Bugs will have a harder time mounding up," I say.

"Bullshit," he snaps. "They can't really do that. Can they?"

"Private Talve, come here," I order.

Private Talve rides over and says, "Yes Sergeant."

"Private, do you see anything wrong with the sentries," I ask.

Without missing a beat, he answers, "Yeah, they're spread to far apart. The Bugs will just climb on top of each other and knock them out."

"I see. Now tell me Private, how long would it take a horde to climb on top of each other to get there," I ask.

He thinks for a second.

"Well Sergeant, I would think a mound that size would only take around five seconds," he says. "If you ask me, I would group them all closer to the wall."

"Well nobody asked you. Return to position," I order, and he rides back to where he was.

"See Sergeant, it's a good thing you're here, otherwise we would have put our guns in the wrong spot," he says.

He might have a point, but as Private Talve proved, any Mongol could have told him about the guns. I really get the feeling that he just wants to say that he is working with a war hero, even though I still hold no claim to that title.

The Lieutenant orders the changes to the sentry guns, claiming that it's his idea. He even went so far as to tell his engineers about the climbing Bugs, like it was common knowledge. This guy definitely has a pompous streak, but babysitting him was better than collecting corpses, so I don't complain.

After setting off towards our next location, the Lieutenant waits a while before finally asking the question that

I know he's been waiting to ask from the minute we met.

"So Sergeant, what was it like?" he asks.

I decide to delay his satisfaction a little longer.

"What was what like?" I answer.

"Fighting on the Bug highway. Taking on all those Bugs with Sergeant Kato. What was that like?" He clarifies with the eagerness of an expectant child.

The question made me hate him. Fighting in a war is bad enough, but listening to non-combat personnel talk about it is even worse. They make it out to be this grand adventure when in reality, most of it is a cold, depressing hell. The few good parts are beyond the comprehension of anyone that's never been in the situation for themselves.

I want to tell him how much of a fucking dork he is for even asking me. I want to have Sleipnir crush his legs and ask him how that feels, but I resist the urge.

Instead, I tell him, "It sucked Sir, and I'm damn lucky that Sgt. Kato and his Samurai were there, otherwise you would have never even heard my name, unless you were reading a casualty list."

He waits for me to continue, and when I don't, he prods me for more.

"What, that's it? Come on Sergeant, tell me what it was really like."

"Hell," I snap at him. "It was fucking hell. Imagine leading your soldiers through fight after fight, and you've managed to keep most of them alive only to be faced with certain death. Imagine looking at a horde of millions of pissed off Bugs and telling your soldiers that, after everything they've done they now need to ride into it. They know as well as you, that if they follow your orders they will die, and they also know that there is a good chance that their deaths will be meaningless. Even though they know that, they still follow you, not because they're soldiers and you gave them an order, but because they respect you. Because after countless battles fought together they both trust and love you. They know that you wouldn't tell them to lay down their lives if it wasn't worthwhile, and they never question you."

I can feel myself growing angrier as I speak.

"Can you understand the pressure that kind of responsibility puts on a leader in the heat of the moment? Can you understand how hard it is to tell soldiers that you love like family, that it's time for you to all ride off and die? And for what? So that the fucking Federation can have better weapons? Can you imagine what that's like?"

I pause to calm myself before continuing.

"Then you charge, and you don't think about much at all. There isn't time to think. You just fight until your brothers and sisters start falling around you. Until your coms link fills with the yells and screams of the people you told to follow you to their death. Then you think of your own death, and you know what the really fucked up part is?"

I wait a pause for the Lieutenant to answer, but he stands quiet.

"Well do you know Sir?" I ask again.

He eventually answers in a whisper, like a child listening to a ghost story, "No Sergeant, I don't."

"The most fucked up part is that all you can think about is whether or not you're dying too soon. You're hoping beyond hope that you've held out long enough that your death will make a difference. Like a dog who only wants to please its master, regardless of its own suffering. You're hoping that you didn't spend the lives of your friends for nothing.

"That Sir, is what its fucking like," I say.

The Lieutenant's helmet blocks all expression from his face, but from the few unintelligible sounds he makes, I can tell that wasn't the answer he was expecting. He wanted some story about honour and bravery. About two warriors standing against a massive horde of evil man-eating Bugs.

Only problem is that story doesn't exist. Not from me at least.

We didn't talk much for the rest of the day. He didn't speak to me much at all after that, except about my opinions on the defenses. For the next two weeks, we went out every day to check the progress of the walls. We made our rounds and tweaked things here and there until the Federation decided that we had used up enough plastanium and called us back to base.

CHAPTER NINE

After two weeks in the field, we are finally heading into base for some much-needed downtime. We haven't been out of these canyons since the drop and are ready for a change of scenery. No matter how long we stay in the canyons, they never become comfortable. They will only ever be a place of death until the Federation mines them into oblivion.

The days since the invasion ended have been pretty quiet. There were still random Bug attacks, which were probably going to be a never-ending reality of life on this planet, but they were small and ineffective. If I were to guess, these encounters were just probing attempts to see what we're up to. Most likely, the Bugs are biding their time until their numbers bounce back. It's one of two tactics that they tend to use. Either they save up warriors and throw them at us all at once, or they will send a continuous stream to lay constant siege to a base. Both tactics require hatching more warriors, and that will take them some time.

As we finally ride out of the canyons, we're struck with the magnificent sight of the newly constructed outer walls of the base. A pair of walls, the inner standing higher than the exterior, rose up from the schythium ground towards the orange sky.

Atop the walls, I see a series of large sentry guns and watchtowers. Between them, the tiny silhouettes of soldiers can be seen patrolling along the tops of the massive walls. They ironically looked like little Bugs crawling around on a structure that was too incredible to be of their own making. But they did make it. This amazing feat of engineering could have only been pulled off by human means. We might not have the most beautiful architecture in the galaxy, but we sure know how to build large and practical.

Approaching the walls, I can't help but feel small and insignificant. I wonder if this is how soldiers felt while walking before the ancient walls of Troy or Babylon, but my thoughts are cut short as the blast gate opens before us. Against the incredible size of the walls, the blast gate appears minor in comparison, but as we ride through it, we realize that it is quite large in its own right. We are able to ride through the gate in a formation fifty riders wide.

Even in these large ranks, it takes us a great deal of time to all ride through the gates. As my turn comes, I ride through, only to look upon the killing field that lay between the two walls. Two hundred meters of razor wire and spiked pits lay to either side of us, between the walls. The razor wire lay in loosely coiled balls that were twenty-five feet high. These balls are designed to snag and entangle any Bugs who were able to breach the first wall.

Walking through this corridor of death, I look up and notice how many guns are fixed upon this path. Any Bugs that found themselves down here would be caught in one hell of a crossfire.

We pass through the final blast door, and I'm floored once again, this time by the colossal scale of the base itself. An entire city now stands where only weeks before, we found nothing but flat, barren rock. The Federation is capable of landing an entire city's worth of buildings in a matter of hours. These buildings are basically specially designed ships that are purpose-built to be landed and then immediately used. Since they are self-sufficient and contain their own water, heat and air, they can be fully operational in about an hour after landing. Even though I understand how they work and have seen them before, I still find myself impressed by the immense scale of the thing.

Sergeant Wenjack rides beside me as we cross through the second blast door. "Well fuck me running. Look at this shit, it's a fucking city, and not one of those tiny hick cities that you find on back water worlds either. Its a real fucking city," he says.

"From what I hear most of it is located in the northern tunnels. These buildings are mostly barracks and supply depots for whichever legions are on standby," I say.

"Fuck," he mutters again as he continues to look

around.

As we head north through the camp, I notice the various legion banners hanging above the different barracks doors. The names that adorn each banner remind me of the size of this operation. It was like all of human history had shown up for this one pivotal war. We pass banners for Cesar's legion, Macedonians, Zulu, Spartans, British expeditionary force, Grande Armee, Navy seal, Danes, Janissary, Rajput, Haudenosaunee, and Hussars.

Seeing the Hussars banner out front of the standby barracks was a relief because it meant there was a good chance we might actually get some downtime. Since there are two cavalry legions on base, I figure that they would rotate us in and out of standby rather than keep both of us activated and burn us out. At least, I hope that is what they are doing. The last few days had been relatively laid back, but I am still itching to get out of this suit.

A battle suit is designed to be as comfortable as possible so that soldiers can stay in them for long periods. Physically, there is no reason that you couldn't remain suited up indefinitely. Although, psychologically, it becomes a challenge to stay suited for too long. After a long enough time wearing a suit and only interacting with others who also wear suits, you start to forget that you're people under the plastanium. You might not notice it, but the little facial expressions and body language people use make a big difference in our personal interactions. When you lose those, a small part of your humanity goes with it.

There are also small things, like eating or drinking. The suit's life support system makes eating and drinking unnecessary while you're suited up, but you still miss it. You do your best not to think about it, but it drags on you. Hell, just the desire to drink a cup of coffee is enough to make you start to go a little crazy.

If we were in line for a bit of out of suit time, it would be fine by me. The Bug war could wait while I have a cup of coffee and take a shit in a toilet, like a normal human being for a change.

Finally, we get to the northern end of the base. In the shadow of the towering cliffs is a building labelled MWS4, which stands for Mongol Wargon Stable Four. We ride into the airlock, and the outside door closes behind us with a loud whoosh. The argon is sucked from the room as air is pumped in to take its place. Once inside, we follow the individual prompts on our HUDs to our assigned pen.

These aren't pens like you would typically think about in a livestock barn, although that's where the name comes from. Instead, these are spaces with equipment designed to lock onto the Wargon's battle suit, holding it firmly in place while a life support system is hooked up. I always thought they looked like a combination of a mechanics bay and a hospital room.

The Wargons don't get time out of their suits on a world like this because there's no practical way to give them enough room. So instead, they are locked into their pens and put into stasis, much the same way as onboard a starship. They stay suited up and ready to go if something should happen. A Wargon can be woken up and prepared for combat in less than sixty seconds.

I lead Sleipnir over to our assigned pen, where I hand him over to the handlers. Separating from your Wargon is never easy. When the jack is disconnected, it feels like a piece of your brain has turned off, and a part of you is temporarily gone. I take a moment to think about the last battle and make sure Sleipnir knows how I feel about going through the ordeal together. Our bond runs deep, and I ensure the Wargon knows that. We stand there together, focusing on our connection.

After a while, I signal the handlers to disconnect the link, and Sleipnir's jack is turned off. We all line up and march back through the airlock, back into the open air of this horrid planet. Once outside, we form back up into ranks and wait for direction.

Captain McArthur walks to the front of our ranks.

I give the command "Attention," and everyone snaps

into place.

Captain McArthur looks at us for a moment before giving us the at-ease command, and we all relax slightly.

"You lot have been through the ringer the past few days," the Captain says. "You went right from the fight of your lives to two solid weeks of patrols. I assure you that the Federation appreciates your hard work and sacrifice."

Someone in the ranks let out an ill-timed "Huha," only to be met by a short awkward silence before the Captain continued.

"As you have probably already heard, the cliff face behind us is filled with tunnels that have been cleared and blocked in with plastanium walls and blast doors. This means that we are in possession of a very large area that has been filled with breathable air. So, you lot are going to get three days of off duty time where you will be given the rare pleasure of not needing your suit."

I'm elated to hear this, and I'm sure everyone else is too.

The Captain adds, "You will be treated with hot food, hot showers and hot coffee."

At these words, you can feel the excitement build in the crowd.

"Enjoy the time off soldiers, you deserve it. Dismissed," he says.

An eruption of chatter breaks out caused by the excitement of the small luxuries that await us in the mountain tunnels. We all eagerly make our way to the airlocks and into the depths of the cliff.

Once we are unsuited and showered, we are given a plain olive drab regulation jumpsuit adorned only with our name, rank and legion. The jumpsuits didn't look like much, but they felt like the most luxurious clothes imaginable after being in a battle suit for over two weeks. Now that I had washed and dressed, it was time to find the mess hall and grab some actual food. After living off life-support for what felt like forever, I was dying for some solid food.

I meet up with Sergeant Wenjack and Privates Talve, Bark and Crang. Together we head down the tunnel to the mess hall. The tunnels are well lit and a lot larger than I initially expected them to be. Most of them look big enough for two Wargons to ride down side by side, which, I guess, must have helped the Hussars when taking them.

The mess hall itself lay at the end of a long tunnel in a section of the cave that opened up into a sizeable cathedral-like cavern. It was far more extensive than I expected it would be, seeing as how it was just sitting here in the rock. It looks to me like the mess hall could easily fit a few thousand soldiers at a time.

We approach the service counter and order our food with a side of boiler grease. Boiler grease is the nickname for the overly strong, bitter coffee that is always found on Federation bases and ships. I remember having good coffee only once since I joined up. It was while spending leave on the small resort planet of Jamaica three. The rich composition of flavours was like nothing I had ever experienced, and I fondly remember them every time I choke down a cup of this hot garbage. Although, even garbage coffee as bad as boiler grease was better than no coffee at all, so I sipped from my cup with pleasure.

The five of us take seats at an empty table against the back wall of the place. I want to sit where we can see who is coming in and out. It was one of the small neurotic habits that are a side effect of always being on alert and ready to fight. Despite where you are, you're never really able to turn it off.

Even though we purposely chose an empty table, it's not long until another group of soldiers comes over.

"Are these spots taken?" one of them asks.

I don't particularly want anyone else to sit with us, but since I can't think of any real reason to say no, I say, "They're yours if you want them."

They thank us and sit down.

"I'm Sergeant Braddock and these are my Mongols," I say as I extend my hand.

"Pleasure to meet you," one of them says, accepting my handshake.

"I'm Sergeant Theron and these are my Assyrians," he says. "Say, you wouldn't happen to be the Sergeant Braddock that everyone is calling the hero of the Bug highway, would ya?"

"Yeah, that's him. Mr. Hero in the flesh," says Private Crang. "Him and Kato fought a trillion Bugs, single handed, while the rest of us idiots stood around and fucked each other."

That got a solid laugh out of everyone at the table.

"Yeah, we know how it is. Federation always has to make something out of nothing," Sergeant Theron says.

"We heard you guys had a hell of a go in those canyons though. Sounded like the Bugs were really ready for you out there," Theron adds.

"They definitely weren't surprised by us, that's for sure," Sergeant Wenjack responds.

"The coms going dead was what really fucked us

though," Private Bark chimed in.

"We lost our coms too. Something about this fucking schythium really messes up the links. From what we've been hearing the coms were the worst in the canyons though. Sounds like you lot definitely had it the worst overall out of the legions at this LZ," Theron says sympathetically.

I look at the other Mongols at the table and then shrug.

"I'm not sure we had it worse than anyone else," I say.

"How about you guys?" Wenjack asks. "How was it clearing out these tunnels?"

Sergeant Theron pauses a while before answering, "It was shit. Think I saw more Bugs in these tunnels than in the rest of my career. The Hussars did a pretty good job clearing out the bulk of the smaller tunnels, but these big caverns turned into cluster fucks pretty fast. We couldn't use explosives without blowing ourselves up in most areas, because of the way Schythium reflects the force of the blasts. So, we were pretty much limited to laser fire. There was never a question of whether or not we were going to win. The only question was how many of us would die in the process."

"Sorry we missed it," Crang says.

"Yeah, me too," Theron says with a laugh.

My attention is drawn to the door as about a hundred soldiers enter the mess simultaneously. They are grouped close together and acting strange. Their jumpsuits bare no legion designations or names, which was against protocol.

"Who are they," I ask, gesturing towards the door.

Sergeant Theron looks over to the door before answering, "Refugees."

"Refugees?" I ask.

"Well not actual refugees of course," Theron says. "They're survivors from landing zone Alpha."

"Survivors?" Private Bark questions.

"That's right," says Theron.

Theron takes a long sip of boiler grease before realizing that we are all staring at him, expecting more information.

"Landing zones Charlie, Echo and obviously us here at Bravo did quite well. We suffered some heavy casualties but achieved our original objectives. Landing Zones Alpha and Delta didn't do so well," Theron said.

"What happened?" Bark asks.

"The Bugs knew they were coming and were ready for them, like always," Theron says.

"They always seem to know when we're coming, clever bastards," Wenjack says.

"This was no different. The Bugs laid in wait and once enough of our troops had landed, they sprung their traps. The exact details of what happened have been kept quiet, but one things for sure, both Alpha and Delta were complete fucking slaughters. Once it was clear that the Landing Zones were a lost cause, the Federation sent retrieval boats to rescue everyone they could, but it wasn't very effective. Only a small handful of legions survived with enough numbers to remain intact. Every other legion was wiped out and only small sections of scattered troops remain," Theron says with a heavy voice.

"How many legions did we lose?" I ask, not knowing if I really want to hear the answer.

"Thirty-seven," Theron says.

We all become silent, struck temporarily dumbfounded.

Eventually, Wenjack speaks, "Thirty-seven legions destroyed in a single day. That makes the Teutoburg forest look like a minor fuck up in comparison."

Theron gives Wenjack a puzzled look, "Teutoburg forest? What planet was that on?"

"Earth, about three thousand standard years ago," Wenjack says.

"Oh, please Wenjack, tell us about it. Like you weren't going to anyway," Crang says sarcastically.

"Well, the Roman empire was in the process of attempting to pacify the Germanic tribes and bring them into the empire. During the process, the Roman governor befriended a Germanic chieftain who had served in the Roman axillary. A man by the name of Arminius. The Roman governor thought Arminius was a loyal servant to the empire but little did he know, this fucker Arminius hated the Romans. He wanted every last one of them dead and to see their empire burn.

"Now, these Romans found the harsh German winters to be unbearable. So, every winter, the Romans would pack their delicate asses up and head to the province of Gaul. Across the river from Germany. This was a long and brutal march through rain and mud that the Romans despised. Arminius knew this and decided to use it to his advantage. He managed to convince the Roman governor that he had a better way that would be less muddy and far easier. Being that the governor was a snivelling little bitch, who was accustomed to a moderate Mediterranean climate and loathed the rain, he agreed.

"Arminius led the clueless Romans down a road through the deep dark Teutoburg forest, which to their surprise was just as muddy as the other trails. Only difference was that this road was much narrower and harder to defend.

"Unknown to the Romans, Arminius had constructed large ramparts on top of a hill beside the road that hid an army made up of warriors from all the Germanic tribes. Once the Romans were right where Arminius wanted them, he sprung his trap. Thousands of Germans came down from the hills throwing spears and quickly encircled the Romans.

"The Romans soon figured out that they were fucked. Not just kind of fucked, where there was still some hope of escape, but straight up, dick is already balls deep in your ass, fucked. They were completely surrounded and were slowly being slaughtered. The pressure from the German forces was so great that Romans in the middle of their ranks were being crushed to death. The massacre took a long time, and those dammed Romans were just trapped there, waiting to die, knowing that all hope was lost.

"The useless tit of a governor, the one who had gotten them into this mess, killed himself out of fear of being captured. The rest either fell to German blades, were crushed, or were captured and sacrificed to Germanic gods.

"All three of the Roman legions were destroyed at once, leaving a scar on Rome that never healed. Even three thousand years later, people are still talking about it as one of the biggest military fuck ups in history. An eternity of shame for losing three legions, and we just lost thirty-seven," Wenjack says.

"No shit," Theron says, followed by a short silence.

"Some of that sounds a little like bullshit," Talve says.

"What parts?" asks Wenjack.

"Maybe it was a big deal once, but to say people are still talking about it is a bit of an exaggeration. I doubt that anyone still talks about it or gives two shits," Talve says.

"We're people and now we're talking about it," Wenjack says smugly. "And you should give a shit about it because learning about fuck ups like these can help us avoid similar mistakes in the future."

"I doubt that were going to let a Bug trick us into following it into a deep dark forest," Talve says.

"I doubt that your mentally capable of understanding the point of what I'm saying," Wenjack says, and Talve gives up because, as we all know, there is no point in arguing with Wenjack.

“So, what’s going to happen with the survivors?” I ask, changing the subject.

“Word is they have been divided among the surviving LZs and will be used to fill the gaps in the rest of the legions,” Theron says.

“I guess there are plenty of those,” I say before asking a question that I didn’t really want the answer to.

As the words leave my lips, I wonder why I’m even asking, but I can’t seem to help myself.

“What’s the total number of casualties for the assault?” I ask.

Everyone pauses because nobody else wants to hear the answer either, but after hearing the question, they now need to know.

All eyes are on Theron as we wait for his response.

“Twenty-three million so far,” he says.

Our mouths hang ajar as we sit like statues, unable to speak. The reality of this war had just hit home in a major way. Until now, we have been focused on our personal losses. Friends that we’ve seen die, legion members lost, but the true scale hadn’t settled in until now. The Federation had just lost more troops in a single day than it had in the past few years.

For the rest of our breakfast, no one else talked. We just sat quietly, ate, and sipped that horrendous coffee. All I could think about was how the Federation could lose so many soldiers. How could a military that was capable of travelling the stars, bringing destruction to anyone we met, be beaten so severely by giant Bugs? Bugs that carried no weapons except the ones they were born with. Excalibur was how. This fucking hell hole of a planet that, by its simple existence, turns so many of our weapons systems into useless trinkets. I told that engineer that fighting on the Bug highway was hell, but what hell had the soldiers at Alpha and Delta experienced. Was it like the hell that the Romans faced in the Teutoburg forest, like in Wenjack's story? More importantly, what hell is waiting for us when we mount up once again.

CHAPTER TEN

Sitting nervously in the chair outside General Carmichael's office with his tablet in hand, Captain Denis wishes that he was anywhere but here. He always hated talking to superior officers, especially ones that weren't from the science departments of the military. In fact, he hated everything about the military other than the science departments. The entire system could fuck off as far as he was concerned. He was a scientist and a damn good one at that. Why should he be subject to the same pointless restrictions and rules as the simple apes that call themselves soldiers?

The only reason he joined up in the first place was the unrestricted funding the Federation offered its scientists. Any private science foundations were extremely limited in their pursuits due to the ever-restricting question of funding. The Federation couldn't care less about cost. They would throw endless amounts of money at anything that had the slightest chance of increasing their galactic power.

Not that he gave two shits about how many wars the Federation wins. It's not that he wanted soldiers to die. He was just so far removed from anything combat-related that it was like a different world to him. The world of wars and combat was as foreign to him as the realms of science were to soldiers. His interest was only in the purity of the scientific process. It just so happened that his field was of particular interest in the current Bug war. After all, he was one of the leading entomologists in the Federation.

Before the Bug wars broke out, entomologists were solely concerned with the study of insects. There were no experts in the species that the Federation had dubbed Bugs because they didn't know they existed. Rather than start training experts from scratch, the Federation decided that it would be easier to shift entomologist's field of study to refocus on Bugs.

Despite popular opinion, insects and Bugs were not actually related. They have independent genetic structures and unique origins. They did, however, share enough in common for the shift in study to be reasonably simple. Specific physical attributes are shared between the species, such as exoskeletons and certain body parts. The Bugs also had a similar social structure to certain insect colonies, with a royalty, warrior and worker class.

That is about where the similarities stopped, and the differences began. The most apparent difference between the species was their size. On Old Earth, an eight-inch tall praying mantis would have been considered massive, while an eight-foot-tall warrior Bug would be deemed on the short side of average. A queen driver ant from Old Earth could reach the whopping size of almost two inches long, while a Bug queen could easily be the size of a Federation dropship.

Another significant difference was the Bugs

somehow managed to spread themselves across the galaxy. However, at the moment, nobody is really sure how this happens. They don't have any spacecraft or technology of any kind. As far as anyone can tell, they simply hatch to meet any basic needs they have. If they need to dig a hole, a hole digging Bug seems to hatch. Due to this ability, they have had little need to develop tools and thus haven't. So, unless there is some kind of Bug that has hatched with the ability to travel through space, it is a complete mystery how they navigate the galaxy.

"Captain Denis, General Carmichael is ready to see you now," the General's assistant says.

His rank of Captain was purely based on his scientific merit, not military ability. He stands up and walks through the door to the General's office without any more acknowledgment of the assistant. As he enters the room, he snaps to attention and fires off a salute. A mandatory requirement of the military that he despised.

"At ease Captain. Take a seat," General Carmichael says.

He takes a seat and places his tablet on his lap. Silently he sits there, waiting for Carmichael to speak, knowing better than to address a General before being asked to. The General sits in silence, giving the Captain an inquisitive look, before pouring himself a glass of scotch.

"Scotch?" General Carmichael offers.

"No thank you Sir, I don't drink scotch," Captain

Denis says.

"Of course you don't," the General replies.

Captain Denis knew that was intended as an insult but was required by rank to take it silently.

"Look. Do you know why I called for you?" Carmichael asks.

"No sir," Captain Denis responds.

"It's about your report," Carmichael says.

"Was it not satisfactory?" Captain Denis asks.

"I couldn't tell you, because quite frankly Captain, I couldn't read the fucking thing. I mean I could read the words, but I sure as fuck couldn't understand what any of them meant. You go on about genomes, chromosomes and genetic fingerprints, like I'm supposed to know what the fuck any of that means. I'm sure you egg heads understand this kind of shit, but you know damn well that I don't," the General says before taking a drink of scotch and leaning back in his chair.

"Son, I'm a combat officer. What I understand are battlefields and warzones. I also understand how to utilize scientific developments to better operate in those battlefields and warzones. What I don't understand or give a fuck about are the complexities that go into making those scientific developments.

"Do you know why the Federation, in its infinite wisdom, chose to put a combat officer in charge of the applied sciences division instead of a science officer?" Carmichael asks.

"No Sir," Captain Denis responds in complete honesty because he genuinely had no idea and, in fact, asked himself that question regularly.

"Because Captain, I don't give a shit about the science. The Federation worries that if a science officer was put in charge, they would be overly concerned with the science itself. They might lose the forest for the trees so to speak. The Federation wants an officer who's only concern is using the science to achieve the mission statement. Do you know what that is Captain?" General Carmichael asks with increasing aggression.

"No Sir," Captain Denis responds.

"The mission statement is to kill Bugs and win this fucking war!" the General shouts.

Captain Denis sinks back in his chair slightly at the verbal assault. This type of shit was precisely why he hated the military. He was doing his job the way he had learned it, and now he was getting jacked up because this gorilla couldn't read a scientific paper. How hard would it be for the Federation to give this guy some basics in the department he's supposed to be running?

"Now, for the sake of all humankind and its allies, could you please explain this report to me in plain Federation standard, before I bust your ass down to private and find myself someone who can?" Carmichael asks.

"Umm, yes Sir," the Captain stammers nervously.

"Well good," Carmichael says happily with a smile

on his face.

All traces of aggression melt away as if the Captain had forced the General to be stern and not that the General enjoyed pushing around subordinates.

"Well Sir," Captain Denis starts. "As you already know, the Bugs have an unparalleled ability to adapt perfectly to thrive in whatever environment they find them selves in. They manage to breathe vastly different atmospheres, consume whatever fuel source is available, and even seem to develop different physical traits in order to maximize their combat effectiveness in each environment. Until now, it has appeared that these adaptations have been reasonably small. I mean, the end results may look like a big change, but on a genetic level, they are caused by reasonably small changes. In fact, most of the time these changes aren't even changes at all. Instead they result from the activation of dormant genes. Think of it like switches that can be flicked to turn on certain traits. Until Excalibur, this theory has been consistent with every sample that we've examined," Captain Denis says.

"Wait, what do you mean until now? What's so different about now?" Carmichael asks.

"Well Sir, we have been going over the samples that were sent to us by the hunter units."

"Hold on," Carmichael cuts Captain Denis off.

"The Federation does not, now, nor have we ever had hunter units. Whoever sent those samples doesn't exist, if anyone asks. Only nobody will ask or else, they, will no longer exist. Do you understand me Captain?"

"Umm, well yes, yes of course Sir," the Captain stammers, confused by the General's defensiveness over the subject.

The Captain takes a moment to gather his composure before continuing.

"The samples that we received from… uh… Excalibur show much more extensive changes than could be reasonably expected from the activation of dormant genes alone. In fact, many of those genes aren't even present.

"For example," he says, regaining composure. "Our original prediction was that the Bugs exoskeletons would be approximately thirty percent stronger than average due to atmospheric pressures. This would be consistent with their typical ability to adapt. We found that the Bugs on Excalibur have exoskeletons that are well over two hundred percent stronger than expected.

"Which explains why they were so easily able to rip their way through the plastanium battle suits. An increase of two hundred percent is far from reasonable based on past data," Captain Denis states.

"No shit," says the General with a slight bit of shock, showing through his normally stoic face.

"There are other changes that I'll explain later, but the important take away is the idea that the Bugs simply adapt through activation of dormant genes is only part of the story. So, we dug deeper and found some extremely interesting things."

"Interesting might be a subjective term Captain" Carmichael interrupts.

"I don't follow, Sir," Captain Denis says.

"It was a joke, Captain. Jokes are something that people with personalities use for amusement," Carmichael says.

Captain Denis found it ironic that this walking stereotype would accuse him of lacking personality, but he resisted the urge to mention it.

"Yes, well," Captain Denis continues. "We compared the genetic structure of the Bugs from Excalibur with past samples that we had on record and found that they were extremely different. Normally the samples very slightly through what we believed to be differences in evolution, but they were basically the same. Like I already mentioned, the structures were the same but different genes would be activated. The genetic structure of the Excalibur Bugs are completely different," Captain Denis pauses for a minute as he searches for the words to explain what they had found.

"Sir, imagine if you built spaceships for a number of years, and became very good at it, but you are always required to build from the same order sheet. Over time, you find ways to build them better and better but because you are always working off the same guidelines the modifications are limited. Then one day your boss comes in and tells you to throw away the order sheet and build the best ship you can. Only catch is it must look relatively similar. Well, you'd finally be able to make all of the massive performance changes that you've been dreaming about all those years. You could completely redesign every aspect of the ship's internals to drastically out perform the old model and then simply cover it with a body that looks original. On the outside it would look the same but inside it would be completely different," the Captain explains.

"That is a terrible fucking analogy, and you clearly know nothing about building spaceships. Get to the fucking point Captain," Carmichael barks.

"The point General, is that on a genetic level, this is what has happened with the Bugs. Their genetic structure has been completely rebuilt from the ground up and the end result is a species of Bug that far surpasses everything else we've seen, by light-years," Captain Denis exuberantly explains.

"Calm down Captain. So what, the Bugs are stronger than anticipated. Our boys and girls on the ground will just have to work a little bit harder to win this one is all. Just give me a list of specific changes that the Bugs have developed and I'll figure out how to use it to our advantage," Carmichael says.

"No!" Captain Denis blurts out, surprising both Carmichael and himself.

He was never one to have outbursts like this, especially about things he didn't much care about. After all, he was only really concerned with the scientific method. So, why did he care what this ape in a uniform thought? Was it possible that he actually cared just a little bit about the military, about the Federation? Did he actually care about those brutish apes that called themselves soldiers?

"Look, Sir. I'm going to put this in the absolute simplest terms possible. If the Bug's genetics have been rebuilt from the ground up, that means their genetics have been built. All this time, we thought the Bugs had been adapting to fit specific planet's criteria for life. Instead, it turns out they have, in fact, been designed to fit those criteria. Someone or something has been developing Bugs for their own purposes. This means that it's no coincidence that the most valuable planet to the Federation, in the entire galaxy, is also home to the toughest species of Bugs, in the highest concentrations that we have ever seen.

"The question of how the Bugs move around the galaxy, that we have been bashing our heads against the wall trying to figure out, could simply have the answer that someone is putting them in our way. The who, how and why is still a mystery, but I assure you General, there is a who," Captain Denis explains.

"Captain are you trying to tell me that there is some kind of something out there that is using the Bugs for their own means?" Carmichael questions.

"What I'm saying, is that something has been designing Bugs to fight in specific environments. It would appear that there is some deliberate intention to the placement of the Bugs as well. Although the how and the why are anyone's guess. I am not able to speculate on that. For all I know, there could be an even higher level of Bug that's doing this, some kind of class above their royalty class. It could be that the Bugs we are fighting are the biological Bug equivalent to drones, fighting wars for the master Bugs. I just don't know."

"Well Captain, I'm not too sure what to do with this information. Of course, it goes without saying that this needs to remain classified and shouldn't be shared with anyone."

"Of course, Sir."

"The one thing that I do know Captain, is that the work that you and your team has done could quite possibly change the course of this war. Fuck, it could change the course of the Federation. You are truly a credit to the human race Captain" Carmichael says with surprising, genuine admiration.

"Thank you, Sir," Captain Denis says, in shock from hearing the first positive comment he's ever received from the General.

"You're dismissed Captain. Get the fuck out of my office," General Carmichael says.

Captain Denis walks back to his quarters, playing his conversation with the General through his head. What happened to him back there? He had always been so focused on the science, but somehow the intensity of the General had brought out something else in him. Something new. When he first discovered the fingerprints of a creator in Bug DNA, he didn't overthink it. Now he was running all kinds of ideas through his head. Suddenly, the why had become something that he knew he would obsess over till he found some answers.

When Captain Denis is almost at his quarters, he bumps into Lieutenant Flores from his research team.

"Hey Captain," she says with a soft smile.

"Save that Captain stuff for the lab. When I'm off duty I'd rather not be reminded of military shit."

"Right, force of habit. Sorry Kayden. Anyway, what's on your mind?"

"Nothing important."

"Nothing important huh? Doesn't look like nothing important," she prods.

"Well, just the future of the human race and our place in the galaxy."

"You're right, that doesn't sound important at all. You want to grab a drink and talk about it?" she asks, brushing her hair behind her ear.

"No, I definitely don't want to talk about it. But, I could use a drink."

CHAPTER ELEVEN

We had been given the luxury of four straight days inside the bunker without any orders. Which has been a very unusual wartime luxury. Typically, we would be performing mindless busy work and attending briefings in order to keep our discipline up. One or two days of on-base leave might be given on the rare occasion, but four entire days is just plain unheard of. We guessed that the only reason we had been given this luxury was because of the massive influx of surviving soldiers from the failed LZs. The Federation had millions of soldiers with nowhere to go that needed to be assigned to new legions.

We didn't complain. Instead, we stayed quiet and enjoyed the unprecedented free time. Our time was put to good use eating, bullshitting amongst ourselves, taking pleasure in the luxury of hot showers, the occasional fucking, and generally just enjoying life outside of our battle suits. After our hellish introduction to this planet, life in the bunker was downright heavenly.

I found that I even had time to do some reading. On Wenjack's recommendation, I read a digitalized copy of an Old Earth book called *The Lord of The Rings*. The story held up well for being over a thousand years old, despite the dated language and writing style, but then again, great stories always do.

From what I understand, the books were written in

response to the author's experience during Old Earth's first World War. A ruthlessly brutal war, even by today's standards. This war saw the once great empires of Old Earth destroy each other in a senseless grab for power. I did some reading about the author afterward. He apparently denied that the books were based on the global events of the times, but I find that unlikely. The connections were far too obvious to deny.

The story is centred around a pair of wars that directly mirror the first and second Old Earth World Wars, but these occur in a fictional land called Middle Earth. In the story, the fading empires of the free peoples of Middle Earth have to band together to fight back the rising power of an evil enemy that threatens to cover the land in darkness. This obviously reflected the rise of the German empire and later the Third Reich, as they threatened to destroy the established European empires.

I quickly realized that another war was alluded to in the story, which was a war between growing industrialization and nature. The free peoples of Middle Earth had rich cultures centred around their ties to nature. In contrast, the new evil empire was only concerned with power and creating weapons of war. I assumed that the world's industrialization at the time of Old Earths' great wars was one of the evils the author used as inspiration for his story.

The story itself follows a group of heroes trying to destroy an evil ring of power that the enemy wants to use to take over Middle Earth. They are put to multiple tests as they go through all of the typical events that have become the standard for the hero's journey that is now classic in most human literature.

I enjoyed the story for much the same reason that anyone would, but what really captured my interest were the parts that talked about a country called Rohan. This country was populated by people whose entire culture was centred around the horse. As you might expect, they were exceptional horse soldiers, which I identified with. Led by their great King Theoden, the Rohirrim rode gloriously into battle after battle, smashing their enemies underneath them. The descriptions of these horse battles made the hairs on the back of my neck stand up as I imagined myself riding with them.

I realize how ridiculous it might seem for a grown man who has fought in countless cavalry battles to be sitting on his bunk, fantasizing like a child about fighting in a mythical war. Although, if you understand what it's like to be a Federation soldier, then you wouldn't find it ridiculous at all. In all of our wars, there wasn't a straightforward issue of good and evil like there was in the books. In our wars, there was always a question of why we were fighting. Sure, the Bugs were mindless hordes of murderous monsters, but they aren't exactly evil. I don't even think they have the mental capacity to think of things like good and evil. They just kill everything that they come across because that's what they were born to do.

I wasn't sure if we were a force for good either. We killed Bugs because they were a threat, but I'm not going to say that the Federation sending millions of soldiers to their deaths to fight Bugs on planets that we weren't exactly entitled to was a just cause.

The Rohirrim that rode with Theoden were honourable and righteous. Fighting against evil without any concern for their own well-being. They were heroes in a war where it was easy to claim such a title. I envied the simplicity of their cause. There was no question of right or wrong. They knew without a doubt that their lives would be given for the purist of reasons, which was truly admirable. I wish our war was that black and white.

I spent a lot of time pondering how the story's author would have thought of our own cavalry. Would he have compared us to the riders of Rohan, or would he have regarded us as the evil Warg riders? The Warg riders were vicious creatures that fought against the people of Rohan, riding the plains looking for prey. They sought to wipe out the free peoples to use their resources to fuel their war machine. Even though we like to think of ourselves as honourable soldiers akin to the Rohirrim, maybe our actions align with the Warg riders. Perhaps our hunger for more planets and resources muddies any claim to righteousness, no matter our cause.

I spent the majority of my time off thinking about this question and concluded that it didn't matter. The problems of our reality aren't as simple as those of a mythical world. We are burdened with inconvenient truths and unpleasant circumstances. I could wish all I wanted that the decisions involved in leading soldiers into combat could be as simple as Theoden's, but they never would be. I had to make decisions that got good soldiers killed without ever knowing whether or not the reasons behind their deaths could be justified on a cosmic scale of good and evil.

I try to put these thoughts from my mind as I walk down the corridor towards General Jaxxon's temporary office. I had been called to report to him for orders, which meant that it was time to settle back into the business of war. It was time to stop asking the question of why and refocus on the question of how. How were we going to take this planet? How was I going to get my soldiers through this mess in one piece?

As I get to the General's office, I am greeted by an assistant at his door.

"You can head right in, the General is expecting you," the assistant says with a smile.

I can't tell if the smile is a standard professional gesture or if he knows something I don't. I enter the office and stand at attention as I salute the General.

"At ease," General Jaxxon says.

I end my salute and stand with a little more ease as I begin to say, "Sergeant Braddock reporting for..."

"Have a seat," the General says, cutting me off, and I do as he says.

"So, I finally get a chance to sit down with the infamous hero of the Bug highway," he says with a smile.

I'm beginning to get really tired of everyone greeting me this way. Although, something in the way the General said it implied a certain degree of humour that made it more tolerable.

"I'm no hero Sir," I say.

"Oh, you're not, and what makes you say that Sergeant?" he asks.

"All do respect Sir, I would have been Bug food if you hadn't shown up when you did."

"Of course you would," he says in good humour. "I know that, and you know that, but nobody else needs to know that."

"I'm not sure I follow," I say.

"Sergeant, the truth is, we need heroes in this war. We're just getting started and we've already sustained heavy losses. As officers, it has taken all that we have to keep moral up. So if people hear a story of a Mongol and a Samurai standing back to back, fighting off a massive horde of Bugs, we're going to do what we can to keep that story going. Our soldiers need inspirational stories to keep them going and let's face it, your story is a good one. We might be choosing to leave out a few details but it's the spirit of the story that counts."

"I understand Sir," I say since I'm in no position to argue with the General.

"I'm sure you do Sergeant," he says, eyeing me carefully. "Look Sergeant. This war is going to be a long one and keeping moral up is going to make the difference between winning and losing. Your story has the ability to do that. It's got two people from different legions working together, ready to give their lives in a last ditch attempt to turn the battle. Its inspiring. Besides, it's not like we're making it up. Sergeant Kato and yourself acted like model soldiers and did the Federation proud. The fact that I saved your asses or that there were a lot of unrecognized people involved doesn't take away from that."

Even though I feel like the idea of me being declared a hero is undeserved, I see where he is coming from and don't protest.

"In order to show that the Federation both recognizes, and values its heroes, it has been decided that Sergeant Kato and yourself will be granted the medal of valor."

"Thank you sir," I say, trying to contain my genuine excitement. "That is a great honour."

Even though I don't think I deserve it, the medal of valour is the highest combat-specific honour that could be awarded to a soldier. The idea of it being printed onto my battle suit fills me with pride.

The Federation no longer gives out physical medals to active duty combat soldiers. Instead, they print the "medal" on the arm of the battle suit just below your symbol of rank. This way, everyone you meet on the battlefield knows your accomplishment. The idea is that this would boost the morale of the soldiers around you and make them fight harder in your presence. Whether or not this is actually the case, I would have to wait to find out.

I was told that, upon retirement, I would be presented with a physical metal that I would be able to hang on my wall or wear to parades. I found the idea ridiculous because the odds of retiring from service were laughable. It's not that I didn't like the idea of retirement. It's just that it wasn't likely.

Due to the Federation wartime act, terms of service were all extended until the war's end. Since the Bugs had seemed to populate the far corners of the galaxy, this particular war would likely last at least another hundred years. That's assuming we don't all die trying to take this planet, which is a genuine possibility.

"Regardless of the circumstances it is an honor to be giving this award to one of my Mongols. You have made your legion proud Sergeant Braddock," General Jaxxon says.

"Thank you, Sir. The honor is all mine," I reply.

"Well, now that we've got the pleasant matters out of the way, we have more business to discuss," he says.

I wonder what business a general would have to discuss with a lowly NCO.

"I lost a lot of good officers on this drop. Hell, not just officers, I lost a lot of good soldiers of every rank," he says in a sullen tone.

An unwelcomed image of Corporal Wilson being

ripped in half enters my mind.

"The high level of casualties has left some noticeable holes in our ranks that must be filled. Lieutenant Jeanceon for example, was one of my best Lieutenants and I relied on him heavily for both his leadership abilities as well as his advice. His heroic sacrifice in the canyons cost me a great officer that will be hard to replace. Luckily for me, the Mongols are now in possession of a war hero, that, in my opinion, has both the experience and balls to make one hell of a Lieutenant," the General says.

All feelings of excitement left from receiving my medal are instantly replaced with dread as I realize he is talking about me. I don't want to lead more soldiers. That brings a weight too heavy for me to carry. Lieutenant Jeanceon was an outstanding combat officer, and he had just led thousands of good Mongols to their deaths. How was I supposed to do any better? I hadn't even been through officers' training. Typically, officers received a minimum of two years at military college to learn how to effectively lead large numbers in the field.

"Sir, I'm honored that you think I would make a good officer, but I lack the required education," I say in an attempt to avoid the promotion.

"You're right, and under peace time circumstances maybe I would give a shit, but these aren't peace time circumstances. This is war, and right now I don't have time to wait two years for my NCOs to go to school and learn a bunch of shit they already know. We have a shortage of officers and the only way I'm going to get more is by promoting my NCOs, and right now you're the best that I've got," he says.

I know that he's right, but the idea scares the crap out of me, and I instantly long for the good Ol days when I only had to worry about the life of the person next to me.

"Look Braddock, have you seen the casualty stats from the drop?" the General asks.

"Yes sir," I answer.

"Good, then you already know how low the survival rates were for the sections that rode the flanks. Every section was nearly decimated, with one exception. The survival rate of your soldiers was far above that of any other section in the flanks. Your two hundred soldiers outperformed the other eighteen-hundred that rode that way. Within your section there was a subgroup that had a proportionally higher rate of survival than the rest. Do you know who they were?" he asks.

"No Sir," I lie.

"Of course you do, because they were the soldiers from your dropship," he says.

I, of course, already knew this because Sergeant Wenjack had brought it up after the battle in the canyons. My opinion on the matter hasn't changed since then.

"Sir, as much as I would love to take credit for our performance, it just wouldn't be right. The reason that we did as well as we did was because I had a large number of experienced veterans under my command. The quality of the soldiers that I rode with were simply unmatched by the other units. It wasn't anything more than that," I say.

"Bullshit," General Jaxxon snaps. "Every section that served under Lieutenant Jeanceon were chalk full of highly experienced veteran Mongols. The only thing that separated them from your soldiers, was that your soldiers had the privilege of training under and serving with you. I've seen your ability to make decisions under pressure firsthand, and I was nothing short of impressed. On top of that you have demonstrated a rare balance of aggression and common sense, a strong understanding of your enemy and an unwavering loyalty to your fellow soldiers. A lesser man would have instantly taken credit for the performance of those under his command, but you did not. You gave all credit where credit was due and that is a sign of a true leader. By taking personal responsibility for the lives of your soldiers, you have helped them outperform, time and time again. Perhaps you don't have the official education of an officer, but you do have all the real-world experience anyone could ask for, on top of a spotless service record. So for those reasons we will be adding a Lieutenant's solid bar to your battle suits arm to go with your medal of valor."

The thought of being personally responsible for the fates of hundreds of soldiers was not appealing to me. In fact, it made me sick to my stomach. I have no problem charging headlong into a horde of murderous Bugs, knowing full well that it might be the last thing I'll ever do. But ordering other people to do it is another thing entirely. An even worse thing than ordering soldiers to go into situations where they might die is ordering them into situations where you know they will die. In this war, that is something that will be unavoidable. Deciding who lives and who dies is not something that I ever signed up for, but what choice do I have. Refusing a promotion was treated the same as refusing any other order, and that wasn't something I was prepared to do.

So, I respond to the General with "Thank you Sir," because that's what a cavalryman is supposed to do.

We handled a few administrative issues regarding the division of troops, and it's decided that I will be taking command of the Mongols seventh brigade. Which will put some five hundred Mongols under my direct command. This was the same brigade that I had spent my entire career in, so I already had a good idea of who I could count on. A few of my NCOs had been transferred to other brigades to fill the gaps created in the drop, but I still had a few solid leaders like Sergeant Wenjack.

We would have twelve more hours of on-base R&R until we switched over to active duty. My orders were to have all of my soldiers suited and mounted in formation outside the West gate at seven o'clock Federation standard time tomorrow morning. As much as I am dreading the thought of taking responsibility for five hundred soldiers. I am looking forward to being reunited with Sleipnir and riding once more.

CHAPTER TWELVE

By seven o'clock, I have all five hundred Mongols of the seventh brigade lined up in perfect formation outside the formidable West gate. Being promoted to Lieutenant wasn't something I wanted, but I admit, sitting on Sleipnir before this many hardened warriors gives me an incredibly powerful feeling. On top of five hundred armoured Wargons, five hundred armoured soldiers are all waiting to follow my command. The crushing pressure of being responsible for all their lives temporarily retreats, and the intoxication of knowing that these warriors live and die by my command takes its place. I feel Sleipnir's demeanour start to shift as he mirrors my sense of pride and power. He holds his head up a little higher and stands just a little bit taller.

With a bit of swagger, I ride Sleipnir up and down the rows of Mongols as I perform the inspection. Inspections are basically a pointless display of military tradition. It serves little actual purpose since every one of these soldiers was thoroughly inspected less than an hour ago when they were suited up by the techs. The act of riding up and down the ranks is more of a chance to demonstrate my authority than anything.

As I ride past each individual soldier, looking them up and down, it lets them see me. See my Lieutenants bar and my medal of valour. The fact that I'm able to move around and judge them, as they have to stand there, still as statues, helps to condition them into knowing that I am in charge. It lets them know that we are not equals, and I have the ability to do things that they do not.

I begin to see the new Mongols that fill our ranks. With the number of cavalry legions destroyed at the other landing zones, there were many Wargons and soldiers looking for new homes. I know from the muster list that about a quarter of my soldiers are transplants of this type. Properly integrating these new soldiers into our ranks will no doubt prove to be a challenge. They all come from proud legions, in which they had fought and bonded.

Soldier's identities are tied to which legion they serve under. Like any proud member of a group, they feel as if their group is superior to all others. This pride is encouraged because it leads to a healthy amount of inter legion competition. However, it can prove to be a severe roadblock when attempting to integrate troops from other legions.

I now have soldiers from the Comanche, Huns, Uhlans, and Cuirassiers, all standing within our ranks bearing freshly minted Mongol insignias.

I stop in front of one such soldier and look him up and down. If these were the old days, the Sergeant McKenzie days, I would have been able to discern what kind of trials this soldier had gone through by the scars on his armour, but plastanium tells no tails. The scars of our trials are now only found underneath the armour. Carved in the deep recesses of our minds.

"What's your name Corporal?" I ask on the brigade's coms link so that everyone can hear me.

"Corporal Ballard, Sir," the soldier responds.

"What legion did you come from, Corporal Ballard?" I ask, purposely using his name as a small gesture of recognition.

"I am, or at least, I was a Cuirassier, Sir," he answers with a tone of remorse in his voice.

"Then you fought at landing zone Alpha, isn't that correct?" I question.

"Yes Sir," he answers.

"What was it like?" I ask the Corporal.

"Sir?" he questions in return.

"Was that not a simple enough question? What was it like being at LZ Alpha Corporal?" I ask more aggressively.

As I do, I can feel him getting irritated. Not in the way that you can sense the tension in a room, but I actually feel it. This Corporal's irritation is shared with his Wargon, which it shares with Sleipnir, and then me. I am directly linked to the feelings of the soldier that stands before me, which is something that has never happened before.

Our links were always limited at best. We can typically use it to communicate with our Wargons and, on rare occasions, get a general sense of the emotions of nearby Wargons but never from another soldier. As far as I know, I had pushed the capability of the link as far as it could go back in the battle for the Canyons. What I was feeling now was strange and off-putting.

"Well, Corporal?" I push.

"It was a nightmare," Corporal Ballard snaps.

As he answers, I feel him shift from irritation to flat-out anger.

"We dropped into a trap. The fuckers somehow knew we were coming. They were waiting for us. We rode right to where they wanted us and then… Then they sprung their trap. We were slaughtered. I saw countless numbers of my friends and fellow Cuirassiers torn apart before my eyes. Some of them were soldiers that I'd known since Boot. I've been in bad spots before, but not like that, never like that.

"What was it like? To be honest Sir, I hope you never know," he says, and among his feelings of anger, I find the hurt that I was looking for.

I didn't enjoy manipulating this soldier to get my point across, but it was necessary. These soldiers needed a reason to fight for me, and it was my job to give it to them. So I continue pushing the Corporal.

"Why are you here, Corporal? Why are you here when so many of your brothers and sisters aren't?"

With this question, I feel him approaching his emotional edge as the loss and hurt turn to anger and frustration. By now, I didn't need my link with Sleipnir to sense it. I could physically see it in the way that he started to shift in his saddle as his body reflected the mental tension that he was experiencing. I expected this question to be a trigger because it's the question that every survivor continuously asks themselves. I figured this Corporal was no different.

I'm guessing that he's probably asked himself, "Why me?" a few times each day since the battle.

Me publicly asking him this question and demanding an answer triggered him to experience the full force of the emotional weight of the question.

I begin to feel the same emotions that Corporal Ballard feels, now coming from others in my ranks. The pure, unfiltered anger, pain and hate are pouring in from all of the survivors of the disbanded units. I have definitely forced them to bring up the emotions that I am looking for. I only hope that it will have the outcome that I intend. This is uncharted territory, and I am unaccustomed to this level of connection. I force myself to focus on my own mind so that I don't get overwhelmed by the cacophony of emotions that now fly through it.

"The only reason why I'm here, is because some hotshot dropship pilot flew his ass off and picked me up in the middle of a colossal fuck up. I just so happened to be in the right place when that ship came in for retrieval. If I happened to be somewhere else, I wouldn't be standing here right now Sir," Corporal Ballard answers with more composure than I thought possible given his level of frustration.

"No Corporal, you're wrong," I say.

"The reason that you're here, is the same reason that all of you transfers are here. Revenge. Your legions were lost, but fate has given a select few of you the opportunity to avenge that loss. Your brothers and sisters, your friends, and comrades, have been slaughtered by the Bugs. Your legions honour and legacy have been destroyed, but you few, have the chance to get some revenge. You have the opportunity to show these mother fuckers, that humankind can't be fucked with. They got one victory over us, but that's the last victory that fate will allow. It's the last victory that we will allow. They took your legions from us, but in turn, we will take everything from them."

My speech is interrupted by a loud "huha" from the ranks.

I can feel the energy of the soldiers rising as I speak.

"Fate has given you the opportunity for revenge by sparing you from death. The Federation has ensured that revenge, by putting you under my command. They transferred away a lot of soldiers that I have fought and bled with, in order for so many of you to be able to have the privilege of fighting for me. Mongols under my command have killed more Bugs than any other cavalry on Excalibur."

I have no idea if this claim is true, but it sounded good, and I can tell they're eating it up.

A loud "Huha" erupts from the brigade.

"I realize that you transfers have come from proud Legions. I also know damn well how much of your identity has been tied to the banners you used to fight under, but that is the past. Those parts of your identities died with those legions.

"Through a cruel twist of fate, you have become Mongols, and from this moment to the end of your short lives, Mongols you shall remain. Whether you die here on Excalibur, or in some other far-off place, you will die with the honor of having ridden with the best cavalry legion in history. You've got a big reputation to live up to, and live up to it you shall. I will give you the opportunity to avenge your fallen brothers and sisters, but in return, I demand that you give me your best, and make me proud. Make me proud to call you my brothers and sisters. Make me proud to have had the honor of leading you."

As I finish speaking, I can feel that the anger in the crowd has turned to excitement.

Corporal Ballard, who I had singled out, and emotionally pushed to the edge of rage, has calmed down, and a stoic silence fell across his mind. He seems to be filled with a new resolve, and a new concern came to me.

I now had no doubt that these transfers were eager to fight, but I wasn't sure if they were eager to fight for me. It is easy to give people a reason to engage in violence, but it is another thing altogether to convince them to work together in that violence. Teams are built through trust and experience. It takes time. Time that you don't always have when the enemy is at your throats.

I ride back to the front of the brigade and turn around to face the troops. The cruel landscape of the Surf lay across the plains behind me.

"Sergeant Wenjack, please brief the men," I ask in a pleasant tone that officers reserved for their chosen NCOs to signal that they held command.

"With pleasure Sir," he responds in a way that lets me know that he's getting as much of a kick out of my new rank as I am. It is doubtful that anyone else picked up on it.

"Listen up you motherless heathens. This is going to be a simple hunt and kill mission. We're going to ride our asses outside the wire and go Bug hunting. Assuming that we don't ride into a trap and get ourselves killed, we should be in the field for the next two weeks. Over that time, we are going to search every cave, every hole, and every tunnel. If we find anything with more than four legs, we kill it, plain and simple. Do you get me?" Wenjack shouts.

"Yes Sergeant!" the soldiers yell back.

"Excellent" Wenjack says.

"Now, Intelligence says that the Bugs have supply stashes scattered across this planet. They believe that this is where they are storing their food and water. We need to find and destroy these stashes.

"Seeing as how they need these supplies to survive, we are expecting them to be well protected. If you happen to see something well-guarded and smaller than a hive, it is likely what we're looking for.

"Don't think about trying any hero shit out there. If we find a stash, we call it in and hit it in force. Do you get me?" Wenjack shouts again.

"We get you Sergeant!" the brigade responds.

"And on the topic of not trying any hero shit. Remember that there are only five hundred of us out here and billions of them. Keep it smart. Keep it safe," Wenjack says.

Turning back to face me, Sergeant Wenjack says, "Lieutenant Braddock. They are ready."

"Mongols, move out!" I order, and without needing to be directed, Sleipnir makes a quick about-turn and takes off.

His pace is easy and comfortable, not slow by any measure, but only about half of what he is capable of. I was expecting his quick start to catch the brigade off guard, but to my surprise, they were on the bounce and immediately followed us in perfect formation. Together we ride, enjoying what will probably be the only flat open terrain on this mission because ahead of us lay the formidable Surf.

As we reach the Surf, we slow our speed considerably and spread out our line. The simple nature of this place will require us to maneuver with more care and caution than usual. Sleipnir moves with surprising ease between the sharp rocky crests and through the short rolling tunnels, but I quickly see why this area was initially taken by foot soldiers. It is possible to move cavalry through this place, but not with enough speed to be combat effective. If we were sent this way on the drop, we would have lost as many soldiers to the landscape as to the Bugs. One miss-step and these schythium ridges could split our suits wide open.

About a half a kilometre into the Surf, we pass our first of three defensive lines. The lines are made up of plastanium pillboxes that have been built into the landscape. Smooth little reinforced buildings that have gunnery slots cut into their sides, just large enough for a soldier to fire out of. On the tops of the pillboxes lay sentry guns protected by their own armoured boxes. I wouldn't want to be one of the poor bastards stuck in these death traps when the shit hits the fan.

The three lines of boxes spread five hundred meters apart from one another. This was supposed to provide an overlapping field of fire that would allow one line to cover the other. I wasn't sure how well this would work in practice, but I guess it could be sufficient if the lines were reinforced with enough foot soldiers and some Goliath suits.

Eventually, we pass the final line of boxes and are officially on hostile ground once more. We release a few drones to scout ahead of us so that we don't end up walking into a proverbial pile of shit. I check my HUD and communication systems to ensure that everything is working correctly. Once I confirm all is well, I give the orders to carry on.

The terrain becomes a little more cavalry-friendly as we make our way farther from our lines. The Surf eventually transitions into a combination of serrated peaks and shallow canyons that pose little challenge to our Wargons. In order to cover ground faster, we break into sections of twenty-five and spread out.

We check every crack, tunnel, and hole, big enough for a Bug to hide in. It doesn't take long for our sections to start making contact. Nothing major at first. Just a few pockets of Bugs here and there that are easily disposed of with a bit of laser fire. According to Intelligence, these small groups of Bugs were scouting parties, sent out to gather information to send back to the hive. I really have no idea if there is any truth to that or not. All I know is they make easy targets that my soldiers are more than happy to use as a warm-up.

About fifty kilometres past the line, we finally start seeing some real activity as our drones pick up a patrol of a few thousand Bugs.

"Sergeant Wenjack, are you seeing this?" I ask.

"Yes Sir. Not too many to handle, but definitely enough that we'd be better off not hitting them head on," he answers.

"Agreed," I say as I bring up the map on my HUD.

I search through the map until I find what I'm looking for.

"Mongols," I call out over the brigade communication link.

"We have a few thousand Bugs up ahead, that need to be dealt with. Your maps have been marked with battle instructions. Move out," I order, and all Mongols begin to move.

There was a time that an order like this would have taken an hour to explain and discuss, as we unfolded maps and individually instructed each section where to go and what to do. Now, all I have to do is tell my computer what I want, and it sends real-time instructions to everyone involved in a plan. The Bugs might benefit from their ability to communicate through their singular hive mind, but with the way we're all connected through our computers, we aren't far behind.

It doesn't take long before I have the bulk of our forces lining the ridges on either side of a small canyon about fifty feet across. It is much smaller than the ones closer to the base, but it's the perfect size for what we need. I hold our forces back, just outside the line of sight of the canyon floor, so that any Bugs that come this way won't see us. With everyone in place, I turn my attention to the feed from the drone that is following Sergeant Wenjack's section.

They meet the Bugs in an open section of terrain, engaging them with heavy amounts of laser fire and grenades. Their orders are to hit them hard enough to get their attention and get out of there, but they're really going for damage. Wenjack has a few transfers with him, and by the looks of it, they're aiming for a bit of payback. I can tell that he doesn't want to deny them the opportunity, although if they miss time and hold engagement too long, it will be us who will be avenging them.

I see Corporal Ballard move towards the Bugs as he fires. Slowly, he moves further and further out of position.

"Get back in line," Wenjack roars, but Corporal Ballard takes no notice of the order.

Instead of moving back, he hurls more grenades at the approaching Bugs, who, at this point, are almost on top of them.

With no more time to waste, Wenjack commands, "Fall back."

At the order, they turn and begin riding hard in our direction. With the Bugs on their asses, the Wargons move with all the speed they can muster. Bounding from rock to rock, moving faster than caution can allow. Each rider and Wargon knowing that the danger behind them outweighs the hazards of moving fast in this hostile terrain.

When they hit the canyon, the Bugs are almost on top of them. The plan was for Wenjack to stay a comfortable distance ahead and lead them into our trap, but now it was doubtful they would make it far enough. Normally, a Wargon would have no problem outrunning a Bug on open ground, but this wasn't open ground. One slip from the lead Wargon, and they would all be fucked. That is if they weren't already fucked.

There is still half a click to go, and the Bugs are right on top of them. Crushing mandibles snap at their heels as they desperately try to put some distance between them. The Bugs begin landing glancing blows on the armour of the Wargons in the rear.

"They're not going to make it," I say to myself.

Just then, a Bug lands a hit square on the back of one of the Wargons. Its sharp leg pierces a hole through the thick plastanium and into the hindquarter of the beast. I can feel the Wargon's outburst of shock and pain as the Bugs barbed leg drives deep into its flesh. With one quick motion, the Wargon is pulled to the ground. As the Wargon falls, the rider reacts with lightning-quick reflexes that only come from years of repetitive drills and training.

She quickly activates all of the grenades she has left without taking the time to remove them from her suit. She falls beneath the endless river of Bugs and explodes into a volcanic burst of pulse energy and shrapnel. Every Bug within a hundred-foot radius is vaporized in an instant. The shock wave smashes into the backs of the Mongols at the rear, but at this distance isn't enough to knock them down. What it does do is create a tiny bit of breathing room between them and the Bugs.

I stay hidden with the brigade on the cliffs, just outside the line of sight, as they make their way into the canyon below. We hold our position and wait. Wait for them to be right beneath us, and then we move.

"Now," I command as every Mongol springs to the edge of the canyon and lets loose a relentless volley of laser fire.

The Bugs are cut down mid-stride as they chase the Mongol bait that has now turned and begun firing on them with vengeful wrath. The soldiers laugh and holler as they shred the Bugs with their lasers. For the transfers, this is revenge. For the others, it is just good fun. The inescapable slaughterhouse we created makes short work of the Bugs as they turn from a few thousand warriors into a slew of bloody mush. Many of the transfers continue firing long after the Bugs are all dead. Their laser fire splashing into the river of bodily material that now lays below.

"Cease fire," I order, and all laser fire immediately stops as cheers break out across the coms.

"Settle down," I command.

"That was a thorough shit kicking but there are billions of Bugs still out here. The hive will probably replace those that we killed by tomorrow," I say just as Wenjack and his men come riding up.

"They are going to be able to replace their dead, but we can't replace ours. The Federation is down a Wargon and a Mongol thanks to Corporal Ballard not following orders and trying to be a hero," I turn and ride directly up to Corporal Ballard.

"What the fuck were you thinking Corporal?" I ask in front of everyone.

"Well Sir. I wasn't. I just wanted to kill those fuckers, make them pay for what they did," he says.

"Corporal, if you did your job properly, they were still going to pay. They were headed for slaughter. The only difference is by you being selfish and trying to deal out the justice yourself, you cost the Federation a good soldier. A woman is dead because of you. Our sister is dead because of you," I snap at him as his head sinks.

"Do you realize that if I demand a court martial you could be executed?" I press him.

"Yes Sir," he responds sheepishly.

"Sergeant Wenjack. Do you believe that this man has any value left for the Mongols?" I ask.

"Yes Sir. I believe he has some value left," he responds.

"Then I don't see the need to shed any more Mongol blood today, but you will be demoted to private and put on probation. Is that clear Private?"

"Yes Sir," Private Ballard says, trying to hide the anger in his voice.

"Good, now back into ranks. There is a spot I marked on our map a short distance from here. That is where we're going to make camp. Mongols, move out," I order, eager to put the day's events behind us.

CHAPTER THIRTEEN

Silently, she tracked the menacing horde as they scurried across the harsh, unforgiving landscape. Their spindly legs easily navigated the jagged schythium. She marveled at how a horde this size can drop in and out of view as if it's temporarily swallowed up by the rock before being spat back out. From a distance, they almost looked like a snake, slithering through the rock. Up close, they looked far less majestic. Thousands of giant, snapping mandibles hissed and clicked as thousands of sharp barbed legs pounded into the ground.

Her camouflaged armour made her nearly invisible, but it was years of experience that truly allowed her to remain unseen. She could have been wearing any standard armour and still stalked her prey because long ago, she had learned how to move without being detected. She learned how to move in the spaces between where anyone or anything looks. Walking within the unnoticed shadows that lay beyond perception.

Not that anything would be looking for her. Bugs didn't ever seem to be concerned about being stalked. Their hive mind was always too focused on the task at hand, never thinking that they might be followed. Not that it would have mattered anyway. They could be as careful as possible, and they still wouldn't see her if she didn't want to be seen.

She had hunted Bugs, beasts, and humans on every planet between here and Old Earth. There was nothing in existence that she couldn't track, nothing that she couldn't kill. Hunting was her trade, and she was a master. That's why she was here.

Military Intelligence had called in all of their top shadow operatives, and she was at the top of their list. Her reputation was revered among the few that knew people like her existed, and she was paid well because of it. On this planet, she had fed more intel and samples back to the Federation than any other hunter, and she was proud of it. She had made it her personal mission to be the first hunter to find a hive on this planet.

Her plan was simple. Track the bigger hordes and try to identify a pattern to their movements. If a pattern could be identified, it should be possible to locate where the Bugs were coming from. So far, the Bugs movements appeared to be random, but that was only because more data needed to be gathered. With time, she knew that this method would be successful.

Through tunnels and over hills, she stalked the horde like a ghost through fog. Carefully moving imperceptibly behind them, observing everything as they went. She noted the size and colouring of each Bug. The way they moved and the speed they travelled. Even when observing a horde of this size, she was able to dial in on each individual Bug and take note of their behaviour. Nothing escaped her observation.

She stalked them through a long tunnel that eventually opened into a low valley, surrounded by tall cliffs. In the valley's center was a knoll, sticking up like an island of stone in a rough sea of schythium.

Behind the knoll, the cliff face formed an unbroken wall, but she could see numerous paths leading in and out of the valley to the east and west.

The valley itself was relatively level by Excalibur standards but was still covered in large mounds of rock. The constant dull orange glow that lit the low clouds made the sight look even more ominous than it otherwise would be. If Excalibur was Hell, then this knoll must surely be the Devil's house. Only, there was no room for the Devil in this version of Hell because it belonged to the Bugs.

Patrolling hordes of Bugs covered the breadth of the valley. The horde she was following headed right through the patrols towards the knoll. She could easily follow the horde and slip past the patrols with little risk, but in this place, any unnecessary risk was too much. She silently slipped away, riding towards the cliffs. She let her Wargon worry about moving across the terrain as she focused on gathering as much information about this valley as possible. If her immediate impressions were correct, the Federation would want as much intel on this place as she could gather.

On the eastern side of the valley, she finds a small path leading up the cliff face. The path is steep and tight, barely wide enough for the hulking Wargon to stand on, but the giant beast effortlessly navigates the tricky terrain.

The two eventually find themselves on an outcrop of rock overlooking the valley. From the rocky perch, she could see the horde as it made its way to the knoll and entered through a tunnel at its base. The tunnel's mouth was guarded by a horde of Bugs that stood unmoving on either side of the opening. Two other hordes patrolled in opposite directions around the base of the knoll.

Between the three hordes, her computer counted fifteen thousand Bugs. Add in the other fifty thousand plus Bugs that were making their way in and out of the valley at any given time, and that's a total of sixty-five thousand Bugs. Not counting however many hordes were hiding in the tunnel and the surrounding cliffs. There was definitely something worth protecting inside that knoll. The numbers were far too small to suspect a hive, but whatever is down there is definitely of value.

For an hour, she watched the valley, recording images of the terrain and taking note of any Bug activity. After that hour had passed, she noticed the horde that she was tracking, exited the tunnel and made their way west into the cliffs. Shortly after they did, another horde of about the same size came in from the south and entered the opening in the base of the knoll. This behaviour confirmed what she had initially predicted.

This knoll was another stash of food and water. She hadn't yet figured out how the Bugs made these stashes, but so far, she had found a number of them on this shit hole of a planet. The Federation put a high priority on these stashes because on a barren rock like Excalibur, the Bugs will be fucked without them. If they could find and destroy the stockpiles, it would severely limit the Bug's ability to take and hold territory.

She didn't disagree, but there were two issues with the plan. For one, there were just so many of the fucking things, and they were all heavily protected. It will cost a lot of lives to clear these stashes out, and even though the Federation has a lot of lives to spend, the quality of soldiers will decrease quickly. They have thrown their best at this planet, which means it is the best that are dying first. This will eventually take its toll on both the fighting power of the Federation and on the morale of the remaining troops. After all, if the veteran soldiers of the legendary legions couldn't survive this place, what hope did the new recruits have.

The second issue was how did the Federation know that whoever built these stashes couldn't create more. So far, nobody knows where these Bugs came from, and it's an even bigger mystery how these stashes got here. It's possible that Bugs could have spread through the galaxy by somehow sending their eggs into space, but how exactly did they cover a planet with stashes of food and water in strategic positions. There were definitely powers at play here that aren't yet understood, and who's to say that they couldn't build more stashes.

Either way, these matters were not of her concern. Her job was to find the stashes and do the necessary reconnaissance. She gathered the pictures and video needed to create a three-dimensional map of the area and documented Bug activity. Anything past that was in the Federation's hands.

She was focusing in on the paths that led down from the cliffs on the other side of the valley when she suddenly got the feeling they weren't alone. With the speed of a rattlesnake strike, she spins her Wargon around, levelling her cut-down Remington battle rifle on an airborne Bug that was leaping for her. Without hesitation, she let loose a thunderous barrage of rapid-fire, cutting the creature down in mid-air. She instantly transformed from hunter to warrior, as a lifetime of experience guides her rifle. Without the need for conscious thought, she shifts her fire down the path towards the rest of the approaching Bugs.

Thanks to the aim assist built into her armour, she

can command extreme levels of accuracy from her weapon. The fully automatic laser fire pounded her assailants as they bared down upon her in the tight corridor.

She noticed that something wasn't right. Under normal circumstances, it would only take one or two direct hits to bring one of these fuckers down, but these Bugs were taking a pounding. Their exoskeletons were far harder to crack than normal. She shifts her aim to where the legs meet their bodies and lets loose. The Bugs screeched as lasers sent bloodied black limbs flying through the air. Her grip tightened on the trigger as if pulling it harder would give her laser a little more punch.

Sliding her left hand down to her hip, she grabs a grenade. In one motion, she uncaps the safety, activates the trigger, and throws it into the approaching mass. A split second later, the grenade blows, sending wet pieces of exoskeleton hurtling through the air. Her limited firepower wasn't enough to hold back the assailants, and the confined space of the tight path gave few options.

She couldn't understand how they had gotten the drop on her when in all her years of hunting and combat, nothing had ever caught her by surprise. Never had she seen anything move as quiet or as cleverly as they had, especially not Bugs. Bugs don't sneak up on their prey. They don't stalk and hunt. They fight as brutes, lacking all the necessary abilities to sneak up on any hunter. Especially one as skilled as herself.

However, it was painfully clear that these weren't any ordinary Bugs. They were larger and tougher. They moved smarter and looked different. Typically, Bugs were deep grey in colour, with bits of black and brown mixed in. The Bugs that were almost on top of her were black with a stripe of bright yellow running down the center of their heads. They were unlike anything she had seen before, but in the moment, none of that mattered. It didn't matter where they had come from or how they managed to surprise her. All that mattered was that she would make them pay for it.

With volcanic ferocity, her Wargon smashed a Bug into the wall with its hulking foreleg before kicking a second off the cliff behind it. She drew her thermal lance, and with an expert strike, severed the upper mandible from an approaching Bug. In a primal challenge, the Wargon rears up on its hind legs showing off its immense size. Unimpressed, a Bug launches at the Wargon's exposed midsection, only to find its face impaled on a thermal lance.

Another two Bugs were crushed as the Wargon brought down its might. Strikes from the Bugs sharp legs landed all over their armour as the hunter and her Wargon fight alone on the cliff. The bugs were strong, but their armour was stronger.

The Wargon used the horn of its armour to throw its opponents into the hard walls of the cliff. The Bug's exoskeletons cracked between the impenetrable schythium walls and the incredible strength of the Wargon. With thermal lance and Wargon might, the two of them fought fearlessly. Cutting, stomping and crushing, they killed without hesitation. Their armour never yielded to the blows of their opponents.

The laser fire, exploding grenades, and falling Bugs didn't escape the notice of the Bugs in the valley. Soon there would be enemies coming up the cliff by the tens of thousands. She might have been able to fight her way through the ambush, but there was no hope of fighting off that many hordes.

The first thought was to fight her way through the ambush and make her exit through the pass in the cliffs behind her. But there wasn't time for that. By the time they fought their way through the ambush, the Bugs from the valley would have been on them. Their only hope was to try something drastic.

She had something that she was saving for an occasion that she had hoped would never come. An occasion like this, where there was indeed no other option. She opened a hidden compartment and pulled out a five-inch-long cylinder that contained a small tactical nuclear bomb. Small though it was, it packed enough of a punch to level a city block. Only she wasn't in a city. She was in the mouth of a schythium corridor where the blast would be reflected off the walls, directing the force in two directions. Wasting no time, she armed the bomb and threw it down between them and the edge of the cliff. She tightened her grip on her Wargon and hung on for dear life.

A split second passed, and then, as if one of the gods of old snapped their fingers, every Bug within range was vaporized in a blinding explosion of light. In a flash, the tremendous shock wave violently hurled the hunter and her Wargon's limp bodies down the passageway and into a wall of solid schythium. They lay there, unmoving as the cliffs erupted with the sound of thunder and a small mushroom cloud rose into the thick atmosphere.

If their suits had been made from plastanium, like standard cavalry armour, they would have been vaporized with the Bugs. Although their suits weren't made from plastanium. Their suits were made from nearly indestructible schythium, and they had just put the indestructible part to the test.

Seconds after being smashed into the wall, their suits, sensing that they were unconscious, injected them with a cocktail of stims and pain killers. They immediately regained consciousness and felt like they had tried to kiss an incoming rocket, but they were alive. She took a gamble that their suits would survive and an even bigger gamble that they would survive in their suits. Luckily it paid off.

They had survived, but it would all be for not if they didn't get their asses moving. The dazed Wargon staggered to its feet and took off down the passageway.

She wanted nothing more than to get a sample from the Bugs that ambushed them, but no traces were left. Every piece of those Bugs had been vaporized in the blast. There was nothing left except the irradiated place where they once stood.

As she rode away, she wondered what kind of new Bug they had just faced and where they had come from. Any answers would have to wait, but she knew that this was just the first encounter with a new enemy that she would meet again.

She was pretty confident that her suit would survive the blast, but she was surprised that her computer wasn't fried. She had worried that the pulse from the explosion would knock it out, but it too was protected by the schythium suit. No wonder the Federation wanted this planet so bad. With this much schythium, they would be truly unstoppable on the battlefield. Or at least they would be until someone came up with something better. That was the nature of war; today's super-weapons were tomorrow's artifacts. There was always something better. It was just a question of who would discover it first.

Once she was a safe distance from the valley, she hailed the dropship that was following her in low orbit. Like a silent bird, it dove down through the thick atmosphere and landed in front of them, opening its blast door. The exhausted Wargon walked into the back of the ship and collapsed on the floor. The hunter unhooked herself from the passed-out beast and fell beside it onto the floor, where she, too, finally succumbed to exhaustion and gave into sleep.

CHAPTER FOURTEEN

The bright sun sits high in the perfect blue sky as I exit the tunnel and come into the open air. I take a second to bathe in the morning light and taste the fresh air. I hadn't remembered how good it feels to be in an environment that isn't continually trying to kill me. Casually, I start walking down from the hills and through a thick green forest. The forest is home to trees that look as if they have stood here for hundreds of years. This place has the pure beauty of somewhere that's remained untouched by the cold hand of industrialization. Only nature has shaped this pristine land.

It occurs to me that I have no idea where this land is, but as I exit the forest and set my gaze on a crystal-clear lake, set against snow-capped mountains, I cease to care. Wherever I am, it fills me with an effortless sense of peace that makes me feel like I am home.

Walking a little further towards the lake, I notice that I'm not alone. About twelve Bugs are casually walking behind me. Not hissing and running in their usual fashion, just walking calmly. I expect panic to take hold of me, but none does. I feel comfortable with the Bugs. In fact, I feel more than comfortable. I love them. I love them as one loves friends and family. It's like we belong together, like we're all parts of a larger whole.

Reaching the lake, I bend down to take a drink. As I do, I see my reflection, looking back at me in the water. Or at least, I see what should be my reflection. But instead, all I see looking back at me is the grey emotionless face of a Bug. The sight doesn't startle me the way it should. Of course, I'm a Bug. Haven't I always been one?

In the mirror-like reflection of the lake, I can see the blue sky that is now home to a few white pillows of cloud. I take a moment to appreciate the sight, and as I do, the clouds burst apart.

Rockets begin raining down through the blue atmosphere, crashing into the mountain tops in explosions of fire. Panic takes me as I quickly turn to the Bugs around me, who are all clearly panicking as well. We turn to run back into the forest as it, too, explodes in a thunderous ball of fire. I look back up into the sky as a group of Federation fighters break through the atmosphere, diving in tight formation. Flying fast and low, they hammer the beach with laser fire.

With nowhere to go, we turn and run into the burning forest, but not all of us make it. Before we reach the cover of the trees, two of us are cut down by laser fire that was smashing into the ground around us. I see their bodies burst into brown mist as the heavy lasers make contact.

Seeing them die fills me with a sense of loss like I've never felt before. I feel like a piece of myself has been ripped away.

I want to stop and mourn, but a voice in my head calls to me, “Come my children. Back to the tunnels.”

I follow the voice’s command as if driven by an invisible force. We run through the burning forest as trees explode from the heat of the hellish inferno. All I can hear is the sound of the flames and the thunder of exploding bombs and rockets in the distance.

We push forward, following the voice that is calling us. As we are about to exit the burning forest, a tree cracks and falls, killing another one of my friends. I stop, and for a second, I want to go back, but the rest keep going, following the voice. Sucking up my ever-breaking heart, I turn from my dead friend to follow the others.

As I turn, a Federation fighter comes soaring in, no more than fifty feet from the ground. It lays down a blanket of laser fire that vaporizes all that I love right before my eyes. I want to break from the pain in my heart, but the voice calls me onward.

I run, and I run. With everything that I have, I run. Barely making it past the laser fire to the mouth of the tunnel. Quickly, I duck into the tunnel, but my efforts are all in vain. Behind me, I hear a rocket enter the tunnel and detonate in a blaze of fire.

Hungry for oxygen, the fire rips through the tunnel, consuming everything with its devilish heat. The fire is so greedy for oxygen that it follows my breath into my body. It cooks me from the inside out and the outside in. I feel the death of my brethren ripping through me as my body burns, and then as if a million screams are silenced at once, I'm plunged into darkness.

Suddenly I awake. Panicking, I try to pat out the flames that aren't there. My HUD flashes warnings that my blood pressure is at one-ninety over one-twenty, which is dangerously high, and my heart rate is at an incredible hundred and twenty beats per minute. Adrenaline surges through my body, making me feel like I'm going to shit in my suit.

I am thankful when my suit finally increases the oxygen level and gives me a mild tranquillizer to bring me back to normal. I am confused as to what the fuck just happened. Obviously, I was dreaming, but it felt so real.

"Shit," I say out loud, forgetting that my coms is turned on.

"What was that Sir?" Corporal Crang asks.

"Nothing. Fuck off," I snap.

I've had some pretty vivid dreams before, what

combat soldier hasn't, but not like this. All my nightmares have always been based on my own memories, but this was something else. It felt like I was living the memory of a Bug. A Bug from a world that we destroyed. The memory felt so real. It felt as if I was actually there as the bombs fell. I remember the feeling of burning, the sense of loss when those other Bugs died.

Bugs don't feel like that though, they don't feel remorse for their dead, and they definitely don't go back for them. Their cold, heartless nature is part of the reason that they're so hard to kill. They will sacrifice thousands of their own just to get one of ours. They have a hive mind. They don't think for themselves. Only, it sure felt like they did. It sure felt like they thought and loved. In that dream, we were the heartless monsters, not them.

"Bad dreams Lieutenant? "Sergeant Wenjack asks.

"Like there's any other kind," I answer, trying to force a small laugh.

"Fuck yeah there are. I just dreamt that I was laying on a big bed surrounded by beautiful women who wanted to serve my every desire," Wenjack says.

"No you didn't."

"Yeah, you're right. I dreamt that I was back on

Yalos, putting down those pointless fucking riots again," he says, and his ordinarily upbeat demeanour fades for a moment.

"Yalos was a bad drop," I say, as memories of the drop run through my mind.

"Yup," he agrees. "Fighting Bugs is one thing but fighting humans is something else entirely. Especially when they're so heavily outmatched."

"I'm not even sure you can call that fighting. It was a fucking slaughter. A pointless waste of life."

"Part of me will always hate those bastards for making us do what we did. If they would have just fucking listened and went home…." Wenjack pauses as he looks for words. "Part of me is relieved that we're fighting Bugs and not people. As brutal as this war is, I've never had second thoughts about killing Bugs."

"Normally I would agree with you… But," I begin to say and then stop because I'm unsure if I want to continue.

"But what? What could possibly make you add a but to that statement?"

"Well, I just dreamt that I was a fucking Bug, living peacefully on some untouched planet. I was walking with other Bugs that I thought were my family. Then the Federation came and obliterated us. I vividly remember the pain and destruction of it all. I remember the feeling of watching my family die," I tell him.

"Shit, you must be going crazy. You know as well as I that these mindless fucks don't have families, and they sure as fuck don't give two shits about each other getting shot up," he says.

"Yeah I know. It was just a weird dream. It all felt so damn real."

"Hmm. It's those damn tranquilizers we take that fuck with our dreams. It's not natural to be knocked out by tranquilizers and woken up by stims. The bad dreams are just our bodies trying to deal with the shit in our system. That's all."

"Yeah maybe. Spending almost two weeks in the field with daily Bug encounters doesn't help much either. I've been seeing so many damn Bugs that I'm starting to think I am one," I say, and we both laugh.

"Consider yourself lucky you haven't had any Bug sex dreams yet," he says, and we both laugh once more.

I adjust the sling on my rifle and check the cartridge.

"Well, I guess we should get this shit show moving. Are you ready to give me my status report?" I ask.

"Sir, yes Sir," he responds in a stupid voice as he throws me a comical salute.

I'm sure he was making a ridiculous face beneath his helmet to go with it.

"Everything is the same as yesterday. All required equipment and supplies were accounted for in this morning's supply drop. All troops are accounted for and are in fighting order. No major Bug movements to report. A few of our NCOs have been reporting a lot of competition developing between the transfers and our original troops. It appears that the two groups feel like they are better than each other and eager to prove it. So far this has just led to seeing who can kill the most Bugs and the occasional Wargon race, but nothing worse than that," he says.

"We need to stay on top of this, disunity destroys combat groups. If we are going to have any chance at being effective on this planet, our brigade needs to be completely unified. Let all NCOs know that any acts of disunity will be dealt with swiftly and severely," I tell him, hating how I was starting to sound like a typical officer.

With the status report out of the way, I screen-share my HUD with Wenjack's and then bring up my map.

"We are supposed to have twenty-four hours left in the field, and we still have to cover this entire section," I say as I zoom in on an area of the map.

"We will ride there together, but once there, we will need to split up into sections in order to clear the area in the amount of time we have left. We're going to log some serious kilometers today, so everyone needs to be ready to ride hard and stay alert. Section assignments have been uploaded to the troops and instructions have been given to all section leaders. Assemble the troops into formation and be ready to move out in ten minutes," I order and shut off the screencast.

"Yes Sir," Wenjack replies in another stupid voice, but this time it was a little more reserved as the seriousness of war was starting to sink back in.

After ten kilometres of hard riding, we come to the top of a hill overlooking the twenty square kilometre area that needed to be cleared. The terrain is made up of a series of small steep rocky mounds about thirty feet in height. The mounds stand like armoured pufferfish, with knife-like schythium spikes sticking out in every direction. Each hill is separated by enough flat ground for five Wargons to ride abreast. From the intel we had been given, it is unclear if any tunnels or passageways lay hidden inside the maze of hills.

I give the command to send out the drones that fly ahead of us, scouting for any significant Bug activity. Normally I would have waited till they had made a complete pass of the area before riding into the maze, but time is a luxury that we don't have.

"Let's do this one by the book. You have your orders, now move out," I instruct over the brigade communication link.

We all break into our sections and enter the maze.

The terrain makes for easy riding, and even a thorough inspection of the area is a relatively simple task from the backs of our Wargons. With our forces spread out, we can cover the large area with surprising speed. Spreading out this much makes us more susceptible to ambush, but with this much land to cover, we didn't have many options. It is an acceptable risk, but we still remain hyper-alert. Our eyes constantly scanning as we make our way through the maze. Always ready and even expecting an ambush. In a place like this, death could be waiting around any corner and probably is.

While leading my section through a particularly nasty area of ground, I suddenly stop dead in my tracks. I get the gut-turning feeling that something isn't right. I sense something, something terrible that I can't quite figure out. Quickly I scan the area for an ambush but see nothing. Then I realize that there is a strong feeling of panic coming through my link with Sleipnir.

Since we landed on this planet, our link has been

growing stronger by the day, and in turn, my link with the rest of the Wargons and their riders grew stronger. It is like having a limited psychic link to my entire brigade. This is a valuable tool as a leader, as it gives me a powerful insight into the state of my soldiers. Right now, the only thing it's giving me is dread.

Moments later, my coms link lights up.

"Medic!" A voice cries over the coms, and a flashing red distress beacon lights up my HUD.

With haste, we ride as fast as possible to the beacon to find a cluster of mounted soldiers surrounding a small crowd of dismounted Mongols who are kneeling on the ground. I quickly leap off Sleipnir and run to the dismounted soldiers to find Private Talve lying on the ground with a massive hole torn through his armour.

"Fuck! Fuck! Patch the fucking hole! Don't just fucking stand there patch the fucking hole," Private Talve screams in an uncontrollable panic.

Looking at the hole, I know instantly that it is far too big to be patched. This far out, there is nothing we can do.

"I'm sorry Private, but your fucked. This hole can't be patched and in about a minute you're going to be completely out of oxygen," I tell him.

There is no point in sugar-coating it, he is going to die, and we are going to have to stand by, helplessly unable to do anything. The reality of the situation turns my stomach in knots.

"I'm fucked? Fuck you! Patch the fucking hole! Don't just stand there," he yells.

"I'm sorry Private," I say, never meaning the words as much as I do right now.

"Fuck you! Fuck all of you! Someone fucking help me. I'm a Mongol for fuck sakes, I'm not going out like this. I can't fucking go out like this. You have to help me. Someone has to help me," he cries out.

His obvious desperation makes me wish with everything inside of me that there was something I could do for him.

"Please! Please fucking help me!" he begs.

"There's nothing we can do. I'm sorry," I say while silently hoping that his death will come quick.

I consider taking my lance and putting him out of his misery, but I am unwilling to cross that line. Even if he is on the brink of death, it would still be considered murder to help him along. So, I steady my nerves and endure his pleas.

"You fucking bastards. You're going to let me die. Fuck you, you dickless fucks."

Something shifts, and his rage turns to panic.

"Please, somebody please fucking help me. What the fuck is wrong with you? Fucking help me," he cries.

Powerless to do anything, we just stand around and watch him as he rages against death until the lack of oxygen makes him slowly drift away. Every Mongol stands by in shock.

We are all about as accustomed to death as anyone could be, but this is different. Watching your brothers and sisters die in combat was hard, but watching this man die helplessly due to a lack of oxygen was crushing. Watching him scream and beg. Listening to him curse us for uselessly standing by, watching as he slips away, makes this the hardest death I have witnessed so far.

We all stand in quiet shock for some time before I break the silence and ask, "What happened?"

A moment of silence passes until Private Ballard speaks up.

"It was an accident, Sir."

"Explain," I command, not surprised to hear Private

Ballard's voice.

"Well, Sir. We were riding out to check the perimeter, and, I guess, we got to racing, and he bumped me and, well, I bumped him back. He hit the wall and one of those schythium daggers got him. It was an accident."

"Sergeant Wenjack, start a recording," I order.

"My name is Lieutenant Braddock. It is twelve thirty five, Federation standard time. The date is March twenty seventh. This recording serves as a record of the court marshal of Private Cameron J Ballard, formerly Corporal Cameron J Ballard, of the seventh brigade of the Mongols heavy cavalry legion of the Federation army," I say before Private Ballard cuts me off.

"Wait, a court marshal? Are you fucking kidding me? It was an accident."

I use my officer override to immobilize his suit.

"Private Ballard, you have been detained on the charge of reckless endangerment, resulting in the death of a fellow soldier. How do you plead?"

"How do I plead? What the fuck? Not guilty, obviously. That asshole bumped me first."

"Private Ballard do you wish to call any witnesses

forward?"

"Witnesses? Who the fuck am I going to call when it was just me and him? It's my word against his and he's fucking dead."

"Private Ballard!" I snap.

"I will only remind you once of the severity of this matter and urge you to show some decorum," I suggest, strongly hoping that he will take my advice.

"Sergeant Wenjack, since Private Talve cannot give his side of the story, please upload the video recording of the incident in question from his suits computer to your own and review it for me," I order.

"Yes Sir," Wenjack answers as he walks up to Private Talve's lifeless body.

We all wait in awkward silence as he downloads the recording and then watches the incident unfold from Private Talve's point of view. I hate that I have to make him do it, but Federation law states that the person holding the court martial can't participate as a witness.

A few agonizing minutes pass before Wenjack speaks, "Okay, I'm ready to testify."

"Sergeant Wenjack, for the record, what did you see

on the recording?"

"Private's Talve and Ballard were riding out to check the perimeter. Private Talve was riding in front of Private Ballard when they set out. They were both traveling at a high rate of speed when Private Ballard came up beside Private Talve. It appears that Private Ballard was trying to pass Private Talve, at which point, Private Talve sped up to stay ahead of him. A race appears to have broken out between the two at this point. Private Ballard couldn't manage to pass Private Talve, so he bumps him with his Wargon. In retaliation Private Talve bumps him back. After receiving the bump from Private Talve, Private Ballard directs his Wargon to ram Private Talve into a jagged wall of schythium, at this point Private Talve's suit becomes compromised," Sergeant Wenjack concludes.

"Sergeant Wenjack, after reviewing the recording, what is your opinion about the intent behind the incident?"

"After reviewing the recording, it appears that Private Ballard intentionally rammed Private Talve into the schythium," Sergeant Wenjack replies.

"Private Ballard, if you have anything to say in your defense, this would be the time," I say.

"Yeah. Go fuck yourself," he snaps, completely ignoring my earlier warnings about the seriousness of this situation.

"This is bullshit. The fucking dipshit bumped me. I'm a Corporal and he's a Private. In my last legion a Corporal would never be disciplined for putting a Private in his place," he says in frustration.

"You, were, a Corporal, but you were demoted due to insubordination resulting in the death of another soldier," I say.

"Whatever, you fucking idiot. This legion is bullshit. You guys are a bunch of weak cowards," he snaps.

"Private Ballard, this is the last time that I'm going to warn you about showing some decorum," I warn.

"Fuck your decorum. Fuck the Federation. Fuck the Mongols and most of all fuck you. This is bullshit. You know what? I plead guilty to the charges. I did it, I killed him. The disrespectful little shit tried to jockey for position with me, so I put him into the fucking wall on purpose. So, call down the prison transport and lock me up. I'm done with this stupid fucking war anyway. I'd rather rot behind bars, than spend another minute on this fucking planet," he blurts out, and every part of me wishes he hadn't.

He just couldn't take a hint to keep his mouth shut.

"In light of Private Ballard's confession, the charges

will be changed from reckless endangerment resulting in death, to murder," I regrettably announce.

"Murder? Wait you can't change the charges," Private Ballard protests.

The time for arguments is over, so I turn off his microphone.

"Taking into consideration the video recording of the incident, as well as Private Ballard's confession, I find the accused guilty of all charges," I announce.

"By the authority that has been entrusted to me by the Federation, I hereby sentence the defendant to death."

I take a second to prepare myself for the next part so that I don't choke on the words.

"In accordance with Federation law, the execution must be carried out immediately by his commanding officer," I regrettably say with a heavy voice.

"Sergeant Wenjack, Private Bark, please lower the condemned to his knees," I order.

The two of them follow my orders holding Private Ballard's shoulders as they guide his immobilized body to its knees and then step aside.

"Private Ballard, do you have any last words?" I ask

as I temporarily unmute his microphone.

"This is fucking bullshit. You can't fucking do this," he screams as I mute his microphone again.

I walk over to Sleipnir and grab my thermal lance. With reverence, I take my place standing beside the condemned and ignite the lance. The soft crackling of the superheated tip is almost deafening in the cold silence of the moment. Raising the lance with two hands above my head, I hope beyond hope that I make a clean strike.

With no more time to stall, I bring down the lance with all the speed I can muster. The hot tip contacts Private Ballard in the back of the neck, cutting through his plastanium armour like butter. The lance easily makes its way through his soft flesh, the intense heat sealing up the cut as it goes. Private Ballard's head rolls to the ground without ceremony as the lance finishes the cut. Held up by his stiff armour, his headless body remains kneeling as we all look upon it with disgust.

Everyone stands silent, afraid to speak. Only the soft crackling of the still-burning thermal lance can be heard. This is not the first battlefield execution I've seen, but I sure as hell hope it would be the last one I have to carry out.

I turn to address the brigade when lights start flashing on my HUD. The scout drones have found Bugs, a shit ton of Bugs, and they are headed our way.

CHAPTER FIFTEEN

The drones had picked up a horde of ten thousand Bugs, only minutes away from entering the southern section of the maze. I set up a limited coms link with my top NCOs.

"We have approximately ten thousand Bugs about to enter the southern section of the maze. They have us out numbered twenty to one, and there is no solid point to form an ambush. We need ideas fast." I say.

"Let's lay explosives around the maze, let them come in, and when they're all inside, we blow the hell out of em," Corporal McQuarrie suggests.

"We don't have the time, or enough ordinance to pull that off," I respond. "Any other ideas?"

"What would Genghis do?" Wenjack asks.

"What do you mean?" I ask, slightly confused by his question.

"You're a military history enthusiast, so ask yourself, what would Genghis Kahn do. If his cavalry was outnumbered in terrain like this, what would he do?" Wenjack asks.

I take time to think on the question and then reply, "He would play to his strengths to maximize effectiveness and minimize risk."

"Exactly," Wenjack says.

"So, the question is how do we do that?" I ask.

"Sorry Sir, that answer I don't have. I was really just trying to throw out some generic advice in hopes that you would think of something. You're the brains here, I'm just the bull shitter," he says with a laugh.

"We'll see how hard you're laughing when those Bugs are on top of us and we're still stuck here trying to figure out what to do," I say.

I think for a moment, trying to come up with a way to turn this situation to our advantage. I analyze the terrain relative to our position, and then something clicks. Wenjack's Genghis Kahn comment gave me an Idea.

"Well Wenjack," I say. "Your stupid advice might have done the trick. Here's the plan."

"I'm uploading a battle plan to everyone's HUD now," I say as I switch over to the brigade channel.

"I know you guys are still trying to process the events of today, but there will be time for that later. Right now we have work to do. So mount up and check your weapons," I say.

I run over to Sleipnir and quickly mount up.

"Mongols move out!" I command as we all ride off towards the south.

We prepare to meet the Bugs just inside the beginning of the south section of the maze. As per my instruction, our line is only stacked three riders deep. This allows us to maintain a wide front while still having three lines of fire, maximizing our area of contact with the enemy. Stretching our lines this thin gives us a substantial advantage in the amount of laser fire we can lay down, but it comes at a cost. We will be highly vulnerable if our lines come into melee contact. Three deep just wasn't enough to outmuscle a force of this size.

Inside the cover of the maze, we wait with weapons shouldered at the ready. The still silence hangs deafening in the air as the tension rises. Soon we hear the scuttling, popping sound of the approaching horde. Anxiously, we wait as the sound grows louder and louder until the bastards finally come into view, and we make a noise of our own. We let the Bugs have it as we unleash our overwhelming firepower. Firing lasers, throwing grenades and launching rockets, we hold nothing back, creating a wall of deadly projectiles and explosives.

Bugs stagger and fall as lasers tare their limbs from their bodies, and blood rains as exoskeletons are burst by grenades. Row after row, we cut them down as they pile into the maze. For a moment, it looks like we might be able to take the lot of them right here, but that hope fades quickly. Each row of slaughtered Bugs provides cover for the next, allowing them to push ever closer. Slowly but surely, they take the ground and push on through our tremendous fire.

I watch as Bugs are blasted apart, and it makes me think of the Bugs in my dream. I remember the way it felt watching them die before my eyes and the hole that it left in me. I remember feeling the pain and suffering of my entire species as the planet burned. I could still feel it in my waking mind, and it hurt. It physically hurt as I remember the pain of the slaughter. Meanwhile, I am leading a massacre of my own. What the fuck was wrong with me.

Sensing my stress levels rising, my suit's computer releases a mild sedative into my blood to bring me down. The drug allows me to regain focus as the Bugs are only fifty yards from our line. It is time.

"Retreat!" I command.

The words are as foreign to me as the previous feelings brought on by the dream. Every Wargon in the line turns around and runs in the opposite direction. With the Bugs on our asses, we need to ride hard to create a comfortable enough gap. Our Wargon's long stride has the advantage over the scuttling Bugs on the relatively flat ground between the spiky mounds, and we get up to speed quickly.

The horde pursues us closely, running hard, trying to catch us as we weave our way through the maze.

Once we have established a big enough gap, I give the order, "Now!"

With that, every soldier spins around on their mounts, facing backward. Levelling our battle rifles, we open fire on the pursuing enemy, catching them completely off guard. The Bugs that we shoot down in the front of their ranks fall and roll, tripping up the ones behind them. Every advantage is ours. With a nearly endless amount of open ground ahead of us, and the Bug's instincts driving them to chase, we have created a shooting gallery. All we need to do now is keep riding and shooting until all the Bugs are dead.

Laying down a constant blanket of laser fire, we continue to make our way through the maze. The mindless Bugs running after us, too stupid to realize or at least too stupid to care, that they are running to their deaths. After all, their royalty commands them to kill everything that isn't a Bug, and they obey. Why would they worry about preserving their own lives? They aren't ordered to kill everything only when it's safe to do so. They are ordered to kill everything, and if that means ten thousand Bugs run to their deaths, in the faint hope of killing a few of us, then that's what they'll do. Follow orders, no matter the cost.

I don't feel the usual satisfaction in the slaughter, as

Bug after Bug falls helplessly to our laser fire. The familiar exhilaration that accompanies crushing the enemy is strangely absent. Row after row, they fall, and it just feels like work. Like any other task that must be completed before moving on to the next. The heat of the moment cools as I kill without feeling. Coldly and mechanically, we finish them all without mercy. The only satisfaction in the end result is that it didn't cost me any Mongol blood to achieve. By every available measure, the encounter is a massive success, yet it really just feels like another day.

"Alright Mongols," I say after the last Bug falls.

"That's it. We've cleared all of our assigned territory and we've still got ten hours to spare. We'll head north three kilometers to the pickup location and then make camp. Tomorrow we'll either get reassigned or sent back to base," I say while silently hoping for the latter.

Even though I've gone months in a battle suit before, I sure as fuck don't want to now, not here. Two weeks is long enough. I want a hot shower and a cup of hot grease.

"Keep sharp and move out," I command.

We get to the pickup location an hour later, which still gives us nine hours of downtime. I assign the watch shift rotation and ensure that all security drones have been launched before making my way around the camp. To call it a camp might be a bit misleading. There are no tents, fires, or anything else one would typically associate with a camp. Instead, it was sleeping Wargons and their riders sitting on the ground with their backs to them. Some people sit together and bullshit, while others just sleep by themselves.

I intended to sleep after doing my rounds, but after seeing Wenjack sitting with a couple of soldiers from our dropship, I decided to dismount and join them. As Sleipnir lays down, I can feel him pass out immediately, without the need for a tranquillizer. I knew that my own emotional stress from the long day had passed onto him, and it left him drained.

Wargons are incredible beasts, but they aren't used to the high levels of stress that humans can sometimes carry.

"Well look who it is. The big important officer, coming down to grace us lowly soldiers with a visit," Wenjack says sarcastically.

"I tell you what Wenjack, how about you be the officer for a while and I'll drop back down to Sergeant. Hell after today I'd be fine with dropping back to Corporal," I fire back at him.

"I'm fine right where I am, thank you very much," Wenjack replies smugly and then laughs.

"What about you two?" I ask, gesturing at Corporal Crang and Private Bark. "Either of you hot shots want to be Lieutenant for a while?"

They both shake their heads.

"No? Neither of you feel like stepping up?" I ask with a laugh.

"Wouldn't Lieutenant Bark sound better than Private Bark?" I prod.

"Maybe one day Sir, but I'm in no rush," Bark answers.

"Okay, fair enough. What about Corporal Bark? How does that sound?"

"That sounds a little more my speed Sir," Bark eagerly replies.

"Good. Corporal Bark it is then," I say. "Hopefully you work out better than the guy who held the position before you."

I instantly regret the words as the image of Corporal Ballard's headless body enters my mind. By the silence that falls over everyone else, I assume that the same thought is in their minds as well. We were all accustomed to the sight of death, but there was a distinct difference between hot-blooded combat deaths and the two cold-blooded killings that we had witnessed today.

"That stupid son of a bitch really gave you no choice. He forced your hand in the matter," Wenjack says in an attempt to somehow make the situation more manageable.

It didn't work.

"I know Wenjack, believe me I know," I respond.

"Everyone knew that it had to be done and nobody disagrees with the outcome. If anything, we respect you more for it, because we know how hard it must have been to do what needed to be done," Corporal Crang says.

"You only think you know how hard it is," I say in a low voice. "But you guys don't really know jack shit. You don't know because you've never been there yourself. The truth is, it wasn't hard at all."

I guess that wasn't the answer they were expecting because an awkward silence settles in.

"Look. Every day that we're out here, I have to make decisions that can get people killed. Whether you live or die is rarely your decision, you just have to play the role that I, or the people above me, give you. It's those decisions that are really difficult because I'm responsible for your life.

"Corporal Ballard made his own decision to die. He had every chance to keep his mouth shut and he chose to continue digging himself into a hole. All I did was deliver the only possible conclusion to his actions. I don't feel bad about it and I don't feel good about it. Honestly, I feel nothing about the matter. If anything, it's the feeling nothing that really bothers me. I hate how easy it has become for me to take life."

We all sit silently for a while in contemplative thought.

"The heaviest of burdens are that of leadership," Wenjack says out of nowhere.

"Who said that?" Corporal Bark asks.

"Me, I said that. Just now," Wenjack says, giving us all a much-needed laugh.

The comment itself wasn't very funny, but the tension of the moment made giving into laughter an attractive alternative to silence.

"Hey, did you guys know that Mat was almost executed once?" Bark says, awkwardly sucking the humour from the moment.

"Who the fuck is Mat?" Wenjack asks.

"Uh, Private Talve," Bark replies.

"Huh. I kind of forgot that people still have first names," Wenjack says.

"They don't, first names are for civilians," I say before returning to Bark's comment. "I know from his record that he was court marshaled for something, but it didn't say what for."

"Yeah he was court marshaled, for reckless discharge of a weapon resulting in destruction of Federation property, as well as reckless endangerment of Federation soldiers," Bark says remembering the charges.

"No shit, he was always a pretty responsible soldier under my command," I say.

"Yeah well, ten lashes and a month in the hole will change a guy," Bark replies.

"Corporal, you better get on with the story before I decide to put you in the hole," Wenjack says in mock seriousness.

"I'll put something in your hole," Crang mutters, but Whenjack ignores him.

"Okay, so we had just finished boot and had a week of downtime on base before heading to cavalry school. We were bored and looking for something to do, so we decided to head on down to the range. We sign out some rifles and take our place on the line and start sighting in. Since we were bored and there happened to be nobody else there at the time, we got to screwing around. I start by shooting rocks and other crap lying around the range. Then Mat shoots my target, and I shoot his, stupid shit like that.

"Now, to understand what he does next, you have to know that Mat always had a different sense of humour. If he thought that something was funny, he would do it, regardless of consequences or what anyone else thought. So anyway, the stupid fuck looks over at me and says, 'You want to see something really cool?'

"Then bends over, sticks his rifle between his legs and simultaneously rips a massive fart and fires a shot," Bark explains.

"What a fucking idiot," Wenjack interrupts.

"It gets worse. He must have had too much dairy or something because he had lots of gas. With each small crack from his ass, he would fire a single shot, and when he let a long one rip, he would give a full-auto burst. It really did look like he was farting lasers. In all honesty, it was pretty fucking funny, and I laughed my ass off. Me laughing so hard just egged him on to keep doing it. Somehow in the shooting, farting, and laughing, the thing got away from him.

"He ended up falling over while still firing out of his

ass. Well, his fart lasers ended up blasting a shit ton of holes through the range building and almost hit the range officer that was sleeping in the booth," Bark says while laughing at the memory.

The rest of us crack up too, thinking about some idiot falling over, farting lasers from his ass.

"Sure enough, the MPs that came running didn't think it was as funny as we did and he got put up for court marshal. Lucky bastard only got ten lashes and a month in the hole," Bark says.

"Shit, he's lucky he wasn't executed," I say.

"I think he came pretty close but Mat always had a horseshoe up his ass. Definitely the luckiest bastard I've ever met," Bark says, pausing for a moment before continuing with remorse. "Until today that is."

"Did you guys know each other before you enlisted?" I ask.

"Yeah, we grew up together, best friends since the age of five. I'm the one that convinced him to enlist, he originally wanted to make holo-movies, but I talked him out of it. So, I guess it's my fault that we're here," Bark says solemnly. "But Mat loved being a cavalry soldier, and always talked about how he would go down fighting, which made it even harder to see him go the way he did. I'm going to miss that son of a bitch."

"We all signed our death sentences when we joined this pointless war," Corporal Crang says.

"You think fighting the Bugs is pointless?" Wenjack questions.

"I do. I think fighting the Bugs is pointless, I think trying to take this planet is pointless, and I think the entire Federation war machine is pointless," Crang scoffs.

"The Bugs are trying to take over the galaxy. They are thoughtless killing machines that won't rest until every planet belongs to them," Wenjack retorts.

"The same could be said about us. We are trying to snatch up every planet, moon, and sizable chunk of space rock that we can get our hands on. I hate to be the one to shatter the fairy tale, but the reason the Bugs are such an issue for us is because we both have the same goal," Corporal Crang says.

"That's a narrow view. The Bugs only want to take worlds for themselves. They are incapable of peace. We have allies, other races that we could have destroyed but instead work with," Wenjack says.

"There are two races that we're allies with, the Wargons and the Hurison. The Wargons were never a threat to us, and the only reason we helped them out was that it benefited us. The Hurison also never posed a serious threat. Their technology was vastly superior to ours, but they weren't a race accustomed to war. We could have and still could smash their civilization without breaking a sweat.

"We only allied with them because their technology would help us conquer the galaxy. If we meet a race of our equal, I promise you that the Federation won't seek a peaceful alliance. Power doesn't share power, and the Federation is only interested in subjects, not partners," Crang says.

"What's your point Crang?" I ask.

"My point is that it's all pointless. The fighting is never going to end. Even if humanity conquers the entire universe, there will still be war. When we run out of other races to fight, we will start fighting ourselves, the way we always do. I signed up because I believed that I was doing my part to bring peace to the galaxy, by stomping out the Bug plague. Now I see that there will never be peace. We fight, we die, and then someone else shows up to repeat the process," Crang says with a heavy defeat in his voice.

"Then why do you fight?" I ask.

"Because it's my job. I signed up to fight, so I fight. Not because I believe in some higher purpose, but because I'm really fucking good at it. Besides, it's not like I've got any other options," Crang says.

"I don't buy that shit," Wenjack says. "For the sake of argument, let's assume that what you say about the Federation is true. If they will only live peacefully with races that aren't a threat, then that means as they become more powerful there will be fewer races that pose a threat. If the Federation gained a massive military advantage, maybe by acquiring a planet full of schythium for example, there would be more races that we could live peacefully with, since they would no longer be a threat. So if you think about it, we are in fact fighting for peace in the galaxy," Wenjack says smugly.

"The Roman empire once thought the same way. Before they fell," I add.

"The Roman empire didn't fall because of their quest for military superiority. If anything, it was losing their superiority that helped lead to their fall. Through sustained contact, their enemies were eventually able to adopt many of the aspects of the Roman legions that made them so superior. If you look at the period closest to the end of the western Roman Empire you will see a leveling out in military technology and superiority between Rome and its competitors," Wenjack says.

"Maybe they wouldn't have had so many competitors if they had adopted a more peaceful type of diplomacy," Crang suggests.

"Doubt it," Wenjack says. "There will always be tension and competition between the haves and the have nots. Rome had what much of the rest of the world wanted and once they were no longer strong enough to defend what they had, war was inevitable. If you look at the most peaceful periods in our history, you will see one superpower that is far superior to the rest. Empires, and Federations, act aggressively out of fear. Remove the need to be afraid and you will have relative peace."

"So, Wenjack, is that why you fight? To help the Federation conquer its way to peace?" I ask.

"No," Wenjack chuckles. "Nothing so high-minded. I fight because somewhere along the line I decided to be a soldier and now I'm locked into a war that I probably won't see the end of. Unlike our friend here, I'm not bothered by this. If I'm going to spend the rest of my life fighting this war, then I'm going to make the most of it. I'm a soldier and I'm here to fight so let's fight. Bugs, reapers, or rebels, I'll fight them all," Wenjack chirps.

"That's putting a sunny outlook on a shit situation," Crang says.

"It's making the most out of the life I have. This is where I am, and war is what I'm here for. So, I'm going to do my job and enjoy myself as best I can," Wenjack says.

"I think that's a good way to live," Bark says before turning his attention to me. "Hey Lieutenant, what's your reason? Why do you fight?"

"I needed a job, and I can't sing or dance," I say.

"No fuck that. Give us a real answer Braddock," Crang says, and I overlook him not calling me Sir for the moment.

"Honestly, I've been asking myself that question a lot lately and I don't have a good reason," I say.

"Bullshit," Wenjack interrupts. "You fight because it's what you were born to do."

"Don't think so Wenjack. It's just the job I chose. Could have just as easily been a construction worker or a shipbuilder," I say.

"No you couldn't," Wenjack argues. "In all my years I've never met anyone as good at this as you. You see things on the battlefield that others miss and anticipate things well before anyone else. Not to mention I've seen you keep your head in situations where the pressure would break normal men."

"Just because I'm good at it doesn't mean that I was born to do it. I would have been just as good at leading construction crews as combat units."

"No, you wouldn't. Don't get me wrong, I think you could do the job and maybe even be good at it. But you wouldn't be great at it. Not like this. Something would be missing. There is an energy I see in you when our asses are on the line, and you're looking certain death in the face. A part of you comes alive in those moments that lays dormant the rest of the time. Now I could be wrong, but I think that it's only in those moments that you are truly being yourself. Truly embracing that raw aggression that burns inside of you that you can only afford to let loose in the thralls of combat.

"If you were a civilian, you wouldn't get the chance to let that part of you out. You would have to keep it stuffed down deep inside, and it would make you miserable. Make you depressed. You would walk through life constantly feeling like something was missing. Like you weren't being true to who you are.

"Soldiering isn't just what you do. It's who you are, and the sooner that you stop questioning yourself, the happier you'll be," Wenjack says sincerely.

"Maybe you're right," I say thoughtfully. "Then again, maybe you're an idiot."

"A man can be both," Wenjack says, and everyone laughs.

"You should have been a guidance counsellor

Wenjack," Bark says.

"Either that or a fucking shrink," Crang suggests.

"Naw, if I wasn't doing this, I think I would be writing children's books," Wenjack says in a way that makes it hard for me to tell if he's being serious or not.

"Right," Crang says. "You can teach kids how they are all subconsciously killers and need to come die in the Bug war in order to find their true selves. I'm sure the Federation would love some books like that."

"Hey now," Wenjack says. "I said that the Lieutenant was born for this shit, not everyone. For example, I think you would have been far better suited as a fluffer. You could just eat sandwiches and wax dongs all day long."

"Yeah? Well it's kind of late for that now, isn't it Wenjack," Crang says, and a silence falls over the group.

I'm not sure if everyone was beginning to think of the lives they could have had if they hadn't signed up or if none of us knew how to bring the conversation back from dong fluffing, but we remain silent.

My mind is occupied with what Wenjack had said. Maybe Wenjack was right, and I really was born for war. There is something inside of me that I only ever let loose in the heat of battle, but I'm not sure if that's something that has always been there. I've been at this so long that it's hard to remember who I was before. Was this thing inside of me always there, hungry for war? Or has it been created by war? Is it just my mind's way of adapting to the trauma of what I've experienced? Does it even really matter?

Even if it's true and there's some primal thing inside of me that has drawn me to combat, does that make it worthwhile? What troubles me has never been whether or not I'm any good at fighting. It's whether or not there is any good reason to be fighting in the first place. Just because I'm good at something doesn't mean that it's worthwhile. Can a person really justify his life based on his ability to conduct himself well in combat? Is that really a valuable purpose?

The more I think about it, the more I wonder if we really are that much different than the Bugs. There is no argument that they are born for the purpose of killing and are pretty good at it. Does that mean that they are doing the right thing by invading planets and doing what they were born to do? After all, they are born for it, and they are, of course, just following orders. If I'm going to justify my existence on the fact that I'm a born soldier and am just doing what the Federation is asking of me, are we not the same?

I roll these questions through my head for some time until, tired of thinking, I trigger my tranquillizers and go to sleep.

CHAPTER SIXTEEN

My suit's stims are triggered by an incoming communication, and I'm blasted into consciousness. It comes as a welcome shock. Once again, I had dreamt that I was a Bug being slaughtered by the Federation. This was a delusion that I was glad to be rid of. The stims instantly clear my head, removing any groggy feelings. Once you get used to the shock of going from a nightmare to being wide awake in a heartbeat, it's actually not a bad way to wake up. I answer the hail on my coms.

"Good evening, Lieutenant," a voice says.

It was Captain McArthur's voice, which meant that we weren't heading back to base for some R and R.

"Good evening, Sir," I respond.

"Lieutenant please switch your HUD to visual link," he asks.

As I switch over to visual, I find myself standing in a briefing room with Captain McArthur, Lieutenant Speers, Lieutenant Prettejohn and another man I didn't recognize. We were all standing around a three-dimensional battle map of a valley surrounded by towering cliffs. As I walk up to the map, I can see one lone knoll in the middle of the valley.

"Lieutenant Braddock, this is Lieutenant Lundholm

of Seal Team Charlie," Captain McArthur says, gesturing to the man that I didn't know.

The Seals were a small force special operations legion named after an Old Earth force from the failed USA. I always found it funny that an elite combat unit was named after a mentally disabled sea dog, despite what the acronym stands for.

"Nice to meet you," I say, extending a hand.

He receives my greeting with a large meat mitt of his own that engulfs my entire hand as we shake.

"Like wise," he answers in a voice that was deeper than the already deep voice that I would have expected from a man of his size.

"Enough flirting, we have work to do," Captain McArthur barks, drawing our attention to the map.

"Intelligence has found several Bug stockpiles, located within a five-hundred-kilometre radius of our base. These stockpiles play a critical role in the Bug's ability to operate and launch attacks in our area, allowing the Bugs to resupply with food and water. We are going to take this luxury away from them.

"The Federation has decided to simultaneously launch raids on every stockpile at once. Hopefully this coordinated attack will catch the Bugs off guard, giving us the advantage of surprise for a change," Captain McArthur says.

He brings up a series of images of an opening at the base of the knoll.

"This knoll is the location of our stockpile and as you can see, there appears to only be one entrance," he says.

"One heavily guarded entrance," Lieutenant Prettejohn interrupts.

"There appears to be about fifteen thousand Bugs standing constant guard, but there will likely be far more in the vicinity," Captain McArthur says.

With Lieutenants Speers and Prettejohn both commanding a brigade, and Lieutenant Lundholm commanding no more than a hundred soldiers, we were sitting at maybe sixteen hundred at most. Once again, we were going to be woefully outnumbered.

"With our numbers as low as they are, we are going to have to focus on speed and overwhelming fire power," Captain McArthur says.

"Speed and fire power might get us into that knoll, but once inside we will be trapped in a hole. It will be a slow brawling fight to get back out." Lieutenant Speers protests.

"Our primary objective is to destroy the stockpile, clearing and securing the area is only a secondary objective. As long as we clear out the stores of food and water, the Federation doesn't really care if we get back out. Understand Lieutenant?" Captain McArthur says.

"Yes Sir," Lieutenant Speers replies.

"Now, the Federation might not care if we get back out but luckily for us, General Jaxxon does. So he came up with this plan," McArthur says.

The map spins around and centers on a path to the west of the valley.

"Drop ships will dump us here," McArthur says, pointing at the path. "From here we will ride into the valley. Lieutenant Braddock and the seventh brigade will lead the way with the rest of us trailing half a click behind."

"Braddock, you will take the seventh and clear a hole through the defence, giving the rest of us a straight shot at the tunnel. Once we are inside you will need to defend the entrance and ensure that we don't have any Bugs coming at us from behind. I will lead Speers and Prettejohn's brigades through the tunnels and destroy the Bug's stockpiles. If we all live long enough, we will come back out and help you clear out the rest of the valley," McArthur instructs.

The map spins again, and five small outcrops are highlighted in the cliffs around the valley.

"Lieutenant Lundholm, you and your Seals will set up in these five locations. From there you will provide a heavy barrage of rockets, lasers, and grenades, to draw the Bugs attention before Braddock hits the entrance. Once they make contact, you will provide supporting fire as needed. The jagged terrain will provide limited lines of site so be careful and keep friendly fire to a minimum. Any questions?" McArthur asks.

"Yeah," Speers speaks up. "How come we're hitting this spot with so few people. There are millions of troops around base, and even reserves in orbit, and we're assaulting a key position with sixteen hundred soldiers?"

"There will be hundreds of raids happening simultaneously and some of them are against much larger forces than this one. On top of that, the Federation wants to launch these assaults without weakening the defence of the base. We've got what we've got," McArthur says.

"Any chance of air support?" Prettejohn asks.

"Negative Lieutenant," McArthur answers.

I consider the plan as it's laid out, and no matter how I look at it, our numbers are just too few. To hold that entrance, we were going to need at least one more team.

"Let me get this straight," I say with more annoyance in my voice than I intend. "You want me to take five hundred Mongols and assault a fixed location, held by over fifteen thousand hostiles, and then give up our advantage of speed by sitting still and defending the location against countless more hostiles." I ask.

"That is correct. Should be doable for a war hero like yourself," McArthur answers while pointing to the medal of valour on my arm.

"Doable. Yeah, I guess anything is doable given the right circumstances. I'm just going to have to think of how to actually do it," I say.

"That's fine. General Jaxxon trusts your judgment and so do I. Do what you think is best, but don't take any stupid chances. Our lives will be in your hands out there," McArthur says.

"How did Intelligence get such good recon of the area? To get images like this they would of needed a person on the ground," Prettejohn asks.

"That's classified beyond your pay grade Lieutenant, and quite frankly it doesn't really matter. Only important thing is that we have it," McArthur answers.

I agree with Captain McArthur that it doesn't matter, but I'm now curious where this intel came from

"Any more questions?" he asks, looking around the room.

Sure, I have questions, like how the fuck was I going to pull this one off, and why the fuck aren't we getting air support, but I keep my mouth shut. I know that I won't get the answers I want here anyway.

"Good. Dropships are headed to your locations with everything you'll need to resupply. Get your brigades ready and get on those ships. I'll see you lot at the drop zone," McArthur says and then disappears from the room.

I turn to Lieutenant Lundholm.

"If you keep those fuckers off our backs, we'll keep their attention off of you," I say.

"Sounds like a fair deal to me. Ya'll stay safe down there," he says and then disappears along with the other two.

I switch off my feed and am instantly back with my brigade.

I trigger everyone's suits to wake them up, and I can see the moment the stims hit as everyone lurches up wide awake.

"Wake the fuck up Mongols. Get yourselves ready, the dropships are going to be here in a few minutes. We've got new orders," I yell into the coms link.

Sergeant Wenjack walks up to me, and on a private link, says, "New orders, sounds like we're in for a good time."

"You wish," I say, turning to face him.

"Get the soldiers ready and make sure that we've got a clear LZ for the dropships. I've got to put some battlefield instructions together."

"Sir, yes Sir," he says sarcastically.

I know that he wanted to give me some stupid salute but knows better than to break field protocol in front of the troops.

About five minutes later, the dropships arrive. We watch as they come bursting through the low cloud cover and slam into the ground. We circle behind them as their blast doors open to reveal a large arsenal of weaponry and munitions.

"Load up with everything you can. Where we're going, we'll be needing every last bit of it," I command.

I grab three extra belts of grenades, an extra bandolier of laser cartridges, and an M73 rotating grenade launcher. The additional munitions were going to weigh me down a bit, but I sure as fuck wasn't going to run the risk of not bringing enough to this party.

I watch as each Mongol follows my lead. I can't remember another time when I'd seen Mongol cavalry load up with this much firepower. Typically, we would want to sacrifice firepower for speed, but seeing as we were going to be sitting still trying not to die, we are going to bring everything. If those fuckers want to kill us, they are going to have to earn it.

"Sir, are we really going to need all this shit?" Corporal McQuarrie asks.

"I never thought that I'd see the day when you'd question whether or not we were bringing too many explosives," I say with a laugh.

"Sorry Sir. What I meant to ask is will we actually have the opportunity to use all this shit. I'm loaded down for a good time and will be more than a little pissed off if this is all one big cock tease," he says in complete seriousness.

"Relax Corporal. You'll have plenty of opportunities to use every bit of it," I say reassuringly.

I look at all the gear hanging from his various straps and bandoliers. He looks like a kid who has brought out every toy gun he owns to play war.

"What exactly are you packing there?" I ask.

"Uh, well Sir. I've got this M73 grenade launcher with eight bandoliers of grenades. Then I've got three belts of standard throwing grenades, a rocket launcher with four boxes of mini rockets, two bandoliers of laser cartridges, a Colt laser pistol with extended cartridges, and a Zephyr high intensity constant beam laser," he says gleefully.

"You know that laser is only good for a thirty second beam, right?" I ask.

"Yes Sir, but it's going to be some of the best thirty-seconds of my life," he says with a chuckle.

"You're a sick man Corporal, but I'm glad to have you with us."

"Thank you, Sir," he says sincerely.

Once everyone is kitted up, we board the dropship and take off. I take the time to send my battlefield orders to the brigade.

"I'm sending the battle plan now. We have nine minutes till we land so use your time wisely and memorize the plan." I say over the brigade link.

A few minutes go by before I hear Wenjack's voice

on a private link. "Braddock, you really think this will work?"

I can tell he is concerned because he never addresses me by name unless he's trying to be particularly sincere.

"I think it's the best chance we have. We are standing still against a minimum of fifteen thousand Bugs. This plan increases our forces from five hundred to a thousand. It also puts the advantage of movement back on the table."

"Yeah, if you can pull it off. Not trying to sound like I don't believe in you but is something like this even possible? This is going to require next level focus in an extremely hostile environment," he says.

"It will, and a month ago I would have said this was impossible, but now I'm pretty confident that it will work."

"How confident is pretty confident?"

"I'd say I'm seventy-five percent confident."

"Seventy-five percent is better odds than we normally get," Wenjack says, clearly looking on the bright side.

"Well it's a seventy-five percent chance that I can do it. There's still probably only a fifty percent chance of the plan actually working."

"Fifty percent meaning that it either works or it doesn't?"

"That's right," I say, and he laughs.

"You're in a better mood than normal," Wenjack says.

"I'm just eager to get after it," I say, not wanting to tell him the truth.

The truth is, I'm trying way too hard to pretend that everything is okay when things are anything but. I don't want the troops to know that I'm terrified inside. Not of being killed, but of leading them to their deaths. The odds are stacked against us as they always are, and that's fine, but I can't stop worrying that I'm taking too big of a risk with this battle plan. If I'm wrong and this plan fails, the deaths and the responsibility for the mission's failure will land solidly on me.

"You know if this plan fails, they will probably court marshal you?"

"I am aware," I say, even though I disagree with him.

If this plan fails, I'll be dead. Wenjack and the rest of the seventh brigade will be destroyed. More than likely, Prettejohn and Speer's Mongols will be dead too. There will be so much death that instead of the Federation blaming me, they will likely make something up. Probably tell some story about how we were outnumbered two hundred to one, but we still fought heroically to the last man. In the end, that sounds better than saying everyone died because some shit for brains Lieutenant, who had no business being an officer, ordered his brigade to do some stupid shit that got them all killed.

"Fuck em. It's going to work. You're turning into one crazy son of a bitch, but I've got a good feeling about this," Wenjack says with surprising optimism.

"I appreciate your confidence."

"Maybe they'll hang you if it doesn't work, but if it does, they'll call you a genius. Hell, you might even get another one of those medals painted on your arm there," he says enthusiastically as the one-minute warning light comes on.

I turn my coms over to the brigade link.

"Sergeant Wenjack, would you ready the troops."

"Absolutely Sir," he says.

"Everybody get ready! We are supposed to have a kilometer of clear riding before we encounter any hostiles, but when the fuck do things ever go according to plan. When these doors open stay sharp, stay alert, and if at any point you decide that it's your time to die, make it count!" Wenjack commands.

CHAPTER SEVENTEEN

"Captain Denis, have you seen this yet?" Lieutenant Flores calls across the office.

"Lieutenant Flores, I'm incredibly busy, I'm sure it can wait," he says in annoyance.

"Sir, I really think you should see this," she says.

"Lieutenant I have an important meeting coming up that I need to prepare for," he protests.

"Sir. you of all people will want to see this," she insists.

Captain Denis releases a big sigh as he rolls his eyes.

"Alright Lieutenant what is it?" he asks as he slides his office chair across the room to look at her computer screen.

"It's a recording that came in from one of the hunters," she says as she goes to play the footage.

Captain Denis shoots her a look at the mention of the hunters.

"Right, sorry Sir. I forgot that we're still pretending that everybody doesn't already know about the existence of hunter units," she says as she begins to play the recording.

"Wow, hang on. Put this on the big screen," he orders.

In silent disbelief, they watch the recording as the hunter is ambushed by the strange coloured Bugs on top of the cliff face. They watch as the Wargon and hunter release hell upon the Bugs in a heroic battle. Then they watched as her bravery turned to desperation as the Bugs from the valley started approaching. With no other options available, she set off a nuke. The charge from the nuke knocked out the feed, and there was nothing more.

Captain Denis's jaw hangs open as he watches the events unfold.

"What happened to the hunter? Was the schythium armor strong enough to repel the blast? Did it block the radiation?" he asks.

"Well, technically that information is classified Sir," she said smugly.

"Yes of course it is, but you and I both know that has never stopped you in the past," he says.

In an extremely rare attempt at charm, he adds, "Everybody knows that you have a very keen mind for detective work. That's why you're such a valuable part of the team."

She sees right through what he is doing but doesn't really care. Compliments from the Captain were hard to come by. So, when one comes along, you just accept it, regardless of ulterior motives.

"Okay but if anyone asks, you didn't hear this from me," she says the way that all gossips start a sentence.

"Turns out she lived. The blast killed all the Bugs, but the hunter and her Wargon were thrown down the path behind them. Their schythium suits lived up to the hype and protected them from the blast, impact, and radiation. They were seriously banged up, but they survived a nuclear explosion, so that's to be expected.

"Their suits filled them with enough stims and pain killers to allow them to get to her ship where they passed out. They're now both in a restricted section of one of the medical ships."

"How did you find this out?"

"Well, you know my friend Joanne?"

"No, of course I don't. Why would I know who you're friends with?" he asks rhetorically.

"Okay, well, Joanne was talking to her sister, who is friends with one of the nurses that works in the restricted medical bay where the hunter is being treated," she says excitedly.

She likes the feeling of finally knowing something that Captain Denis doesn't for a change.

"Hmm. Sounds to me like Joanne should tell her sister to tell her friend that giving away classified information is a capital offense."

"Since when do you care about rules and military protocol. Mr. I'm only here for the science," she mocks.

"Play the recording again," he orders, trying to change the subject.

She restarts the recording, and they watch as the hunter whirls around to face the Bug that's flying at her through the air.

When a clear picture of one of the Bugs is seen, he instructs her to pause the image.

Lieutenant Flores pauses the recording, and an image of a hulking black Bug fills the screen. Captain Denis studies the Bug in quiet contemplation, trying to understand precisely what he is looking at.

"What exactly is this thing?" Flores asks.

"It's a Bug Lieutenant," Captain Denis answers blankly.

"Yeah, but what kind of Bug. I've never seen one that looks like this, and I've definitely never heard of a Bug that could get the drop on a hunter like that."

"You're not suppose to have heard of hunters at all."

"Oh come on. There's almost nothing that happens under a Federation flag that I don't hear about," she says with a smile.

"I don't doubt that."

"So stop stalling, what's the deal with these Bugs."

"The deal is, without samples we will be limited in our assessment of what it is. However, we should be able to discern quite a bit from what it looks like and how it moves," he says, grabbing the controls and rotating the image of the Bug.

"Right from the start there are definite differences in size and appearance. We have seen a few different colorings out there, but never black with a yellow stripe, this is new. These Bugs are also a lot larger than your typical warrior. I would guess about twenty-five percent larger. The larger size appears to give them a considerable increase in strength and speed as well," he observes.

He replays the recording multiple times as he carefully studies everything he sees. Each viewing revealing something that he hadn't noticed before.

"Judging by how close the Bugs got to the hunter before she noticed them, we have to assume that they have the ability to move almost silently," he states.

"They also had the ability to spot a fully camouflaged hunter from who knows how far away," Flores adds.

"Whatever these Bugs are, they definitely aren't products of natural evolution. Further proving our earlier findings. There is no way that a species like the Bugs could go from mindless warriors to fully intelligent hunters in one generation," he says.

"What are you saying Captain?" she hesitantly asks.

"I'm not saying anything yet. We need genetic samples of these things and we need them now. We also need more people working on this. Pick a team to start analyzing everything that we can about these new Bugs. I want a report in two days," Captain Denis orders.

"Yes Sir," Flores answers.

"Is this the only encounter with these things?"

"Um, no," she says sheepishly.

"Why did you hesitate there, Lieutenant?"

“Well Sir, there were two other contacts but,” she says, not completing her sentence.

“But what?”

“It’s just. Umm, its just that the recordings aren’t as useful,” she says.

“I’ll be the judge of what is useful. Play the recordings Lieutenant,” Captain Denis orders.

Lieutenant Flores starts the first recording. They see through the helmet cam of the hunter as he watches a horde of Bugs in the distance. Next thing they know, he is knocked to the ground, and all they can see is a flurry of Bug legs and armoured arms.

Again and again, the hunter tries to get up but is repeatedly knocked back down. His Wargon howls in frustration as it experiences the same. Their impenetrable schythium armour protected them from the Bug’s blows but did little to help them overcome the tremendous combined strength of the horde.

Eventually, the Bugs give up trying to smash their way through the hunter’s armour and end up dragging them away. For almost two minutes, they watch the helpless hunter thrash and scream in frustration and fear before the recording eventually goes dark.

"Do we know what happened to the recording?" he asks.

"We think that the hunter was drug underground," she answers.

The other recording was much of the same. The hunter never saw them coming and was drug off to an unknown fate. The two stood in silence, paralyzed by the horror of what they had just witnessed. They are both military officers in name only. Neither of them is familiar with the cold reality of combat. Neither of them is accustomed to watching someone desperately struggle, helplessly fighting for their life. Like watching someone being swallowed up by quicksand, the helpless hunters fought and struggled to get free, but it was all in vain. Their fates were sealed.

"What the fuck are you standing around for," General Carmichael barks.

"Oh shit the meeting," Captain Denis says.

"Yeah, oh shit is right. You're supposed to be getting ready to meet with some very important people, and yet here you are, watching recordings and flirting with Lieutenant Flores here," General Carmichael says.

Lieutenant Flores blushes at the comment, but Captain Denis stands unimpressed.

"Do you know who we are about to meet with, Captain?" General Carmichael asks.

"Yes Sir," Captain Denis answers.

"Who are we meeting with Captain?" the General demands.

"Chief Fleet Admiral Holoiday and the assembly of Generals," Captain Denis answers.

"That's right, shit knuckle. We are meeting with my bosses to discuss the future of the war effort. This isn't a meeting of your nerd friends, getting together to play dungeons and dildos, this is serious adult shit," the General shouts.

"Sir, I am ready for the presentation, but these recordings may also be of critical importance to the war effort. What we just saw," Captain Denis starts to say before being cut off.

"I'll be the one who decides what is, and isn't, important and right now this isn't important," the General says.

"Sir there's a new breed of Bug out there that appears to be hunting our hunters," Captain Denis insists.

"Like I said Captain that isn't important right now,"

the General says.

"But General," Captain Denis starts to say before being cut off again.

"That's enough!" The General yells as he smashes his weathered fist into the table.

Captain Denis lowers his head in defeat as he realizes that there is nothing he can say to get the General to listen. He is really starting to hate this man.

"Come on, we're going to be late," General Carmichael says, and the two of them leave the room.

Not a word is spoken between them as they walk through the corridors towards the restricted VR room used for classified conversations. The General walked at an uncomfortably fast pace that was intended to set him apart from others. Captain Denis, who was built for the laboratory, had trouble keeping up with the combat-hardened General. The contrasts in the two men's physical nature mirrored the contrast in personality. Even without uniforms or lab coats, a child could identify which man was a soldier and which one was a scientist.

They stop outside the door to the VR room, and the General turns towards Captain Denis.

"Look Captain. These are important people and they

don't have time to waste. I want you to keep everything understandable and to the point. Keep the jargon to a minimum, and above all else stay on topic. I swear that if you mention anything about those new Bugs I will personally take you into a bathroom and beat you to death. Do you get me?" The General asks.

"Yes Sir," Captain Denis answers.

He wants to think that the General was just talking tough but was pretty sure he was serious. The two men enter the VR room, put on their headsets and jack into the meeting.

They find themselves sitting side by side at a large table in a conference room. In the center of the table is a holographic projector casting an image of the planet Excalibur. At the head of the table sits Chief Fleet Admiral Holoiday, with assistance on either side of him. The rest of the table is filled with Generals of various importance.

Next to the General's assistants and Captain Denis, General Carmichael was the lowest-ranked person in the room. Captain Denis could now see why General Carmichael was so uptight about the meeting.

"Ah, looks like the applied science department has joined us," Chief Fleet Admiral Holoiday says, as all eyes land on Captain Denis and General Carmichael.

"General Carmichael, it is my understanding that you have some information that we are quite eager to here," Holoiday says.

"Yes Sir. We have been hard at work over in applied sciences and we believe that we have come up with something that will help us win this war," Carmichael says confidently.

"That's great General, we could use every advantage possible at this point," Holoiday says.

"May I introduce my top scientist, Captain Denis. He is our head entomologist and has been leading this project. Captain Denis if you please," General Carmichael says in a gentle tone.

Captain Denis thought it was funny how proper General Carmichael sounded. He had to remind himself that this was the same man who recently threatened to beat him to death in a bathroom.

Captain Denis stands up and addresses the room.

"Good evening. I know that you are all incredibly busy people, so I'm going to try to be brief. We have been painstakingly analyzing the genetic makeup of these Bugs to try and understand where they come from. We have noticed that the Bugs that we are finding on Excalibur are genetically superior to those found on other planets. To put it simply, the

Bugs on Excalibur have a completely different genetic structure than Bugs that we have previously encountered.

"This has led to the hypothesis that the Bugs aren't a naturally evolving species and have, in fact, been built," Captain Denis says before pausing to look around the room and make sure that everyone is following.

"We also hypothesized that if these Bugs were in fact built, we should be able to find some kind of fingerprint that could identify the creator. This has led us to take a deep look into the genetic structure of the Bugs which led to a discovery," Captain Denis says.

Everyone in the room appears to increase their interest at the word discovery.

"Bugs from different hives have a slightly different genetic structure. The differences are small, but if you know where to look you can see it clear as day. This means we can take a sample from a Bug and know exactly what hive it came from. Does everyone follow so far?" he asks and looks around the room.

"I think we are following just fine, thank you Captain. Please carry on," Holoiday says.

"Okay, so, the reason that this is such a big breakthrough is that we can use this knowledge to figure out a few things. For one, by identifying all of the different markers we find on Excalibur, we should be able to tell how many hives are on this planet.

"We have recorded samples from all over Excalibur and so far we have identified six different genetic compositions, which indicates that there are six different hives."

"How confident are you in this? Are you willing to stake your reputation on it?" one of the Generals asks.

"I'm one hundred percent confident in this Sir. But keep in mind, just because we have only found data to indicate six hives that doesn't mean there aren't other hives hiding out there," Captain Denis answers.

"Fair enough," the General says.

"Getting a count on hives is important, but it is nothing compared to what I'm about to show you. Take a look at this," he says as the hologram on Excalibur grows bigger and begins to rotate.

The hologram shows intricate details, including Federation bases and identified Bug stockpiles. A series of six different coloured dots start to appear on the hologram.

"These dots all represent locations where we have taken samples of Bugs. The different colors represent Bugs from different hives. As you can see, the colors are generally found in the same areas as each other. Reds are found with reds, blues with blues and so on. Look what happens if we draw a circle around every Bug encounter of a similar colour," he says, as six large coloured circles appear on the hologram.

"What happens is that we see these different coloured zones. Now, it stands to reason that if every encounter in each zone is with a Bug from the same hive, the hive must be somewhere inside this zone. For example, the yellow hive is somewhere inside the yellow zone. If we take that yellow zone and start blacking out all of the areas that we have explored, we get an ever-shrinking possible area where a hive could be located. Using this method, pinpointing where the hives are will just be a matter of time," he says, feeling very proud of himself.

Looking around the room, he sees that the Generals are all trying to comprehend what they are hearing.

"How soon can you have this map uploaded to every general in the field?" Holoiday asks.

"Within the hour Sir," Captain Denis says.

"Good, see it done," Holoiday says to the Captain before addressing the group.

"After the raids on the stockpiles are completed and

the new forward operating bases are built, I want a renewed focus on patrols. We need to cover every inch of these zones until we find every damn hive on this planet," Holoiday says.

"Thank you for this information, Captain, this is going to be a major help to the war effort. A promotion may be in your future," Holoiday says. At these words, Denis and Carmichael are ejected from the meeting.

"I guess a promotion is better than dying from blunt force trauma on a bathroom floor," General Carmichael says with a laugh. Captain Denis was not amused by the comment but agreed with Carmichael nonetheless.

CHAPTER EIGHTEEN

I hit the ground with the seventh brigade, ahead of the rest of our forces.

Promptly, I hail the SEAL team, "Overwatch what's your status?"

"Overwatch in position. You're clear to approach."

"Mongols move out," I order, and we take off down the path towards our target.

We ride at a pace of about seventy-five percent, making a compromise between getting there quickly and getting there with enough energy to fight a long battle. Together, we carry that pace, riding three abreast down the trail.

When we are about five hundred meters from where the path empties out into the valley, we begin to hear the SEALs opening up on the enemy. We hear the explosions of their rockets along with the fast-ripping sound of their tripod-mounted automatic lasers. Like planned, they are throwing down enough fire to draw the enemy's attention while conserving enough for the real fight that is soon to come.

Even though there are only a hundred of them, I am grateful to have someone out there to provide covering fire for us. It was a luxury that we often went without.

As we break out of the path, I'm hit with the striking image of the place, made more hellish by the colossal amount of firepower that is raining down from the cliffs. There might only be a hundred SEALs, but the sheer volume of fire makes it look like there is an entire brigade hiding up there.

In the center of the valley, I see the knoll sticking up from the rock. It is sitting there, challenging us, so I turn our ranks to meet it. We ride harder, encouraging our Wargons to build up the speed needed to break through the enemy's lines.

Left and right, we weave through the rocky approach until I see our target ahead of us. Thousands of Bugs lay before us, lined up, side by side. Normally they would have charged, but with the value of what is behind them, they didn't risk moving. We charge hard, building as much speed as we can.

Inside I am hoping beyond hope that this foolish plan will actually work. I hope that I'm not making a big mistake. Faster we ride, as Bugs are cut down by the laser fire that is raining down from the hills. Faster and faster, we go as our Wargons run like hungry beasts chasing their prey. I can feel Sleipnir's excitement growing in anticipation of the impact that's about to come.

We ride with all that we have, and when we are only fifty meters from the enemy's line, we unhook ourselves from our Wargons and dismount. Jumping, we hit the ground with a roll and come up firing as the Wargons smash through the line. In one movement, we have doubled our numbers from five hundred to a thousand.

We stagger our ranks and keep advancing, this time on foot. Firing lasers and hurling grenades, we focus all of our attention on clearing the entrance to the knoll. I take half the men to the right as Wenjack goes left with the rest. We cover and move in a textbook procedure. When we move, Wenjack's troops are firing, and when they move, we return the favour. This ensures that we are constantly closing distance with the target.

I focus on my link with Sleipnir because, in order for this plan to work, I need to be able to communicate directions to the Wargons. Focusing, I direct them to split in two and clear the Bugs surrounding the knoll as we advance up the middle. Luckily the message gets through, and the band of Wargons breaks. Hundreds of Bugs fall dead as the enormous, armoured beasts rip through their ranks.

Behind us, I can sense Captain McArthur coming with the rest of the Mongols. We desperately throw more firepower at the entrance of the knoll. Clearing it just in time, as the two brigades of Mongols blow by us like a hurricane and descend into the tunnels beneath the knoll.

We quickly take position in front of the entrance. We form a half-circle in front of the knoll facing outward. Our circle consists of two lines, the first one taking a knee so that the second can fire above their heads.

Having made their way around the knoll, I direct the Wargons to circle back around and clear our flanks.

By now, the Bugs that were being distracted by the SEAL team had figured out what was going on and turned back towards the knoll. We had pulled off the dismount, and I had successfully kept the link with the Wargons, but now that we have taken this ground, we will have to defend it.

Shoulder to shoulder, we stand together, blocking the entrance to the knoll. Using our bodies to create an unbroken wall to give our brothers and sisters enough time to do what needs to be done. Together we light up the canyon with laser fire, bomb blasts and rocket trails. We unleash a cacophony of noise and destruction as we stand our ground.

"Hey Braddock!" I hear Lieutenant Lundholm's voice call over the coms.

"There's a new horde coming out of the southern tunnel and it's heading your way," he says.

"Copy that."

I search for Sleipnir in my mind, trying to synch my thoughts with his. When I find him, I expect to feel the typical wrath and blood lust that accompanies battle. Instead, I feel overwhelming happiness. The Wargon is leading its kind on a path of destruction through the valley, ambushing and killing Bugs at will.

It occurs to me that this is the first time that Sleipnir and the other Wargons were able to fight on their own terms, unburdened by riders.

They were free to hunt and kill as they pleased, and they were taking full advantage of the opportunity.

I instruct Sleipnir to make his way to the southern tunnel to engage the horde. I feel him instantly respond and head in that direction with an unstoppable hunger for more violence. Any carnage the Bugs have ever delivered against Wargons will be paid back in full once our armoured beasts make contact.

Against my better judgment, I decide to add fuel to the fire, and with all my focus, I think, "Sleipnir, kill them, kill them all."

Sleipnir's rage burns like a fireball straight from hell as he charges the horde.

"Fuck there's too damn many of them," Corporal Crang yells from the left.

"No such thing as too many. Its just more meat for the slaughter," Corporal McQuarrie yells back as he throws a grenade.

The grenade lands perfectly below an approaching Bug that is vaporized instantly.

"Shut up and hold the line!" I order as wave after wave are cut down before us.

It feels strange fighting from the ground for a change. From the back of a Wargon, you're at the same level as the Bugs, but down here on foot, you feel small. Even though we are packing enough firepower to take over a small planet, I can't help but feel like I am unarmed. I feel naked and exposed as the massive Bugs bare down upon us.

What I wouldn't give to be riding Sleipnir right now. I could ride by myself into a horde of Bugs with nothing but a thermal lance and not feel as helpless as I do at this moment. Our line feels weak, like a paper wall trying to hold back a landslide, and yet, despite my feelings, the line holds.

The Bugs break upon our volleys like water upon rocks. A constant rain of fire hammers down from the SEAL team that is now competing with us to see who can deal out the most punishment. We have once again created a meat grinder for the Bugs to charge into. They try to beat our death machine by feeding it more death than it can handle, but it is a fruitless task. No amount of slaughter could ever satiate our craving for carnage.

We are killing so many Bugs that their corpses begin to form a wall that protects approaching Bugs from our direct line of fire. They now have cover as they approach us, and we can't shoot them down until they crest the wall. This causes the wall to grow high and thin and then topple forward.

Each time the wall of corpses falls, it grows a little bit closer to our line. The horde that exited the southern tunnel was weakened by Sleipnir's brutal assault, but there were far too many to kill in time, and the horde has now reached the wall. The increased number of Bugs speeds up the growing and toppling of the wall. If something isn't done soon, the wall will eventually reach our lines, and we will be overrun.

As I try and decide if we should pull back into the hill's entrance or not, Corporal McQuarrie steps forward.

"Cover me," he yells as he charges forward alone, with the massively bulky constant laser in his hands.

He fires the hardware, and a bright beam erupts from the end of the weapon. With carnal delight, he rakes the laser back and forth across the top of the corpse wall. Everything that the laser touches is torn apart, and nothing stands in its way. McQuarrie laughs gleefully like a child as he cuts down every Bug that's unlucky enough to crest the wall. He then lowers the lasers beam and starts cutting down the top of the wall.

I thought he was crazy for carrying that colossal piece of equipment for only thirty seconds of laser fire, but the amount of destruction he delivers in those thirty seconds makes it all worth it. For thirty seconds, he stands out amongst us all, as if it is his battle and we were merely spectators. Like the legendary hero Ajax before the walls of Troy, Corporal McQuarrie rules those thirty seconds of glory.

Then as quickly as it started, the laser goes out, snapping us back to reality. With our man out there in the field alone and exposed, we hammer the top of the wall with laser fire. McQuarrie had taken the wall down a bit, but it still stands and will grow again.

"Fall back in line," I order, but McQuarrie shakes his head.

He reaches up to his shoulder and takes off his last two belts of high explosive grenades. Swinging the belts behind his body, he loads up all the power he can muster before stepping forward, throwing the belts into the wall of Bugs.

In one smooth motion, he completes his throw, drops to a knee, and draws the rocket launcher from his back. Levelling the launcher's sights, he fires all fifteen mini rockets in rapid succession. The mini rockets fly a short distance through the air before finding the two belts of grenades that now lay in the wall of corpses.

With volcanic fury, an entire section of the wall is turned into mist. Blood and chunks of exoskeleton rain down upon the whole area, covering everything in sticky dark slime. The vaporized blood from the corpses fills the air, creating a thick brown mist.

I look through the mist, searching for Corporal McQuarrie, fearing that he was too close to the explosion to survive. Then, through the mist, I hear the unmistakable thump, thump, thump of an M73 grenade launcher. The son of a bitch is still alive and is launching his remaining grenades at the rest of the wall.

"Eat shit you fucks!" McQuarrie yells as he continues firing.

"Don't just stand there, blow that wall down," I order and with a volley of rockets and grenades, we join McQuarrie in taking down the wall.

Once McQuarrie is out of grenades, I yell out, "Get back in line."

Dropping his empty grenade launcher, he turns to follow my order. He doesn't get far before crushing mandibles extend through the mist, grabbing McQuarrie by the ankle. The assaulting Bug is quickly cut down, but not before sending McQuarrie through the air. His body bounces off the hard schythium ground as it lands. I fear the worst, but he gets right back up again. I'm going to make sure this guy gets a medal if we make it out of here.

As he stands and puts weight on his ankle, he falls back down.

"Shit. Fuck. Shit," he shouts angrily into the coms. "My fucking ankles toast."

"Overwatch, we need fire support on the line," I order.

"No can do friend. We are up to our assholes in Bugs right now," Lundholm responds.

"Shit. Second line cover McQuarrie," I order, and the entire second line shifts their fire, and lasers fly all around our wounded man.

Using his rifle as a crutch, McQuarrie staggers back to his feet and makes a mad scramble towards our line as Bugs are being shot dead all around him. Not having success reaching our lines, the Bugs turned all of their attention towards McQuarrie. Like hungry beasts fighting over a wounded calf, they go after him with everything they have. Desperately trying to get a piece.

Stumbling, McQuarrie fights for balance with all his will, trying to make it back. His struggles prove to be in vain. A Bug manages to sink a leg into the back of his neck as it's being shot down. The blow kills McQuarrie instantly, but his body takes a few seconds to drop, lifeless to the ground.

With no time to mourn, we continue to hold the line. In the chaos, I had lost track of Sleipnir. I can feel that he is out there fighting, but I can't tell where, and I can't deliver any more directions to them.

The SEALs were no more help to us because they were now fighting for their own lives, as Bugs have begun to ascend the cliffs.

McQuarrie had bought us some time by bringing down the wall, but it would build back up, and we didn't have enough explosives left to bring it down again. I wonder how much longer we will need to hold the line. How much longer it will take for Captain McArthur to clear the stockpile.

We continue fighting, and sure enough, the wall begins to build back up. Then, like before, it begins to topple and fall towards us.

"How many fucking Bugs are there?" Corporal Bark asks.

The only answer that comes to me is too fucking many. There are too many Bugs in this fucking valley, and there were too many Bugs on this fucking planet.

Out of nowhere, a voice comes into my head. "Give

in. Let them overtake you. Give up. Rest," the voice says.

I wonder where the hell the voice is coming from. I've never thought about giving up a day in my life. The voice doesn't sound like my own either. Was someone or something else in my head. Maybe I'm finally going crazy.

"Lieutenant, they're getting pretty fucking close. What are we doing here?" Wenjack asks.

"Keep fighting! We hold this ground, or we die on it," I order.

Maybe there was another option, but the thought of giving up shamed me into standing my ground, no matter what. We fight every instinct to step back as the wall closes in on us. Side by side, we stand firm, refusing to yield an inch of ground.

Catching us off guard, a series of shock waves come ripping out of the entrance to the knoll. The sound brings comfort to me because it means that even if we die here, we held the ground long enough for the stockpile to be destroyed. We did our job.

"Move!" I hear Lieutenant Prettejohn roar, and we barely have time to jump out of the way as two brigades of Wargons explode from the knoll.

Like a stampede of thunder beasts, they charge past

us in a blur. Without the hindrance of hesitation, they blow through the wall at full speed, sending corpses flying in all directions. With unstoppable force, they charge straight through the ranks of Bugs.

Once they reach the tunnel, the two brigades split off. Lieutenant Prettejohn looping back to charge the horde once more as Lieutenant Speers takes her half up the face of the cliffs to relieve the SEAL team.

Speers drives her brigade up the tight cliffside trails. Like a plow, she forces Bug after Bug from the path, letting their sprawling bodies fall, breaking upon the hard valley floor below. No Bug could hope to overcome the colossal force of the Wargon charge.

My focus is rapidly brought back to the ground as a wave of Bugs comes charging back our way. We stagger our formation and open fire, decimating the small force of assailants. Even though we are holding our own, I need to reconnect with Sleipnir. Splitting up was a good strategy for defence, but now we need to attack. We need speed.

I muster all the focus that I'm able to and call for Sleipnir. Seconds later, he comes bounding over, followed by the rest of the Wargons. Covering each other, we mount up and form a line. Prettejohn is charging the horde to the south, so I turn our ranks to the north.

Once we are mounted, it is only a matter of time before we round up the rest of the enemy. We have an unstoppable advantage with three brigades riding the valley and the SEAL team freed up to provide covering fire.

In no more than a half-hour, we decimate the enemy. We divide up our forces to secure the valley, and then I meet with the other officers by the entrance to the tunnel.

"Has anyone called into command yet?" I ask.

"I just did. They said to stand by for orders," Speers says.

"How many casualties did we sustain?" I ask, thinking of McQuarrie.

"Forty-three from my brigade," Prettejohn says.

"We lost thirty-seven," Speers says.

"I lost seventeen when one of our locations was overrun," Lundholm says with remorse.

"I lost one," I say.

"Only one?" Speers says in shock.

"Only? That death was one too many if you ask me. He was a good man, one of my best," I say.

"I'm sure he was brother. But that is still an

impressively low number," Lundholm says.

"If you guys took any longer clearing that place out, it would have been all of us I think," I say.

"We had our own problems down there," Speers says.

"It was thick. We had to fight for every inch, those fuckers really didn't want to give up that stockpile," Prettejohn says.

"What happened to Captain McArthur?" I ask.

"He fell. The guy fought his ass off but like I said, it was thick down there. The fighting got really up-close and personal, and a Bug managed to get the drop on him. Tore his head clean off and then killed his Wargon," Prettejohn says.

"Fucking hell," I say.

"Captain McArthur killed a shit ton of Bugs down there before he went. Don't think we would have done nearly as well if it wasn't for him. The man died as he lived. A hero," Prettejohn says.

"A lot of good people died today," Speers says.

We all stand in quiet remembrance for a moment before it gets awkward, and Speers breaks the silence.

"Hey, where the hell did you get the idea to dismount like that and fight on the ground?" Speers asks.

"Yeah, and how did you manage to control your Wargons without being on them?" Prettejohn adds.

"The idea to dismount and split up was strictly a numbers thing. We needed more bodies to hold that spot, so it didn't make sense to have our Wargons just stand there. Controlling them wasn't easy but the link doesn't sever until you take your armor off. It gets weaker when you dismount but it's still there, you just need to know where to focus," I tell them.

"Sounds a little two simple for something that's never been done before. You sure you aren't secretly some kind of Wargon whisperer?" Speers asks.

"You assume that it hasn't been done before because you haven't seen it. There are a lot of cavalry soldiers out there doing all kinds of things you don't know about," I say.

"Well I've never seen anything like it. It was definitely impressive," Prettejohn says.

We're interrupted when a call comes in from command.

"Lieutenants. You are instructed to hold the area and wait for the arrival of an engineering legion that is headed your way. Once they arrive you will provide security and assist them in fortifying the location. Due to the physical nature of your location, it has been chosen to be the sight of a new forward operating base. You will all stay on location until the construction of the FOB is complete," the voice says.

"Fuck. We were scheduled to go back to base before this raid started," I bitch.

"Well, any R&R is going to have to wait a while brother because our asses are going to be on babysitting duty until further notice," Lundholm says, slapping me on the shoulder.

CHAPTER NINETEEN

For seven long days, we waited for the engineering legion to show up. Command ordered that we sit tight and secure the area, so that's what we did. We sat, we watched, and we waited. Sitting in combat armour that we have fought and lived in for three weeks straight, watching the barren schythium landscape for any signs of life. I'm just thankful that someone had figured out a way to eliminate the production of body odour when you're in your suit. Otherwise, I think I would have stuck my thermal lance through my own brain by now.

Since our orders were to stay put, we didn't have the option to go out to patrol. The soldiers spent the first few days talking and swapping stories, but after a while, there became fewer and fewer things to talk about, other than how much this place sucks. By day four, we were so bored that we started wishing that the enemy would attack, but none did. We went that entire week without seeing so much as a trace of a Bug. A live Bug anyway, the ground was still littered with the corpses of the dead ones.

It never really occurred to me before because we didn't stick around after killing Bugs, but bodies don't rot on this planet. They just dry up. There were no organisms, micro or otherwise, on Excalibur to eat the bodies. This place was so inhospitable that even deaths helpers couldn't live here. Only the Bugs could live in this place, although that living will likely be a little more difficult with the destruction of their stockpiles. Then again, maybe not.

We had hit many of them, but who knows how many there actually are on this planet. Fuck I hate this planet. In my opinion, they can't mine it into oblivion fast enough. Still, the knowledge that one day it will all be gone is comforting.

To pass the time, I decide to make the rounds. I start by riding the long tight path up the cliff face to one of the lookout points. As I get to the top, I run into Corporal Bark sitting on lookout.

"Good evening, Corporal Bark," I say, trying to sound in good humour.

"Not too sure what's good about it Sir, or if it's actually evening for that matter. Every hour of the day looks the same on planet shit hole."

"Planet shit hole sounds like a bad porno flick," I say, attempting to lighten his mood.

"Or a good one, depending on your preferences," he says with a slight chuckle.

"Yeah, I guess so. How are things going up here?" I ask.

"Boring. The schythium is still schythium and all the Bugs are still dead. Nothing moving and nothing to report. Except for the radiation," Bark says.

"The radiation?"

"Yes Sir. I'm not sure why, but there are heavy amounts of radiation up here compared to the rest of the area. We've got Runkins up the ass up here," he says, and I laugh at the reference to the ancient measurement for radiation.

I check the radiation meter on my HUD, and sure enough, the reading is incredibly high.

"No shit."

"If I didn't know better, I would say that it looks like someone recently set off a small nuke up here, but for the life of me I can't figure out why. I mean if someone was going to nuke anything around here why not the knoll? Why here?" Bark asks.

I look around the area, trying to find any indication as to why this particular spot would have been nuked and find nothing.

"Fuck Corporal, it beats the hell outta me," I say, and we both stare off into the valley towards the knoll.

"You know Lieutenant, normally officers don't spend

so much time talking to us lowly NCOs, and never pay much mind to privates. But you always seem to take the time to talk to everyone, regardless of rank. The troops really respect you for it."

"Yeah? Well, I've only been an officer for a few weeks, so I'm still not really used to the high and mighty shit. Give it a few more weeks and I'll forget all about you peons," I say jokingly.

"I doubt that Sir," Bark says. "I'm serious though, Sir. People really respect actually being treated like we're people and not just cannon fodder. Not that we think we're too good to be fodder because let's face it. It's part of the job, but it's nice to be treated like we're not."

"Hell kid, the way this war is going, any of you that are still alive in a few more weeks might be officers yourselves."

"That might be true for other brigades, but there seems to be less opportunity for advancement in the seventh. You see, we have this Lieutenant that's a little bit nuts, but he's pretty good at keeping us alive."

"Oh you think I'm nuts do you?"

"Uh… No Sir. I was just having a laugh. But to be honest, when we received your battle plan for the raid, we all thought you might be nuts. I mean, who in their right mind has ever heard of cavalry getting off their mounts like that and fighting on foot.

"Let alone, having their mounts continue to battle independently. But fucking hell, it worked brilliantly. I'm not sure if people will ever tell stories about this war, but if they do, that's one of the moments they'll talk about," Bark says.

"Who knows what people will and won't talk about. The Federation tells whatever stories they think will make the most stupid young people sign their life's away. Everyone wants to rush off to become a hero, but they never stop to question why none of these heroes ever come home," I say.

"Either way Sir, I'm glad that I was here for this one. I just wish Private Talve was there with us. He would have loved a raid like that. He really looked up to you," Bark says as we both continue to stare off into the valley.

I wonder if these young soldiers would still look up to me if they knew how over my head I am with all this shit. I'm a career Sergeant, a working man. I'm not really an officer and don't have a clue what I am doing. The only reason that I have done half as well as I have is because I had the privilege of serving under other great officers. Everything I know, I learnt from watching officers like Lieutenant Jeanceon and Captain McArthur. Officers who I greatly wished were still here to shoulder the burden of leadership that I still don't want.

The dull orange clouds that hang low over the valley burst open as engineering dropships come lumbering down. We watch from the hills as the engineers rush from the ships, looking like kids playing war. I wasn't sure why they were rushing when everyone knew we hadn't seen a single sign of a Bug in a week. But I figured for a lot of these guys, this was their first time over the wire.

After all of the engineers had unloaded and were done pretending that they were storming an Old Earth beach, they started unloading their equipment. I marvel as they use the massive engineering suits to offload incredible amounts of cargo. The giant suits always impressed me with their sheer power. I always wanted to take one for a spin, but the opportunity hadn't presented itself yet.

We watch as ship after ship unloads more and more material. Mostly they unload the typical items like plastanium panels, support rods, sentry and defence systems, but then we start seeing things that I've never seen before. After watching these strange items being unloaded for a time, I realize that it's mining equipment. I was going to wait a few hours before introducing myself, but the presence of mining equipment piques my interest, so I decide to ride down and take a look.

Any information surrounding mining is supposed to be kept hush, hush, but I knew that there wasn't an engineering officer alive who would pass up the opportunity to talk to a war hero. Even if it's about things that are supposed to be kept secret.

As I ride through the unloading engineers, I spot their officer.

"Good evening, Sir," I say, giving the officer a wave. Even though this man was a Captain, I usually wouldn't call a non-combat officer Sir out of principle, but since I wanted to butter him up, I figured it couldn't hurt.

"I'm Lieutenant," I begin to say as he cuts me off.

"Lieutenant Braddock, yes I know who you are and I've been looking forward to meeting you. I heard about what you did here and I must say, I'm quite impressed," he says, and I know right away that this guy isn't going to be keeping any secrets.

"Thank you, Sir," I say in mock gratitude.

"I'm Captain Emond of the Ottoman sapper Corps," he says eagerly.

"It's a pleasure to meet you. I just wanted to let you know that my brigade has this entire valley locked down tight so that you and your engineers can carry out your work safely," I say in my best kiss-ass tone.

"Much appreciated my good man," he says.

His manner of speaking makes me want to kick him in the teeth, but I resist for the sake of curiosity.

"Say friend," I say, worried that I might be playing too nice. "What exactly is your work here. I know that you guys are building a new FOB but I'm seeing some equipment that I've never seen before."

"Ah yes, I bet you haven't. Come take a walk with me and I'll fill you in. One officer to another," he says.

I can tell that this loser was absolutely thrilled to tell me anything that I cared to ask. I dismounted Sleipnir, and he walked beside the Captain and myself.

"So Lieutenant, do you know why this location has been chosen to construct a new forward operating base?" he asks.

I obviously knew the answer but decided to play dumb to inflate his ego.

"No sir," I answer.

"Well Captain it's really quite simple. The high surrounding walls, and tunnel access in and out, make this location very easy to defend with minimal reinforcement. Not to mention the knoll behind us will be very easy to install an airlock, making it an ideal location for a base. High security with minimal effort, you see," he explains smugly.

"I see. That's very clever," I say, still stroking his ego.

"Yes, well the Federation does have a few good minds in its engineering corps if I do say so myself," he says with an irritatingly stuffy laugh.

I can feel my curiosity decreasing as my desire to beat this man to death increases, but I let him continue.

"The plan here is very simple you see. We are going to wall up every entrance to the valley with the exception of the tunnel. We are going to install blast doors down there. Then we are going to build an airlock into the knoll so that we can have an area to take off our suits."

"I've never heard of a FOB having an area for soldiers to take off their suits. Normally every soldier is required to stay combat ready at all times".

"Yes, that is normally the case, but this is going to be more than a typical forward operating base and it will be home to more than your typical soldiers," he says, and I know he has a grin under his helmet a mile wide.

"Why is that?" I question.

"This base will be home to a strategic mining operation. Do you know what that is Lieutenant?" he asks.

"No, I don't," I answer, this time in complete honesty.

"As I'm sure you know, this entire planet will eventually be mined for its schythium. After all that is the entire purpose of this campaign. Now this raises the question of where do we start mining? After much debate it was decided that all mining should take place in areas of tactical importance."

I look around at the valley before asking, "What exactly do you mean by tactical importance Captain?"

The Captain stretches out a palm towards the valley and says, "Let me explain our plans for this place and I think you will understand."

Walking towards the front of the knoll, the Captain points to the rough terrain.

"Look at this landscape, its full of ruts, holes and boulders. It provides no tactical advantage to our forces. We can't drive vehicles across it, or even land large aircraft on it. There isn't even enough flat ground to build on. Really all it's good for is providing cover for Bugs. That is why our miners are going to come in and mine it flat. Level the entire valley, save the knoll. That way the Federation gets their schythium and we get a defensible location to build a forward operating base."

I try and picture the valley with a smooth floor that would allow the construction of walls and buildings.

"I guess that does make tactical sense."

"Yes, of course it does. It will allow us to build a base big enough to house enough soldiers to make this place impregnable. But the mining won't be limited to just the valley floor," he says enthusiastically.

"It won't?" I ask, still kissing ass.

"No my boy. We will be mining inside the knoll itself. We are going to open up the space down there to accommodate at least a million personnel. We are hoping for half miners, a quarter support staff, and a quarter combat troops," he says.

"The Federation is going to bring in half a million miners? So this FOB is primarily going to be a mining base then?" I ask.

"Well yes and no. On the Surface it will be a fully functioning military base, but under ground it will primarily be a mining operation. The same thing is happening under the base at Landing Zone Bravo. They have been mining under the base and deep into the hills for weeks now. There are even talks of mining the Surf soon," he says.

"No shit," I say.

I am glad to see that they have already started stripping this shit hole of a planet. At this rate, we might even start seeing some schythium armour come our way before this war is through, but I'm not planning on holding my breath.

"That all sounds like a mighty fine plan Captain. My soldiers will be out on the perimeter making sure you lot are free to do your job uninterrupted."

"Oh, you won't be making camp down here with us?" he asks, sounding disappointed.

"No Sir. We're going to stay up in the hills and make sure nothing comes down and bothers you."

"Okay, well feel free to pop in from time to time to check in on us," he says.

"Yeah of course I will Captain," I lie.

I ride back up into the hills, where I meet with the other Lieutenants.

"What's the deal with the mining gear?" Lieutenant Lundholm asks.

"They're going to mine this entire valley flat. Build a base and then start mining under ground. This spot will be a FOB on ground level and a mining camp beneath," I say.

"About time they started stripping this rock," Lieutenant Prettejohn says.

"My thoughts exactly," I say.

"So, what are our orders?" Speers asks.

"We're going to stay here and protect the construction until we're relieved. Might be a couple weeks or it could be a couple months. So far nobody can tell us shit," I say.

"Well," Lundholm says with a chuckle. "I've got another assignment. My SEAL team is getting picked up in a couple hours. But you guys have fun babysitting."

"Feel free to go fuck yourself on your way out," I tell him.

Still laughing, Lundholm slaps me on the shoulder and walks off towards the hills.

"The rest of you tell your soldiers to hang in there. We might be here for a bit, so do what you can to keep your soldiers from getting restless," I say.

"Easier said than done Braddock," Speers says before

we all ride off to check on our brigades.

For the next two long weeks, we sit in the hills and watch as the engineers work. Quickly throwing up walls and guard towers. They work at a blistering pace, transforming the valley into a stronghold.

The engineers work in complete contrast to the miners who slowly mine the schythium from the valley floor. There is an army of them down there, but mining schythium is slow work. To say they move at a snail's pace would be an insult to snails. Their progress is slow but steady, and they flatten a little more valley floor each day.

Watching the construction of the base is the only thing that we have to occupy our time because there is no action on the line. Day after day, we hope for a Bug attack just for something to do, but none come. I begin to loath all the recruiting videos that show the war like it's an action movie because, in reality, it's a lot of mindless waiting around, staring at rocks. As cavalry, we were used to patrols and movement, but for two more weeks, we just sit. Waiting.

CHAPTER TWENTY

After two straight weeks of doing sweet fuck all, we are surprised when a Mongol command ship descends from the clouds.

"Look alive. General Jaxxon just landed in the valley," I call out over the brigade communications link.

Once the ship lands, I decide that it's better to ride down and meet the General than wait for a call.

As I get to the bottom of the valley, I'm instantly greeted by Captain Emond.

"Hello Lieutenant. Are you here to check on the progress of the base? I'm very busy but I could make some time to show you around."

The way Captain Emond talks sometimes makes him sound like a robot from a holo-flick. If the Federation wasn't militantly against artificial intelligence, I would almost swear this guy was a robo-dork.

"That sounds great Sir, but General Jaxxon just landed, and I need to meet with him."

I wanted to tell him to open his fucking eyes and take a guess why I'm down here, but I resist the urge. Despite

Emond being particularly annoying at times, he isn't a bad guy, and I don't feel like shitting on him.

"Oh, yes of course. Well maybe later Lieutenant," he says, disappointment creeping into his voice.

"Yeah, maybe later," I say, knowing damn well that wasn't going to happen.

I ride up to the command ship. Dismounting Sleipnir, I stand beside him, waiting to be called. I look around, expecting to see the other Lieutenants, and when I don't, I wonder if maybe I should have remained in the hills. These are some of the finer points of officer etiquette that I am clueless about. This should be understandable given that I was still a Sergeant the last time I was on base.

I decide to stand here and wait a little longer when I hear General Jaxxon ask. "Lieutenant Braddock are you going to stand there like a fucking idiot all day or are you going to come on board?"

"Yes sir, coming aboard now Sir," I say like a hapless virgin that was just asked to dance by the hottest girl in school.

Shaking off my awkwardness, I walk up the ramp and board the ship.

Once onboard, I pass an airlock and am approached

by a tech who takes off my helmet.

"Fucking hell," I say in relief as I aggressively scratch my face for the first time in over a month.

"Show some self control you animal," the General's assistant says, but I couldn't care less.

Anyone who's been in a suit this long would understand how good it feels to finally scratch an itch after weeks.

"Come this way," the assistant says coldly, and I follow.

She leads me to the General's office and opens the door. I raise my hand in the air and hold a salute until the General says, "At ease Lieutenant" and I lower my hand.

"Have a seat," he says, gesturing to a chair.

I sit my hulking armoured body into the chair, expecting it to be awkward.

To my surprise, it appears the chair had been specially designed for an armoured individual.

"Would you like some coffee?" he asks.

"Yes Sir," I say, trying not to sound too excited at the prospect of actually drinking something for a change.

He pours a cup and hands it to me, my thick, armoured hand almost completely engulfing the cup.

Instantly I take a sip, not caring how hot it is because I just can't wait to finally taste something for a change. Even if it is the thick sludge coffee.

"Thank you, Sir," I say in complete sincerity.

"Don't mention it, Lieutenant, I'm not too old to remember what it's like to be stuck in a suit for weeks on end," he says. "Although sometimes I think it would be preferable to being stuck behind a desk."

I think about all my soldiers who would kill for a chance to take off their helmets and have a hot cup of grease.

"Sir," I begin to say, but he cuts me off.

"You don't have to tell me Lieutenant. I know how long your brigade has been suited up and how bad they want some R&R. And no, they aren't getting any quite yet. There will hopefully be some time for it in the near future, but we'll get to that later," he says.

"Yes Sir," I say, putting the matter to a close.

"Now, there are a few orders of business that we need to catch up on. I wanted to get here sooner, but there has been a lot of work to do in the wake of the raids. Not every brigade faired as well as yours did.

"The Mongols came out better off than most, but we still sustained some significant losses," he says with remorse.

"All things considered we had an easy go of it," I say, trying to be sincere.

"We will get to that. First though, we need to address the issue of the court marshal and the execution of Corporal Ballard," he says sternly.

I get instantly nervous. Until now, I hadn't questioned the validity of my actions, but somehow, being confronted on the matter by a power higher than myself brings on a new feeling of self-doubt. Maybe I wasn't justified in executing the man, and if not, would I, in turn, be executed for my mistake? I thought I understood the law pretty well, but I had never been to officer school, so maybe I got it wrong. Perhaps I should have just detained him. I realize that I'm not nervous because I fear the consequences of my actions, but because I'm afraid that I might have killed a subordinate unjustly.

"The court marshal and execution of one of our soldiers is a very serious matter. I have had to personally review the report and recording of the proceedings. In my review, I concluded that the court marshal and sentence was not only warranted, but completely unavoidable," he says, and

I exhale in relief.

"Sentencing a man to death is not an easy thing to do, and carrying out that sentence is even more difficult. It's a downright horrible job, and no sane person would ever want to do it. But as a leader, you have to do it because putting that responsibility on anyone else is cowardly.

"That being said, I have seen other officers in your situation do just that. They sentence people to death and then don't have the balls to carry out the sentence themselves. That kind of cowardice hurts the brigade more than the condemned person ever could. In a situation like a court marshal, it is of utmost importance that the soldiers retain respect for the officer. If an officer loses respect, they lose their ability to command effectively.

"After reviewing the recording, I can tell that you understand this, and I have to commend you. You handled the situation as well as anyone I've ever seen. You were quick, courteous, and stuck to the point. When it was clear that a death sentence must be delivered, you did so without delay. You didn't berate the prisoner or make a spectacle out of the situation. You just did what needed to be done and got back to work. Well done," he says.

"Thank you, Sir. Honestly, I was just trying to get it over and done with so I could move on," I say.

"Of course, you were Lieutenant," he says.

Leaning forward on his desk, the General drops his voice to a softer tone.

"Lieutenant do you remember the last time we talked face to face?"

"Yes Sir."

"You didn't want to be promoted to officer because you thought that command wasn't for you. I hope by now you see how wrong you were."

"Yes Sir," I respond, thinking that it wasn't that I didn't think I could handle command. I just didn't want to.

In that respect, nothing has changed.

"Reviewing the things that you have done with the seventh brigade I have to say that you have lived up to the reputation of this legion. I gave you a brigade that wasn't familiar with each other and you quickly produced an effective combat machine. Lieutenant, no matter what you might think, you are a natural born combat leader."

"Thank you, Sir."

"Okay Braddock that's enough fluffing your hog. I need to ask you a serious question and I need you to answer me in complete honesty, leaving nothing out. How the fuck did you manage to command the Wargons remotely in the heat of battle?"

I knew the question was coming. It is probably the only reason he bothered coming out here in the first place. It is also likely why I am in here drinking grease while the other officers are outside, wishing they could scratch their faces.

"It's kind of a long story."

"Good thing I've got time," he says, crossing his arms.

"Well General, on the initial invasion when we lost communications in the canyons I tried to locate the others sections through the link with my Wargon. Since I was linked to my Wargon and the Wargons are all linked to each other, I figured that it might be possible to get an idea of what was happening to the other sections by tapping into that link," I begin to explain as the General cuts me off.

"Hang on, that link is only designed to transmit intent. There is emotion and a few other things that are transferred as a side effect, but you can't tap into the Wargons collectively," he says.

"Sure you can. The Wargons are constantly connected to a collective consciousness with others near by. When we are jacking into our Wargons, we are indirectly jacking into that consciousness," I say, but am cut off again.

"Lieutenant, when you are jacked to your Wargon the two of you are on one wavelength. The connection that your Wargon has with other Wargons is on a completely different wavelength. Think of it like a coms link. If we are on one link, but I'm also on another link, those two links don't become connected," he says.

"No, of course not, but I can ask you what is being said on that other link, right?" I ask.

He thinks quietly for a moment before saying, "Continue Lieutenant."

"I figured that if I focused on the link with my Wargon hard enough, I could sort through which emotions were his, and which ones belonged to the other Wargons. By the strength of the feeling, I might even be able to tell how far away the others were," I explain.

"And did it work?" the General asks.

"Sort of. I was definitely able to sense things from the other sections. I could feel the pain and loss of sections that were being ambushed, and I could feel the excitement and blood lust of sections that were doing well. But the information I received was vague at best.

"Anyway, after the battle I kept focusing on the link,

trying to push my connection deeper with my Wargon. Quickly the connection grew stronger. I even became able to read the emotions of my troops through the links with their Wargons," I say, and I can see the General's eyes widen in disbelief.

"Trust me, it's true," I say.

"So, when the time came and we dismounted, I just had to focus on getting my instructions to my Wargon and he conveyed them to the others. Kind of like he was just another Sergeant of mine. Wherever I needed them, I would focus on the idea of that area and they would go there. It wasn't easy, but it worked," I say, sitting back in my chair and taking another long sip of grease.

"Do you expect me to believe that some nobody Lieutenant, has figured out an entirely new way to communicate with the Wargons? A new way that some of the best minds in the Federation haven't discovered in all the years of working with the beasts?" he questions aggressively.

"I don't expect you to believe anything Sir. You asked a question, and I gave you an honest answer," I reply.

"Bullshit, there must be another explanation for how you did it," he said, pressing me.

"No Sir. That's it," I say, and we sit in silence for a

while as he looks to be pondering what I have told him.

"For the first time in my life I don't know what to say. If what you're saying is true, we need to completely change the way we train cavalry soldiers. This ability could quite possibly change cavalry warfare as we know it. I knew there was something different about you Lieutenant, I just didn't think it would be this," he says in amazement.

"Thank you, Sir," I say, not being able to find any other words.

"Well, I've almost forgot what else I have to tell you after a bombshell like that," he says, scratching his head.

"Anyway, if we're going to introduce this sort of thing into our training, we will have to finish this war with enough Wargons left to be able to train. At the rate we're burning through soldiers, we'll have to wait for the next generation to grow up before we have enough Wargons," he says before pouring himself a cup of grease.

Taking a sip, he looks at me and says, "Speaking of burning through soldiers. It looks like I've got a couple of spots that need filling. I'm going to move you up to Captain and Sergeant Wenjack will take your place as the Lieutenant of the seventh brigade. Do you have anyone that you want to replace Wenjack as Sergeant?" he asks.

I think about Corporal Crang but remember him talking about how pointless this war is and question his long-term reliability.

"I think I would like to transfer Sergeant Rodger out from Lieutenant Speers and give him to Wenjack, and then promote Corporal Cureusot to Sergeant," I say confidently.

"Sounds good to me Captain Braddock," he says, and I'm temporarily thrown off by the use of the new rank.

In less than two months, I've gone from Sergeant to Captain. What does that say about the life expectancy of officers in this war? I push the thought from my mind.

A knocking is heard on the door behind me.

"Come in Sergeant," General Jaxxon says, and a supply Sergeant walks into the room.

"Captain Braddock, in recognition of the heroic leadership that led to the success of the raid on stockpile forty-eight, the Federation has decided to award you with the distinguished medal of the Golden horse. Presented to cavalry soldiers who display exceptional cavalry ability and bravery in combat," he says, catching me completely off guard.

This was the highest cavalry-specific medal that the Federation awarded. The supply Sergeant walks up to me and clamps a large box onto my arm. With a loud thunk, the box adds the image of the golden rearing horse beneath the medal of valour.

“Thank you, Sir,” I say, this time more genuine than when I was awarded my last medal.

“You are definitely welcome,” the General says.

Sir, while we’re on the topic of medals, I would formally like to request that Corporal Macquarie be awarded the medal of valour for his brave stand during the raid. He saved us all,” I say.

“Yes, I read about that in the report and have already made the recommendations to have the medal added to his service record. The actual medal will be sent to his next of kin,” he says solemnly.

“Thank you, Sir.”

“It’s the least I could do.” General Jaxxon says with a gracious nod. “I also passed that section of the report on to the Federation press core so that his sacrifice could be eternalized.”

“He would have liked that Sir.”

Despite the press core being a well-known propaganda machine for Federation soldiers, it was still considered an honour to be mentioned by them.

"With all the pleasantries and ass kissing out of the way, we have a war to fight. How would you and your soldiers like to get out of this shit hole and head back to base?" he asks.

"Sir, we would kill for the opportunity to get out of here."

"I'm glad you're ready Lieutenant, because tomorrow you will be relieved by the Queens own Rifles light infantry legion, at which time you will be heading back to base," he says.

"Thank you, Sir."

"I'm not done yet," he says, cutting my celebration short. "There's a catch. You'll be riding back through the northeastern approach."

There is always a catch to every bit of good news. Still, I'd rather spend the next two weeks riding than sitting around here watching Emond and his guys build this base.

"Sounds good to me," I say eagerly.

"The Federation has rolled out a new plan that they say is going to finally start locating some enemy hives. Our part of this plan is to get out there and clear some territory. In your mission plans, you will find highlighted sections of territory that you will be responsible for searching. You must search these sections carefully for anything that might indicate Bug activity.

"I know your brigades are itching to get back to base but take your time out there and don't miss anything. After all the sections are cleared, you will ride back to the base by way of the eastern mountains. Think you can handle that?"

"Yes Sir."

"Good. You'll be taking all three brigades with you so this should be an easy assignment, but don't get lazy out there. This will be a good opportunity to get some experience commanding multiple brigades in the field, so take advantage of it," he says, and I can't help but feel like he just jinxed us by saying it would be easy.

Why the fuck would he say that. Maybe it was a slip of the tongue, but either way, it cast a black shadow over the upcoming assignment. He was practically asking for shit to go wrong by saying something like that. Nothing is ever easy. Not here, not on Excalibur.

CHAPTER TWENTY-ONE

After being relieved by the Queen's own Rifles, we resupply and form up on the new road leading to the southern tunnel. I sit atop Sleipnir at the front of the line and look at the three perfectly formed blocks of riders. My Lieutenants ride up and down the ranks, inspecting the troops, a task that I was now apparently above.

We were short of three full brigades, thanks to recent casualties, but still stood around fourteen hundred strong. A significant increase from the five hundred that I had barely had time to get comfortable with.

The way this war has been going, a soldier who dropped as a butt fuck private could end up leading the entire legion by the time it was all over. That is if there was still a legion left to lead.

I watch as Wenjack rides up and down the ranks of the seventh brigade, beaming with pride. For a guy who dropped as a Corporal with no desire for leadership, he has definitely risen to the task. He didn't seem happy when I told him he was being promoted to Lieutenant, but seeing him inspect the brigade, I can tell he is warming up to the position. Despite what he says, he likes having the soldiers look up to him. Plus, as he pointed out, we would now both be able to dine in the officer's mess if we ever get back to base. Which was enough silver lining for him.

The Lieutenants finish their inspections and ride up to meet me at the front of the line.

"All brigades look ready?" I ask.

"Yes Sir," they all say.

"That Sergeant Rodger sure knows how to get a brigade ready," Wenjack says.

"Yeah, you're welcome," Lieutenant Speers says, not bothering to hide her jealousy.

"How did Sergeant Cureusot do?" I ask, moving past her comment.

"She obviously doesn't know the finer points, seeing as she's only been a Sergeant for a few hours, but she did pretty good considering," Speers says.

"Well then, I guess its time to get our lazy asses moving," I say before switching my coms over to the company channel.

"All right Mongols listen up. We are about to step out onto the long road home. I know that you're all itching for some R&R, but we've still got a two-week ride ahead of us and a lot to do, so look sharp. I'd prefer it if we could all make it back to base in one piece. But this is Excalibur, and this cold bitch of a planet might have other plans for us. Mongols, move out," I command, heading off at a moderate pace into the tunnel.

At a comfortable pace, we ride through the tunnel and into the rocky hills beyond. After sitting on our asses for so long, it felt good to be moving again. Hell, it felt good just to be somewhere other than that boring fucking valley. As the paths widen, I decide to increase the pace and let the Wargons run. We weren't the only ones that were growing restless in that place. Our Wargons were becoming so agitated from the lack of movement that they had to spend most of their time sedated. Now though, they finally have the chance to stretch their legs, so we let them run for a few more kilometres until we hit the first section.

Once we get within eyesight of our first section, we slow down, taking our time to survey the land ahead of us. Our drones are out front, but with this much un-cleared territory, we need to be careful.

Going into the map, I designate areas of the section for each brigade to clear and upload them to the Company. Each brigade is assigned a section, and from there, the Lieutenants will have to divide their forces appropriately. I debate whether or not I should stick with one of the brigades or hold back in a position where I can support all three.

In the end, I decide that I can better command all

three brigades if I hang back. So, I pick a few privates to ride with me and watch the three brigades ride off in their designated directions.

I head off in the direction of a high path that should give me a good vantage point to observe the brigades from. The path is ideally situated just below the low line of cloud, which makes it the best possible option. It feels strange not leading from the front, watching the troops ride off to find the enemy, while I hang back. If action is to be found, I want to meet it head-on, not stand by and watch like a casual observer. Especially after the boring couple of weeks that we just endured. If there is a fight, I'll be pissed off if I miss it. I decide if any action comes, I'll ride down to meet it. Only, no action came.

All-day, we search every inch of our section, and there are no fucking Bugs. Not even so much as a small patrol. For sixteen hours, we ride and don't find shit. Knocking out the stockpiles was supposed to slow the enemy down, but not like this. Maybe there were fewer stockpiles than we thought, or perhaps we just happened to be too far away from the current ones for the Bugs to reach us.

Most likely, the fuckers were just hiding as part of some larger plan. Draw us out and then ambush us. Still, the complete lack of Bugs is off-putting, and I decide to call camp for the night.

The following day we continue to cover more of our assigned territory. We search through tunnels, down holes, in cracks, up hills, and still, we find nothing. There just aren't any Bugs anywhere. Beginning to think that something must be wrong, I reach out to command.

"Command this is Lieutenant, I mean, Captain Braddock of the Mongols Delta company," I say, waiting for a response.

"What can we do for you Captain?" a voice responds.

"We've been on patrol for the last forty-three hours and haven't found a single Bug. We've covered over a hundred square kilometers and come up dry. I'm starting to think the enemy might be planning something," I say.

"We will pass the information on to Intelligence, but we are seeing plenty of Bug activity in other sections. I promise you Captain, they haven't left," the voice says and cuts off the link.

With nothing else in my power to control, I decide to call camp after another day of zero contact. Silently I hope that tomorrow will bring some kind of action.

I repeat this pattern for another nine days without change. Each day we search inch after empty inch of barren rock. The more we search, the more I'm convinced that something bigger is happening here.

Since there is little actual commanding to be done, I spend most of my time working on expanding my link with Sleipnir. For hours each day I focus on the Wargons mind, and through it, the minds of the others. I want to see how far I can push the link and if it is possible to share more than intention and emotions.

What I find is that each Wargon, just like each soldier has a different voice. Even though they didn't speak out loud, they still had distinct characteristics to their communication. That way, they knew what thoughts were coming from which Wargon. The more time I spend tapping into this connection, the better I get at figuring out who is experiencing what. It might not be a discovery that will yield a great battlefield advantage, but it did bring me one step closer to a goal that I only now realize I have. I want to be able to hold a complete two-way conversation with Sleipnir. Maybe it is an impossible goal, but after days of supervising a search of a barren landscape, I am bored enough to try anything.

After ten days of supervising and trying to talk to Wargons, I grow restless and decide to start searching for myself. I only have a bodyguard of five privates with me, but since I'm on the inside of a fourteen hundred soldier perimeter, I figure it is relatively safe to poke around.

I decide to search out a cave that lay on the edge of a

hillside. I know that this cave had likely already been searched, but I am bored enough that even pretending to do something will be a relief.

I squeeze through the tight entrance to the cave and ride down the narrow passageway. After travelling no more than fifty meters into the cave, I realize that the path quickly tapers down to a width too small for a Bug to pass. I decide that this cave is a waste of time and begin backing out of the tight corridor.

Suddenly I stop as a strange feeling comes over me. No, not a feeling, something else, something stranger. An image of an endless parade of Bugs travelling through an underground highway passes through my mind, and a chill quickly comes over me.

It occurs to me that even though this path is too small for a Bug, there might be something larger beyond it, like an underground Bug highway. That would explain the lack of hostiles on the Surface. It's not that there aren't any Bugs. It's just that they are all underground.

Filled with a new conviction, I dismount Sleipnir and take off any non-life supporting equipment. The gap is too tight to bring anything except what was absolutely necessary. The feeling of laying down your weapons in a place like this is incredibly unnerving, but I realize that if I was to bump into any Bugs down here, I'm as good as dead anyway. Having a weapon was about as helpful as hiding under the covers. It might make you feel better, but it won't do shit to protect you.

Carefully I squeeze through the crack, paying close attention to not get snagged. In a squeeze this tight, brushing up against a jagged piece of schythium could open my suit up like a tin can. Typically, when squeezing through a tight spot, you would exhale your air to make yourself smaller, but that trick doesn't work in a battle suit. Instead, you have to be real careful not to stick something where it doesn't belong.

I move further and further through the tight opening as images of massive hordes go through my brain. I'm convinced now of what is down here. I push further, twisting and bending my way toward the other side of this schythium slit. I desperately try to get to the other side, but I get stopped mere feet from where it opens back up again. I curse as I can almost see the other side. There's something there. I just know it. I fight with all that I have to slip just a little bit deeper into the tight hole, but it's of no use.

After a while, I admit defeat and allow my common sense to return. There is probably nothing down there after all. It is just my bored mind wanting some action. I've been in this fucking battle suit too damn long, and my mind is starting to feel the effects.

I slip back through the crack and rejoin Sleipnir and my bodyguard.

I put my gear back on and check my rifle before saying, "There's nothing here, let's go."

As I ride through the entrance and into the open air, I'm hit with a strong feeling of warning from a Wargon that I don't recognize. Before understanding what is happening, I grab my thermal lance, spin around and cut a giant black and yellow Bug almost in half as it lunges at me.

"Ambush!" I yell as another nasty Bug snips the head from one of my bodyguards before driving its sharp forelegs into his Wargons neck.

The precise blow kills the Wargon instantly. With a speed that could only come from pure reflex, Sleipnir springs forward, crushing another Bug between his monstrous shoulder and the schythium wall.

To my left, two of the strange Bugs drop to the ground as the back of their heads are blown out by laser fire. I can't tell where the laser fire came from, and I don't have time to look. Backing Sleipnir into the wall behind me, I face my assailants, ready to unload weeks of frustration in a primal display. The shredded corpses of my bodyguards lay on the ground. They had been killed so quickly that I didn't even see it happen.

Hardened warriors were slaughtered like children. I can feel Sleipnir is as ready for violence as I am. Without delay, we explode on the beasts with all of our might.

Hurling his body forward with titanic force, Sleipnir sends two Bugs flying into the wall before swinging his deadly armoured horn through the crowd of assailants. Left and right, he sends the smashed bodies of the Bugs airborne, with crushing blows from his powerful horn. Wielding my lance, I sever any body part that gets past Sleipnir's onslaught.

Though we had a noticeable monopoly on brute aggression, it was speed that gave us our advantage. Even though these Bugs were far faster than any other we've faced, we were faster still. Each mandible snap or swipe of leg was just a little too slow and would land just behind where we were. Staying only slightly ahead of each attack, moving mere fractions of an inch out of the way. To a casual observer, it might have even appeared that we were getting hit, though no blows were landed. With each missed attack, we counter with extreme force.

Sleipnir and I move in flawless unison as we smash and rip our way through the advancing Bugs. We move like the perfectly coordinated hands of a champion prizefighter. One hand blocking while the other strikes out. Moving with united intention as we deliver blow after horrible blow upon our opponents. Never before have we so perfectly been of the same mind as we are in this moment.

Any Bugs fortunate enough to be out of the reach of

our carnal fury met a more merciful end as they are expertly cut down with laser fire. The lasers are sailing in from a distance, but I can't see exactly where. Nor can I tell who the shooter is, but I knew it wasn't one of mine. The Wargon on which the shooter rode felt in a way I didn't recognize.

The weapon that fired the lasers was also of a different make than that carried by my soldiers. Even though the lasers came in rapid succession, I could tell that they came from a semiautomatic weapon. The gap between shots was slightly irregular, implying that each laser was created by one trigger pull. It was also clear that each shot was deliberately aimed, as they all found a target with deadly accuracy. Whoever was on the other end of that weapon was nothing short of an expert marksman.

After eighty seconds of brutal violence, there is nothing left for us to kill. We stand victorious and alone, among the smashed and bloodied bodies of our enemies. The ground slick with the pools of blood that pour from the spent black and yellow corpses. Whether it's because of the weeks of endless boredom or something more sinister, I have never felt as satisfied after a fight as I do right now. I had never fought as well as I just had either.

The blissful afterglow quickly retreats as I see a strange-looking figure riding towards me. It takes me a second to interpret what I'm looking at because the figure is near impossible to focus on. As it rides, the colour of its armour is constantly shifting to mirror the environment.

Then it hits me like a brick. This is the mysterious rider from the hanger of the transport ship. At the time, I had mistakenly thought her to be a scout, but after being the benefactor of her marksmanship, I can say for certain that whoever this mysterious woman is, she's much more than a scout.

"Don't step on my sample," she says to me on a coms link that I didn't even know existed.

"Sample? What Sample," I ask, confused.

"Just don't move you fucking idiot," she snaps at me, and for some reason, I listen.

As she rides closer, I realize that I can connect with her Wargon, but I can't seem to get any sort of feeling from her. Reaching the spot where a perfectly intact Bug lay dead on the ground, minus a small hole, she dismounts in one smooth, elegant motion. I marvel at how her armour moves so perfectly, or maybe at how perfectly she moves in the armour.

Kneeling down beside the Bug, she draws a knife and begins cutting into the lower base of the back of its head. After a few smooth cuts, she withdraws a bloody chunk of spinal cord, or whatever the Bug equivalent of a spinal cord is and sticks it into a small container. She keys something into the container, and then it flashes three times. After the flash, she opens the container and empties its contents onto the ground.

She uses a small tool that appears to insert a probe into a spot where the creature's head meets its body and takes some kind of reading.

I watch entirely dumbfounded as this woman takes multiple samples, readings, and measurements. Never before have I seen someone do such things. When it came to Bugs, we would just kill em and leave em. It never occurred to me that someone would actually pay attention to them once they were dead.

Then again, these weren't ordinary Bugs. They were bigger, stronger, faster, and above all else, they appeared to be much more intelligent. They dispatched my veteran bodyguard like they were lambs to the slaughter.

After the mystery woman finishes with her work, she gets up and looks at me.

"So, are you going to say something or just sit there staring at me?" she asks.

I had so many questions that I didn't know where to start.

"What the fuck," was all I could seem to say.

"What the fuck are those things? What the fuck am I doing here? What the fuck is my armour made from? Are those the questions you're trying to ask?"

"It was more of a general what the fuck. But your questions are good too," I say, trying not to admit that those were all questions that I desperately want answered.

"I'm only going to explain these things once so pay attention," she says as she walks over and mounts her Wargon.

"Hang on a second, why haven't my soldiers shown up yet? I yelled ambush and nobody's shown up yet," I say, worried that this might not be the only ambush.

"They haven't come because I jammed your communications," she says bluntly.

"Hold on a second. How and why have you been granted access to the command override for my suit?"

"How about you just shut the fuck up and let me explain a few things before you waste more of my time with your juvenile questions."

Surprised by her blunt attitude, I do as she asks.

"As I'm sure you have guessed, these aren't your run-of-the-mill Bugs. They are something new. I've only run into them once before, and I wasn't able to get samples due to circumstances out of my control. So, to be honest, I don't really know that much about them apart from what you just saw.

"Best I can tell, they are the results of some sort of specialized breeding initiative to produce near perfect hunters." she says.

"When did you" I begin to say before she cuts me off.

"There's no point asking questions because I don't know anymore and won't till the information I just recorded is analyzed."

"Look, I'm going to try and stop you from asking a million more stupid questions. I am a hunter, and I work for Military Intelligence. The Federation has brought me here to scout the planet and collect samples of Bugs for Fleet scientists to analyze. I'm not technically part of the military, and I don't have a rank, so you better not call me mam.

"Since I'm working with Military Intelligence, I have been given access to any and all military assets that I want. Including access to the command override on all suits, except for Generals or higher ranks. That access also allows me to get state of the art technology like this schythium armour that has been equipped with the new active camouflaged nano coating," she says.

I marvel at what the future of cavalry armour could look like. I imagine the hell I could bring with a few hundred soldiers wearing armour like that.

"Before you go asking, no I'm not the only hunter on the planet. There are a couple hundred of us. Although, thanks to these bastards there have been less and less of us. Our job has been to collect samples and scout locations of tactical importance," she says, and I know that she means hives and stockpiles.

"We are the ones who found those stockpiles you all just raided. It was while scouting one of those stockpiles that I first ran into this new breed. I had to drop a fucking nuke to get away in one piece."

"That wouldn't have happened to be on a cliff face overlooking a valley would it?"

"It was. I'm guessing you found the radioactivity and you're proud of yourself because you think you know something," she says coldly.

I decide not to respond to her comment, mostly because she is right.

"I have access to your records and I know that is where you were recently stationed, so you aren't going to impress me with stupid guesses. Anyway, that's about all I'm going to tell you before you answer a couple of my questions."

"Well, I don't know what I can tell someone who already knows everything, but I'll answer what I can," I say mockingly.

"Just before you got ambushed you turned with your lance. How did you know you were about to be attacked?"

"I guess I heard the creature at the last moment."

"No you didn't. These things move in complete silence and have ambushed a number of hunters, including myself, who have far superior hearing devices. There is no chance that you heard it."

I think about the moment for a minute before responding again.

"It was your Wargon. You two were watching me come out of that cave and when the thing was about to attack me, your Wargon had a mild stress response and I sensed it. I could feel that there was something behind me," I say, discovering the information for myself as I speak.

"How the fuck could that be possible? You can't be connected to a Wargon that you aren't jacked into," she says, confused.

"You can't, but I can. Look, it's a long story and if

you want me to explain it, you can ride with me for a while, and I'll tell you all about it."

"Is that your way of asking me out?" she says playfully, catching me off guard.

"I… Uh… No," I say, fumbling my words.

"Relax, I'm fucking with you," she says in an easy tone.

"Right. Me too," I say, even though it made no sense

"Yeah okay. So, you're some kind of Wargon spirit walker or some shit, but that doesn't explain where you learned to fight like that."

"What do you mean?"

"What I mean is, these things have managed to take out several hunters that were some of the most skilled combatants in the galaxy. Who were wearing schythium armour. For fuck sakes, these fuckers almost took me out, and I needed to use a fucking nuke just to get away.

"Now I'm not bragging here and am being dead serious. I'm the best, and I mean the best, Bug killer in this galaxy, and I needed a fucking nuke. But here you are, a fucking cavalry officer. And you just slaughtered an entire pack of these things like it was nothing. How the fuck is that possible?" she questions in sincere disbelief.

"You were the best," I answer plainly.

"What?" she asks.

"You said that you are the best Bug killer in the galaxy. I think what you meant was that you, were, the best, because clearly I'm the best now," I say obnoxiously because I want to see what she will say.

She pauses for a while before answering, "I guess you're right. But I'd still like to know how," she says calmly.

"Don't know really. I've been at this shit a long time and I guess I've picked up a few things along the way," I say because I really don't have a better answer.

"I'd say. The way that you and your Wargon move together is incredible. It's like you're two parts of the same body," she says with just the slightest hint of admiration in her voice.

"Maybe they just fucked with me on the wrong day."

"That brings up another question. Why did they go after you? Normally these packs have been hunting hunters like me. Its like they search us out, but this is the first time that they've gone after regular soldiers. Why?" she asks.

I think for a minute before answering because I want

to be sure of what I'm about to say.

"I think it's because of what is inside that cave," I say hesitantly.

"And what is that?" she asks.

"At first glance nothing. But, at the back of the cave there is a crack in the wall. I tried to squeeze through it but couldn't make it all the way. I believe that there is something on the other side of that wall."

"Like what?" she asks.

"I believe there's a Bug highway down there. That's why there aren't any Bugs up here. They're all underground."

"Do you have any rational reason for thinking this? Did you hear any movement or detect any heat?"

"No."

"Then why would you think there is a giant underground highway?"

"Just a feeling."

"A feeling?"

"Yeah."

"Have you undergone any substantial head trauma in

the recent past?"

"Not that I can remember," I say, making an attempt at humour.

"Okay, well, I'm not sure how much stake I'm going to put into your feelings. I'm going to assume that the reason you were attacked has more to do with those fancy medals you're wearing."

"You think they can read those?"

"These Bugs? Oh yeah," she says. "Well maybe not read exactly but know that they set you apart as important in some way."

I think about the concept of Bugs that are smart enough to recognize insignias, and it gives me the chills.

"I've got one more question," I say.

"Only one?"

"For now at least. What's your name?"

"Dominique," she answers plainly.

"Just Dominique?"

"Just Dominique," she replies.

"Alright Dominique, I've got work to do, but how

about you ride with me for a while and I'll tell you about my link with the Wargons."

"Sure. I am curious how a dipshit like you could have figured out something like that," she says.

CHAPTER TWENTY-TWO

After marking the location of my late bodyguards for retrieval, we ride to retake my position in the center of the patrolling brigades. I spend the next couple of hours filling Dominique in on the finer points of the Wargon mind link. By the time I finish, the daily reports start to roll in. They once again tell me no Bugs have been found.

In light of the day's events, I decide to call in my officers and their lead Sergeants to fill them in.

It takes me a while to explain everything, and there are a lot of questions by the time I am done. Mainly about the mysterious stranger that is now in our midst. Eventually, they are as up-to-date as I am.

"Well, I'm glad someone around here had something interesting happen. There's been so little enemy activity lately that I've started to wonder if they've all gone home," Lieutenant Speers says.

"Only a couple more days and we'll be back at base Lieutenant. We just have a little more uncharted territory to cover and were done," I say.

My attention is drawn away as my HUD flashes with an emergency hail calling for me to switch into VR.

"I've got an emergency hail I need to take," I say to

the group.

"Yeah, us too," Wenjack says.

We all switch on our VRs and find ourselves sitting around a briefing table with a three-dimensional map of base LZ Bravo in the middle. General Jaxxon stands at the head of the table, looking incredibly serious. Everyone in the room is in their uniforms, as is the norm with meetings of this sort, everyone that is, except for Dominique. She is still wearing her full battle armour, and I am disappointed. I want to see what this mysterious woman looks like under that schythium shell.

"Good evening. I don't have much time, so we need to keep this brief and keep questions to a minimum. Intelligence has located two armies of Bugs approaching the base from the south and the west. By our estimates, they will reach the base within the next twenty-four hours.

"Intelligence is saying that the horde approaching from the south is approximately fifty million Bugs strong which won't be enough to break through our defenses in the canyons. We believe the Bugs realize this as well and this is merely a token force designed to tie up our soldiers in the area, drawing our attention from the main assault that's coming from the west," The General says.

I wondered since when fifty million was considered a

token force.

"The main force approaching from the west is estimated to be somewhere in the vicinity of a billion strong. Air support has begun preparation for a bombing campaign to try and reduce this number. It is still believed that close to six hundred million will reach our front lines. Frankly, I think air support will be lucky to kill that many. They still haven't figured out how to get their ship's guidance systems to work correctly in these clouds.

"Make no mistake, this is the largest Bug army we have ever seen," he says, and my heart races at the thought.

I think about the pillboxes that line the Surf that we had seen when we departed LZ Bravo. The soldiers inside them will be sitting ducks if that many Bugs come through. Those small boxes would be their graves.

"The Federation has called in all available drop ships to pick up troops from the field to reinforce the Surf," he says as the defensive line appears on the map before us.

We can see the line of boxes and behind them ten legions of both heavy and light infantry. I see the Samurai are one of the legions. It comforts me knowing that the soldiers in the pillboxes will have Kato covering them. I wonder if he will give them the same speech he had given us, telling them how secure their rear will be in his hands. The idea almost made me laugh, but I held it in.

Mixed in with the infantry lines, I can see a legion of Goliaths that will aid them with some heavy firepower. This is an impressive line, but it won't hold long against six hundred million.

"The line you see here has been nicknamed the anvil, and this here is the hammer," he says as hundreds of legions illuminate to the northeast of the battle line.

"As you can see, we have over three hundred and fifty legions, made up of over three and a half million soldiers, waiting to the northeast. Once the Bugs make contact with the line, we will swing the hammer and crush them against the anvil.

"I will be leading the Mongols and fifty thousand other cavalry as the head of the hammer. This will be the largest cavalry charge since the war for Grimble," he says, and I can instantly feel adrenaline run through my veins at the thought of being a part of such a charge.

"Now for the bad news. You lot won't be joining us," the General says, and I feel my heart sink into the deepest pit of my stomach.

I feel like the air has been sucked out of the room. First, the Federation leaves us out in the middle of nowhere, stuck in our suits for weeks on end, and now we will have to sit out of the biggest cavalry charge of the war. I am ready to kill someone.

"I know you all will want to be with us and believe me, I wish you were, but the Federation needs you elsewhere," he says.

I am generally curious about what stupid fucking order they're about to throw at us.

"Captain, you will take your brigades to the eastern hills above the LZ and secure the area. So far, we have detected armies approaching the base from two out of the three open sides. It is Intelligence's best guess that there will be an army coming from the east as well, but we haven't found it yet. Since the cliffs are so high that they extend into the thick cloud cover, our drones and scout ships are useless.

"That is why you're needed. If there is an army up there, you need to find it and then help destroy it. The hunter asset here will aid you in your task. Any questions?" The General asks.

I have a shit ton of questions, mostly circling around the mental deficiencies of whoever came up with this shit plan, but I decide to keep my mouth shut. Looking around the room, I can tell that everyone else is on the same page.

"Good. Now we all have work to do and not enough time to do it, so let's get moving. Good luck," General Jaxxon says before logging out and disappearing.

We all quickly do the same.

"This is fucking bullshit," Speers grumbles.

"Seriously fucking bullshit," Wenjack agrees.

"What happened to the whole live in the moment and take shit as it comes attitude," Prettejohn asks.

"It's been temporarily suspended. Now I just want to rip someone's head off," Wenjack says.

"Save it for the Bugs. If we're lucky enough to see any. I agree that being left out of a charge like this is the biggest insult a cavalry soldier could endure, but we are still soldiers and that means we follow orders. So, shut the fuck up and get ready to move," I order, the rage in my voice taking them all off guard.

Afraid to say anything else, they make their orders and form up their three brigades.

"Mongols, we are on the brink of the largest battle of this war so far, and we might be sitting it out. The only way that we're going to get a piece of it, is if we find it for ourselves, so keep your eyes open. Intelligence believes there is an army approaching from the east and if there is, we will find it. Mongols, move out!" I command, and we ride towards the eastern mountains.

Eager to not miss out on whatever action there is to be had, we ride with the purpose of hungry beasts. In an impressive show of her Wargon's performance, Dominique takes off to search the terrain ahead. The speed at which she moves is incredible.

We ride hard towards the mountains for the next few hours, still not finding any sign of a single horde, let alone an army. With each passing kilometre, the landscape is as barren as the kilometre before. Although the further we ride, the stronger a feeling grows inside of me. It is a feeling of us not being the only ones heading in this direction.

My mind flashes again to the image of countless lines of Bugs running through an underground highway.

With every hour that passes, the image grows stronger in my mind, until out of nowhere, I command "Halt!" and every Mongol comes to an abrupt stop.

Still and unmoving, I sit and listen. Listen as much to the Wargon's minds as I do to the actual world around me.

"Dominique fall back," I order.

When she returns, she asks, "What is it?"

I wait a second before answering.

"You need to go south."

"What. Why? The mountains are straight a head of us," she protests.

"Yes, But the bugs are too the south," I say confidently.

"And how do you know that?"

"It's just a feeling."

"You're going to put your ass on the line for a feeling?"

"Yes. Besides I'm still going to take the company to the mountains, I'm only sending you to look into this. I also severely doubt that we're going to run into any Bugs up there."

"Are your feelings telling you that too?"

"Yes. Now go. Ride south and report back what you find," I order.

"But how," she begins to say, and I cut her off.

"Go now and be quick about it."

Without another word of protest, she wheels her

Wargon around, and it springs to action, bounding off to the south. I carry on straight ahead towards the mountains.

We reach the mountains and make short work of the steep climb into the clouds. Once in the clouds, our vision is severely limited by the dense orange fog that blankets the path. Seeing no further than ten feet in front of us, we carry on faster than caution allows. Trusting our suits computers to help navigate our way, using the machine to make up for our lack of native senses.

About a half-hour into the clouds, I hear Dominique's voice break over the coms.

"You smug son of a bitch, you were right. You've definitely got Bugs here. Look at this," she says, and my HUD switches to a live view of her feed.

Sure enough, coming out of a massive tunnel is a fucking army of Bugs. Turning her head to the right, the line of Bugs carries forward as far as she can see, and with her visual capabilities, that is really damn far. Like a river pouring from the ground, they keep on coming. An endless line that is easily a thousand Bugs wide. We are looking at millions, upon millions, of Bugs.

"Braddock, this army is likely two hundred million strong, at least," she says with concern in her voice.

"Ride hard and try to find the head of the line. We need to know exactly where they are going," I order.

"On it," she says, and her feed shuts off.

Immediately I contact command.

"This is Captain Braddock of the Mongols requiring immediate orders."

"Copy that Captain, what is your situation?" a voice says back.

"We've found an underground Bug highway that opens up into the mountains east of LZ Bravo. We also found an army of about two hundred million Bugs heading towards the LZ."

The line is quiet for a moment until I hear it switch to a different channel.

"Captain Braddock this is Fleet Admiral Holoiday. Do you have a visual on the Bugs?" the Admiral asks.

"Sir I have a hunter asset tracking them now. She is locating the head of their column as we speak," I answer.

"Very good Captain. Keep her on them so we can track their movements. From what you've told us, it looks like they are going to assault the eastern mountain passes. Those areas are heavily fortified with multiple armored gates in each pass. We have also moved close to five hundred thousand troops that are now dug in deep into those hills in anticipation of an assault. If the Bugs want to hit that section of our line, they will be in for an ass kicking," he says with the confidence of an Admiral.

"Sir what do you want us to do?" I ask.

"Head to the mountains above our lines and wait for the enemy to make contact. When they do, I want you to hit them in the flank with as much firepower as you can muster and try to draw off a portion of their army. Don't fully engage, just hit and run. Your attacks should be enough to take some pressure off our lines," he says.

"Yes Sir," I say.

"If there are any changes to the situation hail my assistant on this line," he says before closing his coms link.

It might not be the job we wanted, but at least we will see some action in this battle. Despite what the Admiral says, I doubt that our lines will be able to hold back the Bugs as well as he thinks. Which means we might have the opportunity to play a more significant role than expected.

"Mongols keep moving. We've got a battle waiting for us!" I yell into our company channel.

A loud "Huha" erupts from our ranks, and we

increase our speed because now we finally have the opportunity for some action.

In our eagerness, we ride faster than expected and arrive at our position far ahead of the Bugs. Dominique is trailing the head of their column, and they are still a little ways from the fork that leads to our eastern lines.

Over the general coms link, I can hear that the battle is about to start on the southern and western lines. It looks like the Bugs are going to time their assault perfectly, hitting all sides at once.

I take a moment to feel the nervous anticipation hanging in the air that always accompanies the calm before the storm. I appreciate the peace of the moment because I know that soon all hell will break loose, and then the dead will be the only ones who will have any tranquillity.

My serenity is shattered as Dominique's voice breaks over the coms.

"Braddock, they didn't turn at the fork," she says in a panic.

"What do you mean they didn't turn," I reply.

"The fuck do you think I mean. I mean they didn't fucking turn. They just kept heading straight."

“Shit! Get back here now,” I order.

“What the fuck are they doing?” Wenjack asks.

“Proving how stupid we are,” I snap.

I switch back to the Admirals direct link.

“We’ve got a serious problem down here,” I yell into the coms.

“Yes Captain,” the Admirals assistant replies.

“Get the Admiral on the line now!” I bark.

“Captain if you haven’t noticed, there is a rather large battle about to start and the Admiral is extremely busy,” the assistant says.

“If you don’t shut the fuck up this battle will be over before it even starts. Get the Admiral now,” I order even though I have no idea what rank this assistant is.

A moment passes before the Admiral answers, “This better be good Captain.”

“The Bugs aren’t going to hit the eastern approach. They’re going for the falls,” I snap.

“Captain, the falls are a five-hundred-foot steep drop. Any Bug that trys to descend it will fall to their death,” the Admiral says with annoyance.

"We aren't dealing with single Bugs here Admiral, we're dealing with two hundred million Bugs! Maybe the first few thousand fall to their deaths. Fuck maybe the first million do, but pretty quick there will be a ramp of corpses that they will be able to run down unopposed. Even if a million die in the process, that still leaves one hundred and ninety-nine million fucking Bugs hitting your walls," I say with all the verbal force I can muster.

It takes a second for the Admiral to respond as he realizes that he might have just cost the Federation the base and a few million of its best soldiers.

"Listen Admiral you need to get every available soldier into that valley now," I say.

"Captain we can move the troops down from the eastern approach, but they are dug in so deep that it will take them a while to maneuver. I'll call in every dropship full of reinforcements in from orbit, but it will be at least ten minutes till they are in position," he says before I cut him off.

"You don't have ten minutes, you have five tops, Sir," I fire back.

"We have three gunships that we can move in, but we will need more time to get more troops into the area," he says.

"You don't have more time," I say, and there is a

quiet pause as I think.

I smile as the only option hits me. I smile not because I'm happy about what must be done but because there is simply nothing else to do.

"Admiral, open the gates on the eastern approach and my Mongols will buy you the time that you need," I say with a dead calm in my voice.

"Captain?" he asks.

"We're going to ride down there and hold them back."

Realizing that even though it was a shit option, it is the only option.

He answers, "The Federation thanks you and your Mongols for their service. Your presence will be greatly missed."

With nothing left to say, the Admiral severs the link.

Around me, Wenjack, Speers, and Prettejohn wait for instructions. Behind them, I see Sergeant Rodger, Sergeant Cureusot, Corporal Bark, Corporal Crang, and all the other Mongols that have served me so well. We might all have different opinions about the war, the Federation, and the cavalry in general, but we have all served together bravely nonetheless.

These honourable men and women have come together, put aside their differences and served as one. Now they surround me, waiting for me to give my final orders. Waiting for me to ask them to ride with me and give their last. I'm filled with more conflicting emotions in this moment than any other in my life, and all I can think of is how damn proud I am. I glance to my right as Dominique comes riding up beside me.

"You're not a Mongol, so I'm not going to try and order you, but will you ride with us?" I ask her.

"Absolutely. Unlike the rest of you, I actually have a chance of surviving this," she says.

Looking over my company, I raise my battle rifle in the air and, with all the breath in my lungs, yell the question, "Who's ready for a fight?"

I get my answer as every soldier in the company releases the loudest "Huha" I have ever heard.

CHAPTER TWENTY-THREE

With all my Mongols formed up behind me, I address them for what is likely to be the last time.

"Mongols! I haven't uploaded a battle plan because we aren't going to need one. This fight isn't going to involve any advanced tactics or ancient tricks. Its going to rely on heart and bravery. We're going to charge down through the gates and onto the planes below where we will hit the enemy in the flank. We will hit them as hard as we fucking can! We will ride over their bodies as far as possible, and if we are fortunate enough to make it through their ranks to the other side, we will turn around and hit them again!" I order with all the fire that I can summon.

"Sir, we only have fourteen hundred and we're riding against two hundred million. We don't have nearly enough to break the assault," Lieutenant Speers protests.

"No, Lieutenant, we do not. But we will charge them just the same. We don't need to break the assault. We only need to buy the Federation time to get more troops into position. Make no mistake, this is a rearguard action. We are not riding so that we can win this battle, but instead to give others the opportunity to win it.

"Mongols! This is where we make our final stand. So let's make it count! Now follow me, let's go meet death before our place is taken!"

At my words, Wenjack rears his Wargon upon its hind legs and yells, "Death!"

At this, every soldier in the company returns his challenge with shouts of their own.

Caught up in the fury of it all, I raise my rifle once more and make my own battle cry of, "Death!"

In a thunderous explosion of primal might, we break into a full-blown charge down the eastern approach. In our wrath, we fail to notice the loud buzzing that fills the skies above us.

****

Three hulking federation gunships hover over the ground at the base of the falls. Their cannons and guns levelled on the ground as the Bugs start to fall. Like an endless river crashing down, their bodies explode as they land. Against the relentless schythium ground, their exoskeletons break like eggshells against the floor.

Since the ground was doing most of the work, the gunships only have to fire the occasional high explosive round to liquefy the corpses so they wouldn't stack up.

Without warning, the thick orange cloud cover bursts

as thousands of flying Bugs come screaming down. The winged creatures quickly fill the skies, turning the orange ceiling of cloud into a buzzing black wall. Frantically every soldier, sentry gun, and heavy weapon shift their sights upward.

Desperately they fire, trying to hold back an unpredicted attack on the new front. Laser fire tears through the air in a horrific light show as blood rains down from the skies. The ground quickly becomes littered with severed limbs and chunks of shattered exoskeletons as the buzzing menace attempts an areal siege of the base. Within the heavily defended walls of the base, soldiers and support staff run out from their barracks with weapons pointed to the sky. Hurling lasers into the air.

It becomes undeniably clear that the assault from the sky won't be enough to penetrate the base. Although every weapon that was now pointed into the sky would be greatly missed on the ground. Until the flying menace is subdued, there will be little help from the walls for the soldiers who fight before them.

The gunships try to turn some of their weapons to engage the Bugs that are now buzzing around them, but they weren't designed to engage this many airborne targets at once.

It's not long before the Bugs land on the hulking ships and begin tearing into them. Piece by tiny piece, they rip through the heavy plastanium armour, digging their way into the heart of the flying war machines. Desperately the ships try to fire upon the enemy that now completely engulfs them, but it's to little avail. Before long, the flying monsters have fought their way into the massive ships.

As the gunships finally fall, the brave pilots steer them towards the mass of Bugs forming on the ground at the base of the falls. Hammering on their thrusters and launching every bit of ordinance that could be fired, they ensure that their deaths would count for something.

****

With breakneck speed, we descend from the clouds of the high country and down through the first gate. Only a short bit of road now lay between us and our fate. Already I can hear explosions echo through the cliffs. Most of them were clearly the results of our rocket fire and grenades, but three of them stood out as something else entirely. I'm unclear what caused the blasts, but I know that it is undoubtedly a sign that the battle isn't going our way. I put the thoughts out of my head and refocus on the task at hand.

As we make our way down the approach, we pass legion after legion crawling out of their positions and frantically trying to prepare a counter-attack. Try as they might, they will be too late. Unless we can hold them back, the Bugs will be over the first wall by the time these soldiers make their way onto the field.

The eastern defence now weighs on our shoulders, so we ride harder as I place all of my focus into encouraging the Wargons to hurry. I focus on their minds and think about how the Bugs invaded their world. Killed their families and destroyed their homes. It works to an extent. They increase their speed beyond anything I've seen before, and we fly down the road like a blast of thunder.

Faster and faster, we ride as we blow past the second gate. Only one more to go. Just one more gate till we reach the monsters and can deliver our payload of pent-up aggression. I grasp my rifle firmly in my right hand in anticipation of the glory that awaits us as we push through the last few turns. We're so close now, and the blood lust increases by the second. I'm fired up to the point that I almost don't notice that Ceasar's legion is fully mustered and almost at the last gate. How they managed to mobilize so fast is beyond me, but I have little time to think about it because ahead of us lays the last gate.

The thunder now blasting from the feet of our Wargons would have deafened an unprotected ear, and I hope that the bastards can feel us coming. Feel the hurricane of rage that is about to crash into their ranks.

With the cry of "Death!" bursting from our ranks once more, we cross the last gate.

We erupt from the schythium walls of the approach with volcanic fury and lay eyes on the chaos before us. Relentless laser fire flys from the base into an army of flying Bugs the likes of which I have never seen. Blood rains from a sky blackened by Bugs and smoke rising from the burning shells of three crashed gunships. By the destroyed ships and the thousands of Bugs that populated the air, I can tell that the dropships of reinforcements won't be coming any time soon.

Unfazed by the hellish sight, we bank left towards the approaching ocean of Bugs that still lay beyond the view of the base. The natural landscape formed two circles, with the falls emptying into the smaller of the two.

This meant that no fire support from the base could be counted on until the bugs had already taken the field and filled the first circle. It is into this circle that we now ride.

Rifles tucked tight against our shoulders, we open fire on the line of Bugs as we hurtle towards them. Our ranks spreading out behind me, forming a wedge as we enter the plain. The growing wedge widening our field of fire that now peppers the enemy's flank. Weakening the line that we are about to smash into. I squeeze my trigger with everything I have in a futile attempt to get as many shots off as possible while the advantage of distance is still in our favour. With less than a hundred meters before contact, every Mongol with a grenade launcher or rocket opens fire. Hurling their payloads into the approaching mass, the explosions send clouds of Bug debris into the air.

With Dominique to my right and Wenjack to my left, we form the tip of the colossal wedge.

One last battle cry of "Death!" flows forth from our ranks as each of us prepares for impact.

Sleipnir lowers his plastanium horn before our armoured wedge collides with the weakened line of Bugs with titanic force. With wrath and rage, we smash into their lines, crushing the enemy between and beneath us. Sleipnir relentlessly uses his armoured horn to break through their hard exoskeletons as he throws them to the side. Even with the colossal size of their army, they can do little against the sheer power of our initial charge.

Our wide wedge formation cuts a significant gap in their forces as we drive onward. Without the desire or ability to quit, we power through their ranks, desperately trying to reach the other side. As effective as this initial charge is, it will do little to slow the enemy if we get bogged down this early. We must get through.

Despite being thrown around as Sleipnir runs through the enemy, I manage to continue to get shots off. Relying heavily on my suit's aim-assist, I keep my rifle pulled tight against my side, letting lasers fly as I shoot from the hip.

Beside me, Dominique holds her cut-down laser rifle in her extended hand as she easily fires off a barrage of lasers into the crowd of Bugs. What I wouldn't give to have a company with suits like hers right about now.

Through either intense luck or brute force, we manage to complete one full pass through the enemy's ranks. Exiting through their southern flank, I bank our forces to the right in a large sweeping motion that turns us back around to the north. Their ranks are growing fast as the river of Bugs continues to pour from the clouds and down the waterfall that is now made safe by a ramp of corpses.

Not quite in sight of the base, I lead our forces in a charge across their front. Staying just outside of their reach, we turn our bodies to the right and unleash a merciless volley headlong into their ranks as we pass. Grabbing grenades from my belt, I begin throwing them into the crawling mass. Each one blowing a sizable hole in their ranks. Seizing what could be their last opportunity, the rest of my Mongols join in, using up their remaining grenades.

In this moment, I find myself being thankful that we hadn't run into any Bugs over the past few weeks. With no chance of resupply, we needed every bit of ordinance that we could get our hands-on. Even with our full supply, we are far short of what was desired. We empty every bit of firepower in that savage pass.

Reaching the end of their lines, I can see Ceasar's legion has set up positions at the end of the eastern approach and has now joined in on the doomed engagement. Their ten thousand men are far overshadowed by the giant Bug army. The odds don't seem to deter them as they heroically fire from behind their phalanx of plastanium shields.

Like us, the near-certainty of death doesn't discourage them from battle, and for that, they will be our brothers in death. Their help is appreciated, but it will do little to slow down the enemy's advance. At most, it will weaken the Bug's northeastern flank.

As I loop our soldiers around to the left, I find that we are within eyesight of the base. The skies are still littered with flying Bugs, occupying all the base's firepower. No fire support could be expected until that menace is dealt with. I wonder what defence the Federation is putting together because as hard as we are fighting, our impact seems minimal.

We ride hard towards the base in an effort to gain enough ground between us and the Bugs. Once far enough ahead, I swing our forces around to face the enemy. Again, we form up into a long wedge formation, but this time we are facing the Bugs head-on.

"With me!" I command as our ranks charge forward for what will likely be the last time.

Each soldier ready to fight to the death, we forsake our rifles for thermal lances. I tuck the end of my lance securely in the pit of my arm like a heavy cavalry soldier of old and lower the tip. The Wargon blood lust is up as we charge with all the speed that can be gained. With all available haste, we ride as the Bugs charge towards us. Both us and the Bugs are hungry for the carnage that awaits our ranks.

I light my lance just moments before our worlds collide in a planet-shaking impact. The force of our two armies crashing together sends Bugs flying up into the air. Their lines break upon our armoured charge as we push deep into their ranks. The initial charge is in our favour as we utilize the unbridled physical force of the collision to create our advantage.

Despite our heavy impact, the incredible numbers of the enemy soon slow us down, and the fight turns personal as I put my lance to work. Not having enough time to swing, I begin thrusting my lance into the heads of the enemy. Bug after Bug falls before me as I drive my lance through their helpless bodies as Sleipnir unloads his own barrage of horrendous assaults.

“Stand fast!” I command as we fight tooth and nail against our foe, but no matter how hard we fight, our casualties quickly start to pile up.

To my right, I see Lieutenant Speers fall as a Bug

strikes from her side, capturing her around the middle with savage mandibles. Tightly, it holds her as I watch its powerful mandibles twitch slightly before cracking Speers in half like a Christmas nut.

While blood still spews, the Bug turns its attention to the now riderless Wargon. But the Wargon falls into a rage at the loss of its partner and begins thrashing in complete madness. In an eruption of uncontrollable rage, it leaps forward, crushing two Bugs beneath its feet before charging off into the sea of hostiles. I lose sight of it, save the occasional Bug that would be thrown into the air.

We fight with superhuman might to hold the line, but against this many foes, it proves to be an impossible task. All of us are prepared to die, but in this line, we are dying too quickly.

"Circle up!" I order, and the outer ends of our line begin to back up as I push the center forward.

Gradually we reposition until we're forming a circle with the ass end of each Wargon fixed tightly to the ones next to them. This allows us a moderate amount of protection as we thrust, stomp, and gore, our enemies. Inside the circle lay a second line that unleashes a punishing volley of laser fire into the Bug's unrelenting ranks. The new position will buy us a little more time, but we will soon be fucked without sizable reinforcements.

I can see on my HUD that Caesar's legion has pushed their phalanx further onto the planes creating a small opening for the infantry that was trying to counter-attack from the eastern approach. Hard as they try, the legion can't force a big enough opening to get enough soldiers through to make a difference. The Bugs are numerous, and no matter how fast they shoot them down, more take their place.

Regardless of their number, the soldiers waiting in the approach can't do much as their ranks are nothing more than grains of sand in an hourglass. Their help was appreciated, but it did little to hold back the approaching army.

Our circle formation stands as an island of destruction in the sea of bugs, decimating anything that washes up against us. Slowly moving just enough to avoid being walled in by the corpses that are stacking up around us. We slaughter our adversaries with expert skill, but it's to a slight advantage. We are no longer holding back the onslaught. No matter how many we kill, most Bugs simply go around us, avoiding our wrath. The gap is too big, and they are too many. I fear that all will soon be lost if more help doesn't arrive quickly.

"Fuck this!" Corporal Crang bellows, fed up with the ineffectiveness of our current situation.

Without warning, his Wargon leaps forward, clearing

the front line of the circle, before jumping again. Pouncing from one spot to the next like a cat playing with a toy, he moves further and further from our lines.

"What the fuck is he doing!" I holler.

I wonder if he has completely lost his mind as I watch him carry on in that ridiculous fashion until he is about a hundred and fifty meters out.

"What's he doing?" I ask again, this time in a whisper to myself.

I see Crang grab something and then lean forward.

"I'm sorry old friend," he says to his Wargon before a titanic blast rips through them both.

The shockwave from the blast sends a hurricane of Bug blood, limbs and plastanium shrapnel hurtling through the air. We are rocked by the blast and the airborne debris, but the Bugs take the brunt of the hit. Crangs sacrifice blew a hundred-meter radius hole in the ranks of the Bugs.

I wonder what he had just done. Was he carrying a bomb that I didn't know about, or was it something more? I wish that I knew because if all of us could make the same sacrifice, we'd have a chance at slowing these bastards down. Unfortunately, nobody else knows how the Corporal had pulled off his suicidal sacrifice, and we are forced to fight on, watching the mass of Bugs that now approach the wall.

The airborne assault has almost been repelled, and the bases guns are now just picking off the few remaining Bugs that dive and dart through the sky. Once they do, they will be able to turn their weapons to the ground, and the dropships can finally land, but it may be too late. The Bugs are almost on the wall, and once they are, it will be a matter of time until they get inside. We fight on in vain as all hope is lost. The Bugs outsmarted us, and we are going to pay the price. I take solace in the fact that we won't be around to witness the aftermath.

"Captain Braddock, we're coming to help," a familiar voice says over the coms.

Then I see five hundred locators pop up on my HUD to the south. The locators tell me they are engineers, but that doesn't make sense. Repositioning Sleipnir to get a view to the south, I realize that the locators aren't wrong at all. It is Lieutenant Drummond leading five hundred engineers, all wearing their colossal construction suits.

They had armed themselves with giant plastanium beams, thick lengths of chain, and other construction supplies. The giant yellow suits wielding their improvised weapons make them look like hooligans heading for a street fight.

In all my life, I never thought I would be happy to see

engineers on the battlefield.

They engage the enemy with tremendous impact, using the titan-like strength of their suits to full advantage. Lieutenant Drummond swings his massive plastanium beam low across the ground, sweeping the advancing Bugs from his path. Meanwhile, the engineer with the chain swings it above his head, its end punishingly ripping through the Bugs with devastating force. Stomping and smashing, the giants make their presence felt with blow after horrible blow.

As the Bugs begin to pile up against the wall, an engineer raises a large water tank above its head and hurls it. The massive tank collides with the Bugs, crushing them instantly, before rolling along the wall, destroying the climbing Bugs. More engineers approach the wall sweeping the enemy from its base. They kick and stomp at the approaching Bugs with brute force, holding them back from the wall.

This motley group of engineers has somehow replaced us as the most effective force on the battlefield, and it looks like they're loving every minute of it. With every massive blow they deal, they cheer and even laugh.

Their devastating presence fills us with renewed vigour, and we fight on with even more fire than before. With their help, we actually have a chance. We can hold these demons back. Maybe we can even make it through this alive.

The engineers are fighting bravely, but it isn't long before some of them start to fall. The Bugs climb up their long limbs and tear their suits apart, piece by piece. If they are going to keep up their assault, they will need our help.

"Fall back to the engineers," I command.

We break ranks and force our way through the Bugs towards the hulking giants that are now beginning to experience the true nature of war. Our breaking ranks removes all forms of defence, and we pay for it instantly as we start taking losses.

We use every effort to fight our way through the enemy, but there is just to damn many of them. Even the god-like strength of the Wargons isn't enough to work us free, as the Bugs crush in all around us. Then, as if on cue, a horrendous barrage of heavy fire erupts from the walls of the base as its gunners turn their focus to the ground. Heavy lasers tear through Bugs all around us, and finally, we have room to move.

With iron determination, we ride through the exploding Bugs and laser fire as we make our way to help our gigantic brethren. The air is thick with bloody mist that bursts forth from Bugs as they are hit. Visibility is terrible as we ride through the gauntlet of laser fire and explosions.

Like the charging Light Brigade, we fearlessly

continue through the hellish nightmare carrying on around us. Each one of my Mongols follows me without question as I lead them through the deadly mess. I think once more of how proud I am to lead such a quality of soldiers.

My thoughts are shattered as to my right, I see Lieutenant Prettejohn's head blown from his shoulders by a stray laser.

"Fuck!" I holler as his headless body, held stiff by his armour, continues to ride beside me.

If we didn't already have enough to worry about, we now must add friendly fire to the list. I try to ignore Prettejohn's headless body and focus on getting to the engineers.

The short ride feels like a lifetime, but we reach the engineers in time to engage the Bugs that are besieging them. We ride between their ranks, firing lasers and slashing lances, trying to clear the Bugs from their feet. The bases guns have put big enough holes in the enemy's ranks that we are now able to move as we fight, which is an advantage that we have dearly missed.

We use our mobility to its full potential as we ride between the yellow giants, cleaning up any Bugs they miss. In the distance, I can see Bugs beginning to pile up once more on the far section of the wall, but there is nothing we can do about that at this point. If the first wall is breached, we still have the higher second wall.

To the south, I can see the first dropships hitting the ground and infantry pouring from them. The soldiers come in the thousands as they quickly form up on the still open section of the plain. As long as the western lines hold out, this battle is ours to lose. Now it is only a question of how many will have to die in the process.

My thoughts are suddenly interrupted as I feel a sharp pain burst into my side. I look down and notice that a Bug has shanked me with its leg, right below my ribs. With a swing of my lance, I sever the limb that stuck in my side. I check my system computer, and even though the leg is plugging most of the hole, the air is still leaking out.

A race has now started between blood and air loss, the winner of which will get to claim my life. With little left to do, I rear Sleipnir upon his hind legs in preparation for my last stand. If this is to be my end, I am going to make it count. I will charge headlong into the enemy and slaughter as many as I can. This is it. I raise my burning lance into the air, challenging all to face my final wrath.

CHAPTER TWENTY-FOUR

Captain Denis once again sits, waiting to be admitted to General Carmichael's office. He hated waiting at the best of times, which these weren't. Ever since the attacks, the lab has been in absolute chaos as they tried to sort out and analyze the flood of data that had been pouring in. For the past two weeks, he had tirelessly slaved over report after report, trying to make sense of what had happened.

In a single day, everything they thought they knew about the Bugs was blown apart, and the task of putting things back together had landed squarely in his lap. He had to forgo sleep many nights and rely on a cocktail of stims just to keep up with the ever-increasing stack of work. Most days, he barely even had time to eat, but now he is stuck wasting time sitting in a chair waiting for a General who he couldn't stand.

Trying to explain scientific findings to such a brash man was an exercise in futility. It always made him feel like Sisyphus, who, according to the Old Earth stories, was sentenced by the god of the dead to push a giant rock up a hill. Every time he got the rock to the top of the hill, it would roll back down again, and the process would need to be repeated. The eternal cycle of futility made him sympathize with the fabled man.

General Carmichael didn't have a mind for

academics. He was a gorilla from a foregone age. The type of man that would be comfortable fighting in dense jungles or leading soldiers through deep swamps on midnight raids. He didn't belong behind a desk on a starship, especially in the applied science division. There was little to indicate that the General knew what the scientific method was, let alone how to apply it. He was an ape that would sooner throw his feces against a wall than look through an electron microscope.

"The General will see you now," the General's assistant says in the same tone that she always used.

The assistant's voice instantly makes Captain Denis more agitated because he has subconsciously learned to associate it with the General. Begrudgingly, Captain Denis gets up from his chair and enters the office.

Upon entering, Captain Denis notices that the General isn't alone. To either side of him stands men wearing the imposing black uniforms of Military Intelligence officers. They hold such unflinching scowls on their stern faces that General Carmichael seemed almost pleasant in comparison. Instantly Captain Denis grows nervous at the sight of the two men.

Intelligence officers had the well-earned reputation of being people you didn't want to cross paths with. They hold almost unchecked authority within the Federation and are rumoured to lock people up, or worse, without explanation or trial. They never smile, never laugh, and never socialize in any way. It's rumoured that all recruits undergo some kind of federation mind control to turn them into emotionless drones, but there was no proof of it.

Captain Denis wonders how many of the stories about them are true. It seems that they have been given the same boogeyman characteristics that every society projects onto its government. Throughout time, there have been stories of men in black and secret police that could snatch you in the night for crossing the government. It was likely that these officers just played into that role because it made their job easier. Fear of being locked up in a secret prison ship did make people more compliant. The Captain is always skeptical of what is true, but he decides that it would be prudent to air on the side of caution in this situation. Story's or not, these officers have an intimidating presence.

"Captain Denis, take a seat," General Carmichael says, gesturing at a chair in front of his desk.

The General appears to actually be happy to see the Captain for the first time in their professional relationship. The presence of the Intelligence officers is clearly as unpleasant to General Carmichael as it is to the Captain. Intelligence officers make everyone feel uncomfortable, regardless of rank. Captain Denis awkwardly saunters into the office and takes the seat.

"Captain, we're here to go over the findings in your last report," the General starts and then is cut off by a third officer that appears behind Captain Denis.

"Some of the conclusions you arrived at in your report are, concerning," the officer says.

"Captain the problem is," the General says before being abruptly cut off again.

"The problem is that your conclusions go against every commonly held belief about our enemy, and we need to be very clear on what you are saying Captain," the officer says, still not introducing himself.

The General grows increasingly agitated with every interruption. The Captain wonders how long a man like General Carmichael can play nice.

"I want you to summarize the report for me in very clear terms," the officer says.

Captain Denis is getting really sick of people asking him to explain his complex work in simplest terms so that any idiot could understand it. He wants to snap on these officers and give them a piece of his mind but fears the consequences. In the presence of these men, he's afraid to do much of anything other than answer their questions.

"Well, Sir... Umm… Where to start?" the Captain

stammers nervously.

"As you know, the Bugs seem to somehow be perfectly adapted for the conditions on every planet we find them on. They can breathe the atmosphere, handle various heat and radiation conditions, etcetera. The question of how they do this has always been one of our biggest puzzles. Our leading theory was that they developed the ability to thrive in these different conditions by activating dormant genes.

"Evidence supported this theory as every sample was basically the same. To put it simply, different genes were either turned on or off to allow for different traits, like breathing carbon dioxide rather than oxygen. But those genes were always there. Small changes were found in samples from different planets, but we thought they were the result of evolution. The changes appeared to be connected to the Bugs time on particular planets," the Captain explains as he looks around the room to make sure everyone is following up to this point.

The officer that had done the speaking appears to be following, but the two that stood behind the General show no indication that they are human, let alone that they followed what is being said.

"Now, from planet to planet these findings appeared to be fairly consistent, and changes happened slowly. That ceased to be the case once we landed here. The first samples that we received from Excalibur were far different than ones from the past. Instead of seeing the typical minor changes, we were seeing massive ones. These Bugs are not only adapted to living on this planet, but they are also far more adapted for war against us. They are bigger, stronger, faster and their exoskeletons are much harder than anything we have seen before," the Captain says, looking for a way to explain things simply.

"Before Excalibur, all the samples we had taken followed a pattern. When we found Bugs that had different traits than previously observed, we could look at previous samples and see that the potential for those traits was there. They just weren't activated. This is not the case with the Excalibur bugs. The changes that we have seen are impossible based on previous genetic samples. These Bugs are no longer the result of the selection if dormant genes," the Captain explains before pausing briefly at the blank looks from the motionless officers that unnerved him to the point of losing his train of thought.

Pausing to try and remember where he was in his explanation, General Carmichael pulls him back on track.

"So, if it isn't the activation of genes, what is it?" Carmichael asks.

Captain Denis looks at the General in shock because not only is this the first time that the General has ever shown him any kindness. It also means he is following what Captain Denis has been saying. Nevertheless, it was the prompt the Captain needed.

"After examining the first samples of the Excalibur Bugs, I had hypothesized that the natural selection of dormant genes no longer fit."

Captain Denis begins to regain his confidence.

"Instead, the Bugs were creatures created based on the same genetic blueprint that held the potential for future requirements. These Bugs were being designed for specific environments, but they were always kept within the capabilities of the original blueprint so that their changes would appear to be natural. However, the Bugs created for Excalibur were made vastly different for some reason," the Captain says proudly.

"And what was that reason Captain?" the Intelligence officer coldly asks.

"Well, the schythium of course. Excalibur is the most valuable planet the Federation has found to date, and if they successfully capture and mine it, the Bugs will no longer pose a serious threat. Whoever is creating the Bugs would obviously realize this and must have wagered that creating a stronger Bug was worth the risk of exposure. Make no mistake, the creator has gone to great lengths to remain hidden from us, but I'm guessing they fear us capturing the planet far more than they fear exposure. The development of the black and yellow hunter class as well as the flying Bugs supports this theory," the Captain explains.

"How exactly is that?" the officer asks with no surprise or shock at the Captain's words.

"Ignoring the obvious physical differences of the two new species from what we consider to be the original design. These new Bugs have an unmistakably different genetic structure. It appears that whoever designed them took no precautions to make them look like natural occurrences. In my professional opinion, it looks as though they started hatching these new Bugs as soon as they were designed, without taking the usual steps to cover their tracks. Looking at these new samples, it is clear that the Bugs we have been fighting on Excalibur were not only created, but created to fight the Federation," the Captain says.

The room sits quiet as the officer and Captain Denis stare at each other. Tension rises to an uncomfortable level before the officer speaks.

"You seem to have all the answers Captain. So let me ask you, who is it that's creating these creatures and why?" the officer asks.

"That I do not know. I can say without a doubt that

these Bugs have been created, and I can confidently say that these ones have been created specifically to fight our troops. I can give you every genetic detail about them, a long list of behaviors and even where they hatched. However, I can't tell you who made them, how they made them, or why they made them. Maybe they were made by more advanced Bugs, maybe it's another species all together. It might even be one of the gods people talked about before the last crusade ended all organized religion. I do not know," the Captain says firmly.

"To the best of your knowledge is there anything in your research that might give you a clue as to who created them?" the Intelligence officer asks.

"No. Well, not really. We can compare genetic structures of different specimens and see if they share the same creator, but we aren't capable of much more at this time," the Captain explains.

"Good than do that," the officer orders.

"Do what exactly?" the Captain responds in confusion.

"Compare the genetic samples with every other organic specimen in the galaxy," the officer orders plainly.

"Do you have any idea how long that will take?" The Captain shoots back.

"Just do it Captain. You will be given any resources that you need," General Carmichael says in a frustrated outburst.

It is clear that having the two officers standing so close to him is pissing him off.

"Captain, given the information…."

"Hang on a second," Captain Denis blurts out, cutting off the officer.

The Captain realizes he has made a mistake by the glair that the General shoots him, but his curiosity overrides his instincts of self-preservation. Luckily for him, the officer was so surprised at being interrupted that he let it go.

"I just told you that the enemy that our species has been fighting against for all this time is likely not our actual enemy. If anything, they are just a weapon that is being used by the real enemy, who's identity and nature is still a complete unknown to us, and you aren't even a little bit phased. You just accept the information like I'm telling you my favorite colour. Is none of this news to you? Am I just sitting here wasting my time, telling you things that you already know?" the Captain asks in apparent confusion and frustration.

"Captain, I work for Military Intelligence and what we know, or don't know, is not of your concern. I am not surprised by your information because it is my job not to be surprised. Now it would serve you well to remember your place," he says coldly, and the words make the Captain both agitated with the secrecy and nervous of the apparent threat.

"As I was asking, Captain," he says, putting new disdain on the word Captain. "Given the information that you have gathered from the newly discovered Bugs, what predictions can you make about future Bugs that we might encounter? We want to be ready for any scenario and need to know how bad it can get," the officer asks.

Captain Denis leans back in his chair and thinks about the question. It had been one that he had asked himself numerous times but hadn't spoken of yet.

"I can not predict what variations might show up in the future because quite frankly, there are just too many possibilities. You see, under normal circumstances a species is limited by the evolutionary restrictions of their environment. However, since these things are being created as opposed to evolving, they are only limited by the supplies available. If there is adequate genetic material and enough food, we could see Bugs that are fifty or even a hundred feet tall. On the other hand, if they saw the need for it, we could see Bugs that are half the size they are now but ten times as fast," Captain Denis explains.

"Captain, we want you to make some guesses on

what you already know," the officer says sternly.

"Scientists don't make guesses, we make hypotheses, and I don't have enough information to do that," Captain Denis snaps.

General Carmichael looks like he is going to say something, but since he is growing tired of these men being in his office, he keeps quiet.

"You will give us your best guess or we will give you a reason to do as you're told," the officer fires back, not playing around.

Realizing that he has used up any good graces he may have had, Captain Denis decides to cooperate.

"Based on what I know about Bugs I'd say they will adapt in ways that will exploit our weaknesses like they did with the flyers. If I were to guess, I would say that there is a good chance of them developing some kind of range ability. Possibly shooting some kind of stinger or needle like bit of bone. The other thing that I could see happening soon would be a larger class of Bug, something in the twenty-to-thirty-foot range, with an exoskeleton thick enough to resist small arms fire. There is also the vary real possibility of more Bugs being able to fly. We could even see flight combined with a range capability. Realistically, if they can find a weakness in our forces, they will likely design a Bug to exploit it," the Captain explains.

This makes the officer pause for a moment. Clearly, he is contemplating what areas the Federation might be weak in. After an awkward silence, he finally speaks.

“I think we’ve heard enough for today. Captain it should go without saying, but everything that was discussed here is extremely classified,” the officer says.

“I understand,” the Captain replies.

“If any of this information is shared with someone who doesn’t have the proper clearances, you will be charged with treason and dealt with accordingly,” the officer says, this time more of a threat.

“Yes, I understand,” the Captain replies as he grows a little more nervous.

“Keep in mind that it’s not only your ass on the line here Captain. If you divulge any classified information, we won’t just be coming after you, we will be paying visits to people you work with too. People like that cute little Lieutenant Flores,” the officer says, now making an obvious threat.

Captain Denis sits completely upright at the mention of her name, his nervousness now evident on his face.

"That's right Captain, we know about you two. It sure would be terrible if she had to endure our interrogation because you decided to let some information slip over drinks. Mind you I'm sure a few of my officers would thoroughly enjoy having the pleasure."

At that, the General smashes his gorilla-like fists into his desk.

"That's enough!" he roars. "Captain Denis is one of mine and I don't have traitors in my ranks. He might be a little puke, but he is a valuable asset to the Federation and definitely someone that can be trusted. I will bet my life on that."

He stands up from his desk and puffs up his chest in a primal display of dominance.

"And if any of you jack booting beauty queens, ever threaten one of my soldiers again, in particular, a fine one like Lieutenant Flores, I will rip your head from your tiny neck...."

"General you might want..." the officer tries to interject but is quickly shut down.

"I'm not finished!" the General bellows, and the two men beside him drop their eyes to the floor.

"After I rip your head off, I'm going to cram your weak little body into a trash shoot. Then I'm going to put your head into a duffle bag so I can carry it around, taking it out at my leisure to use as a fuck puppet!" he screams at the officers as his face turns an unnatural shade of purple.

"And if you think that I'm going to give two shits about what your needle dick colleagues might do to me, you're dead fucking wrong. Because those fucking dickless bags of shit don't have a fucking chance of bringing me in alive. I will shit fuck at least ten of you bastards straight to hell before you can bring me down. I was smashing skulls in the jungles of Karaton before you hamster dicked monkey fuckers were even born. Now get the fuck out of my office," the General yells.

Without a word, all three men walk out of the office, too afraid to take their eyes off the floor. General Carmichael sits back in his chair and stares at his desk. Captain Denis was petrified at the verbal assault the General had just unleashed, but he was also honoured that he would have his back like that. Maybe he had got the General all wrong, and he wasn't such a bad guy after all.

"Are you okay Sir?" the Captain asks.

"Fuck you," Carmichael replies.

"I appreciate what you did," the Captain adds.

"Get the fuck out of my office," Carmichael snaps, but in a different tone than before.

This time there was a hint of affection under the harsh words. With a slight smirk and a little bit of pee in his pants, Captain Denis leaves the Generals office.

CHAPTER TWENTY-FIVE

I wake up with a jolt from another bad Bug dream only to find myself lying in a bed that I don't recognize. Wondering what the fuck is going on, I look around the room in a confused daze. Slowly the mental fog begins to clear, and I realize that I'm lying in the bed of an infirmary, though I have no idea where this infirmary is. I can tell by the schythium ceiling that I must be inside a base, but which one. Was it LZ Bravo? If it is, then that means we had won, and more surprisingly, we survived. At least, I survived.

Maybe this wasn't LZ Bravo at all. Perhaps we lost, and LZ Bravo was overrun. It was possible that I was one of the few, or even the only, survivor of a horrible defeat, somehow found still alive among the piles of the dead. I notice how quiet the infirmary is. All that can be heard is the low hum of equipment and quiet voices talking somewhere out of sight. This definitely isn't the sound of an infirmary after a battle.

Normally the air would hang thick with the screams of the dying and maimed as doctors and nurses scattered around, desperately trying to save as many lives as possible. Unlike most battles on this planet, this one being fought at a base meant the injured and maimed actually had a chance of survival. So where were they? Something here wasn't adding up.

I lift my hospital gown to look at where I had been impaled. Expecting to see a bloody bandage, I'm shocked and confused to find a large, fully healed pink scar. Fresh but fully healed. In a complete fog, I try to piece together what happened. I was impaled while fighting, and then I woke up here. My wound is healed, and the infirmary is quiet.

Possibilities fly through my mind, but I can't land on anything solid. It is clear that some time has passed since the battle, but I can't tell. All I want to know at this moment is where I am and how long have I been here.

"Ah, Captain Braddock, welcome back to the land of the living," a young nurse says, walking into the curtained cubicle where I lay.

"Doctor Boulet, our sleeping beauty is awake," she says into the coms unit that sat almost unnoticeable in her ear.

Looking down at me, she blushes as she realizes that now that I am awake, I can hear the nickname they had clearly given me.

"Oh… sorry Sir… I didn't… well, I mean I'm so used to you being… you know. Shit, I'm sorry," she says, completely flustered.

"I'm a cavalry soldier ma'am. I assure you I've heard much worse than sleeping beauty," I say calmly, trying to put her back at ease.

She gives me a gentle smile that reminds me of what it's like to be a human being. There is just something about the sight of a gorgeous woman that can make a man feel like a man, especially after spending countless weeks trapped inside a battle suit. You begin to forget what a beautiful woman looks like. Hell, you forget what anyone looks like. Even though there are plenty of women in the field, everyone looks pretty much the same in battle armour. We're also given drugs to mute sexual impulses because being horny in a suit with no way to release your frustrations is a recipe for disaster.

My gawking is interrupted as the doctor enters my cubicle.

"Hello Captain Braddock. Nice of you to join us. My name is Doctor Boulet and I've been your attending physician for the past month," he says with a pleasant tone uncommon for doctors.

"A month! I've been here for a fucking month?" I snap.

"Yes Sir," he says with a smile.

"How the fuck have I been unconscious for a month from a wound like this," I ask without trying to hide my agitation.

"How much do you understand about bacterial infections?"

"Not much," I reply.

"Okay then let me put it into common terms. When the Bug jacked you in the guts, it left some tiny shit behind. We thought that we cleaned your new hole well enough but because the shit was so small, we missed some of it. It caused an infection that required us to put you into a coma. By the time we pulled our heads out of our dicks long enough to figure out the problem, you were almost dead. It took a while to bring your ass back from the brink," Doctor Boulet says before erupting in a deep guttural laugh.

"How was that for putting it into simple terms? I could almost pass for a military man talking like that, couldn't I Captain?" he asks, beaming with pride.

"Yeah I guess you could," I answer plainly.

I like the doctor, but just finding out that you've been unconscious for a month has a way of putting you in a foul mood. I consider asking about what happened with the battle but decide to wait till I can talk to actual military personnel. The opinions of non-combatants didn't interest me much at this point. So, I put those questions on hold, save one.

"Is this LZ Bravo?" I ask, hesitant of the answer I

might receive.

"Why, yes Captain. Of course it is," he responds, and I feel a little lighter with the answer.

We had won, and the reason that the infirmary was so quiet is that the post-battle chaos had come and gone.

Eager to be gone myself, I ask the doctor, "How long do I have to stay here?"

"Well, we have a few more tests to run and we'll want to monitor you for a little while to make sure all is well. But I would think we'll be able to release you some time tomorrow," he says.

For the next couple of hours, I lay on the bed as various people came in to do different tests. What they were looking for, I had no idea, but they seemed pretty confident that the test was necessary, so I let them work.

The events of the battle kept running through my mind as I wondered how in the hell I got here. Why wasn't I left to die where I lay, and how did the battle end? It's clear that we had won, but what price did we pay for victory? These questions run through my head continuously, only occasionally being interrupted by the thought of the cute nurse that I had seen earlier. I was hoping that she would come back, at least to pay me a visit.

Soon a visitor came, but they were a lot less attractive than the nurse.

"If you aren't the hardest son of a bitch in the galaxy then I don't know who is," Wenjack says as he steps into my cubicle with a grin that goes from ear to ear.

"Your looking plenty alive yourself," I respond.

"It's not through lack of trying," he says, laughing as he comes to sit on a chair beside the bed.

"Nice setup you got here, like a fancy hotel."

"Fuck. Compared to the last few places I've slept this is pretty good. Just feels good to be out of my suit for a change."

"You got that right," he agrees.

"So how're you doing? Did they put all the pieces back in the right place?"

"Think I'm doing pretty good. I feel weirdly strong for laying motionless in a bed for a month."

"The Doctor said they were juicing you with growth hormone and some kind of testosterone derivative that was supposed to prevent muscle loss," he says.

"You talked to the doctor?" I ask.

"Shit Braddock. I've been here every day since it ended. Checking up on you and what not. Lost enough friends lately, you know," he says solemnly.

"Appreciate it," I say, trying to convey my gratitude with the seriousness of my face instead of my words.

I wanted to say more but didn't know what to say.

"Don't mention it," he says.

"So, how bad did it get out there?" I ask, not knowing if I really wanted an answer.

"Bad. We lost close to a thousand men from our ranks. Think total deaths from the assault were closer to a million," he says with the coldness that soldiers learn to adopt when discussing such matters.

"Fucking hell. A million in one day, and we didn't gain anything from it," I say.

"Not a damn thing. The entire battle was a colossal fuck up. They caught us completely off guard. The Federation didn't see the third army coming, couldn't predict the obvious weak point in the waterfall, and had no idea that the Bugs developed the ability to fly. Needless to say, heads rolled afterwards. Fleet Admiral Holliday was court marshaled for incompetence and will likely be executed," Wenjack explains.

"No shit. If that many soldiers died because of his incompetence he should have to share their fate," I say.

"Exactly," he says, nodding his head in agreement. "In all my years in the armed forces, I have never heard of a rank that high actually being held accountable for their actions. It goes to show how serious the Federation is about taking this planet."

"So, what the fuck happened after I fell?" I ask as the curiosity becomes too hard to ignore.

Wenjack pauses for a time before answering my question.

"You fell as we were trying to free up the engineers to clear the outer wall. Well, we fought with everything we had but it wasn't enough. Even with the added fire support from the base we got bogged down and couldn't free up the engineers enough to reach the wall. Our ranks broke up and it turned into an all-out cluster fuck as we were cut off from one another and forced to fight in small groups rather than one single unit."

Wenjack stops talking for a moment to take a deep breath before continuing.

"We were too bogged down to form a charge or a circle. Our ammunition was all but gone, and we were entirely out of options. So, we just fought on. We fought on as the last of the engineers fell. We fought on as the first wall was eventually breached. And we fought on as our numbers were quickly dropping around us. There was nothing we could do, so we just fought.

"Eventually, enough reinforcements had formed up to the south and launched a counterattack with the aid of five newly arrived gunships. We fought as that was happening too. The Bugs climbed the first wall, but the height of the second wall combined with the razor wire pits proved to be too formidable a defence.

"The counterattack came in from the south and Caesar's legion came down from the northeast and sandwiched the Bugs that remained. Somehow a few hundred of us managed to survive and eventually linked back up with what was left of the rest of the Mongols for the first time in a long time," Wenjack explains in an uncharacteristic melancholy tone.

"I can't believe that we actually fucking did it," I say in disbelief. "Though a lot of the credit has to fall on Lieutenant Drummond and his engineers. In a million years I would have never guessed that those guys would turn out to be war heroes."

"No shit. The brave bastards killed a lot of Bugs," Wenjack says.

"Did any of them survive?"

"No. They fought to the last. Damn shame too, I would have liked to buy a few of them a drink for that stunt," he answers.

"Damn shame. I remember the first time I met that guy. He was acting like a war fan boy, asking questions about what it's like to make a heroic last stand. I gave him the hard truth of it, but that crazy son of a bitch had to go and see for himself."

"Crazy stupid son of a bitch," Wenjack added.

I think for a moment about what those engineers did, and it makes me proud to have shared a battlefield with them.

I adjust myself in the hospital bed and sit up a little straighter.

"I'm almost afraid to ask but."

Wenjack cuts me off, "What about the other two assaults?"

"Yeah well if the death toll was around a million they mostly had to be somewhere else because we didn't have that many to spare on our end," I say.

"No, I guess we didn't. To be honest the south held out like a hot damn. The fortifications that were built in the canyons were substantial and heavily occupied. They repelled the assault without much trouble. It was probably the only part of our defenses that worked like it should have," Wenjack says.

"Another credit to Drummond and his boys," I say.

"Yeah, I guess so. Hadn't thought about that," Wenjack says.

"There we were thinking that we were riding in to save the day, and little did we know some fucking engineers had saved it first. Its all for the best though. I could go a lifetime without having to retake those fucking canyons," I say.

Wenjack laughs, "You and me both."

"And what about the west?" I ask.

"The west? Well, they didn't do as well as they hoped. Most of the casualties were on that front," he says.

"What the fuck happened? I saw the plans and it looked like the odds were going to be stacked in our favor," I say.

"They would have been if things went according to plan, but…" he says, pausing slightly.

"But when the fuck does that happen?" I say.

"Exactly. First of all, nobody ever predicted those flying pricks to show up an tie up the base, so that was the first monkey cock in the gears," he says.

"I think the saying is monkey wrench," I say.

"Don't think so. Monkeys don't use wrenches, but the little bastards are always playing with their cocks," he says, and I honestly can't tell if he's joking or not.

"Anyway, the base being tied up was a minor issue. The biggest problem was that the Bugs out planned us. Our fearless leaders thought they were so smart with their hammer and anvil strategy, but that plan had one major problem," he says.

"Which was?"

"As we swung our hammer, we failed to realize that they were swinging an even bigger hammer of their own. Our troops rushed in, eager to crush the enemy from behind. Problem was that the Bugs had another force waiting to do the same to us. They basically trapped our trap," he explained.

"How the fuck didn't they see another army that big?" I ask.

"How did they miss a couple hundred million up in the high country? Or not realize how the waterfall wasn't as secure as they hoped? Maybe they were blinded by ego, or maybe it was just plane old incompetence. But I couldn't tell you which. All I know is they missed them and good soldiers died because of it," he says.

"No shit. How many of the dead were Mongols?" I ask even though what I really want to know is if we still have our legion.

"About a thousand of them were," he says.

"Shit," I respond in quiet frustration. "Add that to the thousand from our company and the few hundred that died in the stockpile raids and we're at what? Seventy-five hundred?"

"About that," he answers.

"Better than some I guess, but those losses are going to be felt. In more ways than one," I say.

"Like I said, it was a shit show out there. General Jaxxon led the charge as they brought the hammer down, and from what I hear, it was quite the charge. They smashed the Bugs up pretty good. If things went according to plan, the losses would have been relatively low, especially for cavalry units. Their charge tore massive gaps in the enemy's lines. The problems started when that second army hit our so-called hammer from behind. They caught the slower infantry off guard and hit them before they could form a solid line. To make matters worse, all of the best troops were far away at the front of the line, following behind the cavalry. The rear was made up mostly of the reserves, and they didn't stand a chance.

"Jaxxon circled back around, leading the massive charge around the flanks of our own forces in order to hit the newly arrived enemy in it's flank. It was in this move that he started losing people. The battle degraded into a cluster fuck and then eventually into an all-out brawl," he says.

"What a fucking mess. Did the line hold at least?" I ask.

"It did. That line was made up of rows of pill boxes and sentry guns running about three kilometers deep. It was also reinforced with mortars and artillery, a handful of Goliath units, and heavy infantry including our old friend Lieutenant Kato. Who won himself a medal or two during the battle," he says.

"Lieutenant Kato? I guess promotions don't come as quick over there as they do here," I say.

"Lucky them," he says.

"They should have just focused on reinforcing the line. The hammer and anvil plan just exposed our troops and made them vulnerable," I say.

"Yup. The Fleet Admiral tried to blame the lack of

air support, but nobody bought that argument. He fucked up and good people died. That was the only outcome anyone could focus on," he says.

"It's the only one that matters," I add as I begin to remember the faces of those we lost.

Doctor Boulet comes back in with another nurse.

"Visiting hours are over Lieutenant Wenjack, but your friend here will be released tomorrow so you can see him then," the doctor says.

"Shit Doc, can't he stay up a little longer? He's not even tired," Wenjack says in his best attempt at impersonating a small child.

It is clear by their interaction that Wenjack and the good doctor had gotten to know each other during my time here. I feel thankful to have a friend like Wenjack who would check on me every day.

"Rules are rules," the doctor says.

"Okay mom, I'm leaving. I'll see you tomorrow, Braddock," Wenjack says and then makes an exaggerated bow to the doctor as he gets up to leave.

"Wait," I call after him.

"How the fuck did I get here?"

"Your hunter friend brought you in."

"Dominique?"

"You got any other hunter friends? She scooped you up when you fell and rode off with Sleipnir following close behind. I've got no idea why they would have opened the gates to let her in during an assault, but that girl's got serious pull with some powerful people, I guess," he says with a smile and walks away.

CHAPTER TWENTY-SIX

Startled awake, I see a beautiful woman standing beside my bed. She clearly isn't a nurse, and I don't recognize her from anywhere else.

"Put these on and come with me," she says, throwing me a set of infirmary scrubs.

I can tell instantly from the voice that it's Dominique. She is even more beautiful than I imagined her to be. Even though she was wearing standard-issue Federation coveralls, her body still had noticeable curves that eluded to something incredibly exciting beneath that cloth. I stand up, swapping my gown for the scrubs she had given me, and then we sneak out. Quickly and quietly, we make our way through the infirmary.

Eventually, we find a Café that is designated for infirmary staff. The sign on the door calling it a Café might have been a bit generous. It is little more than a storage room with an automatic barista machine, commonly referred to as an automatic BM because the coffee that it produced was straight shit. Small as the room is, it's private and has a hollow window that lets us pretend we are someplace other than here. Dominique grabs us a table in front of the window.

The window is set to an underwater view with various fish and sea creatures swimming by. These underwater views always weirded me out for some reason, but Dominique thankfully changes it to a deep red Tantorian sunset.

I grab us some coffees from the automatic BM and bring them to the table. Sitting down, I look out the window and take a sip of the coffee. Sure enough, it tastes like shit. I would have much preferred a cup of grease because at least grease had a strong flavour to it. This coffee tasted like one part shit and four parts water, but coffee was coffee. After being in a suit for so long, it just feels good to drink something, and I enjoy the moment.

We sit for a while staring out the window before it occurs to me that neither of us has said anything since we left my cubicle in the infirmary.

"It's good to see you," I say, unable to come up with anything better.

She looks at me sincerely and says, "It's good to see you too Braddock. You're looking a lot better than the last time I saw you."

I wonder if she had checked up on me since she brought me back but decide not to ask. Even if she had, I doubt she would admit it.

"How are you feeling," she asks.

"You know what, I feel pretty good for lying in bed for a month. I'm definitely looking forward to getting a little

R&R, "I say, and a strange look crosses her face that I can't discern.

"I guess a little bit of a coma can do wonders for a guy," she says with a small but beautiful smile.

"Yeah, I guess so," I say with a laugh.

"I've always wondered, what's it like being in a coma? Do you dream?"

I think about the dreams that I've been having and wish that my answer was different.

"Yeah, you dream. Wish like hell that I didn't, but I did."

She looks at me with an understanding gaze and asks, "Soldiers dreams?"

"I wish. As terrible as those dreams are I understand them. It's important for a soldier to see the faces of those who have died and even more importantly, the ones they have killed. It keeps it all in perspective. I think of those nightmares as being visited by the ghosts of the fallen. They come to us in our dreams so that we remember them. Remember that they were once soldiers, sons, daughters. People who had dreams, desires, loves, and losses. It's important to remember them."

"That's a pretty well-adjusted view of the matter,"

she says.

"It's something Wenjack said to me that just kind of stuck. Hang around with that guy long enough and some of him rubs off on you."

"I think I'll leave the rubbing off to the two of you," she says, and we both laugh.

"So," she says, her face hardening. "If the soldiers dreams don't bother you than what kind of nightmares could?"

"I didn't say that they didn't bother me, I said that I understand them and accept them. They still tear me up inside, but I realize that it's necessary," I say.

"You can't dodge the question Braddock, because I'll just keep on asking it," she says.

I take a long sip of coffee and look out the window at the surreal sunset, thinking about how I wanted to answer.

"I keep having dreams where I'm a Bug. In every dream, I'm always doing some ordinary activity like gathering food or going for water, boring shit like that. Normally there are other Bugs with me that always feel close to me, like family but a little different. Anyway, as I go about my day, at some point, we get attacked by the Federation, sometimes by air and sometimes by land, but it's always a brutal slaughter.

"I watch these other Bugs, the ones that feel like family, being cut down, burned, and blown up in front of me and its terrifying. Sometimes I fight and other times I run, but I'm always afraid and it always hurts when the others die. Most of the times I'm killed, but sometimes I survive and just walk amongst the corpses, feeling the tremendous pain of losing so many of my loved ones," I say.

I look Dominique in the eyes, trying to figure out what she thinks about what I'm saying.

"The dreams feel so real, almost like they're memories and not dreams at all. I'm also never myself in the dreams, not only am I in a Bugs body but I'm in its mind too. I have no control over anything and I'm just stuck in the Bugs head like an observer. It feels like I'm living the memories of dead bugs," I say.

"But Bugs don't care about each other, they don't have friends and are only loyal to their Queens. If you kill one right in front of another, they barely even react," she says with a little anger in her voice.

"Yeah, that's the confusing part. I know that I'm projecting human emotions onto creatures that don't have them, but why? Is it just the stress of the job finally getting to me or something else? Maybe some part of me feels like we're the same as the Bugs," I say.

"We are not the same as those beasts," she snaps.

"I don't mean the same in the way you think I do. What I mean is the Federation wants something, and a certain amount of Bugs and soldiers have to die to get it. Like this planet for example. The Federation wants it and they need to kill a lot of Bugs to get it, but they also need to kill a lot of soldiers. Every life that's lost on this planet is lost because the Federation decides it's worth it. We're the same in the way that we live and die on the Federations orders," I say.

"You think it's always the Federations decision? Don't you think the Bugs made a choice when they attacked us first?" she asks.

"Of course, they did, and I'm definitely not saying that they're the victims here. They started this mess and the responsibility for this war is on them. But by picking a fight with the Federation they were punching way above their weight class, and that's part of my point. Once they started this war, the fate of their species was doomed. They never had a chance of winning. They can win battles and maybe even capture the odd planet, but they can't win. That puts the control of this war in the Federations hands, which means they make the decisions of who dies and when."

Dominique takes a sip of her coffee and thinks about what I've just said.

"I guess in that context I can follow your thinking," she says. "But I don't understand why that bothers part of you to the point of your subconscious creating dreams like that. Maybe it's something else giving you those dreams."

Not listening to the last part of her comment, I carry on.

"Time after time I've been thrown into situations under prepared, under supplied, and with little or no support. Placed in situations where a lot of good soldiers die because someone deemed it necessary. I've watched people that have been like family to me ripped apart before my eyes and I'm mostly okay with that. I'm a cavalry soldier and everyone I serve with knows the score and what we signed up for. And to be honest, most cavalry soldiers probably wouldn't fit in civilian life anyway. We belong in combat, it's part of who we are and I accept that," I say.

I reach across the table and take her hands in mine as I look into her eyes.

"The part that bothers me, the part that tears me up inside, has nothing to do with me. It has to do with the people who don't know the score. The innocent lives that are thrown into the shit and die for reasons they don't truly understand," I say.

"The only ones that are thrown into battle are

soldiers, people who signed up voluntarily to fight for the Federation. When these people die it's no different than when your people do," she says.

"I disagree. A lot of these people are kids fresh out of boot. They haven't yet learned what it means to be a soldier. They haven't learned what war really is. They sign up at eighteen and think they are serving the Federation and protecting the human race from the monsters that threaten it. Everyone tells them how they're going to be heroes and what a great thing they're doing. Of course, they listen because they're young and dumb.

"Then it's off to training where they think they're going to be transformed into hardened warriors, not knowing that only those deemed good enough receive any real training. If you're one of the masses selected for regular forces, you're given little more than the basics. Then you're given some outdated equipment and shipped off to some fucking backwater shit hole where," I stop for a moment to compose myself.

"Where you're thrown into combat and used as cannon fodder. Because what nobody told you. What nobody ever tells you, is that your only purpose in life is to soak up casualties as the real soldiers get to work. You're no longer someone's son or daughter, you're just a number, a statistic. And if you were unlucky enough to end up here, you're just one of the millions that have been used up. And for what? Because the Federation wanted this resource so bad that they couldn't wait to make better plans. They couldn't figure out how to properly fight on this planet. We don't even have air support for fuck sakes. But it doesn't matter because we have a galaxy full of young life to burn up," I say in complete frustration as I try to hold back the flood of emotions that are rushing up.

I'm on the verge of crying, something I haven't done since I was a child. What was happening to me? I've never experienced an emotional outburst like this before. Had all of this shit piled up and is just now spilling out? Or am I finally beginning to lose my shit?

I look at Dominique as she looks soft and empathetic back at me. Maybe it was her. Maybe being this close to such a strong woman is allowing me to be comfortable enough to express the things that soldiers aren't supposed to. Maybe it was that for the first time in my life, I had actually talked about something I was feeling. Whatever it is, I don't like it.

"I just don't see the point in it all," I say.

She looks thoughtfully at me for a while before speaking.

"Let me tell you why I fight, and then you can tell me whether or not you see a point in this war," she says.

"Alright," I say.

"I was raised by my grandfather. My parents died before I could remember. My grandfather was a tracker and a hunter. Not like me, an actual hunter. He would travel different systems tracking and hunting various species for different clients. Once in a while at first, but more often, as I grew, he would take me with him on hunts. Teach me things here and there.

"He was a master of his trade and had a lot to teach. I was eager to learn. Over time I got pretty good myself. I got so good in fact that I took over the business when he passed on" she stops a moment as if remembering something that she doesn't share, something just for her.

"Time went on, and eventually, I met a man while on a job in the Vartarn system. He was one of those men that still built things with his hands. A man of brass and wood in an age of plastanium. Eventually, we married and moved to Dorisan in order to build ourselves a homestead life.

"It was a quiet planet that was perfect for supporting human life. So, we built a house and a little farm. We were the most cliché homestead family, except I would still take off around the galaxy on hunting jobs from time to time. As things tend to go, I got pregnant, and we had a beautiful little boy.

"He was the most perfect thing I had ever seen. So beautiful and smart, and playful. He had a laugh that would make you want to cry because you just couldn't stand how innocent and pure it was. The kind of kid that would impress you just by being alive," a faint smile grew on her face as she talked.

"Whenever he was happy, he would raise his arms and step side to side doing a little happy dance," she raises her arms in an attempt to mimic the dance as she speaks before turning more serious.

"I don't know if you know what it's like to have someone that you love so completely that it feels like they are a part of you. Like they're a physical representation of all your love and humanity, because that's what it feels like to have a child. And my son was all that and more. He was, everything. My entire universe. And the three of us were so happy, just living. That place was paradise for us. But nothing pure can last in this life and eventually the vail of happiness came down and let the darkness in," her face turns as hard as her schythium armour as she speaks.

She stares ahead as if looking at something far away that only she can see.

"Then one day they came. I don't know where they came from or how they got there, but one day while I was out hunting a merento buck, I saw them. A horde of disgusting

Bugs.

"I ran back to our home faster than I had ever run before. When I got home, I told my husband what was coming and together we quickly gathered our son and what essential items we could carry. The closest town with access to a space port was in the direction that the Bugs had been coming from and I wagered it was a graveyard by that point. So, we ran into the mountains. I figured that in those mountains we could evade the Bugs, until help showed up."

She was fighting hard now to hold back the rush of emotion that I could see welling up in her eyes.

"For two weeks, we ran and hid in those mountains. Any time that wasn't spent running for our lives, we spent trying to comfort our son. He was constantly afraid and confused, too young and innocent to understand what was happening. We had to watch as our son went from the happy kid with an infectious laugh to a quiet introvert who never spoke. It was as if we were watching his innocence die a little more each day, and it broke our hearts. Those were the hardest two weeks of my life, and they felt like they would never end."

She stops talking and takes a couple deep breaths as she tries to hold herself together.

"Then they ended, and I wished with every part of

my being that I could have them back."

Tears well up in her eyes, just one sad blink away from running down her cheeks.

"Up until that point in my life I hadn't had any firsthand experience with Bugs and I didn't know how clever they can be. I was careful to make sure that we always chose terrain that gave us more than one direction to run in case things went bad. I thought that I had covered our bases, but I was wrong. While crossing over a mountain path we were ambushed. I fired on the Bugs, but I was only armed with my semiautomatic hunting rifle, and I couldn't shoot fast enough to fight them off. I watched my son and husband die that day. They died because I couldn't protect them."

Tears now stream down her face, and her voice becomes unsteady.

"I had to watch as those savage beast tore my son's body apart like it was nothing. My entire world, my heart and soul were being destroyed before my eyes and there was nothing I could do to stop it. Those beasts took the most beautiful and innocent thing in existence and slaughtered him like it was nothing. They killed my son! And for what? Nothing, that's what! Just because they're a mindless plague that won't rest until everything that's good and pure in this universe is destroyed."

Tears still streaming, her sadness turns to anger.

"I managed to escape by sliding down the face of a nearby cliff and even though I wanted to die, and believe me, every part of my being wanted to die. Wanted to join my son and husband. I couldn't. I had to carry on and avenge them. I had to stop this from happening to more families. In that moment I promised them both that I wouldn't rest until every last fucking one of those crawling, murdering, mindless fucks were dead. I spent the next six months using everything that my grandfather had taught me to get my vengeance. Building traps and laying hit and run ambushes. Eventually I killed every last one of those fucking beasts."

Her voice levels out, and I see her thousand-yard stair set back onto her face.

"I eventually found a town that had access to a communicator and sent up a distress call. It had turned out that the Bugs hit the small planet so hard and fast that a distress call hadn't yet been sent. I was the only one left. Eventually the Federation arrived, and I boarded a transport for the nearest station. Word got around the ship about how I had taken on a horde of Bugs with nothing but a semiautomatic rifle and some old tricks and eventually someone from Intelligence came to see me. He told me that if I signed a contract with them, he would guaranty that I would be given all the equipment and opportunity necessary to take the fight to the Bugs. So, I signed the contract and never looked back," she says as her gaze falls back to me.

Grabbing my hand, she looks me dead in the eyes.

"The reason I fight is because there are millions of families out there that have shared the same fate as mine. So, if eighteen-year-old kids, who signed up to fight under their own free will, have to be used as cannon fodder so that innocent children can live, then I'm okay with that. Maybe those soldiers didn't fully understand what they were signing up for, but they still made a choice. A choice that my son never got to make. So, I fully support any sacrifice that needs to be made if it means ridding the galaxy of the Bug plague," she says, leaving me speechless.

I want to tell her that I'm sorry for what happened to her family, but despite my wanting it, nothing I say will make anything better. So, I say nothing and instead just sit and think about what she had said.

"That's a hell of a good reason to fight," is all I end up saying.

We sit there for a while longer in silence, drinking coffee and looking at the holographic sunset out the window.

Eventually, she says, "You should go back," and I nod in agreement.

As I get up to leave, I turn to her, "When will I see you again?"

She just smiles at me and says, "Whenever I feel like it."

I smile back at her and leave the Café.

Laying in my hospital bed, I can't sleep because all I can think about is what Dominique had told me. I had never considered things from that perspective before, and the more I think about it, the more things make sense. The more this war makes sense. I had been so busy thinking about the lives of the people fighting that I had forgotten who we were fighting for.

I think back to the words of that old poet who said, "theirs not to reason why, theirs but to fight and die," and I finally understand. Understand that he was wrong because he was writing about combat that he didn't really know anything about. Ours is to reason why, because it is in that reasoning that we understand why. Why we fight and why we must die.

CHAPTER TWENTY-SEVEN

After months of patrols, battles, and being in a coma, I am finally out of the infirmary and getting some time off. I decide that the first thing I'm going to do is hit the mess hall. Since I made officer mere hours before leaving on my last patrol, I hadn't yet had a chance to go to an officer's mess. After all the shit I had gone through since dropping on this planet, I figured I deserved a decent meal.

Upon entering the officer's mess, I am struck with a site that may have appeared on par with the average restaurant to civilians, but to a soldier fresh out of the field, it looks like a slice of heaven. Instead of the long chow line, there were waiters, and the long tables and benches were replaced with tables and chairs. The tables even had tablecloths on them. The plastanium walls were about as ugly as they always were, but they were covered in large holo-windows like the one in the Café. The windows were set to a seaside view on a planet I didn't recognize. If I had known that officer life had this in store, I would have been more enthusiastic about my promotions.

Looking around the room like a lost child, I eventually see Wenjack sitting at a table with a group of Mongol officers.

I begin walking towards them when a voice yells out,

"It's Captain Braddock," and the entire mess hall breaks out into a standing ovation that hits me like a sucker punch.

I stand dumbstruck, not sure of what is happening. Wenjack gets up from his table and walks over to pat me on the shoulder.

"Oh, I forgot to tell you that everyone's calling you the hero of the Federation for saving the base," he says with a deep laugh before leading me to the table.

I sit down to a series of mocking "oohs and awes," from the other Mongol officers before we all break out in a laugh.

"Thanks guys. It feels good to be back from the dead," I say.

Looking around the table, I see the familiar faces of my fellow Mongols, some of which I hadn't seen since just after the drop. In a bid to look like an actual officer and not just a puffed-up NCO who had received too many field promotions, I make a point to acknowledge my superiors at the table.

"Colonel Hou, Major Paterson," I say with a nod.

"Good to see you well Captain," the Major says while Colonel Hou settles for returning my nod.

I notice that Rodger is present, having traded his Sergeant's chevrons for a shiny new Lieutenant's Bar.

"Lieutenant Rodger, it's good to see you at the officers table," I say, acknowledging his promotion.

"Thank you, Sir, I only wish I had gotten here through better circumstances," he says.

"Don't we all," Major Paterson says.

"I'm not sure what circumstances could be better than through excelling in combat. After all this isn't a choir group. People die in war and there is nothing but honor in replacing them when they do," Colonel Hou says.

If that statement came from someone of lower rank, it would have been met by a few objections, but since Colonel Hou was a Colonel, he could get away with saying damn near anything he wanted. Apart from rank, he also had over thirty years of combat experience behind him and a record that intimidated almost everyone.

"Well, I'm just glad to have one more of our ranks back in fighting shape. Even if he is as ugly as Captain Braddock here," Lieutenant Wenjack says, trying to bring the mood up a bit.

"Thanks, Wenjack," I say with a smile, and I'm reminded of how nice it is to see people's faces when you talk to them.

There is so much lost when you're constantly forced to communicate through helmets. You don't really notice the importance of facial expressions until they're gone. It's amazing how far a smile can go towards making you feel like an actual human.

The waiter comes by to bring a pot of grease, and the smell of the thick coffee sludge makes my mouth water. I'm starting to think that the high caffeine content makes the stuff incredibly addicting because I can't get enough of it, despite the fact that it tastes like shit. The waiter also brings me a menu, and I marvel at the choice of food. Not that there was a lot of food to choose from, but the mere fact that we had a choice was a luxury that I hadn't experienced in a long time. I order the meet stake with a few sides. The steak being classified as meat stake didn't bother me because, after months without solid food, it could have been Bug meat for all I fucking care.

"So, who wants to get me caught up on what I've missed in the past month?" I ask the table as I pour myself a cup of grease.

"You got to skip out on your duties in regards to restructuring the legion. We had to shuffle around a lot of troops and give a lot of promotions," Major Paterson says.

"I'm sorry I missed all that Sir," I say with a laugh.

"Yes Captain, I'm sure you are," the Major says sarcastically.

"It's obscene how much paperwork is required to kill things. It almost makes me envy the Bugs. They don't have to do paperwork and shuffle troops. All they have to do is fight," the Colonel says sourly.

"Yeah, but they don't get to sit in fancy mess halls and eat mystery meat, do they Sir," Wenjack says.

"They also have to fight crazy bastards like Braddock here," Lieutenant Rodger adds.

"That's why I said I almost envy them," the Colonel says and then laughs as if he'd just told a joke.

I don't really get what is funny, so I just smile and nod.

All of a sudden, I'm startled by a smack on my back and hear, "How's it going hero?"

The voice belonged to Captain Moreno, a long-time veteran Mongol officer that I had served under multiple times.

"It's been a while."

"Yeah, no shit it has. Good to see you're not dead,"

he says with a big grin.

"Yeah, you too," I say.

"Hell, last time I saw this guy he was just a regular old Sergeant getting ready for this drop and now he's a war hero with a chain of medals down to his dick," he says, and everybody at the table laughs except for the Colonel.

The Colonel only laughs at his own jokes or in the face of a good fight. I think PTSD has messed up his brain over the years.

"I don't think two medals constitutes a chain, Moreno," I say.

"Two? You were at four last time I checked. Did you guys not tell him about the ceremony?" Moreno asks the table.

"It hadn't come up yet. The guys only been out of the infirmary a few hours," Wenjack says.

Wondering what the fuck they were talking about, I ask the obvious question, "What ceremony?"

"Well, if you're going to keep asking about it, I guess I can fill you in," Moreno says with a chuckle and a wink.

Moreno pulls up a chair and takes a place at the table.

"About a week after the battle the Federation

announced that they were going to hold a memorial ceremony for all the soldiers that had died defending the base," Moreno says.

"Really?" I ask, surprised because it was the first time in my life that they've ever done that.

"Oh yeah. It was a really big deal too. They had us all form up in ranks outside the walls of the base and they erected this massive fucking platform for the New Fleet Admiral and the other top brass. We're talking a huge stage covered with flags and giant monitors. The entire thing was ridiculous because it could have been done safer and easier in VR. Anyway, they had military bands with drummers and bag pipers and everything. It was intense," Moreno says.

"It was pretty impressive," Wenjack adds.

"Fuckin rights it was," Moreno says.

"Anyway, Fleet Admiral Schuurman and the other top brass all gave speeches about the importance of this campaign and the sacrifices made by the brave soldiers and shit like that. The band played music and we had a moment of silence for the dead. Then they began the largest medal ceremony in history. They started with giving medals to the living and I think pretty much everyone at this table got one. Then they gave medals to the dead. Stopping to tell stories about how different people made the ultimate sacrifice and what not," Moreno says.

"Did Corporal Crang get one?" I ask as I remember him turning himself into a human bomb to hold back the Bugs.

"Yeah, they gave him the medal of honor for that stunt, and they told the story of how he carried a bomb into the heart of the enemies ranks and made the ultimate sacrifice," he says, putting added emphasis on the words ultimate sacrifice.

"I don't know what he did, but he wasn't carrying a bomb," I say.

"No, but they didn't want to broadcast what he actually did because they don't want people knowing how to do it," the Colonel says.

"And what exactly did he do?" I ask.

"He stacked up a few laser cartridges on top of his Wargon's power supply and then fired through them. Doing so, sends a massive charge into the power supply of the Wargon suit and results in one hell of a blast," Major Paterson says.

"Anyway, back to what I was saying."

"Did Lieutenant Drummond get recognized?" I ask.

"Yes, for fuck sakes. He got fucking recognized. Now can you shut the fuck up for a few seconds so I can talk,"

Moreno snaps.

I knew from experience that it was next to impossible for anyone to stop the Captain from talking, so I gesture with my hands for him to continue.

“Thank you. The Fleet Admiral did a whole speech about Lieutenant Drummond and his engineers, talking about how they were the perfect embodiment of honour and bravery. He then awarded Lieutenant Drummond the medal of Valor. Then they cut to a scene on the big monitors that they recorded earlier.

“The Fleet Admiral and the other brass were standing at your bedside with General Jaxxon. Jaxxon gave a speech about what you did and how if it wasn’t for you the base would have been overrun. The Fleet Admiral said a bunch of stuff kissing your ass and talking about how great you are. Then he awarded you a purple heart for your injuries and the order of the Federation for your contribution to the battle,” Moreno says.

“No shit,” I say, surprised because the order of the Federation was the highest honour that was ever given.

Less than a hundred have been given out in Federation history.

“Yeah, it seems like every time you do anything the

Federation gives you a medal for it. Did the General give you a medal for taking a dump this morning?" Wenjack jokes.

Colonel Hou slams his fist into the table.

"Don't you ever speak of the General like that!"

I think back to my earlier thought about the Colonel having too much PTSD.

Ignoring the outburst, Moreno continues.

"Anyway, the Fleet Admiral went on to make a big deal out of the things you did and he ended up referring to you as the hero of the Federation. Since then you've been a popular topic of conversation around the base. Not for Mongols though, because we all know that you aren't shit," he says, smiling and slaps me on the shoulder again.

"What was the purpose of them doing all of that? It seems like there were more important things to do than hold a massive ceremony, and outside the gates no less. The entire thing sounds like a scene from a holofilm," I say.

"The massiveness of it was the point. It was all about image," Wenjack says.

"It was about recruitment," Major Paterson corrects him.

Not seeing the connection, I ask, "Sir could you

elaborate on that? You know, for those of us that have been in comas."

"You see, Captain, the Federation has substantially stepped up its recruiting efforts since they found out about this planet. Our invasion force was just the tip of the spear, designed to establish a proverbial beachhead. Now that the LZ bases have been completed, they are working on building a series of FOBs. As the FOBs are finished, they will be filled with the next wave of soldiers. This process won't be complete until the entire planet is covered with fully staffed FOBs.

"With the devastating hit that we took during the assault on this base, Fleet Admiral Schuurman and his new administration decided to further increase their recruitment efforts. His goal is to hit a billion new recruits from around the galaxy within the next year," Major Paterson says.

A billion recruits sounds like a ridiculous amount, but after considering that they have over half the galaxy to recruit from, that's a relatively small amount of the population.

"Taking charge after the battle, Fleet Admiral Schuurman realized that he could use the losses we took to gain a boost in recruits," The Major explains.

"Taking advantage of the deaths of our brothers and sisters like a scumbag," Moreno says.

"You mean like an intelligent leader. Our people died defending the base. Nothing was gained by their deaths. However, by the Fleet Admiral portraying the events the way he did, he made their deaths count for something. He made their deaths into a tragedy that was caused by the Bug's blind hunger for human lives. In doing so, he created something for humanity to rally against. An incident that people will want to avenge.

"Hordes of young men and women will join up to the motto of remember the Battle for Bravo. And by portraying those of us who fought in the battle as heroes, he has given young soldiers people to look up to. They will be inspired by the bravery of Lieutenant Drummond and the fearless tenacity of Captain Braddock and his Mongol riders. The Fleet Admiral has done what great leaders have since the beginning of our recorded history. Nothing more," The Major says.

"Wow, Major, you're surprisingly insightful for a guy who rides around on a Wargon, stabbing giant Bugs with a hot stick," Wenjack says as everybody erupts into laughter.

"Whatever helps bring this war to a close faster is fine by me," I say.

"The sooner we kill every Bug bastard in the galaxy the better. As long as I get a little R&R first," I say with a smile.

Everyone at the table starts exchanging awkward looks with one another, and I feel like there is something that I don't know.

"Are you guys going to tell me what's going on or just keep looking at each other like a bunch of schoolgirls?" I ask.

"We thought you knew," Wenjack says.

"Knew what," I hesitantly ask.

"Braddock we're shipping out in eighteen hours," Colonel Hou says bluntly.

My jaw drops.

"Fuck off. There's no fucking way. I've been looking forward to some R&R for months and now we're going back after one fucking day?" I say in complete frustration.

"The Federation gave us a month of R&R. It's not their problem that you slept through it," Colonel Hou says.

"I didn't sleep through it. I was in a fucking coma because I got leg fucked by a Bug while saving this base from annihilation. They go around talking about me being a hero and then give me one day of R&R."

"Welcome to the Cavalry son," Moreno says with a smile.

I decide to stop complaining because it isn't going to do any good. No matter how pissed off I am, it isn't going to change anything.

"So, what's the mission?"

"Oh you'll like this," Moreno says.

"Like what?"

"We don't know what the mission is yet. The powers that be are being vary quiet about it," Wenjack says.

"We don't need to know what the mission is because we know what our orders are. Tomorrow we're going to suit up and board some dropships that will take us to the Knoll," Colonel Hou says.

"The FOB built on that stockpile we cleared out?" I ask.

"Yes. Once there, we're going to link up with General Jaxxon and about twenty other cavalry legions. Then we'll wait for further orders. Seem easy enough?" the Colonel asks.

"Yes Sir."

Of course, it seemed easy because they weren't telling us anything. Things always seemed easy before you get the shitty details that make it hard. I'm not overly thrilled about going back to that valley, but the thought of having two hundred thousand cavalry soldiers in one place at the same time is an exciting prospect.

"With that many cavalry in one place there must be something big happening," I say.

"Something big alright. We just don't know what," Moreno says.

"Its not just cavalry that's being assembled either. We've been seeing a shit load of new recruits and even new legions showing up every day. The dropships have been running nonstop bringing soldiers down to the planet and then moving them around. Whatever is coming, it must need a lot of bodies," Lieutenant Rodger says.

"General Jaxxon has been in meetings and briefings for the past week straight, and from what I hear, so have the other Generals. This is just between us, but I heard rumors that some guy in applied sciences found something big," Major Paterson says in a low, quiet tone.

"Big how?" I ask.

"That is all I know," the Major replies.

"I've never seen a mobilization like this before. It's massive and they aren't taking many precautions to hide it. They're flying dropships low and everywhere in plane sight,"

Moreno says.

"They're flying low under the cloud cover so that our fighters and gunships can cover them in case they run into flyers," the Colonel says.

"Oh, don't forget about the Goliath suits," Lieutenant Rodger says.

"What Goliath suits," I ask.

"They dropped a thousand suits the other day," Rodger says.

"A thousand," I say as if somehow repeating it would make it sound more real.

"They only dropped fifty when we first hit LZ Bravo," I say.

"Like we said, this is big," Wenjack adds.

"Any guesses on what's going on? Someone must have some kind of idea," I ask.

"There are lots of ideas but most of them are shit. The best guess that anyone with half a brain has come up with is that this is payback for the assault. We're taking the fight to the Bugs in a big way. Whether that means a direct assault on a newly discovered target, or we're going to form a line a hundred kilometers long and sweep the planet, is anyone's guess. All we know is its big, and the Federation is putting every resource they have on it," Moreno says.

"Well as pissed as I am about only having one day R&R, I'm ready for a little payback of my own."

Wenjack gives me a questioning look raising one eyebrow.

"Is that right?"

"Hell yeah," I say.

"Hmm, that's a change. Before the assault you were talking about how board you were getting with the Bug war, and you felt like you were just going through the motions. Sounded like you were running seriously low on fucks to give. Now you're all fired up and ready to get some. What changed?"

I think about my conversation with Dominique from the night before. I think about what happened to her family, and I have to choke back a wave of emotions. In a single moment, I feel everything from sorrow to rage, and I don't know if I should cry or put my fist through the table. The wave passes quickly, and everything levels out into a clear sense of purpose.

"I guess you could say I found a new perspective," I say in the steadiest voice I can find.

Hell yeah, I've found a new perspective, and not only am I ready to fight this war. I'm ready to end the Bug's entire fucking species. They failed to kill me, and now they better watch out because I'm coming for them.

CHAPTER TWENTY-EIGHT

If it wasn't for the knoll in the middle of the valley, I might not have recognized the place. The miners had completely levelled the entire valley surrounding the knoll and carved a series of inset walkways and gun platforms into the cliffs. The changes made the place look like it was machined out of a solid piece of dull grey metal, sharing no resemblance to the jagged hell that it used to be. The knoll had undergone substantial changes itself. Its natural uneven entrance had been squared off, and a heavy plastanium blast door was fitted in place. The rough sides of the knoll were smoothed, and platforms have been cut into the schythium where sentry guns now lay.

I'm amazed how the miners had completely transformed this place in a mere six weeks. What was once an evil mess of a landscape is now a near-impenetrable fortress. If any Bugs manage to break through the substantial perimeter security, they will find themselves trapped inside the killing field that the valley now is. Since the base lay encased in impenetrable schythium, the guns that littered the high valley walls could unload a hellish barrage into the valley without endangering the soldiers inside.

As we dismount the dropships, I see the largest assembly of cavalry that I have ever seen in one place. We have become used to seeing large assemblies of troops on this planet, but this was something else. Nearly two hundred thousand cavalry almost completely covered the valley floor, and more were still rolling in. Each legion is lined up in perfect rank and file. Even the Bugs with their hive minds couldn't match the organization and precision that I now saw. An ocean of armour was preparing for war.

Our legion forms up on the side of the main road that leads to the tunnel out of the valley. The road is the only place on the valley floor that has been left unmanned. As we form up in our ranks, it occurs to me that this is the first time our legion has been together since the Bug highway during the initial drop. It feels good to ride up and down our ranks, seeing ten thousand Mongol insignias all in one place. Especially since many of the insignias now had medals underneath them, earned through hard battles fought. So far on Excalibur, the Mongols have been the most highly decorated legion, a fact that I was just now beginning to appreciate.

Inspecting our ranks, I can feel the emotions of our troops. Some of the newer transfers were experiencing some nervous excitement, but our Veterans were all encompassed by an iron resolve. No fear or agitation was felt among any of them. The experience of past battles has burned that away and all that remained was a firm acceptance of circumstance. Through the cruel and unforgiving nature of war on this planet, our soldiers have become as hard as the schythium on which they stood. Whatever fate lay before us, we are ready.

After completing inspection, I ride to the front of our ranks to join the other officers.

"No word from General Jaxxon yet?" I ask.

"Just an order to hold ranks and wait for further instruction," Colonel Hou says.

"Whatever we're doing, I'm ready for it. Seeing this many cavalry soldiers in one place is getting me fired up," Captain Moreno says.

"You're always fired up," I respond, and Moreno laughs.

"Don't get too excited yet. We could be here a while," Major Paterson says.

A light on my HUD flashes an invitation for a private coms link. I switch over and hear Wenjack's voice.

"Looks like we're finally going into a fight with some actual numbers for a change," Wenjack says.

"No shit. I'm still waiting for someone to tell us it's a mistake and we're going to break up into teams of two or some shit," I say.

"By the sounds of it, the new Fleet Admiral is a fan of overwhelming force, so that's good news for us," Wenjack says.

"I'll believe it when I see it."

"Braddock, you're seeing it now. Look around, this is happening," Wenjack says.

"I remember thinking that before the initial assault too. We won't know the reality until the battles over and we see who's still standing."

"Well either way, it's nice to finally have some support from the powers that be, even if its temporary," Wenjack says.

"Ain't that the truth."

"Hey, Braddock. You know when you went down during the assault… I… ugh."

"I know Wenjack, and the feelings mutual," I say.

Our conversation is interrupted as a standby for orders command flashes across my screen, and I switch over to the main coms link. Indiscernible chatter fills the main link, and it is clear that everyone has received the same order.

Shortly after, a command to switch to VR flashes across my HUD, and a shrill voice says, "Your presence has been requested. Please engage virtual reality."

I follow the directions and turn on my VR as quickly as possible so that I don't have to hear that abrasive voice longer than necessary.

With my VR engaged, I find myself in the same auditorium as before the initial invasion. It was a pretty standard program that the Federation liked to use. The assembly of two hundred thousand soldiers that looked so massive in the valley appeared to be a relatively small group compared to the enormous auditorium.

The crowd grows instantly quiet as General Jaxxon walks out on stage and takes his place behind the podium. He could have just appeared directly in his place, but by walking across the stage, he is able to assert his commanding presence over the crowd. Each heal strike of his boots against the hardwood stage echoes through the massive room, drawing all attention to him as he approached the podium. Once he's in position, three more cavalry Generals appear a few paces behind him. He looks over the crowd with an approving expression before beginning his address.

"Good evening. In six hours the Federation will be launching the largest ground assault in the history of mankind. Ten and a half million soldiers, supported by heavy armor and air support, will form a line fifty-three kilometers long in an area that we're calling the valley of death."

A hologram appears over the stage showing a wide valley flanked on both sides by rolling hills. In the valley, we can see our massive line of troops, all marked with their legion's insignias.

"This has been chosen as the battlefield for two reasons. First, is that it is one of the only places we could get this many soldiers into the field at one time. The second, is what lays seventy-three kilometers to the North."

The holographic map zooms out and reveals a massive hive to the North of the battlefield. Instantly, indiscernible chatter fills the auditorium.

The discovery of a hive is a big deal, but I am oddly unsurprised by its reveal. I think that a part of me had already suspected it, based on the massive mobilization of forces. I look down the row of seats at Wenjack, and he indicates that he's as unsurprised as I am. The rest of the auditorium seems to be a little more excited about the situation than we are, and General Jaxxon has to mute all of our mics in order to continue.

"Thanks to Fleet scientists, we have been able to locate the first of the enemy hives. And we are going to smash it. The main force is assembling at the beginning of the valley of death. Once assembled, they will begin advancing across the valley in an attempt to draw the enemy out of their hive and meet us in the field for a pitched battle.

"Having this many of our troops exposed in the field and approaching their hive should draw them out and away from the hive. This will be the only chance that the Bugs have to stop us. They will understand that if a force of that size reaches the hive, it will only be a matter of time till we smash our way in. So, they will hit us wear we are weakest. In the open field. Which is what we want because this force is nothing more than a distraction designed to pull them out from the base. Opening the door for us," General Jaxxon says with sadistic joy.

The hologram shifts to show a series of trails leading from our location to the hive.

"In a brilliant decision, the Federation has decided to leave the assault in the capable hands of the cavalry. We are going to depart from the valley through the tunnel and make the six hour ride to the hive, where we will split into four assault groups and hit it from all sides," he says, and a loud cheer erupts from the now unmuted audience.

"We are going to hit the hive at full speed and force our way right through their front door. Like a river, we will pour through every entrance and make our way inside. Once inside, our mission is simple, kill everything. Everything inside that hive with more than four legs needs to die. We will smash every egg, destroy every supply stash, and slaughter all of their breeders. We will bring an Armageddon of fire into their world!" General Jaxon roars, and the crowd roars back.

"Intelligence tells us that there is a high likelihood

that this hive is home to a Queen. If you find the Queen, do not engage. Kill any bugs with her and cut off her escape, but do not engage. She is the only Bug to be left alive. If you find her, call it in and a special extraction team will come get her. Intelligence has special plans for their Queen, and you don't want to piss them off," the General says before pausing for effect.

"I want to make one thing perfectly clear. This is the hive responsible for the Battle of LZ Bravo. A lot of you lost friends in that battle, and like me, you all lost good brothers and sisters. This is our chance for revenge against the bastards responsible. Not only is it our personal chance for revenge, but it is the chance for the entire human race. We will make them regret their trespasses and like fire bursting forth from the gates of hell, we will consume them. We will ride over them all and crush them beneath our feet. We will leave no doubt in anyone's mind what happens when you fuck with the human race," he stops once more and lets the cheers and shouts of huha fill the auditorium.

"Look at the names of your legions. You're all named after legendary cavalry armies of the past. Armies that changed the course of human history. The Huns, Mongol, Saracen, Dragoons, Comanche, Companions and many more legendary names adorn our armour because we are the descendants of those courageous men. We are cavalry!

"With the great Kahn, we rode as Mongols off the step and conquered half the world. With Alexander, we smashed the vast Persian armies before riding against the ferocious elephants of India. On swift Arabian horses, we proved our might as we rode with Saladin. Even the mighty Julius Caesar sung our praises as we rode as Germanic cavalry against the Celtic rebels. We dominated the battlefields of Old Earth until history thought us finished after we rode as Polish cavalry at Krojanty in a valiant rear-guard action against Nazi armour.

"But we weren't finished. Years later we came back as the Northern Alliance. Riding our wild Afghan horses along side American Special Forces we made the Taliban feel our power. And now, human history hangs in the balance once more and we answer the call. Once more cavalry soldiers will turn the tides of war. As we ride on the backs of our mounts, fate rides on our shoulders. We are cavalry soldiers!"

A loud chorus of "Huha," rises up from the audience.

"Make no mistake, many good soldiers are going to die today in order to give us our shot at the hive. They are willingly throwing themselves into the fray and laying down their lives to buy us the time we need to take out our target. So do not waste this opportunity. Hit it hard and hit it fast. Each minute we take is another son, daughter, father or mother that will never return home. This is it, soldiers. This is what you have been trained for. This is what you were born for. All the battles you have fought, all the trials you faced, have brought you to this point.

"Today, we will make a mark upon history that will never be forgotten. Some of us won't live to see tomorrow, but those that die will be giving their lives to ensure that humanity sees not only tomorrow but carries on till the ending of all things. If I die today, I die happy because I am proud to have lived at the same time as all of you heroes.

"Now ready yourselves for war my friends. Pre-pair to ride. Ride for glory, ride for vengeance, ride for the Federation!" The General roars and the crowd roars back.

Cries of "Death, Revenge" and "Huha," fill the auditorium for a minute and then as suddenly as a light switch being flicked, everything goes quiet, and I find myself sitting in a small briefing room.

Lieutenants Rodger and Wenjack are sitting to either side of me while General Jaxxon sits at the head of the table. Dominique and four other hunters are standing behind the General in full armour. The sudden change of location was a shock to my senses, and I take a few seconds to get my bearings.

"Captain Braddock, I trust you liked my speech," the General asks.

"Yes Sir, very motivational," I say, still a bit dazed.

"I'm glad you found it motivating because you've got a very important assignment," he says, and my heart sinks to my stomach.

If he pulls me out of this assault to do something else, I'm going to lose it.

"You will be given the seventh and third brigade with the special purpose of escorting these hunters into the hive and finding the Queen," he says, and I'm instantly filled with relief.

"You will ride behind me and the first brigade until we get inside the hive. Once inside it will be up to you and the hunters to decide where to go. Your only objective is to find the Queen and get her out alive. Once you find her, the hunters will capture her and haul her out. You and your two brigades will provide cover as they extract her. You think you can handle that, Captain?" the General asks.

"Yes Sir, I can handle that," I answer enthusiastically.

"Look, Braddock. You have proven yourself time and again to be a capable soldier. We are putting a lot of faith in you here, so do me a personal favor and don't fuck this up," the General says.

"Thank you, Sir, I won't let you down," I say.

"Good, now let's go to work," the General says as we are logged out and back in ranks on the valley floor.

"So we're getting a shot at the Queen," Wenjack says.

"Going to bring that bitch down," I say.

"I have to admit, the thought of bagging the Queen is getting me pretty excited," Wenjack says with a laugh.

"Keep it in your pants you freak," Dominique says as she rides up beside me with the other hunters.

"You ready for some payback?" I ask her.

"If you paid any attention to our conversation the other night then you wouldn't have to ask me that," she says coldly.

"I was just... Forget about it," I say, not wanting to argue.

"Let's just go get this bitch. We can make small talk later," she says.

I notice a change in her tone, but I can't pinpoint what it is. There's a coldness that I haven't felt before, and I wonder if it was something that I said or didn't say. Maybe it's just the opportunity to get a piece of a Queen.

The blast doors open, and General Jaxxon comes charging through them, waving a Federation flag. With breakneck speed, he rides down the open road to the sound of two hundred thousand cheering soldiers. He stops in front of our ranks, where he rears his Wargon onto its hind legs as he waves the flag above his head.

"Cavalry, move out," he bellows.

Riding hard towards the tunnel, he leads the way as we fall in behind him. Behind us, the entire valley floor begins to move as all the legions file towards the road. Like a river of armour, we pour out of the valley and into the tunnel. Making our way to the hive and the most important battle of our lives.

CHAPTER TWENTY-NINE

The army's diversion to the south must be working because the ride to the hive goes well, and we run into surprisingly little resistance. Normally it seems that the Bugs know what we're going to do before we do it, but the genius of this plan is that it doesn't matter. If they realize that our army approaching from the south is a diversion and hold tight to the base. Our cavalry charge would be stopped, but our main force would still arrive, and the Bugs would have to face them where they would be pinned in. Whether they know we're coming or not, the only chance the Bugs have against a force that size is to hit it hard with everything they can spare while leaving a smaller defence force to deal with us. Either way, they're fucked.

About a kilometre out, we start to run into increasing resistance as our forces split into our four assault groups. We hear reports of ambushes and the odd roadblock, but nothing seems to be able to stop our violent charge. Even when reports of large parties of hunter Bugs start to flow in, they seem to do little to slow our advance.

As our own group charges, I can see the odd black and yellow limb sticking up from the ground as we hammer down the path towards the hive. Being a brigade back in the line means that we're going to see very little of the enemy until the paths open up. General Jaxxon and the first brigade are making sure that any signs of the enemy that make it back to us have been thoroughly shot, rammed, and stomped.

It's not long before we are winding through the paths just below the base of the hive. Before us, we can see the towering cliffs that hide the filthy lair of the beasts. A shear wall of schythium that lay at the end of twisting paths and tunnels. If we thought that the valley surrounding the knoll looked like an image of hell, then this must be what lay inside the devil's nightmares. Flying Bugs swarm the skies beneath the orange clouds as they form up for their sporadic assaults on our lines.

The Bugs are now pouring onto us from every direction, but our charge powers forward. As we ride, Bugs fall upon us from the rocky outcrops that shadow the paths. At best, they succeed in dishing out only minor damages, taking one or two of us at most. The majority of the Bugs that jump down are shot dead by the thousands of eager soldiers that want a piece of the action. The others are taught the hard way what happens when exoskeletons meet the force of fifty thousand armoured Wargons charging through a tight path. Trying to hold back our wrath is as futile as attempting to hold back a raging river. Many Bugs die in the pointless attempt.

The ground is now slick with the blood and gruesome jelly that has been squeezed from our enemy's flattened corpses. I can feel Sleipnir slipping in it as he runs.

Eventually, the slippery corpses present more challenge than the Bugs do alive, but that doesn't stop them from trying. Our place in the ranks is now assaulted by a constant shower of falling Bugs. Relentlessly they pour over the high ridges that outline our approach. With unshakable ferocity, we fire on them as they fall. Our lasers cut them apart in mid-air, and we're hammered with a combination of raining blood, limbs, and dismembered bodies. The odd black and yellow Bug makes it through our laser fire to land among us, but even they can do little damage before being trampled.

With unstoppable haste, we push through the tight paths towards the jagged opening to the hive. The Bug resistance is now fierce as they pour out of the hive and swarm our forces. Desperately they throw themselves against our ranks, but our hunger for vengeance cannot be overwhelmed, and we push on. No resistance can stop us as the entrance to the hive comes within sight. A giant hole in the base of the cliff, wide enough for ten Wargons to ride abreast. Its rough opening daring us to enter.

"Almost there. Keep moving," I yell, and as one, we drive onward.

With titanic might, we muscle our way through the entrance to the hive and at last, we are inside.

Through the black tunnels, we continue crushing the Bugs beneath the power of our combined charge. Their numbers allow them to push back with great strength, but it isn't enough to overcome the combined power of this many Wargons. Let alone, they have to endure the heavy amount of laser fire that our front line is laying down. They frantically try to jam their bodies together in an attempt at breaking our momentum, but again they fail.

Even without our superior strength, we could have out-pushed them with our sheer rage alone. No force in this galaxy could quench the fire that burns within us now. Our hunger for vengeance and blood cannot be filled. Like all fire, the more it is fed, the hungrier it becomes. Feeding our fire, we rip through the caves. Anything unfortunate enough to find itself in our way is consumed and left asunder.

Caught up in the carnage, I temporarily forget my mission. The wrath coming from the Wargons is intoxicating, and I have to force myself to turn my mind from it. Refocusing, I turn my mind to the task at hand and adjust my attention to finding the Queen. Wherever she is, we won't find her charging down the main path with the General. So, I decide to peel off from the main force at the next fork, and the opportunity comes fast. Ahead I see a smaller tunnel off to the left, and I position myself to take it.

Once at the tunnel, we bank hard to the left and filter down its dark depths. This tunnel is much smaller than the one we were previously in, and we're now only able to ride three abreast. The Bugs are fewer down this direction, and I wonder what that means.

After hammering through the initial couple hundred meters, we break through the enemy lines and find ourselves riding unopposed. I switch my coms over to a private link with Dominique.

"Any idea where the fuck we should start looking for this bitch?"

"In the deepest, darkest part of this place would be my best guess," she says.

"Is that the extent of your tracking wisdom?"

"How did you find the underground Bug highway?" she asks, thankfully ignoring my stupid comment.

"I'm not sure exactly. I knew that it was there."

"How," she asks.

"I just felt it I guess."

"Then just feel it now. Follow your gut and don't think too much."

I focus on keeping my mind blank, trying to let my intuition guide me, but I have little success. Instead, I end up making random guesses at each fork, hoping that I make the right decision. Thankfully my suit's computer is making a map of the tunnels as we go because without it, we would likely find ourselves lost in a hurry. Between the random changes in direction and the waves of Bugs that keep coming, the tunnels are becoming increasingly confusing. The more I try and focus on my intuition, the more I feel like I'm making the wrong decisions.

This pattern of guesses and confusion carries on as we move deeper inside the hive until we reach a crossroads. With three directions to choose from, I stop for the first time since we left the FOB. Through a trick of perception, my body feels like it is still bouncing around even though I am now sitting completely still. I look down all three directions and try to make up my mind. Focusing on my own mind is useless, so I focus on Sleipnir's instead.

I focus on his mind as I look down each of the tunnels, and when I look down the tunnel to the right, I hear a voice say, "Go back."

Instantly I recognized the slithering voice as the one that often calls to me in my dreams.

"Go back," the voice says again. "Only death waits for you. Go back."

Unable to determine if the voice is one of my mind's own making or if it belongs to something else, I decide to do the opposite of what it says and turn Sleipnir to head down the tunnel to the right.

About a hundred meters down the tunnel, we start hitting some serious enemy resistance. Our initial impact goes like the rest, and Sleipnir smashes his way through the Bugs. Crushing them against the schythium walls of the tunnel. The Bugs start jamming themselves up against every wall of the tunnel as they attempt to block our way.

With Wenjack on one side of me and Dominique on the other, we open fire, trying to break the enemy's living wall that is forming in front of us. For the first time since we entered the tunnel, our charge begins to slow down as more Bugs jammed their bodies into our path. This isn't a good situation to be in. If we lose all momentum, this will quickly turn into one bloody fight.

"Turn back. Only death waits for you," the slithering voice says to me again.

The desire to find the owner of the voice drives me forward, and I somehow get Sleipnir to push on. Somehow, we actually begin picking up speed and soon, we are driving through the Bugs at full force once more. Suddenly we break out of the small tunnel and find ourselves in a giant room with a high ceiling.

"Form up," I command, and the troops form into a

wedge as they enter the room.

The floor is filled with Bugs except for the far corner, which is covered in a few hundred thousand eggs, stacked up from the floor to ceiling. In front of the eggs lay four massive Bugs with giant rear ends. I'm not familiar with what the anatomical parts of these are called, but I know without a doubt these are breeders.

Instantly we open fire as we charge forward in our wedge formation. Our lasers ripping through the open horde. Pressed with the imminent destruction of their precious eggs, they fight harder than I have ever seen Bugs fight. They smash themselves against us as they desperately try to halt our assault, but their desperation to protect the eggs made us fight harder to destroy them.

Igniting thermal lances, we continue to slaughter them until a pack of hunters manages to work their way to the front line. Their faster speed gives contest to our slaughter for the first time, and we begin to take casualties.

Along the line, I start to see the first of our ranks begin to fall as the black and yellow demons reach us. The left side of our line takes the brunt of their assault and begins to lose ground.

Raising his lance above his head Lieutenant Rodger roars, "Not one step back!" and his Wargon lunges forward.

Swinging his lance, he delivers punishing strikes upon his assailants. Each strike burning away chunks of exoskeleton and severing limbs.

"Back you beasts," he roars as he leads the left side forward, driven by unstoppable will.

As he pushes forward, his Wargon is impaled through the face by a black and yellow foreleg, killing it instantly. Lieutenant Rodger retaliates with a quick thrust of his lance through the head of the offending Bug.

Then without hesitation, he leaps from his Wargon's back onto the head of one of the Bugs. Violently the Bug thrashes to free itself of Lieutenant Rodger, but he holds on with the powerful grip of his battle suit. He manages to hang on with one hand while using the other to swing his lance. The Bug desperately lurches from side to side as Lieutenant Rodger kills Bug after Bug from his new mount.

As quickly as the display started, it comes to an end as a black Bug snatches Lieutenant Rodger by the ankle and throws him into the enemy horde. Before his body has a chance to hit the ground, it is ripped from the air and shredded by the mandibles of three Bugs. His body comes apart like a pinata at a kid's party, except the filling that burst forth wasn't candy or fun little toys.

Dominique and the hunters use their superior

schythium suits to plow a line straight through the horde towards the stacks of eggs. The large breeders move their bodies to try and protect the eggs, but our hunters cut them down with little effort. The breeder's massive forms do little to stop the punishing laser fire that Dominique and the hunters lay down. They force their way around the fallen breeders and ride right up to the eggs, where they detonate a series of high explosive grenades. Invulnerable to the incredible destructive power of the grenades, they don't bother taking cover as the detonation rips through the eggs and most of the attacking horde.

From across the giant room, I am hit with the concussion of the violent blast, and I feel like I stepped in front of a magnet train. I feel the pain of a great loss echo through the caves as the eggs burst, leaving little more than shrapnel and ooze.

What could have felt deeply enough for the loss of the eggs that I, too, could feel its pain? I felt the loss as clearly as if it had come from one of our Wargons, and I realize that it is coming from the same place as the voice. I was feeling their Queen's pain at the loss of the eggs. We had taken her future children and her ability to replace them. The loss hurt their Queen deeply and feeling that hurt brought a carnal joy to my heart. After all the pain and suffering the Bugs have caused, knowing that their Queens could be wounded by the same feelings made it all feel a little fairer. It also gave us a direction to move in.

"Hard forward," I bellow as we effortlessly overpower the remaining Bugs.

Taking the lead, I ride in the direction that I felt the Queen. We head into a tunnel on the far side of the large cavern. Dominique and the hunters rejoin our ranks as we charge deeper into the hive. Driven by the knowledge that we had a solid direction to go on, I ride as fast as the tight tunnels allow.

Chasing the outcry that filled my mind, we ride with everything we have. Trusting my instincts more than my deliberate thought, I clear my head and let my subconscious direct Sleipnir. Without specific intention, Sleipnir navigates through the forks until he reaches one that brings him to a dead stop.

Neither my conscious nor subconscious mind knows where to go, so we sit and wait. Wait for my mind to pick up on something, anything, that would give us a direction.

Carefully I focus with all the concentration I can muster. I focus on my link with Sleipnir, the link between each Wargon and rider in our ranks and on the dead air in between. I focus on the gaps between the conscious mind and the emptiness that lays beyond, looking for something.

"Captain, we've got bugs approaching up the right tunnel," Wenjack says.

"And the left, just a little further off," Dominique adds.

"You need to pick a direction," Wenjack says.

Ignoring the warnings of incoming hostiles, I maintain my focus.

"Captain, if these Bugs hit us when we're standing still, we're fucked," Wenjack says with increasing urgency, but I keep my focus.

"Captain, we need to pick a tunnel!" Wenjack yells.

"We've got less than a minute here," Dominique says.

"For fuck sakes Braddock, pick a fucking tunnel!" Wenjack shouts in desperation.

Blocking out their pleas, I keep my focus on the link. Then I'm hit with a hurricane of emotion worse than the last. Our troops must have hit another nest of eggs because this bitch was pissed off. The pain of the last outburst is coupled with an intense anger as she realizes that her time is coming to an end.

Without hesitation, Sleipnir and I launch down the

left tunnel, trying to build up as much speed as possible before the wave of Bugs hit. The rest of the forces only take a half-second to react, and soon we are all barreling down the tunnel towards the approaching Bugs. Turning a bend, we smash into the enemy without warning. Luckily, Sleipnir had lowered his head as we entered the turn and met the enemy, horn first. The impact slowed us slightly, but the force of our troops pressing up behind helped drive us forward. With one hand holding onto Sleipnir's armour in a death grip, the other levels my battle rifle and opens fire.

I become disoriented by the chaos of the situation, like a swimmer being tossed and rolled in an oceans violent Surf. All I can do is hold onto Sleipnir and hope my rifle keeps firing in the right direction as we drive through the endless horde. Unable to see much through the bloody mist and relentless assault from severed Bug limbs, I let my instincts guide us through the tunnels. I imagine that somewhere up ahead, the Queen knows that we're coming for her, and I wonder if she's afraid. Does she now feel the fear that Dominique must have felt as she hid her family in the mountains above her home? Or has she excepted her fate, knowing that it was only a matter of time before the metal apes came to kill them all?

CHAPTER THIRTY

Finally breaking out of the tight tunnels, we find ourselves in another large, cavernous room face to face with a horde of Bugs, the likes of which I haven't seen before. Double the size of normal Bugs and with a dull grey and black colouring. Their mandibles and forelegs are thick beyond the scale of their increased size, and their heads bare a formidable exoskeleton armour plate. The giant beasts open their mouths and release a bone-chilling screech that removes all my confidence in our advantage. These hulking beasts will rip our lines to pieces, and I question whether or not our lasers will be powerful enough to crack their hard shells.

"Form a line," I bellow as my troops file into the room and face the beasts.

"Concentrate all fire on the base of their heads," I command, and every Mongol in our ranks opens fire on the charging beasts. Our combined fire in all its fury is only enough to bring down a couple of the giants, and I quickly realize that we are utterly and completely fucked. We are sitting ducks in this formation, and our only chance is to charge.

"Lances!" I order, and a thousand Mongols draw their lances, igniting them at once.

As the beasts are almost upon us, I prepare to give

the order to charge but am halted by a surprise command.

"Now!" Dominique yells, and the four other hunters with her ride forward a pace.

Each of them holding a two-foot green tube that fires a single rocket into the air. I watch as the four missiles fly over the heads of the approaching beasts and split open, releasing thousands of tiny projectiles. Each tiny missile flies on its own path, hitting its targets with pinpoint accuracy, striking the mammoth Bugs at the base of the head. Upon impact, each rocket releases an explosion equal to a small airstrike, and the hulking beasts collapse to the ground.

In one simple strike, our hunters decimate the most formidable adversaries we've seen on this planet. I can't help but feel inadequate in comparison.

As the beasts hit the ground, I can finally see across the room and realize what these colossal warriors were protecting. On the other side of the room, I see a Bug that looks like a cross between one of the giant Bugs and a breeder. Its body is massive and has the larger thorax of a breeder but with the head and long legs of a warrior. Its colossal mandibles drip with some kind of liquid that flies off as it snaps at the air. With each snap, it releases a shrieking chirp that was ear-splitting even through our sound dampened helmets. Instantly I realize, this is the Queen.

"Forward. Don't let her escape!" I order as I charge through the fallen beast to confront the wretched Queen.

With lightning speed, our hunters circle around back of the slow-moving Queen, cutting off her escape. The rest of my soldiers form a circle around her, with each of their rifles levelled on her head. Daring her to make a move.

Realizing that she has no chance of escape, she turns to face me, and my blood goes cold. Her nasty black Bug eyes stare at me, and it feels like they are burning through my mind.

Every ounce of my being wants to drive my lance right through those disgusting eyes, but instead, I raise my hand in the air and give the command, "Everybody hold your fire."

The hunters raise their pulse cannons that had been designed to knock the queen unconscious, but Dominique has them hold their fire as well. Leaving me in a standoff with the beast, eyes locked on one another despite mine being hidden behind my helmet.

"Soldier. I finally get to meet the human who hears my voice," she speaks directly into my mind with a slithering whisper, and I realize that it's her that I've been hearing these last couple of months.

It's been this fucking bitch who has been in my head.

"You are different from the others. You can hear my voice, know my thoughts. After all this time our races can finally communicate. You will be our voice and I will speak through you," she whispers into my mind.

"How about you go fuck yourself," I think back.

"Soldier do not resist me. After all the lives' that have been lost you can bring an end to it all. You can tell your people our story, be the speaker for our kind," she hisses.

"And why would I do that?"

"You have seen our memories, seen the horror that our kind has experienced at the hand of your people," she hisses.

"Memories? You mean my dreams. That was you?"

"Yes. I've been showing you the memories of our kind. Showing you the pain and loss that we've endured. You think that we are the monsters, but there are two sides to every horror. You see monster, but we are just looking for our place in the galaxy, just like you. We are the same," she hisses.

"We are not the same," I snap.

"We are the same," she hisses again. "We both fight so we can have a place in the galaxy. So we can have room for our species to grow and live in peace. Soldier, you can make that happen. Through you, we can talk to your people and find a peace."

"You talk like you're an innocent victim, like you haven't fueled this war with your hunger for more planets to infest. You attacked us first," I think.

Through the corner of my eyes, I can see Dominique watch me very carefully as if she knows that I'm communicating with the beast.

"We attacked you first because we had to. Your species has spread too far too quick. You're taking territory as fast as you can find it, and soon, you will cover the entire galaxy, leaving no room for other species. To grow, to live, to evolve. That is why the creators put us in your way. To stop you from claiming everything as your own. To stop you from devouring their creations. We only go where they send us and they only send us where you need not go."

"Creators?" I question.

"Yes soldier, the Creators. The ones who gave us life, gave many species life. The ones who move us from world to world. The ones who brought us here. They put us on worlds that you might claim, in order to stop you from taking everything. From taking all they create. Your people must stop consuming, you must stop expanding before there is nothing left. Soldier, you must let us use you to find a peace. To end the war," she hisses, and I think to myself, uncaring if she is listening or not.

I wonder what it would mean if she was telling the truth. Was there a creator that was pulling the strings behind this war? It would make sense. It explains how the Bugs get from planet to planet, and it would explain why they always seem adapted to each planet's unique environment. Were the Bugs just a weapon created by some kind of gods to hold us back? Or were they being used to clear out existing life so they could grow their own? Does it really matter one way or the other?

"Who is your creator? Where do we find them?" I ask, trying to seize an opportunity that might not come again.

She makes a sharp hissing sound that I can only interpret as displeasure.

"That is not your question to ask. That is not my information to know."

"You tell me who this creator is and maybe I'll consider helping you out," I think, hoping she can't detect my lie.

"You are not in a place to negotiate. You are also not telling the truth," she hisses in frustration.

I look over at Dominique once more before looking back at the Queen. This Bug definitely knows more than she is letting on, but I doubt that she'll tell me anything she doesn't want me to know. I also doubt that I'd be able to separate what's true from what's not.

"Soldier, you are conflicted, but you don't have a choice in the matter. You are but a drone to your masters, doing what you are told. I am a Queen, royalty to my species and I am requesting to speak to your royalty. The ones who make decisions. This matter is above you. I do not need to explain the way of things to a soldier anymore than your masters need to explain their orders to you. You are to do as you are told. Consider all that I have told you already to be a gift and do as I say. You will call your masters and with them I will form the new peace," she hisses in whispered frustration.

Ours is not to reason why. This bitch said it herself, I am to follow orders. Do what I'm told. So, I guess that's what I have to do.

"Listen here you stupid bitch. I may just be a soldier, but any human soldier is above the highest of your filthy species. You can claim all you want that you're acting out of self defense and it's the human race that's a plague on the galaxy, but you're full of shit. If you haven't noticed, I'm sitting on top of a Wargon. A species whose planet you invaded, unprovoked. They posed no threat to you, and yet you showed up and started slaughtering them. Killing their young, their old, their loved ones. We are the ones who showed up and saved them, like we always do. You fuckers come to a planet and destroy every living thing."

"You don't understand…" she begins before I fire back.

"Shut the fuck up!"

I point over at Dominique, who by now has clearly figured out that I'm communicating with the beast.

"You see that woman right there? She was living peacefully with her family on a small colony planet, and you bastards showed up and took everything from her. She posed no threat to you, and you hunted and killed her son and husband. And for what? How was her helpless child a threat to you?

"Here's the thing that you're clearly to fucking stupid to realize. By killing that child, you fueled hatred in her that has led to the deaths of millions of your kind. She won't rest until all of you are dead, and she isn't alone. Every attack you launch creates more people like her. More people who make it their only purpose in life to kill your kind."

I stop as my thoughts turn to all the friends that I

have lost.

"You're disgusting species has killed almost every friend I have ever had and you dare ask me to help you build a peace?"

"Peace is the only way," she responds.

"Funny that you say this now, when you're on the brink of destruction. Well, I've got news for you. There will never be peace. From the moment that your kind killed the first human, peace became impossible. That single act sealed the fate of your entire race."

Something in the Queen shifts, and for the first time, I can feel her fear, and it feels great.

"You should be afraid because here's what's going to happen. We are going to take this planet. Oh yes, that's inevitable now. And once we take it, we will mine it into oblivion. All this beautiful schythium will be turned into weapons of war that we will use to destroy your entire species, and after every last one of you bastards is dead, we will kill your creators too. We will wipe every trace of them from the galaxy as we claim it all in the name of the Federation.

"It's just too bad that you won't be around to see it happen. You see, we're going to take you and lock you up in one of our ships. Then our scientists are going to drill into every part of your brain and pull out all of your dirty little secrets. You will die slow and alone."

I can feel her fear increase as the reality of the situation hits her like a brick. She is reading my thoughts and knows that I'm telling the truth.

"Before we drag your ass out of here, I just want you to know one thing. Even though I am just a lowly soldier, I have brought you down, and one day other lowly soldiers just like me will kill every other Queen like you. Your royalty means nothing to us. You mean nothing to us," I think and then look at Dominique.

"Bring this bitch down!" I order.

"Now!" Dominique commands, and her hunters fire their pulse cannons, knocking the Queen unconscious. The Queen's long legs fold under her dead weight, and she crashes to the ground.

Without wasting time, Dominique and the hunters draw schythium hooks and cables from their Wargons. Our orders are to bring the Queen in alive, but the condition of her body wasn't ever specified. So the hunters take the opportunity to drive the heavy hooks through the exoskeleton of her mandibles and head. No doubt this would cause excruciating pain when the bitch eventually wakes up. One last fuck you from us lowly soldiers.

Once all the hooks have been driven into her, cables are rigged between the hooks and some of our Wargons. There would be no ceremonial last march for this Queen.

As the last of the cables are rigged up, I give the order, “Alright Mongols, let’s drag this bitch out of here.”

All slack is pulled from the cables as the team of Wargons begins to pull the unconscious, mutilated Queen across the ground. She won’t fit out the way we came in, so we have to drag her through a larger tunnel to the rear of the room. Unsure of how many Bugs are still in the hive, I ride out front with Dominique, ready to defend our prize.

We soon run into more Bugs, but they are a faint shadow of the threat they once were. With the Queen now unconscious, they had no direction, no orders. The thinking part of their brain is no longer awake, and they wander around aimlessly, completely unaware, or at least unbothered, by our presence. Threat or not, we kill them all the same. I had promised the Queen that every last one of her kind would die, and I meant it.

Through tunnel after tunnel, we drag the Queen. Stopping to kill any wandering Bugs that come our way. Eventually, we break out of the tunnels into the open air. As we do, I hear all the channels of my coms link erupt in cheers and celebration. Through the mix of cheers and shouts, I make out that all of the Bugs that had gone to fight our army in the south had met the same fate as those in the hive. Without the Queen, they lost their ability to fight and were quickly slaughtered. We had won the day.

Not wanting to get caught up in the celebration before our job is done. I return focus to completing our mission. I lead the team drawing the Queen to a large dropship that had landed on a small flat bit of path below the hive. Upon first sight, I can tell the dropship belongs to Military Intelligence and my heart races at the thought of what those ruthless bastards have in store for her.

Positioning the Queen behind the blast door of the ship, the crew disconnects the cables from the Wargon and attaches them to a winch. With an electronic grown, the winches drag the unconscious Queen into the back of the ship like a hunk of salvaged equipment. The Queen that thought she was above us all is now being handled like a mere object.

Once she's loaded, I turn towards Dominique to congratulate her on our victory, but my suit won't move. I try to hail her over the coms, but they are dead too. What the fuck is going on? I can see that the only ones affected are Sleipnir and myself, and I realize that we have been shut off by the command override. Desperately, I try to move an arm to signal for help, but the suit won't budge. What the fuck is going on?

I yell at the top of my lungs, "Wenjack!" but not a sound can be heard through my helmet.

The crew from the dropship begin loading Sleipnir onto a dolly, and I realize that the Queen isn't the only one that Military Intelligence is taking.

Dominique sticks her head in front of my immobile visor and I think she is saying something, but without my coms, I can't hear a thing. I yell for help but realize that there is a good chance that she is the one responsible for this. She had set me up. All the time that she was asking about my link with the Wargons and the dreams I was having, she was just plugging me for information. She knew in the hive that I was talking to the Queen. For fuck sakes. I bet she knew that I'd be able to talk to the Queen before I did. How could I have been so stupid to trust someone who works for Military Intelligence?

A cold fear grips me as I wonder what kind of experiments these bastards have in store for us. There's probably a ship full of white coats just itching to cut into the skull of someone who can talk to Bugs.

Realizing what is happening, Wenjack and the others try to intervene. I can't hear what's being said, but there is a lot of pointing and hand gesturing, followed by the raising of guns. It looks like they aren't going to let Intelligence take me without a fight. I'm overcome by a feeling of pride that my soldiers would put their lives on the line and draw guns on Military Intelligence for my benefit. They're going to teach these jack booting ass holes that you don't fuck with the cavalry. Through the corner of my eye, I see General Jaxxon ride in between the lines of cavalry and Intelligence. They were in for it now. Nobody has enough balls to get in the General's way.

The only problem is that the General isn't facing the Intelligence crew. He is facing our soldiers and gesturing at them. My heart sinks into the pit of my stomach, and I realize that the General is backing up Intelligence, not me. Not wanting to face the General's wrath, our soldiers lower their weapons and turn to leave. My heart sinks but despite the feeling of abandonment that is overtaking me, I don't blame them. They have no other option.

Now unopposed, the crew begins loading our immobilized bodies onto the dropship. Once inside, they secure us with cargo straps and close the blast doors. It occurs to me that against all odds, I am leaving Excalibur alive, but what kind of life lay before me is unclear. If my reception here is any indication, it won't be a life I am eager to live. I know as well as anyone. Once Intelligence takes you, you're never heard from again. Out of all the surprises that I've found on Excalibur, the biggest is that I'm afraid to leave.

EPILOGUE

Locked in the confines of my immobilized battle suit, I stare into the darkness of the dropship's cargo hold. Here we sit, only a few feet away from our enemy's unconscious body. An enemy that I fear I will get to know better than any human I have ever met. Through no choice of our own, the three of us have had our fates bound together. From now on, where the Queen goes, so too must Sleipnir and I go. It looks like we will become her voice after all. Just like she wanted. Only she won't be using us to build a peace between our species. Instead, she will be using us to betray her kind as the technicians pull and pry information from her.

She claimed that through us, she could bring an end to the war, and she was right. Through us, she will give up every piece of information the Federation needs to destroy her kind, and her creators. She will tell us who they are and how to find them. We will be her voice as she screams out their names. We will share in her pain as each, and every bit of critical information is drawn from her.

Fear takes me as I wonder what they have in store for us. If they simply want me to be the Queens voice, then they would have asked. I would have gladly aided in her destruction. The very nature of my abduction tells me all that I need to know about their intentions. I'm certain that I'll be her voice, but I doubt it will be in a manner of my choosing.

I realize that this was Intelligence's plan ever since Dominique and I first met. That's why she rode with us. It also explains why she saved my life at the Battle of LZ Bravo. She was so curious about how I knew the Bugs were underground, and she must have pushed that information up the line. Realizing what I was capable of before I did, she played me the entire time, and I ate it up. To infatuated with the mysterious woman in the indestructible armour, to see what she was really up to.

Then again, maybe they were watching me from before Dominique, and I even met. From the assault on the knoll. General Jaxxon could have told them about the way I commanded the Wargons through the link. Knowing that they might have pegged me as a potential asset. Hell, they could have sent me to find that underground highway as a test. General Jaxxon could have been part of it the entire time. He definitely seemed like he was on their side when they were dragging me away. It could have been him who betrayed me, and Dominique was simply following orders. She, too, could just be a pawn in this thing, or she could be the Queen. I really don't know.

All I know is that I'm going to have plenty of time to think about it because the odds of me ever being released are slim to none. I am now just another asset for them to use as they will. No longer a soldier. No longer a person. My fate was sealed long ago. What or who sealed it doesn't much matter because all I can do now is wait. Thinking about what might lay in my future, I stare into the darkness of the cargo hold. Waiting for whatever may come.

APPENDIX

The Charge of The Light Brigade

By: Alfred Lord Tennyson

Half a league, half a league,
Half a league onward,
All in the valley of Death
Rode the six hundred.
'Forward, the Light Brigade!
Charge for the guns!' he said:
Into the valley of Death
Rode the six hundred.

'Forward, the Light Brigade!'
Was there a man dismay'd ?
Not tho' the soldier knew
Some one had blunder'd:
Their's not to make reply,
Their's not to reason why,
Their's but to do and die:
Into the valley of Death
Rode the six hundred.

Cannon to right of them,

Cannon to left of them,
Cannon in front of them
Volley'd and thunder'd;
Storm'd at with shot and shell,
Boldly they rode and well,
Into the jaws of Death,
Into the mouth of Hell
Rode the six hundred.

Flash'd all their sabres bare,
Flash'd as they turn'd in air
Sabring the gunners there,
Charging an army, while
All the world wonder'd:
Plunged in the battery-smoke
Right thro' the line they broke;
Cossack and Russian
Reel'd from the sabre-stroke
Shatter'd and sunder'd.
Then they rode back, but not
Not the six hundred.

Cannon to right of them,
Cannon to left of them,
Cannon behind them

Volley'd and thunder'd;

Storm'd at with shot and shell,
While horse and hero fell,
They that had fought so well
Came thro' the jaws of Death,
Back from the mouth of Hell,
All that was left of them,
Left of six hundred.

When can their glory fade ?
O the wild charge they made!
All the world wonder'd.
Honour the charge they made!
Honour the Light Brigade,
Noble six hundred!

Manufactured by Amazon.ca
Bolton, ON

27669789R00284